Forever,
My Love

Brandy Bennett-Baker

WESTBOW PRESS®
A DIVISION OF THOMAS NELSON
& ZONDERVAN

WestBow Press books may be ordered through booksellers or by contacting:

WestBow Press
A Division of Thomas Nelson & Zondervan
1663 Liberty Drive
Bloomington, IN 47403
www.westbowpress.com
1 (866) 928-1240

ISBN: 978-1-9736-5059-1 (sc)
ISBN: 978-1-9736-5058-4 (hc)
ISBN: 978-1-9736-5060-7 (e)

Library of Congress Control Number: 2019900226

Print information available on the last page.

WestBow Press rev. date: 02/22/2019

Acknowledgments

First and foremost, I thank the Lord who continues to bless me abundantly! When I first felt Him calling me on this journey, I was positive He was speaking to the wrong person. I just knew He had me mixed up with somebody else. Because God gets people mixed up all the time, right?! *But seriously, didn't He realize that I wasn't capable of what He was asking?* I was *certain* of that fact. Yet, faith is believing, even when you cannot see. And though I could never *see* myself taking this journey, I had faith that the Lord knew exactly what He was doing. And so, the journey began.

More than anything, this journey has made my faith in the Lord grow stronger. Never, did I have any desire to write a book, a short story, or even a poem for that matter. But somehow, the doubts and fears that I faced along the way, were pushed to the wayside and replaced with a confidence I could only find in my Savior. It seemed, that no matter what obstacle I ran into, when I turned to God for an answer, a clear and non-obstructed path came into view. I don't know how many times in the beginning that I fell to my knees, filled with doubt in my own capabilities, and begged God to show my stubborn heart whether I was on the right path. And EVERY single time, He lovingly and gently hit me over the head with the answer that I fought to believe. I was being called for God's purpose.

I still don't consider myself a writer, only a vessel through which His love and mercy are displayed. My most heartfelt prayer is that my books will change the lives of many, affect people positively, and give hope to those who maybe have never felt it. A hope that they will only find in the

Lord. I pray that those who know our Lord, will grow closer to Him, as they read about the characters in my stories and relate to their own sorrows and joys, their mistakes and wise choices. For those who don't know Him, I pray through the relatable characters of my stories, they feel drawn to Him, hungry for his love, grace, and mercy.

I would like to thank my editor and dear friend, Kayla Long. I've heard it said that with God there are no "coincidences" and He sure proved that when you showed up unexpectedly as a temporary fill-in for one of my co-workers, and very quickly became one of my dearest and most treasured friends. Girl, the Lord certainly knew what He was doing when He brought you in to my life. Without you, that first manuscript would have remained what it was when I handed it off to you—a jumbled mess of my chicken scratch! How you embraced that, and together we turned it into something I could believe in, something that the Lord could use, something that could positively affect people and change lives, I will always be in awe of. You have been a constant support, and gift of encouragement, Kayla, and I can't imagine taking this journey without you. I hope you know there's no turning back now; you are in it for the long haul!

Kayla, I'm thankful not only for the work relationship we share, but also for the growing friendship between us. I look forward to, and expect, MANY more brain-storming sessions, goose-bump moments and giggles, as we push through future manuscripts.

Your love for the Lord is contagious, girl! I still get chills when I see you on stage belting out songs and praising His great name on Sunday mornings. It is with that enthusiasm and devotion that I am eager to continue working with, as we forge on in His awesome and powerful name! God couldn't have given me a better "forever friend." I love you, sweet girl.

My dear friend, Cindy Evans—You have been my biggest cheerleader by FAR! After reading only a few short chapters of my first, very unorganized and untitled manuscript, you were anxious to share with others how you "loved" my work. Your eagerness to spread the word of how the story came to life, only after I allowed God to lead me down this crazy and unplanned path (unplanned by me, anyway!) was contagious. You were always sharing with our patients and co-workers the news of my writings and how great the books were going to be. I will never forget my final day of work at the office and the words you spoke to me, as both our eyes filled with tears. You told me you were certain I was going to do great things with my books. Cindy, I hope I never let you down and that my work inspires many. While I always knew God placed me at that specific office to be a light and an example to others, I often times forgot how much others were teaching me. Thank you for your enthusiasm and for your confidence in my books. Keep cheering loudly, friend! His work is just beginning. I love you, Cindy Lou.

To the many family members, friends, co-workers, and yes, even patients, that have motivated, supported, and believed in me, I thank you with all my heart. Your uplifting encouragement means everything to me.

Dedicated to

My husband, and very best friend, Tony—You are my rock! I wouldn't be where I am today if not for you. From the very first day that I shared my thoughts about this project with you, you have given me nothing but support and encouragement. Spending countless hours praying with me as I sought God's direction, confirming that I wasn't "crazy" as I chose to follow His direction, and believing I could accomplish the goal with His guidance, you have held my hand through each and every twist and turn, cheered me on when I was feeling overwhelmed, and held me up when it seemed that everything was falling apart! Thank you for all of the crazy-fun, spur of the moment beach trips (even though you hate the beach), and for understanding that it's my "go to" destination when I need to recharge. Unfortunately for you, I see many more trips to the sandy shores in our future! Your love is a constant motivation, Tony, and I cherish our relationship. It took us a while to find our way, I'll admit. But baby we're here! Living out this life, and following God together. I wouldn't trade our journey for anything! I love you with all my heart, "Fred."

My daughter, Brittney—Your relentless faith in God astounds me on a daily basis. As a parent, I always thought I would be teaching *you* all the days of *my* life. I never envisioned how much you could teach me. You have a gift for sharing God's unending love, grace, and mercy to those who seem to need it most. I love how your face lights up with joy, when the Lord works through you and infects people's lives, especially my own. I should have guessed that, as the first born, and by the way you bossed your younger siblings around, you would grow into a leader. And what an amazing leader you are— to so many! I feel so unbelievably blessed that God gave you to me, my beautiful first born (and experimental, mothering guinea pig), and I'm thankful for the bond that we share. I'm so proud of the wife, mother, sister and daughter that you are. I love you, Britt-Bratt!

My daughter, Jordynn—You are a constant inspiration to me as you live out your life fearlessly! The amazing opportunities that you've grasped, and the inspiring people you've met in your worldly travels, renew my faith in this sometimes, dark world. Seeing life through your eyes has been an awe-inspiring journey, and I look forward to traveling many more miles "with you" in the future. Jordynn, you've taught me to grab hold of life, live on purpose, and not to fear failure. I treasure the relationship we have, and even though you are now thousands of miles away, I keep you close in my heart, looking forward to the next opportunity we have to be together. You know the old, familiar story of how you became my "miracle baby", and until I take my last breath, I will thank God for giving you to me as a beautiful gift. I am so proud of the daughter, sister, and soon-to-be wife that you are (I'm crossing my fingers for mother, too—bring on the grandkids!) I love you, JoJo!

My son, Daniel—You've owned my heart since the minute you were born. With your fiery red hair and spunky attitude to match, along with your quick wit and charm, you have always kept me on my toes! You have a heart of solid gold and compassion for those in need, and I thoroughly enjoy watching the Lord continue His work in you. I'm so proud of the godly man you've become, even as you faced trials so dark that many would have turned their back and walked away. You held your head high and sought the Lord and His truth, learning to forgive those who hurt you deeply, both physically and emotionally. You have overcome so many obstacles in your healing process, Daniel. I am so proud of you, and so thankful that God's protection surrounded you that horrible day, and continues to surround you now. He has great things in store for you, my boy! And even though you are all grown up, never, never forget that you'll always be my little man (someone has to open the doors for me, right?). And it's okay to keep the flowers coming too, my thoughtful one! I'm overwhelmed with joy that the Lord brought you into my life. I love you, Bubba!

My beautiful Carrie, I could not love you more if I had been the one to carry you into life myself. You are such a blessing to our family and always a joy to be around. You never, ever cease to make us all laugh, which is the best medicine one could ask for in this crazy world. I absolutely love that you never have a problem standing up for yourself. It takes some of us years to learn how to do that, and you've inspired me with your courage.

You have a spunk, and a contagious, outgoing personality that make you unique and special, and I couldn't be prouder of the wife, mother, daughter, and sister that you are. You may live hours away, but you are always close to my heart and in my prayers. I love you, sassy girl!

Mom and Pops—Your love is an amazing gift that I cherish. You've always supported me, taught me that I am capable of anything I set my mind to, and encouraged me to follow my dreams. Thank you for always believing in me. Mama-Nellie Belle, as far back as I can remember, you've always taught me to enjoy the Creator's beauty and to find joy in the little things of everyday life. I will never look at a majestic sunrise, frozen tree branches covered in pure white snow, or an innocent squirrel searching your backyard for peanuts, without thinking of you. I won't even get into the barrel-rolling! LOL (Get the bird!) You are in the deepest pockets of my heart! Pops (aka Donkey), you have taught me to never back down from something I believe in, and more about unconditional love than anyone I know. You didn't have it so easy in life, but you took that and turned it into a love for me, making sure I never doubted how special and loved I was, no matter what choices I made in life. I hold your love tight within my heart. I love you both!

Sheryl Putnam—Nobody had more of an influence on my life than you! You played the role of a second mother, an aunt, an older sister, and most importantly, a best friend—all rolled into one. You taught me so much about loving others, about caring for those-not just in your own family-but anyone and everyone that needed it. You ALWAYS made everyone laugh with your quick wit and never- ending jokes and shenanigans. Your beautiful smile and snorting laughter are ingrained in my mind, and they're something I seek on a daily basis for encouragement. It's been a rough road since you left us, but I know without a doubt, that you are making all the angels in heaven laugh, and you're keeping my big brother company while you play a game of cards with him. I miss you so much, it still hurts every day of my life. But I look forward to seeing you again, someday soon, and in a much better place. I love you!

Coming from a very small town, we were a close-knit bunch of Maroon and Grey Chargers! So many kind people were examples that helped me to develop into the adult I am now, changing my life with their love and kindness, and teaching me, in unsuspecting ways, about God and His love for me. Thank you for being an example that changed my life in great ways.

Thank you: John Soncrant, Sharon Soncrant, Jeff and Madonna Hilarides, Connie Swain, Dean & Ivanne Spooner, Monte and Bridget Putnam, Bonnie and Jerry Prough.

Prologue

"A*ll packed and ready to* go, Champ?" James poked his head into his ten-year old son's room, hoping the boy had finished the task assigned to him earlier that morning.

Without looking up from the comic book that had been keeping his attention, Gage shrugged his shoulder. "Sure, Dad. I guess."

James watched his son as he closed the book and, with little to no enthusiasm, pulled his suitcase from his Stars Wars adorned bed. Gage shuffled towards the doorway, carefully avoiding the piles of Hot Wheels cars and action figures that covered his floor. James knew what was coming next, as Gage pulled to a stop beside of him, finally looking up into his eyes.

"Dad, tell me again why you never come to Nonnie's farm? Don't you like it there?"

James instinctively tensed at his son's mention of the old woman's ranch back in Iowa. He had been expecting the question, because unfortunately, it had become part of their annual routine. A part that James could do without. Just the thought of that place, and the connection it had to his wife's death, could still bring James to his knees.

Even after three long years.

As if it weren't enough, to consider the farm as the single reason he was now a widower and left alone to raise his only son, it had become a place little Gage cherished and longed to be. Though he hated it more than anywhere else on earth, James tried to keep his feelings hidden as he replied with a forced smile. He surely didn't want to cause his boy anymore pain than he had already endured from the tragic loss of his mother.

James ruffled his son's dark hair as he looked down at him. "There's too much work to be done here, Gage. I have a business to run. A business that keeps you fed and clothed. Now, come on." He nudged Gage through the doorway in hopes of ending the conversation.

"But *mom* loved the farm, didn't she?"

James' patience had finally run out. He'd been playing fifty questions with Gage *all* morning. If they didn't hurry, Gage was going to miss his flight; and James sure didn't want to deal with Nonnie's wrath if that were to happen. Standing in the hallway just outside Gage's room, James bent down and tipped back the straw cowboy hat on his son's head, in order to see his eyes as he spoke. Those sparkling blue eyes that he'd inherited, reminded James of his late wife. Most days it hurt too much to even look into them. In an effort to avoid the pain, James had even gone as far as removing all of his son's and dead wife's pictures from site, turning their once warm and inviting home, into a cold and lonely place that James only went to for sleep at night. He didn't need the daily reminder of what he'd lost. Gage had finally gotten the hint and quit asking to see pictures of his mother. And now when the flyers came home for school photos, Gage knew there was no use in asking. The flyer went straight to the trash.

"Why all of these questions *again today*?" James' irritation seeped through his words unintentionally. It seemed that instead of time suppressing his son's wonder as he'd hoped, Gage's curiosity had only increased with age.

"I'm just going to miss you, Dad, that's all." Gage's lower lip quivered slightly as he spoke, and for a moment James thought his son was going to start crying. That was one thing James would not tolerate.

With an uncompromising tone, James directed his words towards his young son. "Gage, remember what I've told you about men showing emotion?"

The quivering lip immediately stilled, and sad, water-filled eyes turned up to face him.

"I'm s...sorry, Dad," Gage's voice crackled in between little gasps, "I....I know.....men don't sh...show emotion, and I'm supposed to be," he sniffed and stretched the sleeve of his shirt across his nose, "growing into a man like you. *Right*?"

"Right." At least that's what James kept telling himself, trying to convince his mind that his own heart was wrong for shedding tears this long after Glory's death. It was a daily struggle to keep them at bay and his emotions in check. But one thing James had learned a long time ago, was that crying would get him nowhere in life. It was best his son learn that lesson early, and protect himself from a life of heartache.

Pleased, that Gage had kept that important tidbit of information tucked into the corner of his brain, James nudged him once more towards the front door. Gage wasn't quite finished though. He stopped and turned to his father again, this time wearing a small hint of a smile.

"You would love the baby cows at the farm!" Gage's small hands covered his mouth as he giggled briefly, his smile fading slowly as his mind seemed to meander back to a more intense subject. He continued, in a voice barely audible to James. "Nonnie always tells me stories about mom. You would really like that part, too."

James patted Gage on the shoulder, wishing he could say or do more to help his son understand there was no use living in the past. For James, that chapter of his life had been closed for three years and he had no intention of ever going back. He had shut everyone out when his wife Glory died, including Gage, unable to even speak her name most days for fear of falling apart. The pain of losing the only woman he had ever loved still kept him up most nights wondering. Why hadn't he made different choices? Why hadn't he supported his wife when she needed him to? And, most importantly, why wasn't he with her when it happened? If he had been, surely, she would still be alive. James shook his head, refusing to surrender to the guilt. It was the past, and he had no desire to live there. With a tone less harsh, but a facial expression that told Gage the conversation was over, James responded.

"I'll bet Nonnie has some great stories to share with you about your mom, Gage. I'm sorry I can't be there with you; but I know you're going to have a great time, just like you do every summer." James stood back up, determined to end the conversation once and for all, and patted Gage on the head. "Don't worry, Champ. September will be here before you know it, and you'll be back here in New York with me, ready to start a new school year."

"School? Yuck, Dad, I don't want to talk about school!" Gage wrinkled his nose in disgust. Reaching for his father's hand, he pulled him towards the door, completely unaware of the single tear that had escaped and made its way down James' face. "C'mon let's go."

"Now boarding flight 309 to Des Moines," the announcement came over the intercom.

"That's your flight number, Gage," James said to his son as he stood from his seat in the gate area. "Time to board."

With a hint of sadness, James realized how little his son needed him right now. Gage didn't hesitate in making his way towards the boarding desk. He'd made this trip so many times, that he had the routine down pat. Maybe it wasn't so much the lack of being needed that caused the ugly feeling in James' gut, but rather just knowing the excitement that was bubbling over in Gage's heart was due to the anticipation of being at the ranch. The one place that consistently provoked twinges of pain and jealousy in James.

"Hey, Gage?" For fear of disobeying his own rule, James cleared his throat as he tugged at Gage's shoulder, causing him to stop. He was not about to let his concern well up from within, even if he did worry about Gage's safety. He turned his son to face him.

"You know that Max will be there when you get off the plane in Des Moines, right?"

Gage's head nodded in agreement.

"And you know," James struggled for control, "that I love you. Right?" He murmured.

"To the moon and stars, Dad! But I love you more." Gage wrapped his arms around his father's waist and squeezed. "I'm going to miss you, Dad. But I will call you every night before bed, okay?"

"I'll be waiting, Champ." James kissed the top of Gage's head before sending him off in the direction of the stewardess, who stood waiting at the gate entrance.

James saw his son's little hand stretch out in a wave goodbye, just before he disappeared into a sea of boarding passengers.

And just like that, it was all business again for James. Over the next three months, he planned to work sun up to sun down, growing his company and not allowing himself time to think about Gage being gone and the reasons why he was alone. He made his way back to the parking ramp, calling the office on the way.

"Max!" Gage squealed with excitement as he ran to the open arms of the old ranch hand, flinging his arms around his sweat and dirt covered neck, and knocking his tattered cowboy hat to the floor.

Max's smile spread from ear to ear as he relished in the boy's presence. "Wow, Gage," he held him at arm's length, "look at you! I think you've grown at least three inches since you were here last summer. Your Nonnie won't even recognize you!" Max beamed with pride as he reached for his hat and stood back up with Gage in his arms, hugging him tight.

"Yes, she *will*, silly," Gage disagreed. "Nonnie could never forget me."

"You are right about that, young man," Max chuckled, then tweaked the boy's nose before letting him down. "You know, your Nonnie is so excited to see you. *And* she's got a very special birthday surprise for you when we get back to the ranch."

It had become a tradition for them when Gage was just five years old. His annual trip to Iowa always took place during his birthday month, as his mother had requested, and his grandmother *always* made a big deal about it. It had been a sore subject between the boy's parents, he had learned from Nonnie, but Glory figured it was the least she could do for her parents after she'd kept them at such a distance from their only grandson. Max was just thankful to be involved in the boy's life in any way that he could. After all, Gage was the closest thing he'd ever have to a grandson of his own. And, he was the grandson to a couple that held a very special spot in his heart. Max's best friend, Jack, and his wife, Naomi, were the two best friends he'd ever had. He and Jack had been friends since middle school, and when Jack and his new bride bought the old farm of Mr. Hulinga's that sat on three hundred acres, Max had willingly accepted the position of ranch hand, that Jack had offered. Now, some forty years later, Max had spent his entire life as part of their family. He'd been an "uncle" to their only daughter, Glory, right up until the day she died in that a horrific accident. When Jack passed away unexpectedly, Max stepped right into his shoes, and kept the ranch running, so his widow would have an income to support herself. Little Gage had been the joy of their lives ever since the day he was born, and Max was honored to step into his new role as surrogate grandfather alongside of Naomi, who had become known as Nonnie by her grandson.

"A *surprise*? Can you tell me what it is?" Gage's eyes grew with wonder as he looked up into his face. The young boy could barely contain his eagerness as he tried to coax the details out of him.

Max shook his head slightly then pressed his thumb and forefinger together, bringing them to his lips and pretending to zip them closed. "My lips are sealed. Your Nonnie wants to be the one to show you, and I wouldn't want to ruin that for her. *Or* you! Now," his eyes filled with fervor, Max tousled the young boy's hair, "let's get your luggage and head home, okay? The sooner we get on the road, the sooner you'll be able to see that surprise."

Max reached out his hand, accepting the familiar warmth and comfort of Gage's tiny fingers, as the two of them strolled towards the baggage claim to collect the boy's things, and make their way to his old pickup.

After the long drive from the airport, it was a celebration of hugs and kisses when he and the boy finally reached the farm. Nonnie met them at the door with her familiar warm smile and, of course, a plateful of her grandson's favorite chocolate chip cookies. Max certainly couldn't deny the joy he felt watching her face light up at the sight of little Gage. The three of them spent the next couple of hours getting lunch, and trying to catch up on the past year of Gage's life. They hadn't gathered much from the boy, which was usual. Max would never understand how a father could care so little, or barely be involved in his own son's life. But James had *never* been up to standards in Max's mind.

After things had settled down a bit, and Gage was unpacked, Max excused himself from the house, while Nonnie cleaned up from lunch. A short time later, the three of them met up, just outside the back door.

"Ready to see your birthday present, June Bug?" Nonnie asked, a sparkle of excitement in her eyes.

Gage jumped up and down, clapping his hands with eagerness. "I'm ready, Nonnie!"

Max chuckled. He couldn't tell which of them was more excited. Nonnie had been waiting for this day a long time. He walked ahead, allowing the two of them to stroll hand in hand from the back porch of the old white farmhouse, across the expansive backyard, to the large red barn where he began to slide open the massive doors.

Gage stopped when he heard an unfamiliar sound from inside.

"What's that noise?" he asked. His eyes were full of curiosity at the tiniest of whinnies coming from behind one of the closed stall doors.

"That's your surprise, Gage. Go on now," Max motioned towards the stall, "and open the door." From out of the corner of his eye, Max could see the smile spread across Nonnie's face. The excitement in her eyes easily matched her grandson's.

With slow and gentle moves, Gage's little hands worked open the latch on the old stall door, the rusty hinges creaking as he pulled it open, and poked his head inside.

"A *pony*! I have my *very own* pony?" Gage's enthusiasm rang out through the dusty frames of wooden stalls, reaching high above to the rafters. The site of a beautiful, newborn Palomino, was everything Max hoped it would be. Without hesitation, the boy rushed into the stall and wrapped his arms around the neck of the unsteady foal, his face buried in the pony's dark, black mane. Max and Nonnie joined him next to the small horse. "This is the best surprise ever, Nonnie!" Gage quickly hopped over to hug his grandmother and kiss her sweetly on the cheek before turning his attention back to the foal.

"I think you're forgetting someone."

Gage spun around on his heel and looked to Nonnie.

"Max," she pointed in his direction, "was the one who suggested this pony as your present. He said you were just the right age for such a responsibility."

The boy wrapped his arms around Max's legs. "Thanks, Max! I *promise* I will take good care of him!"

"I know you will, Gage," he beamed with pride. "You and I," he looked down into the boy's eyes, still full of excitement, "will be spending a lot of time together in the next few weeks so that you can learn all about taking care of your pony."

"She was just born this morning, and she's all yours, Gage," Nonnie smiled. "You're going to have to come up with a name for her though."

Gage's brows knit together as he processed that thought. "Hmmmmmm," he tapped his finger against his chin and looked up towards the rafters, considering his options.

Giving the boy a moment to think about it, Max's attention moved towards Nonnie. "You doing okay?" He placed his hand on Nonnie's shoulder and looked her in the eye. Gage's arrival was all she had talked about for weeks, but he had known her too long to think that Gage's presence didn't bring with it a flood of memories of his mother, and her only daughter.

"Couldn't be better, Max. My world is complete when Gage is here with us." She smiled and turned her attention back to the source of her happiness as he continued to marvel at his new pony.

Us. Max's heart swelled with joy, as the confirmation of her words settled deep into his soul. Lately, *us* had taken on new meaning for Max. He had always considered his best friend, Jack, as family. But it was something else when his wife, and now widow, acknowledged him in that way. He'd never intended to develop feelings for Nonnie, even after Jack's death. But in the past couple of years, something had changed. Somewhere in the midst of all of their shared meals, or maybe their regular conversations about the ranch budget and staff, something was different between them. There seemed to be a spark in Nonnie's eyes when she talked with him now, regardless of what they were discussing. And he would have to be blind to miss the way her hand seemed to linger, just a little longer on his, each morning when she handed him a fresh thermos of coffee for the day. Their talks had grown longer, their time together had increased, and neither one of them seemed anxious to change back to the way it used to be.

The afternoon sped by for the three of them, full of lessons on caring for a newborn horse. By the end of the day, Gage was an expert on getting his pony to nurse, and he took pride in properly brushing the new foal.

Thanks to Max's help, he'd even been able to walk the pony for the first time inside the corral. Gage was, however, still having trouble understanding why he couldn't ride the little one. Max decided that letting the boy take a gallop with him on one of the older horses would get his mind off the pony. So, they headed out on the trails for a while, leaving Nonnie to prepare their evening meal.

"I sure love it here on the farm, Max. I hope someday, when I'm all grown up, I can live here, too!"

He and the boy had stopped briefly to let Poncho get a drink from the stream, when Gage turned sideways as far as he could in the saddle to look up into Max's face.

"Well, Gage, that's a long way off. But you never know what the future holds. Maybe someday this will all be yours."

"*Mine*, Max? That would be *so* cool!" He paused for a moment, then continued, a slight hesitancy in his voice. "But.......you and Nonnie will still be here........*won't* you?"

Max surely didn't want to upset the boy his first day at the ranch, but he couldn't be dishonest with him about the subject either. Especially after all that he'd gone through when losing his mother. Max took a few moments, searching for the right words.

"You know, Gage, God is the only one who knows how long our time on Earth is. Someday, we will go to heaven, but Nonnie and I would sure love to still be around when you're all grown up."

The earlier enthusiasm Gage had displayed, seemed to momentarily take a backseat to sadness. Raising one shoulder he replied, "I know, Max. Just like my mama, we're all going to heaven someday. I just hope you don't go for a long, long time, because I would really miss you. Like I miss my mom."

Hurt, for all that the young boy had gone through, seized Max's heart like a vice grip. But before he could swallow the lump in his throat, and speak encouragement to the boy, Gage turned towards him again, changing the direction of the conversation, as quickly as a shooting star streaking across the night sky.

"Can we make Poncho run fast again, Max? That was fun!"

Relieved by the new topic of discussion, Max was more than happy to oblige. "You bet, Gage." Max gently pulled the reins, guiding the horse away from the stream, before nudging him and taking off in a fast gallop towards the barn.

Later that night, after sharing dinner and chocolate birthday cake, Max gathered with Nonnie and the boy on the back-porch swing, taking advantage of the clear sky and an opportunity to view the hundreds of stars lighting up the night. It had been a long, eventful day and they were past exhausted. But he thought a little fresh evening air, and the hum of a harmonica, would help them all to sleep better. As he held the instrument to his mouth, producing a relaxing and soothing hum, Max watched Nonnie wrap one arm around Gage's shoulders and lean into him, pointing up at the sky.

"Look there, Gage, I believe that's the Little Dipper. See those four stars making up that square," the boys eyes followed his grandmother's old, wrinkled finger as it traced the shape, "and then the three coming down in a straight line?"

"I see it Nonnie! It looks like a kite with a long tail! Show me another one, please!" Gage bounced happily in his seat.

"All right, June Bug, one more. And then I think it will be time for you to call and say goodnight to your father and get tucked into bed."

"Nonnie," Gage's face turned up to hers, "tell me again why you call me June Bug."

Nonnie leaned back against the swing, pulling Gage onto her lap, and Max knew that she was eager to share her favorite story of her daughter and infant son. Glory might have lived hundreds of miles away from her mother, but that didn't stop them from being close. She called home and sent pictures of Gage to her parents regularly. Max could still remember how Nonnie looked forward to those new letters appearing in the mailbox nearly every week.

And phone calls? Those two would be yacking away every time Max happened to need something from Nonnie or in the house. He and Jack would simply look at each other and laugh at the two women, carrying on like they hadn't talked in years. Glory relayed every little detail to Nonnie, of her only grandchild's life, and how happy she was to be a mother to Gage. Nonnie had shared with Max more than once, that if she did one thing that mattered in life, she hoped it would be sharing her daughter's love with her only grandson. So, when Gage grew into a man himself, he would still remember her. Gage had lost his mother shortly after his seventh birthday, way too early to build many lasting memories, and the guilt Nonnie felt over her daughter's loss, still plagued her every day of her life. Max knew it had taken years for her to finally forgive herself for the fact that she hadn't been driving the truck that awful day. He knew that some days were harder than others for her, but he also knew that Nonnie had a love for the Lord. And Max was certain, that love alone was what got her through the loss of her only daughter and husband, their deaths not even two years apart.

"Well, Gage, that was the first nickname your mother gave you, shortly after you were born. The doctor and your mama thought you wouldn't be born until July, but God had a different plan. You surprised *everybody* when you showed up early on June fifteenth. Your daddy couldn't have been prouder when you arrived on Father's Day. When your mama held you in her arms for the very first time, she called you her little June Bug....... and that name just stuck."

"I love to hear stories about my mama, Nonnie," Gage's little fingers wound their way around a long piece of Nonnie's hair that he continued to twirl. "I wish my dad would talk about her." The sadness in Gage's voice tugged at Max's heart, fueling the fire of anger he held towards James.

"I will never understand how that man—"

"Hey, I know what I'm going to name my pony! Gage jumped up from Nonnie's lap, talking right over Max's negative comment. "June Bug. Do you like it Max? Nonnie?" He looked from one to the other, waiting for their nod of approval.

Nonnie was the first to speak, right after she gave Max a death stare that told him he was lucky the boy had interrupted. "I think it's perfect, Gage. Your mama would love it."

Max nodded his approval and reached for Nonnie's hand, giving it a gentle squeeze. A small acknowledgement that he'd been wrong for his negative thoughts and words that had nearly spilled from his mouth. The *last* thing he wanted to do, was hurt Gage. And speaking about his father that way, would only cause more damage to their already troubled relationship. Someday, when he was old enough to understand the truth, he'd realize the kind of man is father was, without any help from Max.

Chapter 1

“That does it!” Arabella closed her planner with a satisfied look on her face, feeling confident that she was finally starting to make some progress. “The menu has been finalized and decorations ordered. Now, if I could only find someone qualified and trustworthy to help me with the updates for this old building! Then, we’ll be right on track for the formal!”

Beth rolled her eyes and sighed loudly. “I *told you* to call Theo. I’m sure he could take a look at things for you, Ari.”

“I sense some frustration in your tone?” Although there was certainly nothing funny about the work that needed to be completed, or the time frame in which it had to be done, Ari couldn’t help but make light of Beth’s ‘always *too* dramatic reaction’! This was the same song and dance that played out between them every spring.

“Frustration? *Really?* That’s what you sense?” Beth mocked surprise, and chuckled. “Well, you hit the nail right on the head, Ari. I sure will be glad when this event is over and my best friend returns from the land of crazy!”

Arabella had been in charge of the elaborate dance, held in her family’s restaurant, for the past ten years. And it never failed. Every year, two months prior to the function, she could feel herself morph into this aggressively driven lunatic, that couldn’t focus on anything else. And this year? She felt *way* more tense than usual.

“Always have to be the drama queen don’t you, Beth?” Ari stood up with a smile. She walked past her friend to the daily menu board, where she began to write out the evening specials.

"C'mon, what's going on with you?" Beth followed, stopping just inches from where Ari stood and placed a hand on her shoulder. "You're raising the bar on your normal hysteria this year. Is there something going on that you want to share with me?"

"Really, Beth, *hysteria*?" she turned around to face her. "C'mon, I'm not *that* bad.......*am* I? I just want it to be perfect........for *them*. You know, every year is a struggle. But for some reason the milestone anniversaries just seem more difficult."

She let her mind wander back in time to that day, to the moment that had changed her life forever. She'd tried to put it behind her. She really had. But it was constantly there, looming over her like a dark cloud that just wouldn't let her move on. It had affected everything in her life. From her relationship with her father, to the fact that she spent so much time running the family restaurant, not allowing herself the chance to date anyone seriously. And, after all this time, she still wanted just one thing. A family. How she would ever have a family, when she couldn't even make time to date, let alone fall in love, was beside her. With an ache finding its way through her words, Ari continued, "Hard to believe it's been ten years already. *Ten. Years. Beth.* I really wish they were here to see it. I just want them to be proud of me."

Beth moved closer, pulling her into a hug**.** "Ari, your family would love what you do to this place every year; the transformation that takes place!" Beth released her and took a step back, far enough away that she could look into her eyes. "They would be so proud. You *have* to know that."

The problem? Every year Ari thought it *was* perfect. Until the morning after. And then the cycle would start again. Always trying to outdo the previous year, making the event bigger, better, and more memorable. It was an event that had put their little lakeshore town on the map, one that the citizens of their community eagerly looked forward to. An event the Moretti family was known for. Ari had never been shy about the fact that she continued with the yearly event to honor her parents, and their presence in the community. But it had become even more than that. It was a memorial to her sister, Maria, and the senior prom she never got the chance to attend.

"Anyway," Ari pulled away from Beth, "I do appreciate the suggestion. But, *Theo*?" she grimaced. "I'm just not sure I could trust him with a project like this." Ari motioned to the surrounding structure, her family's pride and joy.

The ten-thousand square foot, three-story, brick historical monument, served as the town's favorite and highly recommended restaurant. Arabella's grandparents, Leonardo and Marta, had moved to the States from Italy in their late twenties, and with a newborn daughter, barely a year after they were married. Once they stumbled across the sleepy little town of Rock Haven, they immediately knew they'd found the place where their dreams of owning their own business, and raising a family, would come true. Having barely enough money to pay rent to the tenant, or keep food on their own table, Leonardo and Marta opened a tiny corner restaurant in the heart of one of Michigan's Great Lake shoreline communities. With five family recipes from back home, and a lot of prayers, Francesca's began to grow almost immediately after their doors were opened. Over the next thirty years, they continued watching their dreams come true, as each and every day their business grew in volume and popularity. The regular customers quickly became some of Leonardo and Marta's best friends. When the elderly couple finally decided to retire, their daughter Francesca, Arabella and Maria's mother, and after whom the restaurant was named, agreed with her husband, Eduardo Moretti, to take over the business. Arabella and her sister had lived out their childhoods in the restaurant, learning more from their "hands-on" experiences than any text book could have taught them. It was a no brainer that eventually they would carry out tradition and run the business themselves.

"You could always just search on Google for someone. I'm sure there are plenty of restoration specialists within a hundred-mile radius of Rock Haven. And besides, who wouldn't love a chance to work on a project like this?"

Ari wasn't really listening. She and Beth had been best friends since first grade, and while she respected Beth's opinion, this was *her* family business. When it came to the family business, Ari took on an entirely new set of standards.

"I couldn't hire someone from Google, Beth. It has to be someone I trust completely and feel confident in their abilities."

Beth placed her hand on her best friend's shoulder and looked her in the eye. "And don't forget you need someone that is available on short notice. "Arabella," you *do realize* the formal is just five weeks away, *don't you*?" Beth questioned, her words laced with doubt.

"How could I forget *that,* Beth?" Ari's voice slowly began to escalate along with her worry. "It's only the *single* most *important* thing in my life right now!"

Beth shook her head, and snickered.

"What's *that* all about?" Arabella crossed her arms, just waiting for what was sure to be some snarky comment about her love life. It seemed that her love life, or lack thereof, was what everyone at Francesca's enjoyed talking and joking about most.

"Oh, please, Ari. Don't you think it's sad that the dance is the most important thing in your life? I mean, I get that the restaurant is important; but don't you wish you had someone special in your life to share things with?" Beth's tone became more playful, her facial expressions exaggerated, as she continued. "Maybe someone could twirl you around on the dance floor this year? Instead of you always being the one to sit and watch."

"Please!" Ari refuted. "As if, you and Sam, and the rest of the staff, are not important? I couldn't *imagine* having any better group of people to love."

Beth shook her head. "Seriously, Arabella? You are either extremely naïve or just good at avoiding the real topic." Beth cocked her head and planted her hand on her hip. "When I say 'someone special', I mean someone you can spend the evening dancing with, instead of worrying about refills on the guests' champagne. Have you ever had a date to one of the balls?"

Before Ari could respond, Beth continued. "I already have the answer to that, so don't even try. *Everyone* in Rock Haven knows you've never had a date to the dance."

Ari threw her hands in the air, frustrated with the direction this talk was taking. "Ugh! This conversation is over!" She turned and stormed towards the bar where Sam stood, silently taking in the girls' conversation. "Please, tell me you're on my side, just this once, Sam?"

He just stared at her, a grin slowly spreading across his face, and didn't say a word.

"Ari, you know we only bring it up because we love you." Beth joined them at the bar, slipping her arm around Arabella's waist and laying her head on her best friend's shoulder.

"What I know, is that you two are *impossible!*" Ari gently slipped out of Beth's hold. "I don't have time to be thinking about romance, okay. And, even if I wanted to, there isn't *anyone* remotely close to this town that I would even consider dating."

"Some help please, Sam?" Beth pleaded her case.

Sam looked at Beth quickly before his eyes landed on Ari. He shrugged. "Sorry kid, but I have to side with Beth on this one. I think you are selling yourself short. You deserve to find love and happiness."

Ari groaned in response. Why were they always ganging up on her when it came to her love life? Didn't they get the fact that she didn't have time for dating? *Someone* had to be responsible for the restaurant, and that left little to no time to socialize. More than anyone else, Beth and Sam should recognize that. Sam had been with her family's business for over twenty years. He had been a father figure and mentor to her, especially in the five years since she lost her own father, who happened to be Sam's best friend. Sam and Beth knew Ari better than anyone else. They had to know how much it took just for her to stay afloat most days.

"I truly appreciate that you two think you have to gang up on me like this. Makes me feel *so* loved!" Ari's mocked them both, placing her hands over her heart. Then, in a more serious tone, she dismissed herself and ended the conversation. "Alright, I need to get back to work! The dinner crowd will be here before we know it; and I have a thousand things to get done."

Beth turned towards Ari. "Yes, ma'am!"

"I take it you are still planning on filling in as hostess tonight?"

"Absolutely, just let me get changed." Beth saluted Arabella, a stern look covering her face. "I will be back in a jiffy, reporting for duty."

Ari wrapped her arms around Beth and hugged her once again, the conversation about her love life now forgotten. "You, are a life saver! Thank you so much for always helping out on short notice. I'm hoping to interview a few more applicants this week. If all goes well, I won't need you past Wednesday night."

"You're welcome. Besides you'll make it up to me. I'm sure little Chloe will need to have some Auntie Arabella time in the very near future," Beth teased. Chloe was the cutest little eight-month old cherub, belonging to Beth and her husband Anthony.

"Being Chloe's godmother was the best gift you could've ever given me. You know that, right?"

Beth's face grew serious. "Ari, if something ever happened to Anthony and me, you are the *only* one I would trust to raise Chloe."

"I hope someday I can repay the favor. Ask you to be godmother to my son or daughter." Arabella's eyes were marked with sadness. "That is, if—"

"You will, Ari," Beth interrupted. "Someday you are going to make a wonderful mother, and me a godmother."

"Yeah well, I kind of need a husband to do that. And my prospects aren't looking so great right now."

"Maybe you should try *dating*? I know that is a crazy concept for you, but c'mon Ari. You have to start somewhere. Let the business set on the back burner for a while. It's not going anywhere. And you have more than enough staff you can depend on."

Ari shrugged. "I don't know, Beth. I couldn't even guess where to begin. There isn't anybody in town that I *want* to date and—" she paused momentarily, then, as if a lightbulb clicked on in her mind, she continued, "I thought we were *past* this conversation for today?"

"I'm just saying, keep that option open. You never know when Mr. Right might walk through that door!" Beth turned and started for the restroom. "I've got to get ready, or you won't have a hostess tonight."

As Beth departed, Ari made her way down the hall towards the kitchen, her best friend's words bouncing around in her mind.

Dating? How would I even manage to find time to date? Plus, my focus should be on the restaurant, shouldn't it? Oh, it's always the same excuse. Maybe Beth is right; I should just leave the option open, just in case Mr. Right does come along. Mr. Right? Could there really be a Mr. Right out there somewhere, looking for me?

Ari shook the thoughts from her head. She needed to focus on work; this was no time to be thinking about a relationship!

Gage yawned and shook his head, trying to keep his tired eyes focused on the road. He'd left New York City at five a.m. and had nearly twelve hours under his belt. Passing a rest area sign, he decided to stop and get a quick breath of fresh air to keep him awake and alert. He pulled into a parking spot and headed inside, taking a moment to stop and look at the giant map of Michigan that hung on the wall.

"Not too far to go," Gage mumbled as his finger traced his route across the Great Lake State towards the western edge that ran along Lake Michigan.

"Where you headed, son?" An elderly gentleman shuffled next to Gage, as he continued to stare at the map, trying to decide how much longer his stomach could wait for dinner.

"One of my colleagues recommended the town of Rock Haven. Are you familiar with it?"

"Oh, sure," the old man nodded, "been there quite a few times actually. Nice little lakeshore town. You picked the best time to go if you're looking for some quiet relaxation. By the end of next month, that place will turn into the hottest tourist attraction in the state," he chuckled. "Little too crazy for an old man like me," he elbowed Gage gently in the side. "Oh, and did I mention the good food?" The old man shook his head and licked his lips as if he were sitting at a dinner table staring down at a juicy slab of rare prime rib. "Mmmm, mmmm, mmm. You *have* to check out Francesca's. Fresh pan-fried blue gill all summer long. And barbeque ribs to die for."

The mention of ribs had Gage's full attention. "Really? Francesca's was it?"

"You got it, kid!" The elderly man slapped Gage on the shoulder. "You can't miss the place; it's the most stunning building downtown, sitting just up the hill from the lake."

"So, are you from around the area then?"

The gentle eyes of the old man twinkled, as he replied. "Not too far from here. Just south of Rock Haven about thirty miles. Me and the misses," he thumbed towards the ladies' room, "are on our way east to visit the newest great granddaughter. Two weeks old today."

"Fred, are you rambling on about that baby again?" A petite, grey-haired woman with a wide smile joined them. "Sorry if he's talking your ear off." She shook her head but her smile remained. "The man can talk more than a hair salon *full* of women."

The old man looked at his wife and patted her shoulder before turning back to Gage. "I guess the boss says it's time to go."

"Well, thank you. I do appreciate it. Ma'am it was nice to meet you." Gage shook the gentleman's hand and nodded to his wife, as they slowly walked away, hand in hand. The scene struck Gage in a funny way. Made him think of his Nonnie and Max, and how much he missed them. A thought, almost sad, crossed his mind. Would he ever know what it was like to have that kind of love? According to his father, there was no such thing.

After using the restroom and climbing back into the front seat of his car, Gage pulled out his phone and Googled the restaurant to read the reviews.

"Hmmm...sounds like I will definitely be making a stop at Francesca's tonight," he said, as he scrolled through the menu, reading the positive comments about the food. He turned the key in the ignition and was back on the highway in a jiffy, singing at the top of his lungs to the country music he'd found on the radio.

It was forty-five long minutes later, when he saw the first road sign for Rock Haven.

"*Finally!*" he sighed. "I didn't think I'd ever find this place." Gage followed the signs and turned right off the exit ramp, in the direction of Francesca's. The reviews he'd read about the barbeque rib dinner kept playing back through his mind, as his stomach growled with anticipation.

Maybe if he was lucky, he could still make it to the beach after dinner. He could capture some shots of the sunset over the water, maybe find a vacant room for rent. He'd left New York three weeks early for exactly this reason. He wanted to take his time, enjoy the scenery, and relax a bit. Running an architecture firm was very demanding, more so now since his father's retirement left him as the sole owner. The only time he ever took off work, was for his yearly trip back to Iowa. And he had decided this time, to make his annual trip to the farm more than just a quick run to Nonnie's.

Gage found the restaurant easily enough, but securing a parking spot proved nearly impossible, as he circled around the lot a third time. "I'll take this as a good sign and hope the food is as great as what I'm expecting," he muttered. As if his stomach understood his words, it rumbled loudly in response. Finally, a black Jeep Wrangler backing out, caught Gage's attention and he quickly claimed it's parking spot.

After climbing out of his car and taking a minute to stretch, his eyes were drawn to the breathtaking site of the large brick structure and its surroundings. The extraordinary building stood three stories tall. The lower level opened up to a sidewalk running parallel to a canal, dotted with expensive sailboats and yachts that belonged to homeowners across the channel. The second story had a massive outdoor deck, adorned with white patio lights and high-top tables. All were centered around a four-sided, glass enclosed, electric fireplace. Gage was impressed. He made his way to the restaurant's impressive front entrance, through crowds of people gathered on either side of the massive mahogany doors, hoping the wait wouldn't be too lengthy.

"Good evening, sir. Just one tonight, or will there be others joining you?" A petite brunette, with a name tag that read 'Beth,' greeted Gage with a smile. Noting her cute figure, Gage's eyes roamed towards her left ring finger.

Just my luck.

With a sly grin he responded, "Unfortunately for me, Beth, it looks like I'll be dining alone tonight. How long do you think the wait will be?"

Without skipping a beat, and obviously not interested in his flirting, the hostess looked down at her list and seating chart, before taking a couple steps to her left and peaking around the corner to the adjoining room.

Gage stood in place, momentarily forgetting the pretty girl in front of him, as he directed his thoughts to the uniqueness of the restaurant, mesmerized more by the interior of the building than he had been with the exterior. Directly behind the Hostess' station, and off to one side, was a massive open dining area, that had to be three thousand square feet, and overflowing with dinner guests. He followed Beth's gaze into the opposite direction, noting how the space opened up into a bar area with seating for another hundred or so. This place was an architect's dream come true. It's original red brick, and exposed duct work, paired well with the solid woodwork of bar tops and tables. Industrial lighting and fixtures rounded out the look, creating a warm and welcoming atmosphere. Somebody had really taken the time to keep the history of the place preserved, while bringing it into present day. Gage thought to himself that he would like to meet said person.

"That depends on how picky you are about a seat." The hostess' words pulled Gage's thoughts away from the structure and back to her. "If you don't mind sitting at the bar, there happens to be one stool available. I could seat you right now."

Worried more about the increased rumbling of his stomach than where he sat, Gage happily agreed. "I would love to sit at the bar." He followed Beth through the crowd to the very last seat at the end of the bar where he was greeted by a husky, grey-haired, middle-aged man serving drinks.

"Sam here will take good care of you. Enjoy."

After the hostess turned to walk away, Gage hoisted himself up onto a stool as the bartender placed a napkin in front of him.

"Good evening, young man. My name's Sam. What can I get for you tonight?"

There was something about the older man's pale blue eyes that immediately drew Gage in. "Nice to meet you, Sam," Gage extended his hand in greeting. "My name is Gage. Gage Russell. And I'd like to start with a menu if that's okay?" Gage placed his camera bag on the bar. "Oh, and how about a root beer before I forget? I read some reviews online that mentioned a licorice one that you have?"

"One licorice root beer, coming right up." Sam walked towards the cooler and returned a few minutes later with Gage's drink, giving him just enough time to browse the menu and make a choice. "So, tell me Gage Russell, what brings you to our neck of the woods? Are you vacationing here with family? Here on business, maybe?"

Gage took a swig of his soda and paused for a moment, savoring the taste on his tongue before answering. "Well, first off, let me say the reviews didn't do this justice." Gage tipped the bottle in Sam's direction. "This, tastes delicious. But then again," he smiled, "maybe that's just my opinion after being on the road thirteen long hours today!"

Sam smiled back at him.

"I'm from New York, just on my way to visit family in Iowa."

"Iowa?" Sam questioned with slight concern. "Aren't you a little out of your way?"

Gage nodded in agreement as a chuckle escaped his lips. "Yes, I certainly am."

After taking another drink, Gage continued. "You know, I make this trip every year, and it's always been a straight shot across the highway with one," he pointed one finger in the air for added effect, "thing in mind. Getting to my destination as quickly as I can. But this year, I thought I'd change it up a bit. Explore the world a little and see what's out there beyond big city life. So," he shrugged, "when a colleague mentioned this little beach town that his family visits, I thought, 'why not'?"

The couple sitting next to Gage called over to Sam, explaining they were heading out. Sam took a step to his left and reached out to shake the gentleman's hand. "Chris," Sam's eyes moved to focus on his dinner companion, "Rachel, good to see you as always. You tell that boy of yours he did an outstanding job last week. That was something," Sam shook his head and grinned, "pitching his first no hitter."

"We'll tell him. Thanks again, Sam." The couple couldn't do a thing to hide the pride that came across in their smiles as they waved goodbye to the bartender one last time before walking out. After wiping down the bar where they had been seated, Sam made his way back to Gage, picking up their conversation right where it was left off.

"Well, you've certainly come to the right place if you're looking for something completely opposite of New York City. And you won't find a more beautiful little town anywhere in the country. Of course, after living here fifty-seven years, I *may* be a little biased."

There was something about Sam's warm smile, or maybe just the friendly atmosphere of the place, that made Gage feel right at home.

"So, Gage, tell me about your life back in the Big Apple."

Gage talked about his architecture firm back in New York, about how he'd gone into the business to please his father. He mentioned how he had worked construction jobs during his summer breaks from college; and how he had fallen in love with the creating and building aspect of the job. Now, he felt his talents were being wasted sitting behind a desk, drawing blueprints. He'd rather be on site, building and constructing, along-side his various crews.

Sam shared some small details about the restaurant and the town itself. He shared the story of how the current owner's grandparents had come from Italy over fifty years ago. How they started out occupying just a tiny corner on the main floor of the restaurant, until eventually, it had grown to consume the entire three-story building, and nearly an entire block by itself. It was intriguing to Gage, and he soaked up every morsel of detail Sam provided.

Gage had consumed two additional root beers, an entire rack of barbeque ribs and side of rice pilaf, when Sam wandered back to him with the offer of another drink.

"As amazing as all that was," Gage pointed at his empty plate, "I couldn't eat or drink one more thing. I'm stuffed!" Sam smiled as he watched Gage pat his full stomach. In the last hour that they had spent getting to know each other, the two had quickly bonded like old friends.

"So, no dessert then?" Sam proposed with a grin.

"Actually," Gage focused on the bartender's words, "I would like to head down to the beach and get some shots of the sunset before it's too late."

"I'll tell you what," Sam said. "How about you stop back by after you get your pictures, and I'll hold a piece of our famous bread pudding for you. Maybe then I can introduce you to the owner of this fine establishment."

Sam's invitation held only a fraction of lure, until he pointed out the owner across the room. Gage's heart began to beat wildly inside his chest.

"That's our precious Arabella, right over there." Sam pointed towards a stunning, raven-haired beauty, with a figure that would stop a man dead in his tracks. The way that sapphire dress was hugging her in all the right places, well Gage could hardly catch his breath.

"She......she's the owner of this place?" he stuttered.

Sam nodded. "You might want to wipe the drool off of your chin, Gage." Sam waded a napkin and tossed it at him jokingly.

Gage paid no attention to Sam's words. His mind was on one thing at the moment. He wanted to meet the woman across the room that had taken his breath away. She was a beauty with her long, sleek, black hair, curvy figure that would make any man take notice, and the face of an angel. Just the kind of girl he'd like to meet on his one-day stop. One night, one beautiful woman, and no strings attached sounded like his kind of fun.

"Gage, yoo-hoo!" Sam waved a white dish rag in front of Gage's face until he had his attention once again. "This place will be clearing out in another thirty minutes or so. Maybe I can introduce you to Arabella, and she can fill you in on some more of the history behind the business."

"Think maybe I could get a tour if the boss isn't too busy? This place is just amazing."

And what is even more amazing is the woman that's attached to it. Gage's eyes followed her as she made her way across the room, chit-chatting with the customers.

"Are you sure it's just the building you're interested in seeing?" Sam chuckled at Gage's fascination with Ari. "I'll see what I can do, but she's pretty busy. Now, if you head south out of the restaurant," Sam pointed towards the door, "the beach is about half a mile away. You'll see the lighthouse from the top of the hill. Once you get to the beach, hang a left, and you'll walk straight into the dunes and beach grass. I promise you'll get some amazing photos from that area."

Gage stood up, grabbed his camera bag, and reached out to shake the bartender's hand. "Thanks a lot, Sam, I appreciate everything. I should be back in about an hour or so. If that's okay?"

"Perfect. We should be closing up for the night right about that time. I'll let the boss know you'll be stopping back, and I'll hold that dessert for you, too. By the way, where are you staying tonight?"

"Maybe you could recommend something?" Gage asked nonchalantly. "A bed and breakfast? Or even just a small room," he shrugged. "I didn't make reservations ahead of time."

Sam stared at Gage as if he were an alien with four heads, breathing fire. "You're joking right, kid? This town is booked solid *every* night from now until November first! You did realize you were coming to a lakeshore community, right?"

Gage's heart sank. He wasn't sure why all the fuss over a lakeshore community. But now that he'd found this place, he wished he'd thought ahead. Especially after getting a good look at the owner of Francesca's. He also wasn't very excited about the thought of driving anymore, after all the hours he'd put in behind the wheel today. Sam must have read his mind.

"Why don't I do some asking around for you? Maybe I can talk to a friend or two and see if we can't find you a room for the night?"

"You don't have to do all of that for me," Gage waved him off. "I guess I just didn't plan well. I don't take a vacation very often. It's really no problem. I'll just head out after I see the sunset and I'll find a hotel somewhere along the way."

Sam held his hand out to stop him. "Gage, you won't find any open rooms for miles along the shoreline. This is our busy season, son. Now, you just go enjoy that sunset, and come on back here when you're done. We'll figure something out for you. It might not be anything fancy though. Not like what you're used to out there in New York City," Sam chuckled.

"Well, thank you again, Sam. And don't worry about me needing anything fancy. I left all of that back in the city." Gage tossed his camera bag over his shoulder and headed out the door, looking forward to the walk. It was a beautiful evening. The late-spring air was still warm enough that he didn't require a jacket. He made his way along the canal, the smell of lilacs drifting through the air, and bright patches of daffodils and tulips dotting the walkway.

As he continued down the hill, towards the most stunning sunset he'd ever seen, Gage was thankful he'd remembered to charge his camera batteries. The sidewalks and beach were still packed with locals and tourists, unwilling to give up on the beautiful day before absolutely necessary. Bright dots of color surrounded him, as beach goers and families with children made their way across the sand through the crowd, enjoying ice cream and conversations. As he drew closer to the lighthouse, Gage could see sailboats skimming across the water. The large, orange fireball was slowly making its descent to rest briefly on the horizon. He walked the entire length of the pier, and was able to get some amazing shots of both the newly restored, red lighthouse, and the boats on the water.

Gage's attention was pulled suddenly, when a young boy yelled out to his father for help with reeling in a large fish that he'd hooked. The father's eyes were filled with nearly as much excitement as his son's; as together they reeled in one of the biggest fish Gage had ever seen. Gage snapped a picture of the bittersweet scene, wishing he had a memory like that of he and his father.

Sam hadn't been joking when he told him where to get the best photos. Gage traced his footsteps back to the beach from the pier and turned towards a spot that looked like something out of a magazine. The tall, green, dune grass poked through the silky beach sand in blotches, across an area that spread out farther than Gage's eye could wander. Up on the hill, overlooking the beach, was a line of large beach homes and condos that stretched just as far.

Gage had never seen anything so beautiful; it certainly beat anything he could experience in the city. And though he loved his Nonnie's farm in Iowa, it didn't compare to the scene laid out before him now. He settled into position and began capturing the view around him, click after click. By the time he glanced at his watch, he realized an hour had passed in what felt like seconds. He jumped up and threw his lens cap on the camera, taking note of how quickly dusk was settling in.

Hoping he wouldn't be too late to enjoy Sam's offer of bread pudding, and more importantly, meeting Arabella, Gage quickly made his way back across the beach and up the hill towards Francesca's.

Arabella made her usual rounds, talking to everyone in the restaurant. Regulars and new visitors alike, she made them all feel welcome.

"Good evening, Mr. and Mrs. Spencer. How are you both doing?"

The elderly couple glanced up at Ari, pleasant smiles on their faces. Mrs. Spencer was the first to speak. "We are both well, dear. And how about yourself?"

"I couldn't be better." Ari replied with the same bright and cheery voice that all her guests were used to hearing.

"How are the plans for the dance coming?" Mr. Spencer questioned. He had been a great friend to Arabella's father; and usually at some point in the month leading up to the big event, he had volunteered in one way or another.

"Things are running smoothly, Mr. Spencer, and right on schedule." Ari patted him on the shoulder lightly. "Of course, that doesn't mean you won't be getting a call in the next couple of weeks. Something always comes up last minute, and we're sure to need your help." Ari winked at Mrs. Spencer, letting the older woman know she hadn't forgotten their conversation from the week before, when it just so happened to be mentioned, that Mr. Spencer *loved* being involved in the planning of the dance, just as he had when Ari's father was still alive.

Mr. Spencer blushed. "Well, I'm just a phone call away, dear."

Ari left the couple and continued interacting with guests, making sure that everyone was comfortable and had exactly what they needed. This was the reason her family restaurant was a success. Learning very young from her parents and grandparents, Ari treated each and every customer as if they were family. The same as it had been done for two previous generations. As she excused herself from the Phillips' dining party, Beth caught up to her. Tugging gently on her arm, Beth leaned in, whispering into Ari's ear.

"It's about time I caught up with you! Have you been by to check on Sam lately?" Beth pulled Ari to a stop.

"No, why? Is there something wrong?" Concern hung on Ari's words until Beth's frantic expression changed.

"Not exactly." Beth teased with a smile. "But there might be if you don't go check out our most recent newcomer to Francesca's, who happens to be sitting at the far end of the bar chatting with Sam."

"Okaaaay," Ari's face scrunched up with confusion as she tried to sneak a peek over Beth's shoulder.

Beth took a step to the left and nudged Ari past her, in the direction of the bar, and whispered into her ear as she passed. "Hottie doesn't even begin to describe him! Oh, and did I mention that he isn't wearing a ring?"

Oh, I should have known! Ari took a deep breath and exhaled long and slow. *When will everyone stop trying to play matchmaker with me?*

Ari tried, as always, to convince herself she wasn't interested in their suggestions. But that was a battle she was sadly losing. Admittedly, at twenty-six, she thought she would have long been married and started a family by now. If only she could take a break from working so much, like Beth and Sam suggested. But then again, she wasn't sure true love even existed for her. Not if any of the guys she'd met were any indication. Maybe work was just a safer bet.

Ari meandered around a few tables and peered toward the nameless stranger at the end of the bar.

Well, I guess it couldn't hurt to casually stroll in there. Just to make sure Sam and the guests are all doing okay. 'Keeping the option open'. Beth's words drifted through her mind again.

His well-styled, jet-black hair and backside were the only things she got close enough to see.

"Arabella, dear, come here." Mrs. Maxwell flagged her over to a nearby table.

"I'd like you to meet my grandson, Robert. He's here visiting for a week."

Ari turned to greet Mrs. Maxwell's dinner guest. "It's nice to meet you, Robert." She reached out to shake his hand.

"It's nice to meet you too, Arabella. My grandmother has had nothing but wonderful things to say about you."

Of course, she has. Here we go with the matchmaking! Again!

"But, I will say, she didn't come close to describing your beauty."

Ari felt the heat rush to her cheeks. "That's very kind of you, Robert."

"You know, dear," Mrs. Maxwell gave Ari 'the look,' "Robert is free tomorrow afternoon. Maybe you'd like to give him a tour of the town? Enjoy lunch somewhere together?"

Ari gently patted Mrs. Maxwell's wrinkled hand. She knew the old woman had her best interest at heart, but this was the *fourth* grandson of hers that Ari had to turn down! And this one wasn't even close to her age. He had to be at least ten years her senior. Ari played it off the best she could.

"Now, Mrs. Maxwell, how fair would that be to your *other* grandsons?" Ari sent a teasing grin in the older woman's direction, hoping to keep the mood light. "I couldn't possibly agree to a date with Robert and cause strife within the family." Ari placed her hand on her heart, pretending to be slightly offended.

By the time Ari was able to excuse herself from the old woman's matchmaking fiasco and wander towards the bar, she noticed the dark-haired stranger had disappeared. Slightly disappointed, but almost relieved at the same time, she resigned to the kitchen to assist with closing duties.

Chapter 2

Arabella's feet were killing her! She slipped out of her three-inch pumps and sighed, as she slumped into a chair, briefly resting her head on the four-top. It had been busier than usual tonight, and she couldn't wait to get upstairs and draw a hot bubble bath for herself. But first, she needed to catch up with Sam and help close out the books for the night. Slightly irritated that he'd pick tonight of all nights to disappear, which wasn't like the bartender at all, Ari contemplated starting a search for him. She stood, trying to decide which direction might get her to him the fastest, when she heard footsteps behind her. Expecting to see Sam, she was caught off guard when she turned to find Beth standing before her.

"Hey, what are you still doing here? I thought you left a while ago?" Ari questioned with slight concern. Beth was usually out the door and on her way home to her husband and precious daughter long before Ari finished up.

"I was just helping out in the kitchen for a bit. Besides," Beth's mischievous smile reached her sparkling eyes, "I wanted to find out if you introduced yourself to Mr. Hottie, and what his story was."

Ari chuckled and leaned back in her chair. "You weren't helping in the kitchen at all were you, Miss Nosy Pants?"

"Guilty," Beth raised her right hand in the air. "But for good reason."

She smiled her award-winning, cheesy grin that usually made Ari cave and give into giggles. But not tonight. Ari was going to dish it right back to her best friend, and teach Beth a lesson, for always trying to meddle in her love life.

"I'm sorry, but you will be disappointed to know that I never even got the chance to introduce myself. The back of his head was the only thing I got close enough to see. And now....... I'm afraid he's gone."

Beth just stared at Ari, her mouth hanging wide open.

"Oh, c'mon Beth, you know how it is. First the Smith's, next the Harrison's, and then on to the Olsen's. Oh, and let's not forget good 'ole Mrs. Maxwell and her grandsons. I get pulled in every direction, talking with the people that keep my restaurant in business." Ari held her arms out, palms facing up, "What was I to do?"

"Hmmm, figures!" Beth crossed her arms over her chest, not even trying to hide her frustration. "Well, I guess there's no reason for me to hang out here any longer then. I will see you tomorrow?"

Ari was always happy when Beth agreed to help out at Francesca's. She knew more about the restaurant than any of the other staff did. In fact, she'd mentioned to Beth on more than one occasion that she could probably run it better, if Ari just stepped out of the way. Beth wouldn't even let Ari add her to the payroll. She instead, just volunteered her time whenever the restaurant was short-handed.

"As usual." Ari stood to hug her friend goodbye. "Hey, thanks again, Beth, for all of your help." Ari turned in a circle, taking in the room around her. "I guess I need to go hunt down Sam to help me close out the books. Have a good night, and tell Anthony thanks for letting us borrow you again."

"No problem. I will see you tomorrow then. Goodnight, Ari."

As Beth walked away, Arabella reached for her glass on the table and took a long sip of water. Before she could swallow, another noise behind her caught her attention.

"Ahem," Sam cleared his throat, "excuse me, Arabella. Do you have a moment? This is the boy I was telling you about earlier tonight. I would like you to meet Gage."

Arabella spun around and water spewed from her mouth as she choked and sputtered.

Boy? Uh, this is definitely not a boy. This is a very attractive, full-grown man, with biceps that....oh, my! And a smile that nearly reaches his brilliant blue eyes! Wow!

Ari's thoughts were all jumbled, as she stood drinking in his sight from head to toe. Once, then twice, then.....

"Ari? Is, something wrong?"

Trying to maintain her composure, Ari straightened and cleared her, suddenly dry throat. For a very brief moment, she allowed her gaze to travel to Sam.

"When you said boy, I…I wasn't expecting someone," her eyes roamed toward the dark-haired stranger once more, "quite this *old*."

Oh no, what am I even saying? Ari couldn't seem to make her mouth work the way she wanted it to.

"I….I mean….you're not old, I just thought…well, Sam said boy, and I thought, you know, someone much younger than me, like just out of high school young, which you are definitely *not*." Her eyes remained glued to his upper body.

"Arabella, are you okay?" Sam, looking perplexed as Ari floundered around in front of them, stopped her before she could make an even bigger fool of herself. Her reaction didn't appear to be lost on Gage, however, and his smile only deepened.

"Wh…what?" she whispered, slowly pulling her gaze from the stranger's eyes and looking towards Sam, as if she just realized he was standing there. "Oh, yes……yes, I'm fine, Sam.

"Good. Now, as I was saying. Gage, this is Arabella Moretti, the owner of Francesca's. Arabella meet Gage Russell. Gage is on his way to Iowa, all the way from New York City."

Arabella extended her hand to Gage, but instead of the expected handshake, he pulled her hand towards his mouth where he placed a gentle kiss across her knuckles.

Arabella couldn't move. Couldn't think. Couldn't speak. And if her knees didn't quit shaking she might—

"It's a pleasure to meet you, Arabella. Your restaurant is quite charming, I must say." He released Ari's hand, his gaze still fixed upon her.

Her fingers instantly missed the warmth of his touch. "I…um…yes, um…well, thank you. Yes, I do really love this place."

Why won't my mouth work like I want it to?

Sam jumped in, and Ari couldn't have been more relieved. At the moment, she couldn't control her mouth *or* her eyes, let alone try to carry on an intelligent conversation.

"So, I made a few calls. Unfortunately," Sam shrugged, "I wasn't able to find a room for Gage. I was wondering if you would be open to him staying at your place for the night, Ari?"

"Mm…*my*…….place?" The color drained from her face.

Gage shook his head immediately. "No, I could never ask you to do that for a total stranger. It's really not a problem. I can just jump back on the highway and—"

"No, no, no!" Sam dismissed Gage's refusal and continued. "That's not what I meant. I would never suggest *that*. Arabella stays in the loft on the third floor *here*," he pointed towards the ceiling above them, "but she also has a house on the shoreline overlooking the water. In fact, you were probably looking at it tonight while you were down there taking pictures, Gage. Anyway, the house is empty. R*ight,* Arabella?"

Sam looked towards Ari expectantly.

"Yeeeesss." She responded slowly at first. But then, the idea seemed to catch up with her and, a spark came to life in her eyes. "That's correct Sam. In fact, I think that's a brilliant idea. It won't take much to get some clean sheets and toiletries around, and I'll have the place ready in a jiffy." Suddenly her feet, which seemed so tired a moment ago, were now aching in a different way; aching to find a place for Gage to settle in, so that he wouldn't leave town tonight.

"I really didn't mean to intrude on you both like this. Are you sure it won't be a problem? I would be more than happy to pay for the use of your home, Arabella."

Again, the inviting eyes drew her in, and Ari found it hard to even form words. "No.... problem.... at..... all."

Arabella couldn't remember a time when she acted so tongue tied in the presence of the opposite sex. That just wasn't who she was. She was all business and no time for play, and had been ever since tragedy struck her family, the year she turned sixteen. She grew up fast that spring; and became the rock that her father depended on for everything. By the time she turned eighteen, Ari could run a home, and a business, more efficiently than anyone she knew. But noticing a good-looking guy like Gage? That was just something she didn't do. Those closest to Ari knew she dreamed of being a wife and mother someday. But getting her to cut back on her work, and actually take a step in the direction of dating? Well, that was another story. And it appeared Sam was very willing to help.

"Arabella, I promised Gage a piece of our famous bread pudding. Why don't you sit down and join him while I grab that?"

"Sam, I've got to get the books clos—"

"Now, now. I will take care of the books tonight." Sam shushed her, then pulled out a chair from a nearby table, prompting her to sit down with Gage. "Don't you even worry about it. In fact, after you two share dessert, why don't you take Gage over to the house and get him settled in?" Sam suggested. "And then maybe tomorrow he could come by for that tour we talked about, huh?"

"Tour? Sure, I guess we could do that. I mean, if Gage doesn't have to leave town too early tomorrow?" Ari's eyes were full of hope as she prodded Gage for an answer.

"No," he responded quickly. "In fact, I'm not in a hurry at all. I promised myself I would take my time and enjoy the trip. So," he continued with a smug smile, "a tour tomorrow sounds perfect!"

"Sounds like a date to me! Now, let me go grab that dessert and a couple of forks." Sam quietly dismissed himself.

After two hours of friendly conversation, and a piece of bread pudding that he continued to rave about, Arabella and Gage made their way towards the parking lot.

Arabella yawned and stretched her arms above her head. "I can't believe how late it is."

"Sorry, I didn't mean to keep you so long." Gage apologized.

"No, I'm not upset with you, Gage," Ari reached out, placing a reassuring hand on his arm. "I'm just sort of surprised at *myself.* I don't……well, I usually don't take time like this to get to know many people. My life is pretty busy with the restaurant." The warmth of his skin had her mind spinning. When he didn't respond, she feared she had somehow, unintentionally, crossed a line.

"Gage?"

"Oh, sorry," he shook his head as if he too were struggling to focus. "If you just give me directions, we can take my car."

"It's easy really. Just down a couple blocks," Ari pointed towards the lake, "and over a couple more." She followed him to his car where he opened the passenger door. He began to pull his camera bag out of the way, making room for her to sit.

"You're into photography?" By the look of all the different bags and lenses, it appeared to be more than a hobby. "Are you a photographer by profession?"

"I wish! No," he shook his head, "it's just a hobby." Ari watched Gage's grin turn into more of a frown as he continued. "I actually own an architecture firm in New York. It's a family business my dad started when he was young. He has since retired, leaving me in charge."

Gage certainly didn't look thrilled as he spoke about it.

"You say that like you don't enjoy it?" Ari questioned. She situated herself in her seat, and pulled the safety belt across her shoulder as Gage made his way to the driver's side.

Once he had fastened his buckle, Gage continued. "Don't get me wrong, I enjoy owning my own business." He paused for a moment, as if searching for the right words. "It just wasn't what I saw in *my* future. I love the feel of getting my hands dirty, constructing, building, remodeling, you know. I feel like my talent is being wasted sitting behind a desk, drawing up plans, and worrying about who's working on what project. Management has never been my dream, but it seems to be working out, since the business has continued to grow and expand under my direction. I guess my father knew what he was doing after all, by keeping me in the office," he half-heartedly shrugged.

"I can understand that," Ari responded. "Growing up, I always knew it was expected that I be involved with the restaurant to some degree. There was never any thought given to any dreams I might have had to try something different."

Ari stared down at her hands as they rested in her lap. She remembered how, as a young girl, she desperately wanted to be a stay at home mother with a house full of children. Her hope had always been that her older sister would be responsible for their family business. Unfortunately, that dream was pushed to the wayside when her sister was killed.

After a quiet moment, she continued. "But it was my parents and grandparents dream; and I could never say no to keeping their dreams alive."

"Your restaurant is amazing! Now, getting to work on a project like *that,* would be a dream come true for someone like me," Gage turned the direction of the conversation slightly. "The building was constructed back in the day, when things were built to last, and people took pride in their work! I can't *wait* for the tour tomorrow."

"Turn right here." Ari guided him in the direction of her house.

"Hey, thanks again for letting me crash here. I really appreciate it."

"Turn here." Ari motioned to her left this time. "It's the second place on the right."

Once Gage had parked and grabbed a suitcase from his trunk, Ari pulled the key from her pocket and led him into the small cottage.

"It's not much. But it was always just right for our family." She made her way through the living room, turning on lights along the way, stopping as she came into the dining room. She opened up a set of French doors that led to the deck. "This is what we loved most about it." She continued onto the deck, taking in deep breaths of the invigorating smell of fresh lake water drifting on the breeze, a hint of fresh lilacs adding to it. This would never get old. Arabella had the best memories of growing up in this small beach town. She couldn't imagine ever living anywhere else, and she hoped someday to raise her own family here.

Gage came to stand next to her at the railing, overlooking the beach and great expanse of water. Although it was dark, the glow from the lighthouse, and the sound of the waves as they rolled onto the shore, was hypnotizing.

"Wow, *this* is amazing," Gage whispered. A comfortable silence filled the space between them as they both relaxed, surrendering to the tranquility.

After a few minutes, Gage initiated conversation again. "If you don't mind me asking, with a view like this, why don't you live *here*? Why stay at the restaurant?" Gage gazed at Ari, waiting for her response.

Caught off guard by his question, and the emotion that quickly welled up inside her, Ari lowered her head in silence. Even after all these years, the reason why the house remained empty could still shake her to the core.

"I'm sorry, I didn't mean to pry."

Not looking up, Arabella let out a breath and began to speak. "It's okay. I guess," lifting her head, Ari's eyes connected with Gage's, "it just made sense for me to stay at the restaurant instead of here, after my father passed away. It was hard to come home to this empty house after all the loving memories I'd shared over the years with my family. Emotionally, it was just too much for me to handle. And besides," she lifted her shoulder, "I'm always working late, so it was convenient to just turn the third floor into a loft for myself. Problem solved."

"What about your mother, Ari? Or any siblings?"

So much for tip-toeing around the subject. I can't believe I'm about to share this with someone I just met.

For some unexplainable reason, Ari was feeling something she'd never felt before, and something she certainly couldn't explain. Ari felt *comfortable,* and safe, talking with this man. Even though she'd only known him a few short hours.

"My mother and only sister were killed in a car accident when I was sixteen. It was just my father and I after that. Until he passed away, five years ago."

Gage reached his hand out and placed it over Ari's where it rested on the railing. The warmth of his touch sent a shiver down her spine, and instantly she felt connected to him on a deeper lever.

"I'm sorry, Arabella. I didn't mean to make you uncomfortable."

She turned to look at him, a sense of peace washing over her. "It's really okay, Gage. I just haven't talked about it in *so* long. My mom and my sister were my two best friends. I still miss them terribly."

Not sure how to even explain the sudden ease of discussing her past with a stranger, Ari continued to share the details of the horrific day that claimed her loved one's lives. How, in a blink of an eye, her life had changed forever. By the time she finished, Ari felt as if she had been sucked right back into that ugly day, the moment the police officers stood in her doorway, breaking the news to her father. Her emotions were running rampant in her mind. It had been a long, long time since she'd talked about the accident, and Beth was the only one she'd ever shared her feelings with.

Until now.

"I lost my mother to a drunk driver when I was seven," Gage mumbled, his head appearing to sag. "I know how it feels to have your world ripped apart."

Not expecting a response of that magnitude, and still struggling with her own emotions, Arabella was at a loss for words. "I'm so sorry, Gage," she whispered.

Eventually, the quiet between them grew uncomfortable for Ari, prompting her to go. "I think I should probably head home now."

She slowly turned and walked into the house, ending any thought of continuing the difficult conversation they had treaded into. Ari waited for Gage to catch up to her in the dining room before giving him all the information he would need for the night.

"The master bedroom is down the hall on the left. There should be clean sheets in the hall closet along with clean towels for in the morning. You picked a great day to show up here," Ari smiled and a hint of sparkle returned to her eyes. "On Saturday mornings, Sam always fixes breakfast for the restaurant employees, so be there at eight if you'd like to join us. You won't be disappointed. Sam's a great chef." Ari continued towards the front door.

"Why don't I give you a ride back to your," Gage paused, and appeared to be struggling to come up with the correct words, "well, your *other* place?" Gage offered as he followed Ari outside and down the porch steps.

"That's okay, Gage. It's just a few blocks. And," she added, "this is probably the safest neighborhood in America." She grinned in his direction once more, before continuing down the sidewalk and heading towards the restaurant.

"Must be if you're comfortable letting a complete stranger from New York City stay at your place." Gage chuckled. "I'll see you in the morning, Arabella."

"Goodnight, Gage."

A quiet walk home was just what Ari needed. She took in a deep breath of fresh air and exhaled slowly as she tried to wrap her mind around everything that had happened in the last four hours. There was something about Gage that awakened feelings in her that she'd never felt. Some desire from within causing a stir and a need to get to know him more. Something that was drawing her to him. Beth's words from earlier came to mind again.

"You never know when Mr. Right might walk through that door. Maybe you should try dating."

As if her best friend could sense the conversation she was having with herself, Ari's phone rang and Beth's picture appeared on her screen.

"Hey, Beth. What are you still doing up? I figured once Chloe's head hit the pillow yours would too. And by the way, thanks again for covering tonight. I really appreciate all of your help."

"Girl, I didn't call to talk about work! I called to find out about the hunk that's staying at your cottage! Last I knew, you hadn't even met him! What gives?"

Wow, thanks for that, Sam. By now the entire staff was probably aware of her 'hospitality'. *I'll be so glad when the day comes that I'm not the center of everyone's attention.*

"It was all Sam's idea, Beth," Ari blew it off. "It's really nothing. He just needed a place to crash for the night. He'll be leaving tomorrow sometime."

"According to *Sam*, you were pretty speechless around the guy tonight. In fact, Sam said he's never seen you so tongue-tied, or so googly-eyed over someone. I do have to admit, though, the guy is easy on the eyes. What about his personality? What kind of vibe did you get from him?"

"You two aren't going to let this rest, are you? Just can't stop playing matchmaker." Arabella took in a breath and exhaled, trying not to get upset over her friend's eagerness. "He's just a stranger passing through, nothing else to say."

"Nothing else, huh? Even after you took two *long* hours to share one piece of bread pudding?" Beth challenged her.

"Really? Did you and Sam have a timer set or something? Got a camera set up to spy on me? You've really outdone yourself this time, Beth!"

Beth switched gears, obviously trying to throw Ari's thinking off track.

"So, how about a double date for tomorrow night with your *best* friend and her husband? That way, we can all get to know Gage together!"

"Have you not heard a word I've said? He is leaving town tomorrow, Beth."

"I'll bet you could convince him to stay just one more night. Or two," Beth prodded.

"Goodnight, Beth."

"Fine!" Beth grumbled. "Goodnight, Ari."

As Ari changed into her pajamas and climbed into bed that evening, Beth's words from earlier kept running through her mind.

"You never know when Mr. Right might walk through that door."

Had her Mr. Right walked through the door today? Or, was Gage just a stranger passing through town? How would she even know this quickly, if he *was* Mr. Right? Wouldn't that take weeks or maybe months to find out? And, even more, Gage wouldn't be here long enough to figure that out.

Ari collapsed onto her pillows, staring blankly at the ceiling. No man had ever caused her to think this deeply or to lose sleep. She didn't understand why she couldn't get him off her mind; or why she felt so comfortable talking with him about personal topics. Regardless, there was definitely something that felt different about this man.

Over the years, Ari'd had plenty of opportunities to date. That was never the problem. In fact, she was certain just about every single guy at church had asked her out, at least once. But there had never been anyone that piqued her interest enough to want to get past the first date. At one point, she questioned whether her expectations were unreasonably high when it came to the type of man she wanted to spend the rest of her life with. But she'd ruled that thought out rather quickly.

And then there was the restaurant. How could she ever find time to keep a restaurant running smoothly if she was caught up in some romance? And let's not forget her promise to God. That was more important than anything. Even the guys from church that had asked her out, seemed to think casual kissing was okay. Boy, had she told them! Poor Tommy Perkins was never the same after their first date. He'd eventually joined the ranks of Ari's rejected admirers; and there were enough of them to start their own small group at church. It seemed like she would *never* find a man that matched up with her list of qualifications. And maybe that was best. Maybe God didn't intend on sending that certain one in her direction. Could it be possible that she was to be single the rest of her life? But then again, why would God want *that* for her? And not a loving husband, and a houseful of children, like she desired? Isn't He the one that *gave* her that desire? It just didn't make sense to Ari. But she did know one thing. She needed a good night's sleep! And right now, even that didn't seem like it was going to happen for her.

"Ugh!" She reached over to turn off her bedside lamp. Frustrated with herself for not having the ability to get Gage off her mind, she prayed quietly before closing her eyes.

Beth turned her phone off and placed it on the night stand before sliding under the covers.

"One of these times you're going to get burned playing matchmaker, you know." Beth's husband, Anthony, teased.

He was such a good sport when it came to her matchmaking ideas; and he *always* had Ari's back. When Ari lost her sister, she and Beth went from good friends, to very *best* friends, and Anthony always included Ari in he and Beth's plans, no questions asked. They had become known as "The Three Amigos," and neither Beth nor Anthony would have wanted it any other way. Now, if only Beth could find her a husband.

"Well, someone's got to find a man for the poor girl. She sure isn't handling that job very well on her own. For such an intelligent person, she can't seem to get *anything* right when it comes to men!" Beth snuggled up to her husband, laying her head on his shoulder. "Besides, I want Chloe to have some cousins to play with eventually."

"Cousins? Cousins would be *okay*, but I was thinking more like little brothers," Anthony teased.

Beth knew exactly what was on her husband's mind, as he pulled her face up to meet his.

"C'mon, Anthony!" She drew back several inches, looking him in the eye with all the seriousness she could muster. "Help me figure out a plan to get Ari and Gage on a date tomorrow night! He seems like a really nice person. What would it hurt for them to go out one time? Or a few times?" Beth's lips began to curve upward. "You know, if he should decide to stay a while."

"Sorry, my mind is still on little brothers for Chloe," Anthony teased.

"Ugh! She huffed in frustration, crossing her arms across her chest. "Okay, fine! How about this? You promise to work on a way to get those two on a date tomorrow night, and I will think about little brothers for Chloe?"

"Aren't you worried that Ari might really start to like this guy? I mean, he lives in New York, Beth. What kind of relationship could they even have with that distance between them?"

"Love conquers all, sweetheart. Even distance. I know Ari will never leave Rock Haven so we will just have to convince Gage to move here!"

"Wow! Now we are really getting too far ahead of ourselves."

"Do we have a deal or not, Anthony? I'm feeling *very* sleepy right now," she stretched her arms above her head and yawned. "I think I'll just turn out the light and—"

"Deal!" Anthony exclaimed. "How about we up the ante to a whole baseball team of little brothers?"

Beth swatted him on the arm as he trailed kisses down her neck. "A whole team?" she giggled. "I know you can't be serious! How about one? Or possibly two?"

"I'll take whatever you'll give me," Anthony kissed the tip of her nose. "But we better start working on it tonight!" He pulled the covers up around them and held her close. As his kisses grew more intense, Arabella's love life became a mere distant memory.

Chapter 3

A*ri tossed and turned throughout* the night, never really finding sleep, as Gage's face kept sneaking back into her thoughts. Finally, around six a.m., she'd given up and decided to go for a run on the beach. A good run always helped to clear her mind of thoughts that weren't welcome. And her thoughts of Gage, definitely weren't welcome! She didn't have time to be thinking about a man.

Any man.

Not even one with eyes so blue, he could make a girl's heart turn to mush in five seconds flat.

Ari brushed her long, black hair into a ponytail, threw on shorts, a t-shirt, and running shoes, and was out the door ten minutes later. She headed straight towards the beach. Her favorite place in the world; where her worries all disappeared, even if only for a brief time. The beach was where she always worked through her problems. It was shortly after the loss of her mother and sister, that she'd taken up the hobby accidentally. She'd raced along the sandy coastline, trying to outrun her anger and fear, and she'd immediately been drawn in by the peace it brought her. Shortly after, it had become part of her morning routine. There was just something about the solitude, surrounded by the beauty of her Creator, that drew her near to God. And this morning, she needed *that* more than anything.

An hour later, after a good run, lots of praying, and clearing her mind of everything but the upcoming dance, she found herself at the end of the pier. Bent over, sucking in huge gulps of air and trying to steady her heart rate, that's when she saw him. Sitting on the pier with his camera in hand

and his back to her, Gage was focused on the horizon. Mellow blues mixed with majestic streaks of cotton-candy pink, the light of the sun filtered through the clouds with a salmon hue, as the great, orange fireball inched its way higher and higher above the water. Ari was certain she'd never seen anything so beautiful. It was quiet and serene. Way too early for tourists or even locals to be at the beach, with the exception of two other joggers she had passed, taking advantage of the cool morning air. Not wanting to disrupt his work, Ari quietly made her way along the pier until she was mere inches from him.

"Gage?"

He spun around, surprise written all over his face. It was obvious from his reaction, that he had been so deep in thought, he hadn't heard her approach.

"Arabella! What are you doing up and about so early?" Gage stood quickly, pushed his fingers through his hair and straightened his shirt. The joy he felt from her presence became evident in his smile.

"I didn't sleep well," she shrugged, "so, I thought I'd get a quick run in before breakfast. Try to jump start the day and get the brain pumping." Ari's eyes wandered to the sketch pad and equipment at Gage's feet. "I see you wasted no time in capturing one of our great sunrises. Best place in the world to see one is right here in our sleepy little town." She reached down, picking up the pad that contained a partial sketch. "I wasn't aware that you were an artist too?"

Gage blushed. "Not an artist, really. I just like to doodle once in a while." He reached towards Ari to claim his drawing, but she refused to release it from her grip. She began to flip page after page.

"Gage, this is not just doodling. *This*," she pointed at the sketch pad as her eyes met his, "is amazing work, and you should be proud of it." Excitement danced in her eyes as she handed the pad to him. The touch of his hand as it brushed against hers, caused a stirring deep within her soul.

After a moment of awkward silence, Gage gently pulled it from her hands back towards him.

"I appreciate the compliment, Arabella." Gage turned and, kneeling on the pier, began to tuck the sketch pad into his satchel.

Ari waited, not making a move or a sound, until Gage stood and faced her once again. But after what felt like a very awkward and uncomfortable eternity, Ari couldn't stand the silence.

"So, that's' it? You don't have anything else to say about your art work or photos, and why they aren't in some gallery in New York? They're that good you know."

"It's just for fun, Ari, not to be taken seriously."

Ari couldn't figure out why someone with Gage's talent didn't want to pursue something more, especially after the conversation they'd had the night before. She distinctly remembered him talking about how much he disliked his "real" job, operating and managing an architecture design company. But, from the look on Gage's face, he was finished with the conversation. And not knowing the man all that well, Ari thought it best to move on to a lighter topic.

"Okay, then. Are you coming to breakfast? Sam will be really disappointed if you don't, you know." Ari dipped her head and smiled in a flirtatious way that only deepened the smile on Gage's face.

"I hope he's not the only one that would be disappointed," Gage returned her smile. "I wouldn't dream of missing it. I just need to drop my stuff off, grab a shower; and then I'll head that way."

"Great, I'll see you there." Ari waved goodbye and jogged towards the restaurant.

Ari made her way through the loft to her bathroom, hoping the steam and scalding hot water from a shower would wash away her thoughts of Gage.

No. Such. Luck.

Never had Arabella felt this drawn to a man, and it made absolutely no sense to her that her emotions were all over the place at just the sight of him.

So much for clearing my head of thoughts about Mr. Handsome! How can any man look that good first thing in the morning? What is going on with me? Why can't I get him out of my mind? Focus, focus, focus! The dance is just a few weeks away, and there is so much to still get done! I certainly don't have time to be thinking about anything else, especially a man! I've got to get my mind on something else, and NOW.

Determined to divert her attention from Gage, Ari called out to her Echo Dot, "Alexa play Chris Tomlin's greatest hits." She began to sing along, worshipping God, and pushing all other thoughts to the back of her mind.

"*There's a place where mercy reigns and never dies. There's a place where streams of grace flow deep and wide*"

"*Where all the love I've ever found, comes like a flood, comes flowing down..*" The hair on Ari's arm stood on end as she thought about the sacrifice that had been made for her.

"*At the cross, at the cross I surrender my life, I'm in awe of you, I'm in awe of you….*"

As the song continued on, describing the greatness of God's love, Ari was overcome with emotion. She was barely able to choke out the last few words of the final verse before she began to pray.

"Thank you, Father, for the gift of your Son, and for the mercy and grace that I have received." Ari let the hot water continue to pour down over her, as she reflected on the depth of that love.

Feeling ready to tackle the world by the time she said 'amen,' Ari turned off the water and reached for her one of her plush bath towels. She quickly threw on denim shorts, a fresh t-shirt, a touch of make-up and, lastly, her favorite pink flip-flops. As she ran the blow dryer over her long hair, the idea came to her to call a short staff meeting during breakfast. That way, she could get an overview on the progress being made for the upcoming dance.

She made her way downstairs fifteen minutes later. But her plan to keep her mind off of Gage completely disintegrated, when she walked into the breakfast room and saw him standing next to Sam at the head of the table, looking even better since he'd showered. Sporting fresh jeans and a plain black t-shirt that did nothing to hide his sculpted biceps, Gage looked more like a calendar cover than an architect or part-time photographer. Ari tried to swallow the knot that had formed in her throat, as she made her way towards them.

"Good morning, Arabella." Sam embraced her and placed a quick kiss upon each of her cheeks, but Ari's attention was in one place, and on one person only. The smell of Gage's cologne wafted through the air, causing her stomach to flip-flop, as if she were on the front seat of a roller coaster, beginning it's spiral downward.

"Morning, Sam." Ari stepped back and turned her attention to her new friend. "Gage."

"You look beautiful this morning, Arabella." Taking her by surprise, he too pulled her close and kissed her first on one cheek and then the other.

Sam stared at the two of them for a long moment, in shock more than likely, before clearing his throat and grabbing everyone's attention.

"Um...okay, why don't we all take a seat and I'll open with prayer."

The staff quickly found seats surrounding the hand-carved, twenty-foot, oak table that was used for this purpose alone. The table had been crafted by Arabella's grandfather many years ago when the restaurant was barely big enough to house it. The four leaves that it held was his way of forecasting their future success. He'd shared with his granddaughters at very young ages, that someday the restaurant would be so successful, the number of employees they'd have would barely fit around the table in its expansion. In the meantime, their family had used it for holiday dinners and gatherings.

Beth quickly claimed the chair across from Arabella, and sat down with a little bit of attitude. It seemed, she was feeling left out, as Gage and Sam had already flanked her best friend's sides.

Ari reached for Gage's hand, following tradition of course, as Sam opened with a blessing over their meal.

"Amen! Now, dig in!" Sam exclaimed upon completion of his words of thanks.

Gage took his time releasing Ari's hand, and while she immediately missed the warmth of his touch, she quietly wondered if either of her friends would notice. She glanced up just in time to get her answer. Beth and Sam exchanged an undeniable look that said the three of them would be discussing this subject later.

Many conversations quickly began amongst the employees, as they passed bowls and platters filled with a variety of breakfast foods and began to eat.

"Wow, this is fantastic!" Gage took another bite of Sam's famous blueberry crepes, and appeared to be savoring the deliciousness of the sweet cream filling mixed with fresh berries. "Sam, you really do this every Saturday?"

"Absolutely! Every Saturday from May until October. It's our way, at Francesca's, to thank the employees for all their hard work throughout the hectic weeks of tourist season. It's a tradition that's been carried out for years now."

"Well, you sure can cook. This is the best breakfast I have *ever* tasted. I'm surprised Ari lets you hide behind the bar and doesn't put you to work in the kitchen." Gage swallowed another bite of sausage before addressing the group again. "I would just like to say thanks again to all of you for including me." Gage received a table full of smiles and nods as he glanced at the faces surrounding him.

A few minutes later, Ari stood and tapped her fork against her glass to quiet the small talk. "Alright, let's compare notes on where we stand for the ball. Joe, let's start with the menu and food prep."

An older gentleman with dark hair and tender eyes, sitting at the opposite end of the table, began to speak. "The menu that you finalized is being reviewed, Arabella. I will be working with the kitchen crew starting next week to go over the order of prep that will take place."

"Great! Now, how about RSVP's Gretchen? Do we have a solid number yet?" Ari turned her direction to a middle-aged, petite woman, with short red hair and glasses, sitting next to Beth.

Gretchen responded politely before Gage piped up.

"Is this ball some fancy event that you host *here?* At the restaurant?" He questioned her.

The room grew quiet and every eye turned to him, as if they expected him to know the answer. But, it was Ari's eyes he locked onto and held as she explained.

"Exactly, Gage. Every year Francesca's hosts an elaborate ball, and we sell tickets to raise money for charity. The citizens of Rock Haven have made it tradition to attend for over twenty years now."

"So, where does this elaborate ball take place? I mean, this place is big, but not *that* big. *Is* it?" Gage looked around the room, as if picturing in his mind how the restaurant would look when transformed to accommodate such an event.

Beth happily chimed in. "The lower level of Francesca's is actually where the event takes place. You will get to see the space on your tour this morning! And, you haven't seen an elaborate event until you see the way Arabella hosts her annual dance. It's really too bad you couldn't stick around town a while longer and attend." She winked at Gage.

Gage smiled in return, but Ari quickly moved on to another subject.

"Okay, let's stick to the menu and decorations for now, Beth."

Over the next half hour, Ari took turns interacting with the staff and gathering all the information she needed to continue to push forward with her plans on making this year's gala the best one yet. Despite all the talk of party food and decorating details, it seemed to Ari that Gage really was interested in the event. More so than she would have thought a New York stranger to be.

After the employees had finished their breakfasts, the table was cleared. When the last of them headed out, Beth spoke up about the renovations Ari had been contemplating.

"Arabella, have you found anyone to put the finishing touches on the interior of the building? I know you weren't excited about doing a Google search to find someone, but we have to get the process started, and *soon!*"

"Ari," Sam jumped in, "why don't you talk to Gage about the work that needs done? I'm sure he is more than capable of completing the task. After all, that's what you do for a living, right Gage?"

Gage raised his left shoulder. "Well, it depends. What exactly is it that you need done, Arabella?"

"No, no, no. That's okay Gage." Ari brushed the idea off with a wave of her hand. "I know that you have plans to leave town today, and I wouldn't dream of asking you to stay and put your plans on hold for me."

Beth, making sure her two cents were heard, interjected. "Why don't you let Gage make up his own mind about it, Ari?"

Ari extended her leg to meet Beth's knee under the table, letting her know how much she appreciated her friend's boldness.

"Ouch! What was that for?" Beth hissed as her eyes narrowed in Ari's direction.

Ari shot a fake smile in Beth's direction.

Meanwhile, Gage seemed oblivious to what was taking place between the two women.

"Yeah, in fact, you owe me a tour of the place, remember? Why don't you just show me around and explain the work you need done as we go? I told you before, I'm not in a time crunch."

"I'm sure Ari wouldn't mind if you extended your stay at the cottage while you are in town, right Ari?"

"That's a *marvelous* idea, Beth," Ari managed through her clenched jaw. She would definitely talk to Beth later about her "helpful ideas".

She turned towards Gage, and instantly the tension on her face disappeared. "Well," she lifted one shoulder, "it's up to you. What do you think?"

"I think a couple of extra weeks in this sleepy little town could be just what the doctor ordered. Now," he extended his arm to hers, "let's get started on that tour, shall we?"

Ari linked her arm through his, and they made their way towards the front of the building. All the while, she tried to figure out what his stay really meant to her. On one hand, she would love for him to stick around another week or two, and help out with some projects at the restaurant. On the other hand, she wondered if her "way too eager" emotions, that were *already* in overdrive, could handle being around the dashing bachelor that long. She'd known him less than twenty-four hours, and she was already struggling to keep her mind intact. But the way she felt right now, with her arm wrapped around his, Ari was pretty sure she'd already made up her mind. Nothing would make her happier than Gage hanging around Rock Haven a while longer.

Arabella had been the only thing on Gage's mind since Sam first introduced them the night before. Now that he was walking arm and arm with her through Francesca's, he was certain that he couldn't make himself leave Rock Haven. Not yet any way. Gage wanted just a little more time to see where this "thing" with Arabella was going. He really wasn't looking for a girlfriend. But maybe a pit-stop in Rock Haven with Ari each summer, could work out for his benefit. Much like Jenna had in Iowa over previous years. Only time would tell.

Gage had been captivated by Ari last night, as he'd watched her interact with her customers. She carried herself with confidence and grace. Success radiated from her. But, it was her figure that had Gage ogling over every move she made. He had learned quite a bit about Ari from his conversation with the bartender, enough that made Gage want to know her more. She was single, and that was a good start! And the way that her shiny, black-hair fell on her shoulders? Well, Gage would love nothing more than to get the chance to run his fingers through it. She was stunning; no doubt about it. Gage had been drawn to her, once again this morning, as he watched her take control of the conversation, securing the details of the dance with all those involved. There was power in her voice, but also a gentleness that others seemed to admire and respect. Gage found he was even more attracted to her as the morning went on.

The connection he'd felt with her last night when she had opened up her heart, and talked about losing her mother and sister, was something Gage couldn't explain. He knew then, that there was something about this woman that he needed in his life. Never had he felt so captivated by someone. In fact, Ari made him feel better emotionally than anyone had in his past. This morning on the beach, the way she'd talked about his artwork? Gage had never felt comfortable sharing his art with anyone except his art teacher. But Ari made him feel good about himself, and he hadn't felt that way in a long time! And physically? Well, that was a no-brainer! There wasn't a man alive that wouldn't turn in her direction, Gage was sure of that.

Beth's words at breakfast, about the dance, wormed their way into his mind.

"It's really too bad you won't be in town long enough to attend."

Maybe staying right here in Rock Haven, just a little while longer, wouldn't be so bad. The thought of Arabella in an evening gown, her long black hair flowing across her shoulders, peaked his interest. With he in a black tuxedo, spinning her around on the dance floor, holding her tight against him, there may be a possibility of something happening after the dance. And *that* was appealing more to him with every second. Remembering her touch from earlier this morning, as she'd passed his sketch pad back to him on the pier, sent a chill down his spine. Maybe he should just take what he wanted as quickly as possible and head west, before she inched her way any deeper into his heart.

I don't know what it is about you, girl, but I know I want more of it.

Gage shook his head in wonder. He couldn't remember another time in his life when he'd felt so undecided.

Ari came to a stop, pulling her arm free from his and turning towards him, drawing Gage from his thoughts.

"Well, what do you think?"

"It's truly amazing, Ari," he responded, trying to focus on the purpose for the tour. "I can only imagine what this space will look like the night of the dance." Gage was almost as fascinated by the character of the building, as he was with the girl giving the tour. The old barn wood ceilings, exposed brick walls, and original architectural details had been partnered with updated and modern artwork and fixtures, creating a warm and inviting atmosphere. Photos lined the walls, showcasing the changes that had taken place within the restaurant itself, and in their small community, over the past fifty years. The historical aspect nearly had Gage drooling by the end of the tour.

"So, do you think you would be willing to give that list a shot, and get the work done before the dance?" Ari leaned back against the coolness of the brick wall as they finished their tour of the lower level ballroom.

"I think I can get most of it accomplished," he responded, an intensity burning in his eyes as he stared deep into her soul. Placing a hand on her arm, he drew closer, pouring on the charm, hoping to penetrate any wall of doubt that remained in Ari's mind. "But that's going to mean me staying in town a couple of weeks. Are you sure that's what you want?"

She must have been oblivious to his intentions. "You are welcome to stay as long as you wish, Gage," she said sweetly. "I think you'll find our little town to be quite charming. And, if you agree to stay, I will even throw in free lunch and dinner daily if you don't mind our menu. It's the least I could do."

"That sounds like an offer I can't turn down."

Before he could reach out his hand to shake on it, Ari wrapped her arms around his neck and hugged him, rendering him speechless.

"Thank you *so much*, Gage! You have *no* idea what this means to me," she whispered.

Almost as quickly as she hugged him, Ari released her hold on Gage and took a step back, staring at her feet and nervously tucking a strand of hair behind her ear.

"I, uh.....I'm sorry. I didn't mean to...... I'm just really....."

"Excited, I get it." Gage slowly moved closer and, not one to waste an opportunity, reached towards her face, running a finger along her cheek. "I'm not complaining."

Gage leaned in close enough that he could smell the coconut shampoo Arabella had used that morning, putting his senses on high alert. This was his moment and he wasn't going to let it pass by. Tilting his head slightly, and focusing on her perfectly shaped rosy lips, Gage closed the slight distance left between them, as he pushed forward to kiss—

"Hey, what would you say to a tour of our downtown area?" Ari slipped out from under his touch. "The restaurant doesn't open for a couple of hours, and I'd be happy to show you around. You're definitely going to need to know where the hardware store is. And don't worry. We have an account set up there, so if there's anything you need, just let them know to add it to my tab."

"Okaaaaay," Gage said reluctantly, as he took a step back. She seemed nervous, almost skittish, as she rattled on. But, why? There was obviously an attraction on both sides. He was certain he hadn't misinterpreted that. Slightly defeated, he decided he could be patient a little longer, if that's what it would take. "Another tour would be fine, I *guess*," he shrugged.

Over the next three hours, as the pair made their way through the crowded downtown streets, Ari filled Gage in on the history of several local businesses. They stopped for ice cream, met the owner of the hardware store, and visited at *least* twenty novelty shops during their outing. Gage had never met such kind people. This little town was the complete opposite of what he was used to in New York City. People actually liked and cared for each other, and wanted to invest in each other's lives. It seemed the more they explored, the more he realized how sheltered he had been growing up. Even at Nonnie's farm, he had never experienced anything like this. Nonnie's ranch was so large that she had only one neighbor, old Mr. Bivens. Their land expanded so far, their houses sat five miles apart. Gage didn't bother going to church with her on Sundays, once he was at the age he could protest. So, he knew very few people other than Max and a few ranch hands that helped out during the busy season. And then, of course, there was Jenna. It was purely coincidence that he'd met her, one hot summer day, driving back to the ranch from running errands in Des Moines. Gage would always remember that day fondly. Her old blue Toyota had a flat and she was stranded out in the middle of nowhere when he'd come along and 'rescued her'. Boy, had she paid him back in a way Gage would never forget.

"Gage, are you alright?"

"What? Oh, yes," he replied, shaking thoughts of Jenna from his mind. They'd finally arrived back at Francesca's.

"I should probably start a list of what I'm going to need to complete these projects." Gage said as they entered the back door of the restaurant. "I'd like to get a start on things today, if you don't mind?"

It seemed his stomach had other plans, as it rumbled loudly in disagreement with him. The sound caused Ari to smile in his direction.

"I think lunch might be a better option at the moment. You can't work on an empty stomach now, can you?" she teased.

"Will you join me?" Gage asked, hopefully. If he was going to have to postpone starting the job, lunch with Arabella was a good reason for it. Working on this historic building would be a project he thoroughly enjoyed. But to have more time with Arabella? Well, that was the best part of the deal. Gage couldn't believe his good fortune. There was something different about this girl, something he couldn't quite put his finger on, and it caused a stirring deep within him, that he couldn't ignore.

"I think I could manage that. Let me grab a menu for you while you get a seat." She disappeared through the kitchen, making her way towards the Hostess' station.

The moment she was gone, Gage slumped down into the closest booth, planting his elbows on the table, and resting his head in his hands. His mind was exhausted from all of the conflicting thoughts he was having.

What are you doing? Surely, you are setting yourself up for failure. Nothing good can come from sticking around here. You should run for the hills now, before it's too late! Get what you want from her and get out of dodge! Better yet, don't wait around, just get out-NOW!

And so, the battle continued. His mind was clear that only *one* thing could come from this new "friend" he'd become interested in. His heart, however, for the first time in his life, was trying to convince his brain that this woman had already passed the "just a quick physical relationship" phase.

This girl was nothing like the girls he'd dated in New York. Girls that threw themselves at his feet, starved for a man's attention, with no respect for themselves. But not Ari. No, this girl was reserved, sure of herself, and confident in who she was. She was a no-nonsense woman, that obviously didn't *need* a man. Gage would bet his life savings that when Ari fell head over heels for a man, it would be because she *wanted* him. And, he also had a feeling that Ari always got what she wanted. Now, he just had to figure out how to convince her that *he* was what she wanted next.

Chapter 4

The moment she exited the room and was out of Gage's view, Arabella stopped to take a deep breath, trying to calm her nervous self and gather her roaming and unpredictable emotions.

What am I doing? I almost kissed him! Remember, he is only here for a short time; and you have made a promise to God that needs to be kept. You are worth the wait; and so is finding true love.

Ari was becoming more aware that Gage helping with the project, and thus staying in town, was not a good idea. The closeness of him sent her head screaming in one direction, while her heart entertained what it would feel like to be kissed by the handsome handyman.

Her heart was winning at the moment.

Ari's thoughts were diverted, when she was pleasantly surprised by Beth and baby Chloe strolling through the front door of the restaurant. Happy for the distraction, she met them halfway across the room.

"Well, what have I done to deserve this unexpected visit?" Ari reached for the little angel in Beth's arms, kissing her all over her tiny face, which caused the baby girl to giggle loudly.

"Sorry, Ari," her friend grimaced as she handed the baby over to her, "Anthony had a meeting that he couldn't take Chloe to. I hope you don't mind. She will only be here for an hour or so while I help Cindy with some final decoration details for the ball."

"You're joking right?" Ari looked absolutely appalled. "When has it ever been a problem for my goddaughter to visit me?"

"Thanks." Beth looked around, as if searching for something, or someone. "Where did your hunky new handyman go?"

"Ssssshhhhh!" Ari put her finger to her lips, looking around to make sure that Gage had not followed her. "Don't call him that out loud, Beth."

"Oh, please, Arabella. There isn't anyone close enough to hear me," Beth rolled her eyes. "So, where is he? Did you put him to work already?"

It was obvious Beth was not going to let it go. "No, I didn't put him to work.....yet. I took him on a little tour of downtown. *And,* we are getting ready to have lunch together. Do you and Chloe want to join us?"

Arabella had just been struck with the idea, and immediately, realized it was a smart move. Having Beth and Chloe eat with them would be a safeguard to keep some distance between she and Gage.

"You must be kidding!" Beth exclaimed. "I've been waiting too long for this! There is *no way* I'm going to intrude on the little love fest going on between you two!"

"Seriously, Beth? Love fest? C'mon, you know me better than that." Ari shook her head at her friend and then turned her attention back to the child in her arms. "Your mommy is being silly. Isn't she, Chloe?"

"Whatever! You can't deny it, Ari. I've known you your entire life, and I've never seen you so smitten with a man. You're falling head over heels for him, aren't you?"

Arabella threw her head back and sighed loudly. "I've known him less than twenty-four hours, Beth. Don't you think you're being a bit dramatic?"

"Say what you want. But you can't deny there's something going on between you two. Ari, it's no secret that you've never had a boyfriend. But there is some kind of spark going on between you and Gage. What is it about him that has you so gaga?"

"You have looked at the man, haven't you, Beth? A woman would have to be blind not to notice him. But, I don't know," she shrugged and paused momentarily, "it's more than his looks. A man's face can't compete with his heart, and you know I don't care about the exterior. But with Gage, it's the whole package. From what I've seen, he has a kind and compassionate heart, *and* he got blessed in the good looks department. It's like he stepped out of a Hallmark movie and onto my front steps. I've got to admit, Beth," she looked her directly in the eye as she confessed, "I'm having feelings I've never had to deal with before. I'm way out of my league with this."

"And it's about time." Beth laughed and reached for Chloe. "Now, you go on and enjoy that lunch with Mr. Hunky. We'll talk soon, okay?"

"Oh," Ari's eyes widened as she nodded in agreement, "I'm sure we'll talk soon, Beth. You'll be going crazy waiting for a play by play of our lunch, won't you?"

"Well, *somebody* has to keep tabs on you."

"Right!" Ari rolled her eyes. "How could I forget that you, my dear sweet friend, are the town informant?"

"Hey, I can't help that I'm good at what I do," Beth smirked. "Or that everyone in town already has bets placed on how long this relationship will last!"

"What?" Ari stomped her foot in frustration. "Beth you can't be serious!"

"Not really," Beth snickered. "I was just trying to get you fired up. I see it worked. Enjoy lunch." Beth turned to Chloe. "Time for us to leave little pumpkin. Kiss Aunt Ari goodbye."

Ari pressed a kiss to the baby's cheek, gave her friend a look that would scare most people, and headed back towards Gage.

And did she *ever* enjoy lunch! Her lunch *date* more specifically. Caught up, not only in the conversation, but in his charm as well, two hours passed before she realized what time it was. Apologetically, she excused herself, explaining she needed to pay attention to the restaurant for a few hours before the dinner crowd arrived.

"Do you think I might see you later tonight?" Gage asked before she got too far away.

She stopped and turned, twirling the ends of her hair as she thought about her answer. Not wanting to seem too excited about the possibility, she answered nonchalantly. "Hmm, maybe. At least you know where to find me." With a small, teasing grin and a pep in her step, Ari turned and disappeared.

Ari's fingers trembled as they skimmed down the silky dress in her hands. She stood facing the full-length mirror in the corner of her bedroom, pondering her attire for the evening. The possibility of seeing Gage again made her nervous, and she wanted to look her best if she did. This was all foreign to her. Ari had never met a man that piqued her interest enough to put much effort into impressing them.

Her phone rang in the background and she dropped the dress on her bed as she ran to answer the call.

"Are you sure you aren't going to need me tonight?"

It was Beth, making sure the hostess spot had been covered. When she and Anthony had been surprised by their neighbor's daughter, who offered to babysit for the night, Beth had approached Ari about finding a replacement for her evening shift at Francesca's.

"Positive! Sara has it covered tonight. Besides, you and Anthony deserve a night out by yourselves. Go enjoy!" Ari walked back towards her closet and thumbed through her options once again, the phone still pressed to her ear.

"Okay, if you insist." Beth conceded. "Hey, I know Francesca's will be packed as usual tonight, but do you think there's any way Anthony and I could steal a quiet booth for dinner before we head to the movies?"

"Do you even have to ask, Beth? Of course, there's always a table for two of my *favorite* people." Ari's eyes turned to a burgundy silk, spaghetti strap, mini dress her fingers had landed on. She pulled it from the closest and held it up to her in front of the full-length mirror, imagining how she'd look in it; and if by chance, Gage would be around to see it.

"Thanks, Ari," Beth squealed with delight. "We have a babysitter until *midnight,* and we want to take full advantage of every minute. It's not like we get this opportunity every day. We'll probably be in around five or so, okay?"

"Perfect, I will see you then." Ari smiled to herself as she ended the call. She easily recognized the anticipation in her friend's voice and she couldn't be happier for Beth and Anthony. If any two people deserved a night alone to enjoy each other's company, it was them. Not only were they amazing parents to their young daughter, but they both were always making others happy, working and volunteering their time wherever there was a need. Especially at the church that all three of them had attended since their youth.

Directing her attention back to her wardrobe, Ari tossed her phone on the bed and pulled the burgundy dress from its hanger. Holding it against her, she looked into the mirror one more time. This time, when she envisioned herself wearing the dress, she was holding on to the arm of a very handsome, dark-haired man with dazzling blue eyes. And just like that, her thoughts were filled with Gage once again.

Ari took a deep breath and sighed, allowing herself to fall back onto her bed. Just thinking about Gage made the butterflies in her stomach begin to flutter again. What was it about him that stirred so many emotions in her? She lay there, thinking about him longer than she realized. When she finally sat up and turned to look at her phone, Ari panicked.

"Four thirty-five already!" she shrieked, scrambling to her feet. "What am I going to do with my hair?"

She gathered up her long black tresses with one hand, scrutinized the look, then decided leaving it down would be better. She strode to her bathroom and turned on the curling iron, allowing it to warm up while she got dressed, and applied the make-up that she rarely used. Twenty minutes later, she nervously walked downstairs to many turning heads, taking in her sight. Gage's was one of them. Ari was well aware that Gage had seen her. She was doing her best to remain calm and not seem too eager, as she took a moment at each table chatting with guests, and avoiding his stare. Finally, she made her way towards the booth in the back corner, where Anthony and Beth were seated, pausing just long enough to steal a quick glance towards Gage. Out of the corner of her eye, she could just barely see the look on his face. But she was certain, based on his smile, that she'd picked the perfect outfit.

Beth let out a low whistle as Ari reached their table. "Where have you been hiding *that* dress, my friend?"

"Oh, this old thing?" Ari teased, batting her eyelashes at Beth.

"And *make-up*?" Beth shook her head. "This *must* be serious!"

"Ignore my dramatic wife," Anthony stood and greeted her with a hug. "Ari, you look beautiful."

Before she could respond, Anthony pulled her tighter and whispered into her ear, "Man on the move at twelve o'clock! Don't look now."

"Excuse me." She felt a gentle tap on her shoulder. "Arabella?"

"Oooh, too late," Anthony whispered, slowly releasing his hold on her.

Not sure who to expect, Ari was slightly disappointed when she turned around to find Mrs. Maxwell's grandson, Robert, to her left.

"Good evening, Robert," Ari managed, wearing the friendliest smile she could muster. "How are you tonight?"

"I'm fine, thank you," he smiled. "And may I just say, you look quite lovely tonight!"

Ari could feel the heat as it crept up her neck and into her cheeks, but she kept her voice calm as she responded. "That's very sweet of you, Robert."

"Um, I was wondering if maybe—"

Please, don't let him ask me to join him for dinner tonight! Ari selfishly thought.

"Well, if I might have the pleasure of your company for dinner tonight." Robert reached for her hand, pulling it towards his mouth.

"Robert, it's very kind of —"

"You wouldn't happen to be hitting on my date now, would you?"

That's the voice I've been eagerly waiting to hear!

Robert immediately released her hand and raised his head, turning to the deep voice behind them. Ari couldn't have been more relieved.

"Oh....no.....um...I'm so sorry, sir. I had no idea." He stumbled back a step, looking nothing but embarrassed, as he found Gage's possessive glare focused on him. "I didn't mean......I'm so sorry. Please excuse me."

With Robert's back to them, as he made his rather quick escape, Ari turned just in time to catch Beth's look of shock as Anthony slapped Gage on the back. "Very well played, my friend!"

Beth was quick to chime in, shamelessly satisfied over what had just taken place. "Well," she gloated, "I suppose that since the two of you are *officially* on a date, you'll just have to join us for dinner and a movie." She slid over in the booth, patting the spot next to her. "Anthony, why don't you slide in over here next to me?"

A small chuckle escaped Anthony's lips, as pure joy spread across his beautiful, meddling wife's face. He slid into the booth next to her and placed a kiss on her cheek. "Nice work, dear."

Gage reached for Ari's hand, gently pulling it towards his mouth, and planted the kiss Robert had intended. Ari was breathless.

"You look absolutely stunning, Arabella." Gage lifted his face and fixed his eyes upon hers.

Ari swallowed. She was certain everyone in the room could hear her heart beating inside her chest.

Could this really be happening?

"It sure would be a shame for you sit around here all night, looking as good as you do." He motioned towards the booth, his eyes never leaving hers. "What do you say we take Anthony and Beth up on their offer?"

Work would have to wait until tomorrow. The scent of Gage's cologne had the butterflies in Arabella's stomach, fluttering like mad. Her pulse had kicked up a notch at the feel of his lips on her hand. She was more than happy to share a booth, *and* an evening out, with the man that was rapidly working his way into her heart.

Arabella had taken his breath away the moment she walked into the room. Gage was certainly not going to let her slip away again tonight. As he'd watched that man stroll across the room and take her hand in his, he couldn't help but react. There was no way he was going to let another man hone in on what he had going with Arabella. It had all fallen into place perfectly when Beth had extended the offer to join her and Anthony for the evening. The four of them had a great time at dinner, and now Gage found himself sitting in a dark movie theatre, his arm around Ari's shoulders, sitting close enough to feel intoxicated from the scent or her perfume.

"Would you like some popcorn, Gage?" Ari held the bucket towards him.

Popcorn? That was the last thing on his mind! He was too focused on the woman sitting next to him. The one he'd known less than two days, but felt like he'd known his entire life. The same one that was creating feelings in him he didn't know existed, and *definitely* didn't know how to handle. For the first time in his life, Gage found himself looking at relationships with a whole new perspective, drawn to the attributes that made Arabella more desirable than any woman he'd ever met. More than the dazzling color of her eyes that made him weak in the knees, her contagious smile could light up a room. The coconut scent of her soft hair made his hands tremble at the thought of touching it. Arabella was humble, yet confident in herself. Her heart was filled with love and compassion for others. And, from what he'd witnessed over the past two days, the joy and happiness she exuded, was infectious to those around her. Arabella was *it*! The total package. And *that*, scared him to death.

His father had warned him about girls like this. Girls that would sneak into his heart, turn his world upside down, and leave him feeling more hopeless than a convict sitting on death row, counting down his final minutes. More defeated than an alcoholic stumbling through a dark alley in search of just one more drink. More desperate than a patient diagnosed with a fatal disease the doctors cannot find a cure for. The kind of girl he had stayed away from his entire life.

Until now.

"Gage?" Ari shook the popcorn bucket again, gaining his attention.

"Hmmm?" He turned towards her, momentarily pulled from his thoughts. "Oh, sorry! No thanks, I'll pass on the popcorn."

"You okay? You seem to be pretty deep in thought?"

"Just caught up in your beauty," he responded with a teasing grin. His reward was a smile that he felt all the way to his toes.

"Are you having a good time tonight, Arabella?"

Her smile grew even larger, melting his heart.

"Gage, I'm having a wonderful time. I haven't felt this relaxed in so long. Thank you for this evening."

"I should be the one thanking you, Ari."

"If you two can't be quiet during this movie, we might have to separate you," Beth warned in a semi-joking tone.

"Okay, okay. We get the hint." Ari turned to face the big screen; Gage's eyes staying fixed on her for the majority of the show. He would have flunked any pop quiz about the flick, that was for sure. The movie seemed to drag on forever, until finally, the credits rolled across the screen, and the four of them made their way to the exit. Standing outside the theatre, Beth was the first one to break the group's silence.

"We really need to get going and relieve our sitter. We don't want to take advantage of her, or we might lose her. And Chloe adores her! So," turning directly towards her best friend, Beth continued, "do you want us to drop you off at the restaurant, Ari?"

Gage was quick to answer for her, hoping she would agree to a little alone time with him. "It's such a beautiful night, Ari. You and I could walk back together. It's only a few blocks, what do you say?"

Gage sensed Ari's hesitancy as she remained quiet. He watched her eyes wander towards Beth's, as if asking permission.

"If that's what *she* wants to do, that's fine with us," Beth responded. Quickly she glanced towards Anthony before looking back to her friend, and waited for her response. "Ari?"

They all waited for her answer.

"Um, sure. I.....I guess that would be okay. It's not *that* far." Looking down at the three-inch heels on her feet, Ari smiled and shrugged. "Looks like I'm going barefoot."

After a round of goodbyes and comments about the good time they'd had, Beth and Anthony headed towards their car. Feeling spirited, Gage gently reached for Ari's hand. It couldn't have been a more perfect spring night. Milder temperatures in the sixties meant the evening sky would be filled with thousands of bright stars. The luminous and brilliant full moon, gave off just the right amount of light to make their walk home a bit romantic. Not having been prepared for a walk home tonight, Ari shivered as a slight breeze blew in from the lake. Gage was quick to offer his jacket, and used it as the perfect excuse to hold his arm around her, keeping it place.

"Just lean in to me, Ari. I will keep you warm."

If he thought his heart beat double time last night, it was surely going to beat right out of his chest tonight. Gage had never seen anything as beautiful as Arabella was this evening. When she'd floated across the dining room at Francesca's, her dark curls framing her face and spilling onto the burgundy dress that complimented her figure, his brain had gone to mush. Then, sitting next to her in the darkness of the movie theatre, Gage thought for sure he would go insane! The scent of her perfume and the touch of her hand in his as he'd intertwined their fingers, caused him to lose all train of thought. And now, here they were, walking home together in the light of the moon. He zeroed his attention in on her and only her. With his arm secured around her, and her head leaning on his shoulder, they made their way back to her place.

Gage was hopeful this night would end on a positive note.

Chapter 5

"*Don't worry, he'll show up.* Service doesn't start for another ten minutes," Beth said from the adjacent pew. Ari had shared her reservations about inviting Gage to church, and Beth must have read the angst on her face.

"Maybe he only agreed out of courtesy and doesn't plan to show up." Ari twisted her shaking hands in her lap before returning her gaze, once more, towards the door at the back of the church. "What if I've scared him off? He could be packing up to leave town right now, as we speak!"

"You're just being silly, Ari. Now, sit down and relax while I run Chloe to the nursery," Beth demanded.

"You know, I saw the way he looked at you during dinner last night. I don't think the guy's going anywhere," Beth's husband, Anthony, added.

Ari smiled at the man that was as close to a brother as she could get. She loved both Beth and Anthony like they were family. In fact, other than Sam, they were the only family she had now. Anthony and Beth's relationship—now that was a love story to write about. They'd been together ever since Mrs. Watkins *forced* them to sit next to each other in seventh grade science class.

It was during frog dissection week. Anthony had saved Beth and her squeamish stomach, taking control of the experiment, allowing her to receive all the credit for it. Mrs. Watkins never even caught on. They'd received an A on the project; but more importantly, they'd found their soulmates. Their love had only grown stronger as they entered high school.

Neither Beth nor Anthony, were interested in dating anyone else. There was never a doubt that they would end up married.

Ari admired the closeness the two of them shared. It was a deep bonded friendship. And the fact that God was at the center of it, was what appealed most to Ari. It was the kind of marriage she had dreamed about, late at night when she couldn't sleep, as her mind wandered over the course of her life. As a young girl, she had often dreamed of finding a love like what her parents, and Beth and Anthony, had. But after losing her mother and sister her junior year of high school, Ari's father had completely fallen apart, leaving her to grow up faster than she'd planned. Ari, all too quickly, had to step up and become responsible for their home, and the business as well. There had never been time to date or fall in love. But still, she dreamed about it.

"Look who I found in the hallway."

Disengaging from her thoughts, Ari looked up at the sound of Beth's voice. She was, immediately and pleasantly, surprised to see a pair of fresh khakis, and a white button down staring back at her. She didn't know how Gage managed to do it, but he looked even better this morning than he had last night when he'd kissed her goodbye at the back door of the restaurant.

Beth slid into the pew, brushing past Ari and pulling her from her reverie, as she took a seat next to her husband.

"Great to see you again, Gage." Anthony reached across his wife for Gage's hand.

"Good to see you too, Anthony." Gage took a seat next to Ari, bidding her a good morning before leaning closer and whispering into her ear. "You look amazing."

"Good morning, Gage," she grinned. I'm really glad you could make it."

The praise team began singing before either of them could speak another word, but it didn't stop Ari's mind from wandering. Her first thought? A tiny celebration that he'd even shown up for church this morning. Relief washed over her, and she relaxed a little in her seat. Maybe this *was* right. Maybe *he* was right. It certainly was beginning to feel that way. Ari thought about Beth and Anthony's relationship; about their dynamic relationship with God. It seemed almost natural to her, to envision similar happenings for she and Gage. Fantasies of attending church with him as her husband, of marriage, and kids flooded her mind. She was momentarily entranced, until suddenly, the reality of her surroundings snapped her focus back. She had completely missed what Pastor Ron was even talking about.

Get yourself together, Ari!

Her eyes drifted to the man sitting beside her. The guy sure did make it hard to think straight. She let herself study his chest and arms a few moments more before nonchalantly checking to see if she had been caught. She hadn't. Gage looked like he hadn't even noticed. In fact, his face sort of lacked expression, almost disinterested even.

Wait! Is he bored? Is he sorry he came to church?

Arabella sat on that thought, her previous fantasies slowly feeling less and less tangible. It wasn't before long, that she noticed Gage fidgeting in his seat, the uneasy look in his eye, impossible to misread. She continued to watch him out of the corner of her eye, as he twitched and fiddled throughout the remainder of the service. Thankful that neither baptisms or communion were taking place and lengthening the service, Ari was relieved when the worship team wrapped up with another two songs. Had they not, she was convinced Gage would go screaming from the pew, and run out the back door. It was painfully obvious to Ari that this was not something Gage did on a regular basis, and that thought caused another twitch in her stomach. This was just the opposite of the happy butterflies she'd been feeling for the past few days.

The words she declared to her father on a very special night many years ago, rushed to the forefront of her thoughts.

I promise I will keep myself pure until my wedding day, when I marry the man of my dreams. And surely, he will be a godly man.

Based on the way Gage had twitched in his seat like a cat on a hot tin roof throughout the sermon, Ari had to wonder if "godly man" was, or ever would be, a phrase used to describe him.

Chloe had been picked up from childcare and Ari was off talking to the pastor, as Gage stood at the back of the sanctuary with Beth and Anthony, while they tried to figure out lunch plans. In the end, Beth was kind enough to invite all of them, including the pastor and his wife, back to her house.

"So, what do you say, Gage? Will you join us?" Beth questioned.

"You know," he shrugged slightly, hoping Beth didn't catch on to his dismay, "I didn't really get too far on my projects at Francesca's yesterday. It might be a good idea for me to just head on over there and get started. I do appreciate the invite, though."

Please let that be believable! I need to get out of this place. And FAST!

Gage had enjoyed the time he'd spent with them last night, especially the part where he and Ari split and went on their own. But after church this morning, he was certain his mind couldn't handle much more. What was all the hype about this "God" that they kept going on and on about, anyway? It reminded him of his childhood days with Nonnie, and her talks about God. He'd been forced to sit through a few uncomfortable Sunday services with her as well, and it didn't make any more sense today than it had back then. These people were actually worse than what he remembered from his childhood. What, with their loud worship and calling out, like they were doing. And what was with all the hands being raised in the air? Did they really think this 'God' could see what they were doing? It all seemed a little far-fetched to him.

"Francesca's isn't open today, Gage, and I highly doubt Ari would want you working, anyway." Beth's eyes narrowed as she shook her head in Gage's direction. "Sundays are all about church and family around here. Always have been and always will be! They take care of their employees at Francesca's and put them first. You don't find that many places these days."

"No, you sure don't." Gage replied with a half-hearted smile as the wheels continued turning in his mind. Who didn't go to work on Sunday because of *God*? If his father had taught him one good thing, it would be his work ethic. It didn't matter what day of the week it was, if work needed to be done, you did it. This all seemed a bit much for Gage to take in. He was more certain now, that skipping out on lunch with the "godly gang," was in his best interest. Ari alone he could handle, but he had no interest in lunch with a pastor breathing down his neck about sin.

Just then, Ari called out to him from across the room, saving him further questioning from Beth.

"Hey, Gage! Come over here. I want you to meet Pastor Ron."

Wonderful! From the frying pan to the fire.

Gage turned and walked towards them, an award-winning, "hope it's believable," smile on his face. He met the two of them halfway across the room, where Ari stopped and introduced him.

"Gage, this is Pastor Ron. Pastor Ron, I'd like you to meet Gage."

"Good afternoon, Pastor. It's nice to meet you." Gage extended his hand to the pastor, while still cursing himself mentally for not fleeing sooner.

"Nice to meet you, too, Gage. What brings you to our little town on the lakeshore?"

"Oh, I'm just passing through on my way to Iowa."

Gage caught Ari's frown out of the corner of his eye, just as Beth and Anthony joined them. Beth was quick to react to her friend's discouraged look.

"*But,* he's decided to extend his stay for a while in order to help Ari out with some updating at Francesca's before the dance. Isn't that right, *Gage?*"

Gage nodded in response. It was becoming more evident, with every conversation, that Gage would be facing serious retribution if he hurt Ari in any way. Beth was a fierce protector. Maybe he had better rethink he decision about joining them for lunch. If he was going to get where he wanted to with Ari, he knew he'd better stay on Beth's good side. Hopefully, if he played his cards right, it wouldn't take long to have Beth's alliance.

Gage watched as Ari's face lit up, explaining to the pastor some of the plans the two of them had come up with for the restaurant, during their extended lunch together yesterday.

"That should keep him busy for at least a couple of weeks, anyway," Beth added.

"So," Pastor Ron rubbed his hands together as he changed the subject, "I hear we've all been invited to lunch at Beth and Anthony's?"

"Well, Gage...."

"Wouldn't miss it!" Gage interrupted Beth, his sudden change of plans about lunch gaining him a confused look from her.

"All right, then. Let me grab the misses and we will meet everyone there."

The pastor walked away, followed by Ari, who went to grab her jacket, leaving Gage with a perplexed Beth, and an open door to question his change of heart.

"So, what happened to going back and working at the restaurant, Gage?" The look Beth gave him sent a chill down his spine. But he was ready. He hadn't missed her expression when he made the announcement.

"It seems to mean a lot to Arabella that I come to lunch," Gage flashed another charming grin, "and I wouldn't do *anything* to disappoint her." Gage didn't wait for a response; simply turned and navigated his way towards Ari, feeling confident that he'd made peace with Beth on the topic.

Until he heard Beth's distant mumble from behind and it sent a shiver through him as cold as an artic wind.

"You better not do anything to disappoint her, my friend, or you will have me to contend with."

Gage caught up to Ari just in time to help her slip her arms into the sleeves of her jacket. Another look at her in the short apricot sundress she wore, the way it shaped her figure, and the way those long dark curls framed her gorgeous face, he was convinced he could handle a short lunch. Maybe if he played it just right, he could gain some brownie points with Beth and an evening alone with Arabella.

Beth called across the room as she welcomed Ari and Gage into the house. "Chloe, Auntie Arabella's here." The small tot crawled towards them, a tooth-cutting, drooling grin on her face, and Ari happily bent to pick her up, giving her a squeeze.

"Oh, you are just the sweetest little girl in the whole world," Ari squealed.

"Come on in guys! Lunch will be ready in a few minutes. Something to drink? Anthony just made a fresh pitcher of lemonade." Beth took drink requests before disappearing into the kitchen, leaving Gage and Ari alone with baby Chloe.

"Isn't she just the most precious little thing?" Ari looked up into Gage's eyes, not one bit aware of the storm brewing behind them.

Man, what have you gotten yourself into now? The woman is baby crazy, too? If this doesn't scream RUN I don't know what does!

Before he could utter a negative word about his feelings on children, little Chloe reached up and patted his cheek, causing Ari to gush.

"I think she *likes* you!" Ari beamed. If he had to admit it, a woman holding a baby had never looked better to him. As long as it wasn't *his* kid, he could put on a smile and pretend the comment didn't scare the pants off him.

Another knock on the door had Beth returning to the living room.

"Pastor Ron! Karen, welcome! Make yourselves at home while I finish getting lunch ready." Beth hurried to the kitchen once again.

"Something smells absolutely delicious!" Karen commented. "Why don't I come help you?"

Anthony strolled into the room shortly after. "Ari, why don't you leave Chloe with me and the guys? You and the girls go have some bonding time in the kitchen before lunch."

"Sure, if you don't mind?" She questioned Gage with her eyes as she leaned in and handed Chloe over to him.

"Ummmm.....no...not at all. You go on with the ladies and....." he paused briefly as he looked at the little girl's father, who he hoped would be retrieving the tot soon, "we can handle Chloe." His instantly queasy stomach, said otherwise.

"Are you sure, Gage?" She questioned again.

Well, he was sure of one thing. He was doing a lot to impress the woman standing next to him; and he didn't quite know why. She was beautiful, no doubt. But he'd been on dates with plenty of beautiful women. Never before had he been willing to compromise the man he was. And yet, in this moment, he found himself holding a small child in his arms for the very first time, after willingly going to a Sunday church service, no less! There was definitely something wrong with this picture.

"Um, yeah, I guess we'll be fine." He searched for confirmation in Anthony's eyes.

"No worries, Ari. I'll be right here to help him."

After a lunch filled with Q & A's about his life, and trying to decipher through Beth's confusing expressions of approval and distaste, Gage had enough and needed a breather. He decided to approach Arabella with a proposition of spending a quiet evening alone. Moving in behind her as she discussed Chloe's teething trials with Beth, Gage swept Ari's hair to one side and drew in close, whispering softly into her ear. "Hey, beautiful, how about you and I spend a little time together, *alone*?" Gage caught Beth's expression out of the corner of his eye, but dismissed it quickly. The warmth of Ari's body against his as he sidled up to her, and the way her perfume tingled his senses, was all the approval he needed.

Ari turned in his arms, looking deep into his eyes. "I think I would really like that, Gage."

Your making headway! She's already leaving her friends to spend time with you. Just keep it up a little longer and you'll get exactly what you want.

Gage couldn't even hide the smirk on his face, as he and Ari said their goodbyes. The two of them drove separately back to Ari's lake house to drop off their cars.

"So, where should we go first?" Ari asked, seemingly unaware of Gage's thoughts. His plan involved never leaving the house at all.

Patience, he told himself. *Let her think she's in charge.*

"It's still early and we have plenty of time. Why don't you decide, Ari?"

She led him downtown again, checking out some of the stores he'd missed on their first voyage. An antique store, a second-hand furniture warehouse, Clara's clothing boutique, which Ari said was her favorite little shop, and a knick-knack store where you could buy anything from bubble gum to bath towels, kitchen dishes to the newest electronic device. He purchased a new handbag for her at Clara's that she raved about. By the time they were headed back to the cottage, Gage realized he was actually having fun. Shopping with a woman had never been high on his 'to do' list, but there was something special about Ari that was comforting to him.

On their way back to the cottage, they passed an empty store front on the corner for rent. Out of the blue, Gage thought aloud that it would be perfect for a small art gallery. He wasn't sure where that thought came from, or why the thought of putting down roots in this town kept fluttering through his mind. But he'd been pushing them aside all afternoon. He'd never been so confused in all his life. One minute he was ready to split and hit the road to Iowa, and the next minute he was picturing how a future in this quiet little town would look. Provided Ari was by his side.

The two of them made their way to the beach where they sat on a blanket, surrounded by the frequent sounds of laughter and happy conversations from the many beach goers. A while later, they walked along the edge of the water, hand in hand, sharing an ice cream cone and more conversation. Ari talked about the restaurant mostly. Gage was quiet, listening more than talking, as late afternoon turned to evening. They eventually strolled back to the cottage with take-out pizza and a bottle of wine.

Ari was slightly hesitant to accept Gage's invitation back to the cottage. Perhaps she was stepping too far out of her comfort zone. She'd seen the look on Beth's face when Gage had asked her to leave lunch earlier in the afternoon. And, if she wasn't mistaken, there was a warning included in Beth's gaze that said, "Danger Ahead." Gage's words sang like a melody to her heart, however, and before she knew it, she'd agreed. Now, with it being too late to change her mind, Ari was walking through the front door of the house with him. Alone.

The day had been a mixed bag of emotions for Ari. Certainly, she was happy that Gage had come to church that morning, but it was obvious that it made him uncomfortable. Ari had known her entire life that she would never get serious with a "non-believer." Being unequally yoked was something her parents had spent many hours discussing with she and her sister, Maria. And now, Gage had asked her to leave her friends in order to be alone. With him. Ari had always put her friends first. Especially since they were the only family she had. Was being alone with a man that was practically still a stranger, a wise choice?

Before she could spend any more time debating the situation in her mind, Gage gently guided her through the front door. Once again, she let her defenses drop. Walking straight through the house and towards the kitchen, Arabella hesitated only briefly before opening the French doors that led outside.

"It's a beautiful night, Gage. Would you like to eat out here?"

"I would love that, Ari."

She brushed past him on her way to the kitchen where she poured them each a glass of wine and grabbed some paper plates. Staying outside would probably be smarter, based on how fast her heart was pumping at the moment. Alone with Gage in the house might be more temptation than she could handle after the day they'd spent together. Ari had been lost in a dream ever since he took his seat next to her in the pew that morning; and temptations had only grown stronger as the day progressed. No man had ever made her feel this way!

Gage followed her out the door to a small patio table, where they spent the next twenty minutes, eating pizza and making small talk.

"I don't think I could ever get tired of the sunsets here." Gage mused, his voice draped with awe.

"I admit it's beautiful, but it's still a little chilly this time of year." Arabella shivered and pointed towards the gas fire pit. "Would you mind starting a fire?"

Gage took another bite of pizza before jumping up to start the fire, then disappeared into the house without even a word. Moments later, he emerged. A warm, fleece blanket in his hands.

"Come sit by the fire with me, Ari."

He reached out, gently tucking her small hand into his, and led her to the couch near the fire. Gently, he placed the blanket around them and snuggled in next to her.

Her mind was racing in a thousand different directions, thinking about the scene unfolding around her. The beautiful sunset, the sound of the water crashing on the shore, and the warmth of not only the fire, but of the man she felt next to her. She'd never allowed herself to get this close to someone. She'd never had a boyfriend, had never been kissed, and yet here she was sitting next to this....this dream boat that made her oh, so crazy inside. It was silly to think that after only three days she could be falling for him. She kept trying to warn herself that he couldn't possibly be the right man to fall in love with, but even still......

Gage quietly slipped one arm around her shoulders, and with his free hand, pulled her chin in his direction until they were face to face. She knew his intention. Just as she had earlier that morning. He wanted to kiss her.

Lord, what am I doing here? This cannot be a decision you would have me make, can it? I'm so confused by the feelings I have for this man. Please, help me to be strong and make the right choice.

There was no audible response, but Ari knew in her heart, the truth. God had been trying to tell her since yesterday.

She slowly began to pull away, but Gage's grip around her shoulder only tightened.

"Arabella, what's wrong?" Gage asked, frustration in his voice. "This is the second time I've tried to kiss you, and you've pulled away. Have I misread your feelings about me?"

"Gage, I know that this might sound silly to you, but," feeling suddenly shy about her reservations, Ari lowered her eyes, focusing on her hands in her lap, "I've never had a boyfriend. I've never even been kissed. This is all new to me. I'm not sure what to do with all these feelings I have for you. I mean.....I only just met you. Doesn't this seem *crazy* to you?" She looked up, waiting for his response with anticipation.

Gage gently brushed a few strands of hair away from her face. "Ari, it's just a kiss. It's not like I'm asking you marry me."

When a single tear slid down her face and landed on his hand, Gage wrapped both of his hands around her cheeks.

"Talk to me, Ari."

"Gage you and I are different in so many ways, and that becomes more evident the longer we spend together. I've built my life around a relationship with the Lord. And in that relationship, I've pledged my purity to him. When I experience a physical relationship with a man, I want that man to be the husband I spend the rest of my life with."

Gage leaned back and let out a long breath as he shook his head.

"Wow, Ari, I don't even know what to say to that. I've never met a woman that cared about her purity enough to *not* kiss me. In fact, I'm pretty sure this is the first time I've ever heard the word purity in a relationship. Heck, all the girls I've ever dated are usually the ones trying to kiss *me*!"

Ari could sense frustration in his words, but she knew she had to honest with him. "Maybe I should just go, Gage. This was probably a bad idea."

Once again, Gage held onto her, not allowing her to move from the spot next to him.

"I'm sorry, Ari. I don't know what else to say. I like you……. a lot. I've enjoyed the time we've spent together and I look forward to more of that. Kissing you is just the next logical step for me. I had no idea that you had never….well, that you were so *pure.* It's not my intention to hurt you."

"But you're leaving in a couple of weeks, Gage. What will happen then? I mean, you live a thousand miles away. Will I ever see you again? I can't give my heart away to a man that doesn't stick around. I've spent my entire life trying to avoid *this exact* situation."

When he spoke again, his words were soft and tender, and *very* convincing to her heart. "Ari, I can't guarantee what the future holds, but I'm starting to care a lot for you. And I would never do anything to hurt you."

She could feel herself slipping further and further, as Gage ran his fingers through her hair, and reached in to kiss her on the cheek. It was more than she could say no to, and very quickly she found herself wanting to feel his lips against hers.

You're no better than all those girls in high school that gave themselves away so easily. All these years you've held yourself to a higher standard, and for what? Now you're just going to give in and throw it all away. This is not what you want, Ari!

"Stop! I can't do this." Ari pushed away from Gage and stood up, turning her back towards him.

Gage rolled his eyes in defeat and sighed heavily. "C'mon Ari. You can't tell me you didn't like that."

She turned back long enough to respond. "Gage, I think it's best if I leave now." She started towards the house, needing to put distance between them. "Why don't you meet me at the restaurant in the morning? We can go over your schedule then."

Gage raised his hands in surrender. "Fine, Ari. You know, I'm not trying to hurt you, but if you want to wait, then I will respect you for that." He reached out to take her hand as he stood and walked to her. "Let me at least walk you out."

As soon as her hand felt the warmth of his, Ari seemed to forget the confusion in her mind, suddenly wanting to be in his arms again. After all, it was just a kiss he was expecting, she was sure. Would a kiss be so bad? He'd seemed sincere when he said he'd respect her. Maybe.....

Keep walking towards the door, Ari. You can do this! Put distance between you and Gage, it's for the best.

Gage turned towards her once again as they came to stand at the front door. "Hey, how about we meet on the beach before breakfast tomorrow? There's something I want to do."

Ari reluctantly agreed, unsure of what he had in store, but wanting to spend more time with him. As long as it was out in public, and temptation was easier to avoid. She said goodbye and made her way back to the loft, not feeling an ounce of reassurance until she reached the safe haven of her apartment. She couldn't dial Beth's number fast enough.

"Well, I'm glad you stood your ground, Ari. Maybe, with feelings this strong, you and Gage shouldn't put yourself in a position like that again? Maybe you need a chaperone to kind of put a damper on those desires."

Thinking back on how close she'd come to kissing Gage, not once but twice, Ari readily agreed. She wasn't ready to give up on the relationship quite yet, but a little distance might be good. "Probably not a bad idea, Beth. *So*...... does that mean I might talk you and Anthony into joining us for dinner tomorrow night?

Beth chuckled. "I think we might be able manage that. *If* I can find a sitter, that is. *And* if you can find a hostess."

Ari could hear Chloe's baby jabber in the background, which always brought a smile to her face. She allowed a calm to wash over her, momentarily forgetting the stress she felt regarding this *thing* with Gage.

"Thanks, Beth, for always being here for me. You know I couldn't love you more than I already do."

"I love you too, Arabella, and I'm proud of you. I know you want to find the right man, but you will never regret your decision to stay true to God. Gage isn't the right one for you, if he doesn't support that."

"You're right, Beth," she sighed. "It's just weird, that's all. I mean....I've always dreamed of finding Mr. Right, but I've never really pursued anyone because I never wanted to make the effort. I guess I was just too afraid of the commitment. But there's just something about this guy—"

"Ari, I want you to be happy. And, I see that you are happy when you are with Gage. But I want you to honor God more than I want your temporary happiness. Your relationship with Christ is more important than *anything*!"

Beth's unsympathetic words were solid truth. Ari had nothing to argue against them. "Okay, I get it! Loud and clear."

"Good, that's what I wanted to hear!"

"Tell Ari goodnight, dear."

Ari heard Anthony's voice ringing out in the background.

"You can talk to her tomorrow."

"Why didn't you tell me Anthony was waiting for you, Beth? I didn't mean to take away from your time with him. We can talk later."

Ari shook her head as her best friend responded to both she and her husband.

"Sorry. He's been patiently waiting for me to get off the phone and pay some *serious* attention to him."

"Seriously, Beth? I *did not* need to hear that. Goodbye." Ari shuddered in disgust as she disconnected the call and made her way to the bathroom for her weekly charcoal face mask and exfoliation. Afterwards, she spent an hour poring through her Bible and reaching out to God in prayer. She once again recited her vow to Him, pledging her purity and asking the Lord to give her the strength and insight to handle her relationship with Gage in a godly manner. Romans 6:12-13 really sank into her heart, so she jumped up to grab a notecard and pen.

"Therefore, do not let sin reign in your mortal body so that you obey its evil desires. Do not offer any part of yourself to wickedness, but rather offer yourselves to God as those who have been brought from death to life; and offer every part of yourself to him as an instrument of righteousness."

Feeling more confident with her choices, she scribbled the verse onto the card. At the bottom, in all capitalized and bold letters she wrote, "I AM WORTH THE WAIT!" and taped the card to her bathroom mirror, making a promise to herself that she'd read it each morning.

Anthony watched as Beth set her phone on the nightstand and climbed under the covers, scooching up next to him. He wrapped his arm around her and pulled her tightly into a hug. When she remained silent, which was rare for his talkative wife, Anthony knew she had more on her mind that she needed to talk about.

He released his hold on her, pushed his pillows up against the headboard, and leaned back against them, thinking it might be a while before he had his wife's attention to himself.

"What's on your mind? I'm guessing it has to do with Ari and Gage?"

Beth sat up next to him. "I'm so worried about her, Anthony. I really do want her to be happy, and at first Gage seemed like a great idea, but now—"

"And now *what*? Is this about him not being a Christian?"

"Absolutely!" Beth's concern rang out in her words. "I mean, he was pressuring her into kissing him tonight, and that's a huge step for Ari." Beth crossed her legs, sitting Indian style, and turned to her husband as she continued, talking with her hands as much as her mouth. "Don't get me wrong, Gage is nice enough and all, but you *know* what the Bible says about being unequally yoked. I think she's sliding down a slippery slope and *fast*! How could I not be worried about her?"

Pulling his caring and compassionate wife into his arms, Anthony placed a kiss on her forehead before releasing her. "Beth, I know you love Ari like a sister. But, honey," he tilted her chin with his finger and looked her in the eye, "you can't make her decisions. You can gently and lovingly give advice and be there for her when she needs you. Other than that, this situation is out of our hands. Why don't you just let it go, put your trust in God, and see what happens?"

Beth was quiet for a long moment, and Anthony wasn't sure if that was a good sign or not.

Finally, with a long, drawn out sigh, she responded. "How did I manage to find such a smart and handsome guy?" She leaned in and gently rubbed her nose to his.

"Just luck I guess." Anthony chuckled. "Now come here and let this smart and handsome guy have some of your undivided attention."

"You got it, babe." Beth leaned into his embrace and planted a kiss on his lips.

Chapter 6

The next morning, Ari attempted to start her day with her normal routine, beginning with time in the Word. This was the part of her day that she'd come to count on and looked forward to, bringing with it a calm and peacefulness that compared to nothing else. This morning, however, felt different. Something, or *someone* rather, was filling her mind and distracting her. This someone had dazzling blue eyes, jet black hair, and a magnetic personality that continued to pull her to him.

Gage had asked her to join him on the beach this morning; and for Ari, seven o'clock couldn't come fast enough. She paced back and forth, trying to decide what to wear. Having been awake since six a.m., she'd already tried on eight outfits, straightened her hair, then changed her mind and curled it, until finally deciding to put it up in a clip. Her hands were trembling so bad, that she could barely pick up her phone and check the time, for what felt like the hundredth time.

Convinced if she walked slow enough, she could leave now and not be too early, Ari stepped into her favorite flip flops and headed towards the beach. She couldn't help but notice what a beautiful day it was going to be. There wasn't an ounce of humidity in the air and the temperature was perfect for this time of day; the sun already brightening the beautiful blue sky. Living in this little beach town her entire life had been a blessing, and Ari couldn't imagine another place that would ever mean this much to her. Her thoughts began to wander towards Gage again. If this thing between them developed into something serious, would he be willing to give up his life in New York? Or, would he expect her to give up her life here, to make a life out east?

Realizing, once again, that she was thinking too far into her "relationship" with Gage, Ari tried to get her mind on something else. Something less serious. Something less scary. Something. Anything. But once again, her mind betrayed her. She tried to tell her feet to slow down and not be as eager as her heart, but it seemed her mind and body were in cahoots. She made it to the pier in record time, a little nervous but excited too, just as Gage was arriving.

"Good morning, beautiful." Gage's deep smile put her at ease immediately.

"Morning, Gage." She took a couple of steps in his direction. "So, what do you have planned for us?"

"I'm going to sketch you, Ari."

"You're *what?*" Ari's eyes grew wide as she coughed and sputtered, certain she had misunderstood. "*Sketch me*?"

Gage chuckled as he came to her. "Yes, Ari. I want to sketch you." Gently, he reached up and tucked a wisp of hair behind her ear. "Will you let me?"

"I…uh….I," she cringed slightly, "guess, *maybe,* it would be okay." Ari looked to her left and then to her right, wondering just where this sketch was going to take place; and hoping there was nobody around to witness it. She definitely wasn't model material. So, the fact that Gage wanted to draw a picture of her, was beyond her comprehension. "What exactly did you have in mind?"

Gage took a step back and surveyed the area around them. "There," he pointed. "On that rock. Do you think you could sit up there long enough for me to do the sketch? The way the sun is just sitting on the water, directly behind that spot, would be perfect if we could get started."

Ari looked at the rock and shrugged. Stepping closer, she could see a partially flattened spot on the top where she might be able to get comfortable. "I guess I could try. No guarantees, though."

"No worries. C'mon, let's get started."

Twenty uncomfortable, and back-aching minutes later, when Gage helped her down and turned the sketch in her direction, it brought tears to Ari's eyes. Backpain? What backpain? The giant red lighthouse in the background, and the sun on the horizon, hovering just above the water, with its bright rays easing around the rock where she'd sat, gave it a "golden halo" effect. It was not the image Ari had anticipated. What Gage had captured was stunning.

"Gage, this is absolutely beautiful."

He smiled, reaching up and brushing his knuckles lightly across her cheek. "I had the perfect subject."

Ari blew off the comment like it meant nothing. "I mean your drawing, silly! Not me. Why aren't you selling your art, Gage? You have a gift, that's for sure. I mean....I just can't take my eyes off of it!"

Gage was slow to respond, and she could see he was having a difficult time processing her words.

"You know, Ari, only one other person has ever complimented my art before."

"One person, Gage? I find that hard to believe."

"It's true, Ari." Gage looked down at his feet, the sand slipping through his toes as he made circles in it, obviously uncomfortable with where this discussion was going. "In fact, you're the only person I've shown it to since I was in high school."

"Gage, why? I don't understand. You should be proud of your art!" When his only response was shaking his head, Ari moved closer and placed a reassuring hand on his arm, sensing his unease. "Do you want to talk about it?"

He was quiet for a moment, then simply reached for her hand, and pulled her to a bench facing the water. He stared straight ahead, never once looking her way, as he began to speak.

"When I was a freshman, I took an art class because I thought it would be a no-brainer. An easy credit class," he shrugged. "But that first week, my views on art changed, and it suddenly became a way to express myself. I had nobody to talk with, to share my feelings with. My father was always at work and even when he managed to come home, he never had much to say to me. He always taught me that men weren't supposed to show their feelings, that I needed to keep them bottled up. Art became an outlet for me, a way to share my feelings, even if nobody was listening. I was always happy with a paintbrush or pencils in my hand."

Ari shuddered at the thought of what Gage's childhood had been like. She had been fortunate to have, not only happily married parents that doted on her, but a sister that she adored and shared every little secret with. Maria had been her very best friend. Sadness tore at Ari's heart for the hurt Gage must have endured.

"I'll never forget the day my father first found my sketch pad and colored pencils."

Gage turned to face her now, and Ari was certain he was trying to keep the shimmer in his eyes from becoming tears. His jaw trembled slightly as he began again.

"He tossed them in the garbage, and told me he never wanted to see them again. Told me art would never be a way to pay the bills."

Ari reached for his hand and tucked hers inside. "Gage, we don't have to talk about this if it's uncomfortable for you."

Instead, Gage turned his attention back to the water as he continued, his grip on her hand becoming tighter.

"I kept it hidden, and by my Junior year, I had begun to think that I could see a future in art. I knew my father would never agree to it, but I dreamed about it every day. That year, our class held a small Art Expo to raise money for our Senior trip. My teacher, Mrs. Brown, encouraged me to invite my father. But up until that very day, I was scared to even mention it, for fear of his reaction."

Ari could feel the tension in Gage growing stronger, as his arms stiffened. "But, you did invite him, didn't you?" Ari ran her other hand along Gage's arm, showing her support, and trying to comfort him as he spoke.

"Yes," he turned his head towards her again, "after days of listening to Mrs. Brown tell me how proud my father would be of my hard work, I was actually foolish enough to believe it. I left a voicemail for him that morning at work, letting him know the event started at 6:30 that evening."

It was silent for the longest, most uncomfortable few moments. Finally, needing to know the answer, Ari nudged him and asked quietly, "He didn't show up, did he?"

"Oh, he showed up alright," Gage shook his head, "at 8:30, just as we were packing up for the night. He marched right in, with angry fists clenched at his side, and tore into me before he even bothered to take a look at the best picture I had ever painted."

"What is this non-sense about an art fair, Gage? For the last time, you are not an artist and I don't have time to waste on silliness like this." His father's words escalated in volume as he continued. "I have a job to do, which you have now pulled me away from! If you needed money for your senior trip, all you had to do was ask. I have always provided for you." James stood next to the easel where Gage's canvas rested, not even recognizing the young man and father featured in the picture were the two of them. Nor did he realize the volume that the scene spoke, boy and father sitting on a dock fishing together. Gage knew his father would never understand his desire to be an artist. And he certainly would never understand his son's need to have a real relationship with his father.

Surrounded by his classmates, Gage dropped his head in embarrassment. He felt like a ten-year old being scolded in front of them. The sting of his father's words cut deep, leaving shards of his self-worth scattered on the ground.

"But...um...dad...I...um," Gage stammered, feeling like a fool for believing he had an ounce of talent. His artwork must be horrible, and that was why his father disliked it so much. Why had Mrs. Brown told him it was good? Was she just trying to be nice?

"I'm sorry, Gage, I haven't had the opportunity to meet your father." Gage felt the warmth of Mrs. Brown's hand upon his shoulder.

"Oh, sorry Mrs. Brown," Gage mumbled as he pointed at his old man, never moving his gaze from the floor, "this is my father, James. Dad, this is Mrs. Brown, my art teacher."

James threw his head back, a single, wicked, chuckle of disgust escaping from his mouth. "Oh, art teacher. I see. That explains it all."

"I'm sorry?" Mrs. Brown cocked her head and narrowed her eyes in James' direction. "I don't understand?"

"You artsy people are all alike. Gage's mother thought she had talent, too. But you people need to realize there are real jobs in the world that actually pay the bills. Art is fun, I suppose, if you like that kind of thing. But it's not something you can make a living with."

What? My mother liked art too? How did I not know this? His father's words burned inside Gage's mind. It was as if his mother had been in an entirely different world, the way his father kept everything about her a secret. How many more secrets has he kept from me about her?

Gage wanted desperately to believe this night wasn't happening. His father's 'not so pleasant' words had caught the attention of his classmates and fellow staff members, who all stared in their direction.

Mrs. Brown cleared her throat. "I'm not sure what your wife's talent was or how familiar you are with art yourself, Mr. Russell. But your son, Gage, has talent. You should be very proud of the work he's done and the effort he puts into all of his pieces. Your son is my best student; and he can most definitely look forward to some nice scholarships in his future."

I knew this was a mistake. Things are about to get REAL ugly! Gage's stomach churned with fear. If only I could turn the clock back a few hours and change my mind. Calling my father was wrong and, judging by the look on his face right now, we're all going to pay for it. Poor Mrs. Brown.

An evil laugh erupted from James' throat. Gage's classmates all had enough sense to see what was coming. They looked at each other in horror and began to take steps backwards, hoping to escape before the explosion.

Too late.

"You must think you're really something, Mrs. Brown the 'art teacher,'" James sneered. Then, pointing his finger in her face, he continued his tirade. "But let me be very clear. You don't know the slightest thing about

my son and his 'talents'. So, don't you go planting some scatter-brained seeds into his head about making a living with his so-called 'art'. My son, and all of his talents, will be working with me," James pointed his thumb towards his chest, "and me alone, to build and grow the company that I've worked my entire life for!"

Don't argue, Mrs. Brown. Please, it will only make things worse. Gage knew that much from experience.

His classmates now stood frozen in their steps as Mrs. Brown placed her left hand on her hip and glared right into James' eyes.

"Mr. Russell, do you even realize the talent that your son has, and what he could be throwing away if you don't let him choose his own path? He is nearly an adult and has a mind of his own. A brilliant one at that!"

Her best student? Brilliant? Scholarships? Could that really happen? Wow. Nobody has ever stood up to my dad like that, especially when it comes to me. Gage's thoughts were interrupted by his father's retort.

"Don't you worry your pretty little head about my son's future!" James turned to face his son. "Gage, get your things. We are going home! And, as of right now, you are finished with art class!"

Mrs. Brown nodded at Gage, indicating it was okay. He knew that she would take care of his artwork and supplies.

The ride home had been eerily quiet. In fact, the next two days proved to be one of the longest weekends of Gage's life. His father never spoke a word to him, making him feel even worse by Monday, when Gage couldn't wait to escape to school. Unfortunately, his day turned ugly fast when he realized his father had been serious about art class. He had been transferred to Advanced P.E.

"Hello, Gage. Are you in there?" Ari's hands waved back in forth in front of his eyes, pulling his thoughts back to the present.

"You know, when I was younger…" he paused momentarily and looked down at the ground, his face contorted with grief, as if confessing his desire was somehow wrong, "I dreamed that one day my drawings and paintings could be good enough to sell. But that was so long ago," Gage shook his head, "and you're the only one, besides my art teacher, that I've even shared this dream with." He looked up and turned towards her, shifting his weight and leaning in closely to her as he ran his thumb along her jaw line. "Ari, you've brought out so many things from my past, things that I thought I was done with. But I realize now, how much I've missed them."

Ari stilled, allowing the warmth of his hand to comfort her. "You've got a talent, Gage, there's no denying that. You should really consider it." Ari picked the canvas up from the bench and held it in her hands, staring at it. "Can I keep this one?"

"You really like it that much, Ari?"

"I *love* it, Gage. Nobody has ever given me anything so special. It would mean a lot to me."

"It's yours."

Their morning started and ended just like it would every day for the rest of that week. They met first on the beach, where Ari would watch Gage sketch, then later they'd have breakfast at the café down the road. After heading home for showers, they would meet up again at Francesca's and the work day would begin. Even though they both put in eight or more hours each day, they were always in each other's company. Gage taught Ari about the work he was doing at Francesca's, and Ari shared details about running her business. They'd break for long lunches in the afternoon, continuing to grow deeper in their relationship.

Usually by dinner time, they would find themselves sharing a meal at Anthony and Beth's house, or sitting at a quiet table near the bar, where Sam would conveniently join them. Beth's face was seen at Francesca's more than usual these days; she never hesitated to sneak a few scriptures into their daily conversations. And Sam? Well, he hadn't been shy in voicing his opinion about their relationship, either. How they needed to take it slow. Although, it appeared that Sam found himself liking Gage more and more the longer they were around each other. More than once, Ari overheard the two talking about a relationship with the Lord, and Sam teaching Gage things you'd expect a father to pass down to a son.

Privately, Sam had shared some concerns with Ari, about she and Gage being unequally yoked. But he'd also mentioned, more than a few times, that Ari's friends and church family would be the ones likely to draw him into a relationship with the Lord. At least that was the hope.

The following week the same routine continued, until Sunday when Anthony and Beth had to go out of town for the afternoon. Feeling confident that she and Gage had made positive strides in their relationship and could handle the pressure of being alone, Ari had agreed to have dinner at the cottage with him. By now, Gage certainly understood how important her promise was to God, right? How could he not after they'd spent so much time discussing it?

After a second church service and another lunch with Pastor Ron and his wife, Gage had taken Ari to the beach where he'd sketched yet another picture of her. This time, sitting on the pier, with the bright blue sky and a few white, fluffy clouds floating through the air. A number of brightly colored sailboats were captured in the background. Nobody had ever made Ari feel so loved, as when Gage lavished her with his attention.

It struck her then, that with everything Gage had shared with her, she'd like to share something with him. Reaching for his hand, she pulled him away from his sketching, and led him across the road to the base of the highest sand dune.

"Are you going to ask me to climb this thing?" Gage asked, with a curious look, first at the massive hill, and then back at her.

"It's really not as bad as it seems. Besides," she shrugged, "look how much fun it is coming down!" Shielding her eyes from the bright sun, Ari looked towards the top of the dune and pointed. Three teenagers had just begun their fast descent, their laughter filling the air, as they sped towards the bottom.

Gage's eyes wandered to a few other beach-goers that had stopped mid-way up the hill, resting on a large piece of driftwood.

"You really want me to do this?"

"C'mon, Gage. I promise it won't be that bad. There's something I want you to see on the other side."

"Okay, then. Let's do it!" Gage allowed Ari to lead him toward the dune.

By the time they made it to the top, Ari was certain Gage was going to pass out.

"Seriously, Gage? You are way too dramatic!" She watched as he bent over, gasping for air.

"Dramatic? You....you.... force me... to walk in deep sand..... up a mountain.... and you call me.... dramatic?"

Ari rolled her eyes and giggled. "Boys! Such non-sense! Well, the hard part is over. Follow me, you're going to love this."

Gage held out his hand to her and Ari pulled him gently behind her through a small patch of trees and high grasses.

"Okay, close your eyes, Gage."

"Close my eyes? Just what have you got planned for me, Ari? Is there a band of pirates around the corner, ready to take me out to sea?"

"Pirates? Are you delirious from too much sun today? Just trust me, Gage. And quit being so silly."

"Well, it made you smile," he argued. "Okay. Let's get this over with. My life is officially in your hands."

Gage closed his eyes and Ari reached for his hands, gently pulling him towards their destination.

"Okay, on the count of three you may open—"

"Three!" Gage impatiently hollered, then opened his eyes. Together they stood in absolute silence, looking out over the water.

"It's beautiful, huh?"

"Stunning!"

They stood on the top of what looked like black volcanic rock, forming a half circle around an inlet of bright blue water.

"This is how our town got its name. It's a story that's been passed down from generation to generation. In the old shipping days, the captains would depend on this little inlet as a protection from storms while they made their way from the Upper Peninsula to Chicago. Eventually, they named the spot Rock Haven, as settlers began to take up residence nearby. This is where I come when I need to think, or just feel like being alone."

"It was definitely worth the trek up here, Ari. I'm sorry I made such a fuss about coming. Promise me that we will come back some day soon, so I can bring my sketch pad?"

"Oh, definitely. Just wait until you see it at sunset. Are you ready to head back?"

Gage followed her back to the top of the dune and they raced down the hill, side-by-side, as fast as their legs would take them.

They stayed on the beach, soaking up the summer sun most of the day. Later, they joined in on a game of volleyball until dinner time, before heading to the cottage where Gage had a surprise waiting for her. He'd seemed overjoyed when she'd accepted his invitation on Friday, and truthfully, it was all she had thought about since then.

As Gage gently guided her through the doorway, Ari couldn't have been more surprised. Gage had thought of everything, including the small candles that were scattered throughout the house, giving off a romantic glow. The lights were all dimmed, and in the background soft music flowed through the room. She stood in the doorway taking it all in, speechless, as she thought about the effort he had put into it, and how much he must care for her.

"Gage, this is beautiful," Ari whispered as she motioned to the room around her, the candle light glowing softly in the reflection of her eyes.

Gage pulled her into a hug and rested his forehead against hers. "I want this night to be special for you, Arabella."

Slightly uneasy about their close proximity, Ari gently pulled loose from his embrace, using the excuse that she needed to freshen up.

"I'm going to get a quick shower if you don't mind? I need to get this sand out my hair," Ari grabbed her bag and headed down the hall.

He just smiled towards her as he watched her walk away. "Great idea, Ari. I'm going to get dinner going while you do that. Take your time and relax."

The refreshing, cool water of the shower, washed away the worry and stress she was feeling about being alone with Gage, leaving her more confident and at peace with the situation. Certainly, they were mature enough to handle one night alone, weren't they? Staring at her reflection in the mirror, Arabella could only hope so, as she prayed for strength.

Twenty minutes later, Ari stood in the doorway of the kitchen. She wore a simple, but very flattering, pink summer dress, her still-damp hair pulled back neatly into a bun, and her pretty bare toes sporting a fresh new color that matched her outfit.

"Mmmmm, something smells delicious! What's on the menu for tonight?"

Gage turned at the sound of her voice and smiled brightly. His reaction was everything she'd hoped it would be.

"Ari, you look wonderful!"

She swallowed past the lump in her throat. Her nerves were short circuiting everywhere in her body. Gage offered her some wine and, hoping it might help to calm her just a bit, Ari gratefully accepted the glass he handed to her. Along with the tender kiss he planted in the crook of her neck.

"So?"

"So, what?"

"What's for dinner?"

"Oh," Gage seemed to quickly switch gears as he turned back towards the stove and began whisking some concoction in a saucepan. "Just a simple tortellini and prosciutto in a basil cream sauce, along with salad and cheese filled bread sticks."

"Wow! It sounds as delicious as it smells," she grinned. "You better be careful Mr. Russell, I might put you to work in the kitchen at Francesca's."

Arabella made her way across the room and found herself toe to toe with Gage, as he turned towards her, and away from the stove. The way he smiled at her, those deep dimples, and that sparkle in his eye, had her senses on high alert.

Flee Ari, you are treading down a path you don't want to go! The words were loud and clear in her mind, as if God himself were standing next to her as He spoke them.

"Would you like another glass of wine, Ari?" Gage's crackling voice sounded as nervous as she felt. Even though wine was the last thing on her mind, and her glass was still nearly full, Ari was happy for the distraction.

"Sure, a little more wine would be nice, Gage."

After topping off her glass, Gage led her to the dining room table that he'd already set. A vase of fresh flowers and additional candles adorned the center. He seated her before he returned to the kitchen to plate their dinner. Ari was lost in thoughts about him once again, as she stared into the candlelight, the sound of the waves crashing upon the shore, flowing in from the open patio doors. This was something she could really get used to.

"Dinner is served!" Gage waltzed back into the room, first carrying their bowls of salad and breadsticks, then returning with their plates of pasta.

It was after her very first bite, that Ari commented. "Gage, this tastes amazing! How many more hidden talents do you have that I need to know about?" Ari gushed.

"When you grow up an only child with a workaholic father, you have to fend for yourself. A lot. What can I say?" he shrugged his shoulders. "I watched a lot of cooking channels."

"Well, you're going to make some girl a very happy wife someday."

Gage nearly choked on his pasta. There was much less talk after that.

Following a chocolate mousse dessert, they found themselves on the sofa in front of the fire, where Ari happily accepted Gage's arm around her shoulders. The night had been a dream for Ari. She knew that she'd fallen in love, and began to envision Gage sweeping her into his arms and slow dancing with her around in circles across the living room floor.

"Gage this night has been amazing. I still can't believe you did all this for me." Ari rested her head against his shoulder, very aware of the effect his body was having on hers.

Ari, you're getting too close. Put some space between you before one of you loses control.

There was that voice again.

"Ari, this entire week has been wonderful. Each day that I spend with you, I find myself falling deeper and deeper for you." Gage sat his wine glass on the coffee table and reached for hers as well. Then, turning towards her, Gage cupped Ari's face in his hands, sending a shiver down her spine. "Ari, I have never felt this way about anyone. I can't imagine how I will ever be able to leave you when my work here is done."

"Stay, Gage. Make a life here." Ari spoke before she even realized what she was saying. "I know it sounds crazy since we just met, but, I don't want to think about life without you now."

Ari you're moving too fast. This is not even the relationship you saw in your future. He is not a believer!

But no matter what her conscious told her, Ari couldn't stop. She had no control when it came to Gage.

The first kiss landed softly on her cheek. Without another word, Gage's kisses slowly found their way to Ari's lips. And this time, she didn't even try to pull away. He was gentle with her, first kissing her very softly, over and over, until she responded with a hunger that she couldn't contain. Their lips continued to meet time and time again, leaving Ari breathless and scared, until finally Gage pulled back. A smile from ear to ear, lit up his entire face.

"See, that wasn't so bad, was it?" Gaged wrapped his arm around her, kissed her gently on the top of her head, and held her against his chest.

A five-alarm fire burned inside of Ari. And it felt good! *Didn't it*? But the way Gage was holding her and had kissed her, her very first kiss—and one she would always remember—had opened her mind up to all sorts of confusion. And that scared her.

A lot.

She eventually let herself relax and lean back against him, savoring how it felt to be in his arms, and pushing all thoughts aside that were not a confirmation that what she was doing was right. She didn't realize how relaxed she'd become, until Gage gently nudged her quite sometime later, and woke her as he whispered in her ear.

"Ari, I think I'd better get you home. It's past midnight, and we both have a busy day tomorrow." Gage pulled the blanket off of them and reached for her hand, pulling her to a stand next to him as she yawned.

"Are you okay?" Gage looked down tenderly into her eyes. "I mean with what happened, Ari?"

Without a word, Arabella reached her arms around his neck, drawing him to her, and placed a kiss on his lips that she hoped would convey her message, loud and clear.

"Thank you, Gage, for everything. I had a wonderful time with you tonight." She reached for his hand as they made their way to his car.

Later that night Gage lie awake in bed, staring at the ceiling, processing the day's events and trying to figure out how he felt about it all. He'd only wanted one thing when he'd first met Ari. The same thing he usually wanted from women. Fun. And a physical relationship that he had no intention of making into something more. But what he was feeling now, was all new to him. Scoring a home run with Ari was the constant thought he'd had since the first night he'd laid eyes on her. But tonight, when he kissed her, somehow all of that changed. Not that he didn't still plan on getting to home base. That would definitely happen. But now, he had all these emotions swirling around in his head that he didn't understand. Like how good she made him feel when talking about his art, and how nice it was getting to know her past. And the way she kissed him was something magical and more than he was prepared for. It had completely turned his brain upside down, and inside out, leaving him more confused than he'd ever been.

As she'd stood in the kitchen doorway, fresh out of the shower in that cute little dress, with her pretty painted toes, his heart had exploded inside his chest. She was the most beautiful woman he had ever seen. And dinner with her, here in her home? Well, dinner took on a whole new meaning now. As they'd sat across from each other at the table, the candlelight reflecting in her eyes, it felt......well, it felt right. It felt like he had found the part of his life that he'd always been missing. It reminded him of dinners with Nonnie and Max, and what a home *should* feel like. He was starting to have feelings for Ari. Feelings that he was scared to admit, even to himself. Could he stay the course and just get what he wanted from her, like he originally planned? Or was he already too involved to leave?

Memories from his childhood played like a recording in his mind.

"Don't be foolish enough to believe that real love exists! His father had voiced his concerns often. *"Girls will only mess with your brain and make you think things you shouldn't."* James had forced his opinions on Gage from a very young age, starting shortly after his mother died. *"You need to work hard and build a future for yourself, Gage. Don't let any woman talk you into changing your mind. She will only hurt in you the end and leave you with nothing."*

The bitterness held captive in his father's heart had seeped out and bled into every part of Gage's life as a child and young adult. By the time he turned eighteen and rented an apartment of his own, Gage was so scared of relationships that when he finally did start to date, he had one thing on his mind, and one thing alone. And that one thing did not include real emotions, or feelings.

Jenna had been the closest thing to a real relationship that Gage had ever had, and even she didn't matter to him. Not really. She was a convenience, someone he could have fun with and not have to answer to, knowing he would only be around during his summers at Nonnie's.

So, what was he supposed to do now with all these thoughts running through his mind? Thoughts of a future, thoughts of what making a life in a small beach community would look like. Thoughts of what love could really mean. Love? That was a scary word.

Gage tossed the covers aside, got up, and strolled across the bedroom to grab his laptop from the dresser. He had to get his mind off of her and what she was doing to him. He opened up last month's spreadsheets and submersed himself in a safer subject, and one that he'd been neglecting. Work.

Chapter 7

Beth was waiting for Ari to join her the next morning, as usual, for their regular get together at Luna's coffee shop. The second Monday morning of every month, the girls treated themselves to some alone time, catching up on each other's personal lives with the promise that work was not to be discussed.

The minute Ari set foot in the cafe, Beth knew that something was different.

"You kissed him, didn't you?" Beth grilled her, feeling both excitement and, at the same time, apprehension about the situation. Anthony had gently reminded her just before leaving the house this morning, that she needed to take a step back, and just be happy for her best friend. She was definitely trying her hardest.

"Sssshhh." Ari looked from her left to her right and then at Beth. "You don't need to say it so loud!"

"I've already ordered for you so sit down and quit stalling." Beth motioned to the chair across from her. "Hurry up and tell me all about your night with Romeo." Beth silently prayed that a kiss was all she would be hearing about.

"Okay, okay, relax!"

But Beth couldn't relax, as she eagerly attuned her ear to how the afternoon with Gage had gone.

"We spent the afternoon relaxing at the beach. You know, just another day." Ari was stringing her along, and Beth knew it. She wasn't about to let her best friend get away with it.

"You've got about five seconds to get to the juicy details, before I call Gage himself and ask for his version!" Beth was so torn between the excitement she had longed to share with Ari, when finally finding "the one," and the unsettling truth that Beth didn't think Gage *was,* 'that one.'

"You wouldn't dare, Beth!"

Beth picked up her phone, knowing Ari would panic and start dishing out details.

"Fine, okay. Just put the phone down," Ari's voice trembled. She took a deep breath and leaned forward in her seat.

"Yes, we kissed. A lot!" Arabella sat back in her chair and crossed her arms. "There, does that make you happy?"

Beth might have been mistaken, thinking Ari was upset, if it weren't for the huge smile that covered her face. Beth shook her head, "Well, I know you got it bad then, girl. Your first kiss, huh?" She released a heavy sigh. As much as she wanted to be happy for her best friend, Beth couldn't help but wonder if Ari was making the biggest mistake of her life. Trying to tamp down her uneasy feelings about the situation, and heed to her husband's advice, Beth faked a smile and continued, trying her best to convince Ari that she shared in her excitement. "Well, how was it? Was it worth waiting twenty-six years for?" she teased.

"What do *you* think, Beth? I mean, you've *seen* the guy!"

The excitement grew in Ari's smile. It was the change in the tone of her voice as she continued, however, that Beth was worried about.

"He's probably kissed more girls than I can count on all my fingers and toes. I'm the only inexperienced one in this picture."

"There's nothing wrong with that, Ari," Beth was quick to defend the high standards that Ari had kept in place for so long. "You were waiting for the right guy, and now you *think* you've found him. I'm," Beth looked down at the twisted-up napkin in her hands, struggling against every negative thought in her mind, and trying to stay up beat. "I'm happy for you."

Ari didn't misunderstand the hesitancy. "Buuuuuuut?"

"But what?" Beth looked up again. "I said I'm happy for you."

"C'mon Beth, it's *me* you're talking to. We've been friends for too long for you to pretend nothing's wrong. What's going on in that head of yours?"

Happy for the invitation to share her feelings, Beth jumped right in. "Did you guys talk about what happens when his work here is done? I mean, this all happened so quickly. Have either of you thought that far ahead? I just don't want to see you hurt, Ari. You've kept your heart protected for so long, and I'm a little worried about you. Happy! But at the same time worried. If that makes sense?"

Arabella's gaze drifted out the café window, her soft voice void of the excitement from earlier. "We talked briefly about it," she shrugged, "but all he would say is that he cares about me and 'who knows what the future holds'. That's it."

"Hmmm. Well, I do think he really cares for you, Ari. I can see it in the gentleness and kindness he shows you. And, I can see how the relationship is growing between the two of you." Beth reached her hand across the table and covered Ari's, as Ari turned her attention back towards her. "There's no crime in what you've done, Ari. God is not going to be angry with you for kissing a man. It's not like you slept with him. Just be careful it doesn't tempt you to go any further in that direction."

That, was Beth's biggest concern. She was torn. She desperately wanted to support her friend and celebrate the relationship that was growing between she and Gage. But in the depth of her soul, Beth was more worried than she would admit. She could see the changes in Ari. And Beth knew her friend's struggle to remain pure and keep her promise, was something she had to overcome on her own. No matter how much Beth wanted to do it for her.

Ari exhaled and looked into her best friend's eyes. "I know, Beth. It's just so hard. I really do think he's 'the one,' and I want to make sure I do everything right. The way God would want me to. Thanks for talking me through it, and for always being here for me. I love you, you know."

"I love you too, sweetie. And that's what best friends are for! You've been there for me so many times I've lost count."

The conversation quickly turned in another direction. "You mean like when John Mackovich tripped you in the lunch room our first day as freshman, sending you face first into your mashed potatoes? What a dumb initiation to high school."

"Why is this, the *one* story you always remember?" Beth laughed and rolled her eyes. "But, yes, like that. I don't know anyone else that would take a suspension from school, and a grounding from her horrified parents, just to get even for their best friend."

"Well," Ari grinned, once again showing her pride for the choice she'd made that day so long ago, "John really had it coming. It was best that the school remember him with a face full of mashed potatoes as well! Besides," she smirked, "it never felt so good to trip somebody."

The girls laughed so hard at the memory, soon they both had tears streaming down their faces.

"Ari," Beth grew serious again, "I hope you know, I will always be here for you."

"I know," Ari nodded. "And I will always be here for you, too."

A moment later their breakfast was being served.

"Eat up! We have a lot to get done today." Ari grinned.

"No talk about work! Remember?"

"Always a stickler for rules aren't you, Beth?" Ari took a bite of cantaloupe from her fresh fruit bowl.

"Somebody has to keep us on the straight and narrow path."

"Your bagel is getting cold. Let's call a truce and agree to no more talking."

"Agreed."

Later that afternoon, while Gage and Ari slipped away out of town for a couple of hours, Beth called both Anthony and Sam, asking them to join her at the restaurant. Surprised by the others' attendance, for what they thought was a late lunch, both looked at Beth in confusion, as she sat at the bar with a glass of Sprite in her hand, and a grin on her face.

"I think we've been had, Sam." Anthony was the first to recognize that his scheming wife was up to something.

"I should have known," Sam chuckled as he walked behind the bar and pulled a root beer from the cooler. "Anthony, what can I get for you? It looks like we might be a while."

"Go ahead and grab me a root beer as well. I think you're right. She's got that look in her eye that something big is on her mind."

Beth swatted her husband on the arm as he pulled up a stool next to her. "Boys, this is serious! I'm worried about Ari and the direction her relationship with Gage is going!"

"Sweet, beautiful, wife of mine," Anthony looked directly into her eyes and patted her hand, "how is it possible that you barely passed high school drama class with a D?"

Beth's eyes narrowed. "Don't make fun, Anthony. You boys don't seem to realize how serious this issue has become!"

"Okay, okay," Anthony lifted his hands in surrender, "I get it. This means a lot to you, I won't tease."

"Smart man," Sam chimed in and then turned his attention from Anthony to Beth. "So, what's got you so upset, Beth?"

"Don't either of you see what's going on? Ari is slipping further and further away from us. She's spending all of her time with Gage, and I'm not so sure that's a wise decision. I mean, after all, she's already kissed him, and I'm certain he's trying to get her to compromise her beliefs. What are we going to do? Just stand by and watch her world fall apart, when he's done using her and walks away?"

"Whoa, now. Don't you thing you're jumping the gun *just* a little, Beth?"

"Jumping the *gun*, Anthony?" Beth crossed her arms over her chest. "I thought you were on *my* side with this?"

Sam jumped in, apparently to play peacemaker between them.

"Beth, I think we are all on the same side. None of us want to see Ari get hurt. And yes, I think we all sense that she's deeper into this relationship than she ever has been before. However, we can't do anything to stop her. She is an adult. Unfortunately, the most we can do is sit back and wait for the chance to give Godly advice when the opportunity arises. And," he placed a reassuring hand on Beth's shoulder and looked straight into her eyes, "be here when she needs us."

"Agreed. And we've talked about this before, Beth." Anthony crossed the room to Beth and wrapped his arm around her waist, turning her towards him. "If we push too hard, honey, Ari is going to turn her back on all of us. And I know you don't want that." Anthony placed a kiss on the top of her head before releasing his hold on her.

"I just feel so helpless," Beth pouted. "It's not that I don't like Gage. I really do like him, and I know Ari is head over heels for him. But—"

"But you're worried about his relationship with the Lord." Sam cut in. "Personally, I think Gage is a great kid. He just needs a little nudge and some encouragement. Beth, you have to remember, not everyone has been raised in a home with Godly examples."

"I've talked to Gage a few times, and have gotten to know him a little," Anthony began, "and I agree with Sam. He's had a pretty tough life, losing his mother so young and all. It doesn't sound like his father was very active in his life. I think it's safe to say he doesn't have, or desire to have, a relationship with the Lord."

"But, that's where we come in!" Sam smiled now, eagerness showing in his eyes. "We all need to come alongside of him and lift him up, encourage him."

Standing at the bar, Anthony took a drink of his root beer, waiting for his wife's response.

"So, you're suggesting I forget the fact that Ari has lost all common sense, and my fear that she will compromise her beliefs and toss her pledge to God, out the window? I don't think I can do it!"

"No, honey," Anthony set his soda bottle down on the bar. "I think what Sam is saying is to just continue loving her. Pray for her. And, don't be judgmental when it comes to Gage. Right, Sam?"

"Right, Anthony! And I think you and I," Sam pointed at his chest and then Anthony's "need to purposely include Gage in some one on one time."

"I'm sure the guys from church wouldn't mind if I asked him to join our basketball games on Monday nights," Anthony offered.

"Fine," Beth conceded with a huff, "I guess what you're saying makes sense. I'll try my hardest. But I can't guarantee anything. My first thought to run him out of town still sounds easier to me."

"You know you don't mean that, Beth. You want Ari to find happiness," Anthony stood up and reached for her hand. "Now, where's this lunch you promised me?"

"Hold on. She promised me lunch too!" Sam added as he came around from the back of the bar.

"I guess this meeting is adjourned then," Beth replied with just a hint of disagreement in her voice. "I still think you are both living with blinders on when it comes to Ari. But, if you don't want to listen, then we might as well head on over to Nina's for lunch."

"Nina's? Great choice. I can taste those chicken enchiladas already!"

Beth lightly elbowed her husband in the stomach and narrowed her eyes in his direction. "Don't even think this conversation is over. And don't believe for one minute, that you won this round."

"Wait up, Sam! I think I'll catch a ride with you," Anthony called out. He tossed a smile towards his wife, before taking off in a slow jog towards the door.

"Men!" Beth shook her head and rolled her eyes as she picked up her car keys off the bar.

Chapter 8

"Hey, Max. *How are things* at the farm?" Gage held the phone to his ear, reluctant to have the conversation, but knowing it had to happen.

"Things are good here, Gage. What's going on with you, though?"

This was the second call Gage had placed to Max within two weeks. He knew Max well enough to know that he would sense something was going on. Gage had never missed his yearly trip to see his Nonnie. It was as close to being set in stone as it could be, the same time every year.

"Well, I just wanted to let you know that this project I'm working on is taking a little longer than I planned." Gage paused, still uneasy about his decision to put off his trip to his grandmother's. "I guess what I'm saying, is that it's going to be another couple of weeks before I get to Iowa, Max."

"Well, I'm sure sorry to hear that Gage. I know your grandmother is really looking forward to your time together, as am I. So...."

Oh no, here comes the guilt.

Gage hated the thought of disappointing Nonnie and Max. They had been so good to him over the years, and he really did miss them. But the thought of telling Ari goodbye, of not being able to wake up in her beach house, the thought that he wouldn't join her for lunch, or share dinner with her every night, well, that seemed to feel even *worse.* This past week being with Arabella, had been one of the happiest Gage had ever encountered, and one he had never imagined would happen to him.

"Is she worth it?" Max asked.

"Huh?" Gage asked, puzzled by Max's question.

"The girl that's stolen your heart. Is she worth it?"

Gage stuttered, trying his hardest to disguise his feelings. "I…I um…I'm not sure what you're talking about, Max? I'm helping out a friend that I met on my trip, and the project is just taking longer than I planned."

That's believable, right? And it's not really a lie.

"Gage, how long have I known you?"

Gage could feel the conviction in Max's voice. "You've known me my entire life, Max. What's up with the questioning?"

"Yes, I've known you your entire life, Gage. That's why I know, right now, that you're not telling me the whole truth. And since you've never kept secrets from me, or Nonnie, I'm thinking this has to be pretty serious. So, I ask the question again. Is she worth it?"

Gage sighed. It would sure feel good to talk to someone, and share his feelings about Arabella. He had always been able to talk to Max. Max had been more like a father to him than his own dad had. Gage respected Max, and knew he would speak honestly to him.

"Her name is Arabella. And I think she's worth everything in the world, Max. I've never felt like this about a woman, and it scares me, I must admit. She's not the typical, 'date once or twice and have a good time with' kind of girl. She is different. Innocent. And has the purest heart I've ever known. And you know me. I've always been the love 'em and leave 'em kind. No reason for those emotions and promises of a future that will only rip your heart out. But this time, I don't think I could do anything to hurt her, even if that means I get hurt in the process." Gage was startled by his own words. He wondered if Max could read his emotions through the phone line.

"Well, you really have it bad, don't you, kid? Sounds like you might even be falling in love."

That word got Gage's attention. "I'm not so sure I would say—"

"So, why don't you bring her with you? To the farm, that is. Nonnie and I would love to meet the woman that's stolen your heart, you know."

Max had interrupted before Gage could tell him, there was *no way* he was in love. He had never even entertained *that* thought. Love was not a feeling he was all that familiar with. But, he was certain he didn't *love* Ari.

He'd always kept his life private. Something he learned at a very young age by watching his father. But the thought of sharing his love for the farm, and his Nonnie and Max with Arabella—well, that was the perfect idea! The thoughts began to spin in his mind, as he processed all the things he wanted to share with her and show her.

"Max, that is a *brilliant* idea! I'm going to have to discuss it with Ari, but I can't imagine her saying no.

I will call you and Nonnie when I have an answer. But, this doesn't change the fact that I'm going to be later than planned. I've got to finish this project up for Arabella first."

"I would expect nothing less from you, Gage. You go on and finish up with your commitments there, and give us a holler when you're on your way to the farm, okay? I will let Nonnie know what's going on with you." Max paused for a moment before he continued. "You know, Gage, your Nonnie is going to be so happy to hear that you've found someone that you really care about. Your happiness is all she's ever wanted."

"Thanks, Max."

"Gage, there's just one other thing."

Gage stiffened. He didn't like the change of tone in Max's voice. "Yes, Max?"

"You should probably know before you bring this girl home for a visit, that someone else has been waiting here for you."

Gage's enthusiasm was briefly deflated. Jenna.

"She's been by the farm three times in the last week. She knows your routine as much as we do, you know."

The red-haired, blue-eyed, long-legged, beauty flashed through Gage's mind, along with all the nights she'd spent in his arms over the past three years. They had an agreement. Sort of. She was always waiting for him, every June when he arrived; and even though his days were filled with Nonnie and the farm, his nights would be filled with her. She knew where things stood, though. He had a life in New York that he was going back to, and that part of his life didn't include her. In fact, she didn't even have his cell number. The farm was their only connection, and it had been *quite* a connection. One that Gage remembered with a slight smile.

But things were different now. Gage rested his elbow on the table, running his fingers through his hair.

"I never promised her anything, Max. I'll just have to get ahold of her once I get there and explain things to her. I'm sure she'll understand."

Max cleared his throat. "Gage, women look at things a little differently than us men do. Are you sure she understands things the way you do? It's been three—"

"She'll have to understand!"

Max remained silent, and Gage allowed his anger to calm slightly before he continued.

"Sorry I raised my voice, Max. It's just.....I don't want *anything* to ruin my time on the farm with Arabella. Jenna is just a friend. That's all she will ever be."

"I'm pretty sure she thinks of you as more than a friend, Gage," Max argued. "Most *friends* don't spend their summers together the way you two have. Might be wise to give her a call and talk things through as soon as you get here." His words were met by Gage's silence. "Of course, that's just my opinion."

"Sure, Max. I'll do that." Gage hung up the phone, thinking Max had simply misunderstood the relationship he shared with Jenna. There really wasn't a reason to call her. She understood the rules. They had fun for a few weeks every summer, and then went back to their separate lives—no big deal. He refused to let this black cloud overshadow his excitement about Ari's visit to the farm. He'd get all of the projects completed for Arabella by the end of next week. Then, there would be no reason for her to say no, and nothing standing in the way of her visit.

No thing, and no *one*.

The dance was now just one week away, and promised to be the biggest and best one yet. Arabella had even let Beth talk her into a purchasing a gown this year, and that was something she had never considered before. But that, was before Gage. And, as with so many other things that had changed since Gage's arrival, so had Ari's desire to have a man on her arm for the evening. Ari had played it over and over in her mind a hundred times, if not more. Gage would twirl her around on the dance floor, telling her how beautiful she was, and then pull her in tight against his chest; everyone in attendance "oohing and aahing" over what a perfect couple they made. After the past two intimate weeks they'd shared getting to know one another, she had been certain Gage would stay. After all, how could he not realize how important this night was for her? That being said, she could hardly believe the conversation they were currently having.

"No, Gage, absolutely not!"

"But Ari," Gage pleaded, my birthday is in *three* days, and I've spent my birthday on the farm every year since I was five years old! It's a tradition I don't want to break. Why are you being so unreasonable?"

"You're seriously asking me that?" Arabella huffed, slamming a stack of menus down on the bar. Everyone, including Sam, had left for the evening. Ari was just about to have a glass of wine and close out the books for the night when Gage approached her.

"You know how much this ball means to me. My family has provided this event for our community for nearly forty years, and they've come to depend on me! And not only that," she placed a hand on her hip, continuing to look stern, "but you *know* about my sister, Maria, and how this dance is a memorial to her. Especially *this* year! *Ten years*, Gage," Ari was speaking as much with her hands as she was with her mouth at this point. "She's been gone *ten years;* and this is going to be the best dance yet! How could you even suggest I not be here? Are you *that* insensitive? I mean, what do you think I've been doing with all my time the past two weeks?"

"You mean, besides falling for me?" Gage moved in behind her, wrapping his arms around her waist and kissing her on the neck, as if he didn't realize the seriousness of their conversation.

"Gage, stop." Ari pulled away and turned to face him, determined not to fall for his charm. "The dance means *everything* to me. Why can't you just leave for Iowa in the morning, spend a couple days with your grandmother, and be back for the dance?" Tears threatened to spill down Ari's face as she spoke, the emotional rollercoaster she'd been on for the past several weeks seemed to be spiraling out of control, headed for a crash landing.

"Ari, please. Don't make me choose between you and my Nonnie. It's not fair! What if we flew out together, instead of driving, and just spent two days there for my birthday? I promise I will have you back before the dance. And the night of the dance, it will be just us. No talk of work or renovations. Just you and me." Gage moved towards her again and, using all of the charm he had to convince her, pulled her into a deep and passionate kiss.

What had started with a few innocent kisses a couple of weeks ago, had now developed into a thoughtless routine between them. As usual, Arabella's defenses fell apart the moment his lips touched hers. She'd found herself giving in, more and more, to him over the past two weeks than she was comfortable with. The only thing she hadn't compromised on, was their living arrangement. She continued to keep him at a distance when it came down to that aspect of their relationship, although it hadn't been easy. Her loft above the restaurant had always been her safe haven, her only real personal space. She refused to allow him into it, no matter how much he begged.

The promise ring she wore on her left hand was also a constant reminder of her pledge to God to remain pure until marriage. She'd spent countless hours, praying for strength to keep that promise. The relationship with Gage had grown deep, and developed fast, leaving Ari with her head spinning, and constantly questioning her beliefs and morals. She often found herself wondering if giving in would be that bad after all. God would still love her, right? And Gage loved her. There was no doubt in her mind, even if he hadn't spoken those *exact* words. But their disagreements about their living arrangement were making her crazy! Gage continued to attend church with her. And, he had talked briefly about the future, as well as possibly extending his stay indefinitely. Gage had even found an empty space to rent downtown. He talked of using it as an office space, where he could continue to run things for New York and possibly even showcase his artwork.

Ari was in love and happier than she thought possible. But it was still so soon, and the question of marriage had never been mentioned. He did care about her though. Of *that* she was certain.

Gage continued to kiss his way down her neck and Ari, once again, found herself in a position where she was ready to give in to his request.

"Leave the books for tomorrow, Ari." Gage intensified his kisses along her neckline, nearly sending her over the deep end.

"Gage, c'mon," she pulled away slightly using every ounce of strength she had, "you're making this hard on me. We have to come to an agreement about this." She struggled to focus on the conversation they were having instead of how much she missed the warmth of his body against hers.

"Then, say you'll go with me, Ari. And we can end the conversation! It's that easy."

"Easy? None of this is easy, Gage. I can't go with you! Not now, anyway. Why don't you go for a few days to celebrate your birthday? You can come back for the dance, and then afterwards, we will drive out together and spend a week there. Can you at least agree to that?"

"If I go alone, Ari, I'm not rushing back for the dance. Sacrifice is a two-way street in relationships. I want to enjoy my time there. So, you can fly out after the dance and spend a week with me then." Gage's stern attitude came as a surprise. Ari had never seen this side of him. She began to wonder how many more things there were about Gage that she didn't know. Even after spending nearly every single minute over the past couple of weeks with him, she was sure there was much more to learn.

The picture that had played out so many times in her mind over the past week of the two of them, dressed up and dancing together, was shattered. But what else could she do, but agree? She didn't want Gage to break his tradition, knowing how much it meant to him. And she certainly wasn't going to miss the dance.

"Fine," Ari conceded, "then you'll go to Iowa alone and I'll stay here for the dance," she pouted. "But I really wanted to spend your birthday with you."

Seemingly pleased that they had agreed to disagree, Gage found his way to Arabella once again. Sweeping her into his arms, he whispered, "We could celebrate my birthday together tonight, Ari." He slowly made his way to the stairwell that led to her loft.

"Gage, no! We can't do this. You *promised* me you would never push me to do something I wasn't ready for." Ari tried to squirm free of his hold, but Gage's grip only tightened, as he began to climb the stairs.

"Ari, I need you," Gage pleaded. "Let me stay with you just this once! I don't want to waste one more minute of the time I have left with you before I leave in the morning! *Please*," he begged, "let me stay with you tonight. I just want to hold you, nothing else, I promise. I won't hurt you, Ari. I care about you."

It was those last four words that gave her heart permission, to forget all that she had promised God, and let the man she loved carry her through the door of her loft, and into her private world. A world she had never shared with anyone.

Arabella woke the next morning to find herself alone in her bed. Instead of the happiness she had anticipated that she would feel, she was met only with more confusion, when she realized Gage was gone.

He'd been a gentleman and never forced her to do what she wasn't ready for. He'd been true to his word and held her—nothing else—fully clothed, all night long. She'd fallen asleep in his arms, only to dream about their life and future together. So, where was he now? Was he angry because she hadn't allowed their relationship to advance to a new level? Had he left her, without even a goodbye? Frustrated, thinking she never should have let the relationship go as far as it did, and confused by how deep the pain went at the thought of losing him, Ari threw back the covers, ready to go in search of him. She hadn't even made it from the bed when he strolled through the doorway, carrying two steaming mugs of hot chocolate.

"Good morning, beautiful." Gage set the cocoas on the nightstand and leaned down to kiss her, instantly putting her mind at ease.

"Where were you? I was scared you'd left me." Ari was surprised at her boldness, that she'd admitted her fears to him. This too was new, like everything else in this relationship had been.

Gage gently pushed her back onto the bed where he joined her once more, lavishing her with kisses. Breathlessly, but so intent, he responded, his face hovering just inches above hers. "Bella, I told you I wouldn't leave you and I meant that. I was just checking out the loft. This place is amazing. It's just an empty pallet waiting for an artist to create it."

Ari's thoughts hung suspended on the name. "What did you call me?"

"Bella. You know, short for Arabella. I'm surprised nobody else calls you that." Gage kissed the tip of her nose.

Ari froze. Completely powerless to move, she tried to wrap her mind around that single word. Gage couldn't possibly know. There was absolutely no way. Ari was certain it had to be a coincidence. Sam and Beth were the only ones that knew about it, and she was positive they hadn't shared that information. Ari's mind raced back in time to the day she'd last heard her nickname.

Bella.

"Hey, you okay? Why so serious all of a sudden?" Gage pushed a lock of hair away from her face, his smile now diminished.

"My sister, Maria, called me that," she choked out in a brittle whisper.

Gage rolled onto his side facing her, a tender and loving look in his eyes. "Ari, I'm sorry. I had no idea. I promise, I won't call you that again." Gage trailed a finger gently down the side of her face, his gaze never leaving her eyes.

It had been ten, long years since she'd heard anyone call her by that name. Since the day her sister and mother had escaped for an out of town shopping trip, hunting for her sister's senior prom dress, only to be killed on their way home that evening in a freak accident. One that left their family and the entire town shaken to the very core.

It was a tragedy that Rock Haven had suffered greatly from. Francesca and her husband had been loved by, not only the friends and neighbors that knew them, but by strangers stopping to eat as they passed through town, as well. Their business, nicknamed the "Friendliest restaurant in the state," by Governor Halstead many years ago, had been like a second home to many of Rock Haven's residents, and served as a welcoming committee to thousands of tourists a year. And Francesca, with her pretty smile and warm heart, had been the center of it all.

Not only did Arabella lose her mother in the accident, but she also lost her sister and best friend. The sister that she'd shared a room with since the day she was born, shared her deepest secrets and hopes for the future with, and the only one that ever called her, Bella. Nobody had dared to call her by that name since. In fact, she was pretty certain that Sam included that in every new employee's interview. It was the unwritten rule at Francesca's. *Nobody* called her Bella.

Ari felt the bricks of her defenses slowly begin to crumble around her. She couldn't deny it sounded nice to hear again. Especially coming from someone she loved as much as Gage. Yes, she was in *love.* She couldn't deny it any longer.

"I like it, Gage." A tear slipped from the corner of her eye as she thought about her love for her sister, and now for him. Gage's gentle smile and the tenderness in which he pulled her into his arms, only confirmed her decision. "In fact, I love it. As much as I love you." It was the first time she had said those words to a man. And the last man she would ever say them to. Her heart was so full of joy, it felt like it would burst inside her chest.

Chapter 9

Gage had left for Iowa and taken Ari's heart along with him. Beth was sure of it. She'd never seen her friend look as lost as she did today. For over five weeks, Ari and Gage had spent every waking minute in each other's presence. Whether they were working or just hanging out, they were together. Ari had taken more time off work in those five weeks than Beth had ever seen her take. She had witnessed the connection between the two of them, as they spent hours, working at the restaurant and hanging out on the beach during the day. Ari had gushed about the quiet dinners at the cottage she and Gage shared, and watching sunset after sunset disappear on the horizon. They hadn't missed a Sunday church service yet, which Beth was happy about. And it seemed that Ari and Gage had grown quite close. Much faster than Beth expected.

"Are you going to be okay?" Beth asked, drawing Ari's hi-jacked attention back to the details they had been discussing regarding the dance. Today they'd agreed to meet and work on decorations, so while Beth hung strings of light, Ari was writing out the name cards that correlated with the seating chart for the dinner portion of the event.

"Oh, yeah," Ari looked up from her work, nonchalantly waving off Beth's question. "I'll be fine........once Gage comes back." She paused for a moment and when she looked up again, frustration was written all over her face. "I just wish he could make it in time for the dance."

"Come on, Ari. I know this is a big deal for you, but he's not going to be gone forever." Although Beth wasn't sure if that was such a bad thing to hope for. She couldn't tell which was upsetting her more. The fact that

Gage had gotten Ari's hopes up, and then left before the dance? Or, that he would be coming back and likely sweet talking her into compromising herself even more. The only good thing that had come from the situation, was that she'd finally been able to talk Ari into dressing up, and being a part of the celebration, instead of sitting on the sidelines observing, as she did every other year.

"And *you're* still planning on dressing up for the dance anyway, right? After you spent a fortune on that gown, you'd better be!" Beth stepped down from the ladder, as she finished with another string of lights, and made her way towards Ari.

"I don't know, Beth. Maybe it's just better that I put the dress back for another year.

"Nope. No way, Ari," Beth shook her head. "This year is going to be the best by far, and you are going to enjoy it! Girl, you have outdone yourself once again." Beth stood, admiring the details that were transforming the room around them.

"Well, I couldn't have done it without you," Ari smiled, but Beth just rolled her eyes.

"No, I mean it, Beth. I know my brain has been pre-occupied lately with Gage and all, and you've put in so much time and effort. None of this would be possible without you! Thank you!" Ari took Beth's hand, and squeezed it gently.

"All in the name of love," Beth replied and the girls both laughed.

"Yeah, *love*."

"So, it's true then? You love Gage?" Beth questioned her with a hint of desperation in her voice. "When I heard him call you Bella the other morning, I knew you'd gone and given your heart away. And, I get that. But….."

"But, *what*? I sense there's more?" Ari asked.

"Well, I saw Gage coming downstairs from your loft and, I have to admit, I'm worried about you, Ari. How far have you let things go? What about your promise to the Lord?" She'd meant to talk with Ari that very morning, but time had gotten away from her. And now, Beth knew she had held her tongue for too long. She had to confront Ari about her choices.

Ari's frustration from the inquisition was evident on her face.

"Is anything I ever do, going to be right in your eyes, Beth? I mean, aren't you and Sam the ones always preaching to me about spreading my wings, finding love, and someone to settle down with? Just yesterday Sam cornered me and gave me the speech about being unequally yoked with Gage! And now, you're coming at me with this? Give me a break!"

"Wow! Okay, then." Beth placed the candle she was holding on the table. "Maybe I'd better go, and give you some space to work out your anger."

As she turned to leave, Beth felt Ari's hand on her arm. "Beth, no. Please don't go. You didn't deserve that, and I'm sorry."

Beth turned back to face her friend, a sadness in her eyes that wasn't there before. "Ari, we are supposed to hold each other accountable and that's all I'm trying to do. I want you to be happy. Please, you must know that. But—"

"You're right, Beth."

"I am?"

"Yes, you know you are." Ari took a seat at the table and motioned for Beth to join her. It was still early afternoon, long after the lunch rush, and too soon for the dinner madness. So, the restaurant was quiet, giving the girls an opportunity to talk.

"You know me better than I know myself most days, so I shouldn't be surprised by your line of questioning."

"Meaning?"

"Just that I've questioned how fast this relationship is moving, too," Ari sighed. "But, Beth, I don't know what it is about Gage that I can't say no to. It's almost like he's cast a spell on me, and I'm mesmerized by everything he does."

"What exactly can't you say no to?" *Oh, Lord please tell me she hasn't made the one compromise that means the most.* Beth felt a shiver travel down her spine.

Ari held out her left hand flashing her promise ring under Beth's eyes. "Don't worry, Beth. I'm still wearing the ring."

"But you allowed him to stay all night with you?"

"I did, but it's not what you think. I mean, we did sleep in the same bed, but—"

"What!"

"Chill, Beth. Nothing happened. Gage was a perfect gentleman."

Perfect gentleman is not quite the word I would use to describe a man that sweet talks his way into a woman's bed! Beth wanted so desperately to say those words out loud, but refrained knowing they would only hurt her friend.

"Ari, we all like Gage. We just want you to be careful, and it seems to me that you might be setting yourself up for failure when you compromise so many of your beliefs and allow yourself to be in situations where you know you are weak. I'm not trying to sound like your mother, but, maybe while he's in Iowa, you should take a couple of days to think about your relationship. And I don't mean, to think about not seeing him or ending the relationship. I just mean maybe think of a way to slow things down a bit, and give God an opportunity to work."

Ari reached across the table and placed her hand on Beth's.

"It's so easy to sit here and talk to you about it. And it makes perfect sense, what you're saying. Thanks for having the guts to speak up to me about it."

The girls both stood and embraced in a hug.

"Ari, I just want what's best for you. You deserve all of the happiness in the world, and you will never regret doing it God's way. I promise."

"Okay, okay. Enough about relationships. We have less than twenty-four hours to get this place ready for the dance. Back to work!"

"Yes, ma'am!" Beth agreed as she climbed back up the ladder with another string of lights in her hand and a smile on her face. The conversation had gone better than she'd imagined, and she was hopeful that Ari had taken her words of advice to heart.

If she was completely honest with herself, Ari would admit, that yes, she had questioned her own actions more than once. She recognized that she had absolutely no control when Gage was around. She'd prayed about it many times since the first day she'd met him, but after allowing him to stay all night with her, and following Beth's recent confrontation, Ari realized she was pulling away from God. She was making excuses and compromising in ways she'd always promised herself she wouldn't. And that was definitely not what she wanted.

Beth had been right to question her. Accountability was just one of the reasons they had always been such good friends. And now, Ari was certain, that when Gage came home, she would sit down and tell him they had to draw the line. They'd made a mistake that night, and it *wouldn't* happen again.

Surely Gage would understand that God needed to be placed at the center of their relationship. After all, he'd been attending church each week with her, and listening to Pastor Ron preach. How could he not see it? And how could he disagree if he loved Ari? Certainly, he would want to do what was right for their relationship. Wouldn't he?

Ari plopped down on her couch and, with the touch of a button, turned off the television. She hadn't really been paying attention to it, anyway. She had much, *much* more on her mind today. She grabbed the nearby photo album from the coffee table and held it tight against her chest, taking in a deep breath and exhaling, preparing herself for the emotional rollercoaster she was about to ride. The very second her trembling hands turned back the cover, Ari was lost in her distant, happy past. A time when her family was still together. The images came to life as she recalled so many happy memories she had shared with her parents and sister, Maria. She had been raised by two very loving parents, with a marriage so strong it was what she had dreamed about having someday as a child. She and Maria had often talked late into the night, in the small bedroom that they shared, about their futures and the type of men they hoped to meet and marry someday.

"He will be handsome like Daddy, and have dark hair like him, too," Maria giggled quietly into her pillow. Mama had warned them twice already that it was way past bedtime.

"He has to love the Lord like Daddy, too, Maria. That's most important," Ari added as she turned the flashlight back on her sister.

"Don't shine it in my face, silly! I can't see you."

"Well hurry up, Maria. It's your turn again," Ari turned the flashlight off and impatiently waited for her older sister.

"Hmmm," Maria tapped her finger against her chin, "I think he is going to have blue eyes and lots of muscles!"

Ari chuckled at her sister's comment. Maria had always been the funnier one of the two, usually causing the girls to break out in giggles so loudly that Mama was bound to hear.

"The boy I marry is going to love children. Someday I'm going to have a whole houseful of babies!"

"How come so many, Bella? Don't you like having just me for a sister? Do you wish you had more sisters?"

"No, silly, I love having just you for a sister. But I want to have lots of baby boys and girls to love, that's all."

"I bet Mama isn't going to babysit for you if you have all those babies, Bella!"

Sure enough, within seconds, the girls' giggles had their mother tapping softly on their door and peeking her head inside their room.

"I bet there are lots of dishes still to be washed at the restaurant if you two girls can't get to sleep. Shall we get dressed and head back over?"

"No, Mama," the girls said in unison.

"We'll get right to sleep," Maria added as the girls both snuggled under their covers and rested their heads on their pillows.

"Goodnight, Maria, I love you."

"Goodnight, Bella, I love you, too."

Ari closed the photo album and leaned back against the couch. She and Maria had so many dreams for the men that they would someday marry. Ari couldn't help but wonder what her sister and parents would think of Gage. Would they like him? Would they think he was the right man for her to share her life with? She missed her family so much, it hurt to even think about it.

Chapter 10

"*Happy Birthday, Gage!" Nonnie and* Max joined him at the old farmhouse table, to share a piece of the chocolate birthday cake that Nonnie had baked that morning. Her famous, "secret recipe," chocolate buttermilk frosting, had *always* been Gage's favorite. And favorites were the theme of the week. Nonnie had made sure to cook all of Gage's preferred dishes when he arrived. In part, out of celebration, but also as a token of gratitude. The past two days at the farm had flown by in a whirlwind of activity for Gage, as they usually did when he first arrived. Max had wasted no time in taking advantage of Gage's presence and his strength the day before. He'd had him riding the fence line most of the morning, mending what needed repaired to keep the cattle safely corralled. Later in the day, it was putting a fresh new coat of red paint on the old barn. The finishing touches were added early this morning, before Gage and Max cleaned up and headed into town for breakfast. They'd barely been seated when Max started in.

"You've been acting pretty pathetic ever since you arrived. I suppose that has something to do with the fact that you showed up here alone?"

"Is it that apparent?" Gage scowled, his frown growing deeper. He'd had plenty of time to think yesterday as he'd worked the ranch. The peacefulness and calm that he usually found at the farm, was skewed by thoughts of a beauty with bright green eyes, and a dance that she would be attending without him. Just imagining Ari all dressed without him by her side, was tormenting his mind. He didn't even want to think of her dancing with another man!

"So, what happened? Did you and your girl have some sort of disagreement?"

"Not exactly." Gage turned his menu over and leaned back in his seat, unable to think about anything but Ari, even as his stomach rebelled and rumbled from hunger.

"Coffee, boys?" The waitress walked up to their table with a hot pot of the dark roast in her right hand.

Max was quick to cover his cup with his own. "I think we'll stick to orange juice this morning, Miss."

Gage nodded in agreement. He didn't care what Max ordered. Coffee, or even breakfast, was the last thing on his mind.

"Two orange juices coming up," the waitress replied as she set the coffee pot on their table and pulled a pen and order pad from her apron. "Do you boys know what you want to eat or do you need a few minutes?" She looked from Gage to Max and waited.

"I'll take the breakfast special with scrambled eggs and bacon," Max answered, then nodded in Gage's direction. "Why don't you give lover boy here the same! Seems he's too distraught to decide at the moment," Max chortled.

The waitress turned and raised a brow towards Gage.

"Very funny, Max." Gage looked up to the waitress as she waited, and smiled slightly. "I'll have what the old cowboy is having."

The waitress tucked her notepad back into her apron, picked up the coffee pot, and headed towards the pass-thru window to the kitchen as she hollered out, "Two specials, scrambled with bacon, and two O.J.'s."

"Well, do I have to drag it out of you?" Max rested his elbows on the table and leaned in.

Gage's mind had already gone back to Rock Haven and completely missed what the old man had said.

"Boy, you really do have it bad, don't you?" Max said just a little bit louder. "Why on earth did you even make the trip out to Iowa if you didn't want to be here?"

"That's just it, Max," Gage replied, sitter up straighter in his seat. "I do want to be here." He paused a moment before continuing, still deep in thought. "I just want Ari here with me. That's the problem."

The waitress arrived and set two hot plates in front of them, covered with eggs, hash browns and bacon. "Can I get you boys anything else?"

"No, I think we're good ma'am," Max answered.

"Alright then, just holler if you need something. And you," she nodded in Gage's direction, "might try to smile once in a while. It won't kill you!"

Gage's mega-watt smile spread ear to ear. "Yes ma'am. Thank you."

Max waited until the waitress had disappeared, and he'd tested his first bite of eggs. "So, what stopped her from coming?"

Gage was spreading blackberry jelly over his toast when he replied. "It's this dance at her family's restaurant. It really means a lot to her." Gage went on to explain the story of Ari's family and the loss of her mother and sister, Maria, and why the dance meant so much. "It's been ten years since her sister died, so this year is kind of a big deal. Ari is trying to honor the fact that Maria missed her Senior Prom."

"I see," Max said. "And you don't want to disappoint your Nonnie. *But*, you left your heart back in Michigan." He fiddled with the scrambled eggs on his plate, separating them from the hash browns, as Gage picked up his glass of orange juice and took a long drink.

"I'm pretty sure your Nonnie would understand, Gage. Have you talked to her at all about this?"

"No, and I don't plan to, Max. I need to be here. This is our tradition and I'm all she has." It took a long moment of Max's silence for Gage to realize what he had implied. "Sorry, I didn't mean it like that, Max. I know Nonnie has you, and believe me, I'm thankful for that. I just don't want to hurt her, and I know she counts on our time together each summer."

With their plates now empty, Max reached across the table and picked up the check. "I reckon we better head home and get busy on some more projects, or your grandmother will be having a hissy fit.

"Yes, sir!" Gage pushed back his chair and stood up. "I'll meet you in the truck," he called over his shoulder as Max headed towards the cash register.

"What's on your mind, June Bug?" Nonnie asked.

After twenty-eight years, that nickname still brought a smile to his face. Gage realized then, that he'd been lost in thought, missing Arabella. He desperately wanted to be in Rock Haven for the dance tomorrow evening. The fact that he wouldn't be, was the only thought taking up space in his mind. Not even the small celebration he was having with Nonnie and Max to recognize his birthday, was a contender. He knew how special the dance was to Ari, and he couldn't help but wonder if he'd been wrong for making the trip to Iowa at such a crucial time. And now that he was at the farm, how could he possibly think about leaving? Surely, it would break Nonnie's heart?

"Oh, nothing." Gage shoved the last bite of chocolate cake into his mouth, before he stood up from the kitchen table and walked over to plant a sweet kiss on his grandmother's forehead. "The cake was delicious as always. Thank you." He turned around and made his way to the kitchen sink where he rinsed his plate and washed his hands.

"What are the plans for tomorrow, Nonnie?" he asked.

"Well, I think *you* should be buying a ticket for a plane trip back to that little beach town." Nonnie said, motioning for Gage to rejoin her at the table.

"I think that's my que to leave you two alone." Max winked at Nonnie as he stood and pushed his chair up to the table. "I'm going to go finish up some chores."

Gage watched Nonnie's eyes follow Max to the door. He was thankful that she had him at the farm to watch over her. Her age was really beginning to show, and Gage hated the thought of her being alone out here if it weren't for Max. He reminded himself to mention his gratitude to the old man before Max left and went home for the evening.

"Gage," Nonnie's eyes found his again, a tenderness in them only a grandmother could have, "I know you miss her and want to be there with her. It's okay if you go."

"No, Nonnie, I want to be here with you. This is our tradition, and I'm not breaking it! That's my final answer."

"Gage, do you remember the story of how your parents met?" Nonnie placed her hand over his as she began.

"Yes, I remember it well, Nonnie. She was on a field trip to New York City her senior year in high school, studying interior design. She fell in love with my father the moment she set eyes on him, and they lived happily ever after." The smile on Gage's face disappeared. "Well, happily until she died, anyway. Then my father's world fell apart. And mine did, too."

"You're right about the love at first sight. Your mama had never been away from the farm, and she wanted to go on that trip more than she'd ever wanted anything. She had big dreams of being a designer for the rich folk in the city, and making a name for herself. For weeks before the trip, it was all she could talk about. And that smile that she wore every minute of every day? Well that made the trip worth every last penny." Nonnie paused for a moment, looking away from Gage.

"I'll never forget the call I got, the fourth night she had been gone. She talked with so much excitement I could barely make out a word she said. But she had met your father her first day in New York, and they had been inseparable since. There wasn't much I could say, but, 'be careful.' She hadn't graduated yet, but she was already eighteen and stubborn as a mule. So, I kept quiet, wondering if things would change once she came home."

"But things didn't change, did they, Nonnie?" Gage prompted. He could hear this story a million times and never tire of it. He missed his mother so much and had very few memories of her, outside of what Nonnie shared. So, every year during his visit, she would fill his mind with the memories he loved. Memories to help him understand his mother's love for his father, and him, her precious June Bug.

"No, Gage. To my surprise, they didn't. Your mother was on the phone to New York every minute that she wasn't in school. You should have seen our phone bill!" Nonnie laughed, lifting her hands to her face. "Back then they didn't have all the computer technology they do now, so the phone was their lifeline. It wasn't long until your mama had completed her classes. In fact, your father came to Iowa, the *only* time he ever came to the farm, a month later, to watch your mama stand on the podium and receive her diploma. Two days later, they were married at the courthouse and left for New York City on a train the next morning."

Gage could see the tears welling up in his Nonnie's eyes, and feel the hurt she obviously still had in her heart.

"But mom loved this farm, Nonnie. Why didn't my dad just move here and make it easy for her?"

"Oh, honey, your mom loved everything about this farm and had a wonderful childhood growing up here. But she loved your father more! And that love is what kept her in New York, supporting him in every way that she could."

"I still don't get why my dad never attempted to come back and visit the farm with her. Why does he hate it here so much?"

"Your mom always told me he was jealous. He was scared that if she came back and stayed any length of time, she would leave him to move back home. He knew how much she loved it here and sometimes he felt she loved it more than she loved him, the way she always talked about her happy childhood."

"That just seems silly, Nonnie. My mom loved my dad so much. If I remember one thing about her, it would be that." Gage still couldn't understand the resentment his father held, even after all these years. Even though Gage's memories were few, he knew that he'd been happy as a child, until his mother died. There were no memories of arguing or disagreements, only happiness and joy were linked to the memory of his parents' relationship.

"Your father didn't have such a happy childhood, Gage. You have to remember, he grew up with a single mother and no father figure. He didn't know what to model his own marriage after." Nonnie patted Gage on the hand. "He did the best he could, sweetheart. And you were always well taken care of."

"I know, Nonnie. I just have a hard time letting go of the anger I have sometimes. If he had just given in and come to the farm with her, maybe she would still be with us today."

"Now, that's something only the good Lord knows, and we can't make assumptions." Nonnie's tone of voice had changed quickly, coming across very sternly to him.

"But, Nonnie, if they'd come together, maybe she wouldn't have been on that road when the truck hit us. She might not have been on that road at all! And if my father's not to blame, then the blame falls on me. We were on our way to the airport after she picked us up at the farm, and *I* was the *only* reason she was at the farm. Don't you see, Nonnie? Maybe.....maybe it really was my fault."

Nonnie stood up, a fierce look on her face. "Now you listen to me, young man," she pointed her finger at him, "you are not to blame for your mother's death and neither is your father. The Lord had her life planned out long before she was ever born. You need to remember that, and be thankful for the time you had with her." She paused, the tears now spilling from her eyes, her next words softer and gentler. "You're the best gift she could've ever given me."

Gage stood and took his grandmother in his arms, kissing her on the cheek. "I'm sorry I upset you, Nonnie."

"Gage, life is too short to be angry. Promise me you won't make the same mistakes your father has. Enjoy your life and allow yourself to love."

"I don't know what love even looks like, Nonnie. All I ever learned from my father was anger and how to survive being alone."

"Well, you're an adult now, Gage. You need to forge a path of your own. Do you think you love this girl, Arabella, that you've met and spent so much time with?"

Gage shrugged, not sure of the answer himself. "When I first met her, Nonnie, I was so taken by her beauty. All I could think about was holding her in my arms, the way a man and woman are meant to hold each other. But, over the days and weeks, I've begun to care for her feelings, care about what makes her happy. I never intended on staying this long with her, but being here at the farm, she's all I can think about. My heart aches when I'm away from her. Is that love?" He looked up to his grandmother in question. "I don't have a clue."

"Only you can answer that, Gage. But the fact that you care to put her feelings above your own says something. Here, come with me."

She stood up and held out her hand to him, pulling him towards her bedroom, where she took out a small brown box from the back of her closet. She opened the box with slow, loving movements, pulling out a stack of torn and tattered envelopes that she placed in Gage's hand.

"I was waiting until the right time to give these to you. I think you're ready now." She returned to the kitchen, leaving Gage staring at his mother's handwriting. He sat on the edge of Nonnie's bed, opening one after another, from the stack.

Oh, Mama, Christmastime is so beautiful in New York. I wish you could see it for yourself. And don't worry, James is such a good man. Tell Daddy that he works very hard every day to make a better life for me and this little one we will be having soon. Someday, James is going to be known all over this city for his good work. Maybe the whole state even.

Mom, you won't believe it. Baby Gage has cut his first tooth! And my, oh my, does he look more like daddy every day. I'm sending you some new pictures. I know you'll see the resemblance. It would be nice to see Gage and Daddy's picture side by side in a frame, don't you think? I love you and miss you and Daddy and the farm so much, Mom.

Mama, he did it! Little Gage took his first steps today. James and I couldn't be prouder. He's growing so fast, it's hard to believe he's already a year old.

Gage took his time, poring over the different letters again and again. Just the feel of them, was like a healing salve over his "little boy" broken heart as he was transported back in time. His mother's love for her husband and her family in Iowa were evident. But the love she had for her only son, and the way she delivered that message, was overwhelming. He read about his first words, first haircut, and first day of pre-school, along with all the silly things little boys do. His mother had shared all of that with Nonnie, no matter how many miles apart they were. She'd made sure that Nonnie was a part of Gage's life.

The letters were a treasure that Gage would always hold dear to his heart. They were the only thing he had left of his mother. Somehow the anger he felt for his father had slowly morphed into empathy as he'd continued to read his mother's words. He couldn't imagine having a love like his parents had. And then to lose that love? Well, that was just unfathomable. Maybe, if his father could just read these letters, it would change his heart too, make him less bitter. Help him, maybe, to remember the happiness he once felt. Gage knew that he felt different after reading them. He began to look at his relationship with Ari on a different level. One that he had never planned for.

Thirty minutes later Gage joined Nonnie at the kitchen table once again. "Thank you, Nonnie. These mean more to me than you'll ever know."

"You just tuck those away and always remember you have them when you need them."

"But, Nonnie, what about you? Don't you want to keep them? They're all you have left of her too." Gage felt sick to his stomach at the thought of taking the last thing of his mother's that Nonnie had.

"Gage, I have you. And that's more important than those letters. I know your mama loved me."

"So, that's where the old phrase came from, huh?" Gage asked.

"You noticed—in the letters? Yes, your mom always told me that, 'home is where the heart is,' and her heart was both here and in New York City. Somehow she made that work."

Gage smiled, feeling more at peace and satisfied than he ever had. Funny enough, New York was not even a thought in his mind. There was nothing there but an empty shell of a life and a business he didn't want. Maybe it was true for him too. His heart could be both here and back in Michigan. He couldn't wait to share this with Arabella. His thoughts slowly drifted from the farm to the restaurant and the woman he'd left behind. He imagined she was a basket case right about now, with all the last-minute touches needing to be completed before the dance tomorrow evening. If only he could be in two places at the same time.

"Gage, honey?"

"Yes, Nonnie?" Gage struggled to pull his thoughts from Francesca's and all that was happening there.

"Don't you think it's time for *you* to go home?" Nonnie asked.

Gage turned to face her, confused by the statement. "I don't understand, Nonnie, I'm not going anywhere? This is our time to be together."

"Oh, my little June Bug," she stood up to face him and patted his cheek with her old wrinkled hand. "You've left your heart back in that little town in Michigan. Take your mama's advice and go home to where your heart is."

"Nonn—"

"Gage, I'm not going to argue with you about this." Nonnie walked towards the back door, pausing momentarily as her hand rested on the handle. "I'm going to help Max finish up with the evening chores. When I come back in, we'll have dinner. In the meantime, you go on and get a flight booked. Once this big dance is over, you and that special girl head back this way. I'll be anxious to meet the one that's captured my grandson's heart. She sure is one lucky gal."

Gage couldn't love his grandmother any more than he did at that moment. His heart raced with excitement, as he went in search of his phone. Arabella was going to be so surprised.

Chapter 11

A *rabella made one last walk* thru of the kitchen, inspecting everything from the dishes, to the food, to the additional staff that she'd hired for the evening. The appetizers were ready, and the champagne was chilled. The servers stood, dressed sharply in black tuxedos, waiting for the guests to arrive. Ari worked her way into the ballroom where she found Anthony and Beth.

"Wow! Don't you both look sharp?" Ari hugged them both and thanked Beth again for all her help. "You have no idea how much I appreciate you, Beth. I owe you a lot of babysitting time!"

Beth threw her head back and laughed. "And don't think I won't collect."

Anthony nodded in agreement. "I will make sure of it."

"Well, are we ready, then? The doors open in fifteen minutes."

"Not hardly, Ari. You need to get dressed. Hurry up now, and get ready. Anthony and I will do the greeting while you're upstairs."

"I don't know guys. Maybe I'll just stick to tradition an—"

"Oh no, you don't!" Beth turned Ari right around. "You *promised* me you were going to wear that beautiful gown. It doesn't matter that Gage is gone. You are going to put on that dress and have fun with us tonight. You are officially off duty! March!" Beth gave Ari a not-so-gentle shove towards the stairwell.

"Fine, you win!" Ari crossed her arms over her chest, frustration dripping from her words. "I'll get dressed up and play nice, but only because tonight is all about Maria and remembering her. Just don't think I'm going to dance with anybody because I put on a stupid dress!" Ari's immature behavior as she stomped towards the stairway, left Beth and Anthony laughing.

"*Stupid* dress? She loved it the minute she laid eyes on it!" Beth argued. Then, turning towards her husband, a mischievous grin crept across her face. "Think she's going to be surprised?"

"Oh, she's going to be surprised alright."

"This is going to be the best! I can't wait to see her face when she finds out!"

"Especially with this being the ten-year anniversary," Anthony added. "This couldn't be more perfect if we planned it."

"I've had my doubts, but I have to admit, this was a good move."

Anthony put his arm around his wife and pulled her in close so she could see his eyes. "Just make sure you remember who is responsible for this, dear."

"I know, I know," she rolled her eyes dramatically. "As much as I don't want to, I will make sure to give credit where credit is due."

"That's my girl." Anthony stepped back and reached for Beth's hand. "I think it's time we open the doors and get this event underway."

"I seriously can't believe I let them talk me into this!" Ari grumbled as she tugged at the zipper, on the dress she had been so excited to find, just two weeks ago. Turning to face the mirror, her attitude took a hundred-and eighty-degree turn. "Okay, so it *is* a beautiful dress." She ran her hand over the prodigiously flattering bead and sequin-embellished top. "And," her hand traveled to the soft tulle at her waist, "I might possibly be acting a *little* immature." Her frown slowly morphed into a smile. She had been looking forward to this evening for months, long before Gage had come into the picture. Even though she was disheartened that he wouldn't be on her arm for the night, she decided a change of heart was in store. She vowed to enjoy her time with her friends, and the community that made the event a success. With a newfound excitement, she pulled out her make-up bag and got to work.

Twenty minutes later, Arabella made her grand entrance from the top of the restaurant stairs. Suddenly nervous, as she looked down at the sea of people below, Ari wondered if the emerald green, floor-length, form-fitting gown had been the right decision. By the sounds of the gasps in the room, she had chosen well. She felt like a movie star cascading down the stairs, with her long black tresses pulled neatly into a bun, littles wisps framing her face, and an emerald necklace draping her neck. The sequins on the dress alone could light up a room.

"Arabella, you are breathtaking." Sam was the first to greet her and offer his arm, escorting her across the room to join Beth and Anthony.

"Thank you, Sam. You clean up pretty well yourself. Where is your beautiful wife, by the way?"

"She's over gossiping with some of the ladies from bridge club," Sam replied, just as they caught up to Beth and Anthony.

"Wow! You look fabulous, Ari! I knew that was the dress the moment I saw it on you." Beth gushed.

"You do look lovely, Ari," Anthony added, as he reached for her hand and pressed a kiss to it.

"Thank you, both. And look at the two of you. You have to be the most charming couple in the room, I must say." Ari complimented the pair. "I love the dress, Beth. You would never know that you have a nine-month old at home, that's for sure. Anthony, you are one very lucky man."

"I'd have to argue that I'm the luckier one."

A chill ran down Arabella's spine at the familiar voice behind her. "Gage?" Her voice was nearly a whisper, as she spun around to face him, clad in a black tuxedo and emerald green bow tie that matched her dress perfectly. "What are you doing here?" Pure bliss radiated from her face, as she turned to see the man she loved, standing in front of her. "I thought you were staying in Iowa with your grandmother?"

Gage didn't respond with words. He simply swept Ari into his arms, and met her lips with his own.

"Okay, then. Why don't we leave these two love birds alone for a minute to catch up? I mean it's been, like what, four days since they've seen each other? Who knows, this could take a while." Anthony grabbed his wife's hand, put his arm around Sam's shoulders, and guided them both towards their table.

"Bella," Gage took her face in his hands, "I've missed you *so* much. You're all I have been able to think about. I'm thankful my Nonnie is such a smart woman. She knew how bad I wanted to be here with you, so she forced me to pack my bag and come back. I'm sorry I ever left in the first place. I should have listened to you when you wanted to waited until after the dance and make the trip together."

"Oh Gage, you've made me the happiest woman in the world by being here tonight!" Ari threw her arms around him and hugged him again.

"Well, that was my plan. I'm sure glad it worked." He grinned sheepishly, and Ari was lost in another world. A world that belonged only to she and Gage.

"This," Gage pointed as he took in the site of the room around them, "looks spectacular."

"Well, I have you and Beth to thank for that. Gage, the work you've done on the lighting and updating is really phenomenal."

"So, this is the man responsible for the amazing updates?" Gage and Ari turned and directed their attention to the gentleman behind them.

"Oh! Mr. Spencer, good evening." She turned sideways looking from Gage to the older gentleman. "I would like you to meet Gage. Gage, this is Mr. Spencer, an old friend of the family."

Mr. Spencer reached out to shake Gage's hand. "It's very nice to meet you, young man. And, I will say, I think you've done a fantastic job here." Mr. Spencer motioned from one end of the ballroom to the other. "The lighting alone made a world of difference. But the way you've restored the old fireplace, and built that mantle around it? Astounding."

"Thank you, sir. That's very kind of you."

"So, what brings you to our sleepy little town of Rock Haven?" Mr. Spencer inquired.

"Well, I was actually just passing through," Gage turned, his eyes on the beautiful woman standing next to him, "but after meeting Arabella, I've decided to extend my stay, indefinitely."

"That's the rumor I've been hearing," Mr. Spencer chuckled. "Glad to hear it, Gage. It's about time our Arabella met a nice young man like yourself. At least that's what Sam's been telling me. Anyway, I've got a few projects that I would like you to take a look at, if you don't mind." He patted Gage on the back. "It sure couldn't hurt to have an extra income while you're in town, right?'

"Well, that's very kind of you, sir." Gage offered. "And I would be more than happy to take a look at what you've got. But...."

Ari swallowed nervously as she waited for Gage's answer. Something didn't feel right to her.

"It's going to be a few weeks before I can get to it. Ari and I are going to be in Iowa for a while after tonight."

What? Without talking to me first? How dare he tell Mr. Spencer before we even agree on a plan?

"Iowa, huh?" Mr. Spencer gave a slight smile in Gage's direction. "Well, just don't keep our precious Arabella gone from her home too long now."

"I'll look you up when I return, Mr. Spencer. You have my word." Gage extended his hand to him once again, and then quickly wrapped his arm around Ari, pulling her into a corner to talk.

But she wasn't going to give him the opportunity.

"Gage, I know we *talked* about going to Iowa together, but we hadn't made anything definite. Don't you think you should have talked with me before sharing that news with everyone in town?"

"Everyone, Ari? It was just one person. And besides, I came back tonight to attend the dance just for you! Can't you agree to come to Iowa with me now? My Nonnie and Max are dying to meet you."

Arabella instantly regretted her attitude towards him. He was right. After all, he had come all the way back to celebrate this special night with her.

"I'm sorry, Gage, you're right. Tomorrow after church we will sit down and plan our trip to Iowa. We can leave on Monday if you want. I can't wait to meet everyone there."

Gage picked her up and twirled her around in a circle. "Thank you, Ari. This means the world to me."

The rest of the evening went off without a hitch. The word had apparently spread fast about the work Gage had done at Francesca's and about his business in New York. He'd been approached by a number of guests, requesting bids on jobs they had available, and Ari couldn't have been more pleased. Gage couldn't possibly leave Rock Haven any time soon with so many jobs to complete.

The food had turned out perfectly, and all the guests seemed to be having a wonderful time. Ari made her way around the room, chatting with everyone, the music playing softly in the background. Gage had remained glued to her side the entire night, as if he was afraid to leave her. And she wasn't complaining. He'd come back from Iowa for her. *Just* for her. From the moment she'd first heard his voice tonight, Ari had been on cloud nine. There wasn't a shred of doubt left in her mind that Gage loved her, and he was the man she would spend the rest of her life with.

"Gage, you've made me so happy tonight," Ari looked up at the man next to her, her sparkling, electric-green eyes giving away the feeling of joy she couldn't contain. They'd finally stopped for a breather from interacting with the guests. "You have no idea how glad I am that you decided to come back to Rock Haven for the dance. I've dreamt about this night for weeks. And," she lifted one shoulder, "I missed you terribly while you were gone."

"Good. Does that mean you'll quit socializing and come spend some time on the dance floor with me?"

Gage pulled her close and gently trailed kisses down her neck. Ari was suddenly a bundle of nerves. Not only had she never danced with a man, but what were people around the room thinking as they watched Gage kiss her like he had?

"If you're worried about what everyone's thinking, why don't you just agree to dance with me? Let's show them all what a princess and her knight in shining armor look like! I promise to keep it respectful," he added.

Ari tried to swallow the bundle of nerves that had made their way from her stomach to her throat. But, before she could even entertain the thought to protest, Gage took her hand in his, and led her to the middle of the dance floor.

She was completely unprepared for the way she soon began to feel, as Gage held her tight against his body, twirling her around the room and whispering to her how beautiful she was. Arabella's emotions were all over the place. If she hadn't noticed it before, tonight she was well aware of his muscled arms as they held her tight, and the scent of his cologne filling the air. Gage kept her out on the dance floor until she could barely stand. She'd carelessly tossed her heals aside a while ago, around the same time Beth and Anthony said their goodbyes and headed home to relieve their babysitter. Sam and Karen had called it a night a short time after that, and now the clean-up crew was the only thing standing between she and Gage being alone.

She covered her mouth as she yawned, pulling back from his embrace. "Gage, I think I'm ready to call it a night."

Surprising her, Gage pulled her tighter and leaned into her, a firm grip around her waist. "The night is young, Bella. There's still time to make more dreams come true. Why don't you let the staff go home and we will finish this upstairs?"

Ari had meant to talk to Gage when he returned from Iowa, about the night they'd spent together and how guilty she'd felt about it after, but his surprise return tonight had left her without an opportunity. Her conversation with Beth replayed itself in her mind, as she struggled to come up with an answer.

"I'm glad you stood your ground, Ari. Maybe you and Gage shouldn't put yourself into a position where you are alone with feelings this strong. You know, maybe you need a chaperone to kind of put a damper on those desires."

"Gage, I don't think—"

"Arabella, have I done something to upset you?" His hold only grew tighter around her waist. "I mean after everything we've shared, I thought you felt the same way about me as I do for you. I've told you I'm not going anywhere. Isn't my return tonight, enough proof of my feelings for you?"

"I know, but Gage, I promised—"

"Arabella, I love you." Gage lowered his mouth and claimed Ari's, as she fought to keep control.

Lord, I've waited my entire life to have a man say those words to me! I knew it! He loves me as much as I love him!

Gage deepened their kiss, and Ari felt herself quickly slipping. His kisses made her feel things she had never felt, and she had missed him so much while he was gone. The war waged in her mind, where she tried to convince herself that there was nothing wrong with what they were doing.

Run, Ari! This is not what you want. Think about what you are risking!

The voice was strong in her mind, but the feeling in her heart was stronger. How could it be wrong? They loved each other! Ari knew, they would be married *someday,* and Gage had been so patient with her already. Didn't she owe this to him?

Their passion for each other continued to grow, and the kisses became more intense. Until finally, her promise to God, was the farthest thing from her mind. When Gage picked her up in his strong arms and carried her towards the stairs that led to her loft, this time, Ari didn't protest. And as he opened her bedroom door, to the space that had always been hers and hers alone, all thoughts except his love for her disappeared.

"I'm scared, Gage," she whispered, as he gently set her on the bed and pulled her hair loose from the bun she'd knotted at the base of her neck just a few short hours ago.

Gage took her face in his hands as he joined her on the bed. "Bella, I'm not going to hurt you, I promise. I just want to love you."

"Forever, Gage?"

"Yes, Bella. Forever. Please, let me stay with you tonight and show you in every way what your love means to me." Gage leaned in and kissed her lightly on the cheek and then slowly made his way down her neck, each kiss becoming more passionate than the last.

Arabella could resist the temptation no longer. She'd prayed, she'd argued with herself, and she'd begged her heart to cooperate, but nothing had worked. She was drawn to Gage and his touch, like a magnet. Desire inched it's way deeper and deeper within Ari, until the cost no longer mattered. She *wanted* to be with him. She wanted Gage to love her in *every* way that he could. Without an ounce of resistance, Arabella finally allowed Gage to pull her into a place she'd never been. A place where broken promises didn't exist.

Gage had been waiting for this moment all night. Arabella had filled his thoughts for days, weeks even, and now, finally, she was in his arms again. Gage was right where he wanted to be, and he had no intention of stopping. All of the time that he'd spent in Rock Haven, had been building up to this very moment. He'd been fairly certain that Ari would no longer debate the level of their physical relationship once he said those three little words to her. And he'd been right.

Gage knew that Ari had never been with another man, and he had promised himself he would take his time and be careful with her. The last thing he wanted was to hurt her. But her purity and devotion to God was driving him mad, and had consumed his thoughts for too long. Being with her now, he had only one thing on his mind. It didn't help matters that he'd had to be patient all night, watching the way that dress hugged her body like a glove. Her long, silky, black hair once knotted into place, now slipped through his fingers as he pulled the neatly styled bun from the back of her neck. Her emerald green eyes, full of innocence and fear, searched his for an answer. Gage was quickly losing control.

"Gage, I—"

His fingers rested on the zipper of her dress. "Bella, please," he cupped her face in his hands, "we've been through this. I love you, and I know—"

Arabella pressed her finger to his lips and whispered, "I only wanted to say I love you."

When he woke up in the wee hours of the morning, with Arabella fast asleep in his arms, Gage couldn't have felt more complete or satisfied. It had a been a night of passion he would never forget. And, there was not a doubt in his mind now, that Arabella loved him. She would *always* love him.

After what they'd shared, God had to know how right this relationship was. Had to know that their love for each other was real, and their relationship would only grow stronger. Gage bent forward and kissed the top of Ari's head. He had never felt so alive.

Chapter 12

When Arabella opened her eyes the next morning, she felt the warmth of Gage's body entangled with hers, and she quickly remembered how they ended the previous evening. Thoughts of the passion that they shared filled her mind, right alongside of the promise she had broken. Guilt. Happiness. Fear. Joy. Shame. Love. Regret. They *all* were at the forefront of her thoughts.

She'd broken a promise.

But Gage made her so happy!

She'd broken *the* promise.

But Gage loved her, didn't he?

How could it be wrong if they loved each other? The questions whirled through her mind like a category four tornado.

Not wanting to face the truth she was painfully aware of, the truth she'd been taught over and over during her teenage and young adult years, Ari buried the truth deep within the chambers of her heart and locked the door. A door she refused to open.

Tears stung her eyes, as she slowly slid her legs over the side of the bed, never taking her gaze from the simple diamond adorned heart that served as the centerpiece for her promise ring. Slowly, she slipped the crisscross band, given to her by her father on her fifteenth birthday, off her finger and quietly dropped it into the drawer of her bedside table. Mournfully, she remembered that day.

Her mother had purchased and surprised her with a beautiful, ankle-length, apricot colored dress and white wrap for when the evening grew cool. Maria, her older and much more of a fashionista sister, had done her hair in a long French braid, but only after hours of Ari's begging.

"Mom, can't you please make Maria do my hair? She's so much better at it than me," Ari swung the hairbrush in her hand towards the floor in frustration. *"And tonight, is the most important night of my life!"*

Her mother cast a death stare across the room to where Maria defiantly refused.

"Mom, I don't have time! I have plans to meet April and the rest of the girls in fifteen minutes!" she stomped her foot for added effect.

Their mother's words were as calm as usual. *"I remember when the two of you were little and, Maria, you would spend hours brushing Arabella's long hair. It used to be one of your favorite things to do, you know."*

"That's because she's the best at it," Ari added, hoping to finally convince her sister. *"And tonight, is really special Maria,"* the pleading continued.

The guilt eventually took its toll, and Maria gave in. *"Fine, I will do your hair! But we need to do it quickly, so bring the brush and come on."* The girls marched towards their bedroom, as their mother looked on with a fondness in her heart. The girls had always been especially close. At least until a year ago. Once Maria had turned sixteen, it was suddenly as if her little sister, and once best friend, had become an uncool thorn in her side. Francesca took advantage of every opportunity she could to bring them back together.

It would end up being one of the most precious memories Ari held of her sister. Maria's frustration had seemingly dissolved, once the girls sat in front of the vanity in their room, and she ran the brush over her sister's long locks. Years of their close relationship soothed her anger, and before long the two of them were laughing together like old times.

"You know, this night is going to be really special for dad, too." Maria looked at her younger sister's reflection in the mirror as her fingers wove through the strands of her hair. Ari could tell Maria was referring to when their father had presented her ring the previous year. *"Your purity and relationship with God are the most important things to he and mom."*

"It's a special night for me too," Ari responded, *"and not just because I'm getting my ring. It means the world to me that mom and dad love us both enough to care so deeply for our futures."*

"Yeah, we're pretty lucky. Some kids will never have the kind of love and security our parents have given us. I think the best way we can pay them back is by keeping our end of the promise and staying pure until marriage."

Ari nodded in agreement. She had no intention of ever breaking that promise.

Eduardo had made dinner reservations for them at Casa's, one of Arabella's favorite Italian restaurants. They shared a wonderful meal, all the while her father had told stories of how he'd met and fallen in love with Ari's mother. His voice grew thick with emotion, as he expressed the love that he and his wife had for their two daughters, and how much their relationships with the Lord meant to them.

"Arabella, the most important thing in your life should always be the Lord."

Naïve of the world around her, and the temptations she would encounter as a young woman, Ari smiled and patted her father's hand. *"Oh, Daddy, I promise to never stray from the Lord. He will always be the center of my life."*

It was then that Eduardo held out the small, black-velvet box across the table to her. *"Arabella, your mother and I want to give this to you, as a reminder of how much we, and the Lord, love you. Every day, when you look down on your hand, this will be a constant reminder to you of your worth. Of what the Lord gave for you on the cross."*

Ari opened the box and gasped. It was the most beautiful piece of jewelry she had ever seen. She held the band in her hand as she read aloud the inscription her father had designed it to include. "True Love Waits." Her father gently removed the ring from her grip and held her left hand in his, as he slid the ring on her finger.

"Arabella, my dear, may you always remember how valuable you are. Your mother and I love you so much."

"Oh, Daddy," she wrapped her arms around his neck, hugging him. *"I love you and Mama so much! And I promise. I will keep myself pure until my wedding day, when I marry the man of my dreams. And he will surely be a godly man."*

He will surely be a godly man.

Oh, what have I done? How could I let this happen? How could I break my promise? Ari questioned herself, as the reality of the previous night's actions crashed in around her. A stabbing pain pierced her heart, just as she felt the pressure of Gage's hand upon her back.

"Good morning, beautiful."

When she turned, the smile on his face and the way he pulled her back down to him, planting soft kisses along her cheek and neck, made all thoughts of the ring and her broken promise disappear.

"Good morning, Gage," she returned his smile. "Did you sleep well?" The sparkle in his blue eyes charmed its way into her heart very quickly.

Gage tossed his head back, allowing a loud chuckle to escape. "You mean when we finally went to sleep? Bella, I've never slept better in my life." Gage pulled her hand to his lips. "I love you. Now, come here," he teased, pulling her body down to meet his. The next time Arabella woke up, the clock read half past ten.

"Bella, get up. We are going to be late for church." Gage nudged her before climbing out of bed.

Did he really just say that? Church? How can I even think about setting foot in church after what I did last night?

A small voice cried out inside her mind. *Sinner! You can't take back what you've done. God will never forgive you. You broke your promise and gave yourself away to a man who doesn't love you enough or respect you enough to marry you first. You're tainted. Everybody is going to know what a sinner you are.*

An overwhelming fear paralyzed her, taking her mind captive and refusing to let go. "Gage, I think I just want to skip church today. I'm not feeling so well this morning."

"What? Bella, is something wrong? Wait, did I hurt you?" Gage quickly came around the bed to her side and pulled her hands into his. When his thumb brushed over the area where her promise finger once fit, he looked up at her in confusion.

"Arabella, where's your ring?" he demanded. "This is about what we did last night, isn't it!" His voice began to escalate. "I thought you were okay with our relationship and what happened?"

"Gage, please calm down. I'm fine! I'm a big girl. I knew what I was doing last night and I'm.....I'm fine." Maybe, if she convinced him that she was okay with what happened, she might start to believe it herself. She paused briefly before looking up at him. "I love you, Gage."

Gage remained quiet, but he stood and began to pace from one side of the room to the other, as tears welled up in Ari's eyes.

"But......I did break a promise, and I couldn't look at myself in the mirror if I continued to wear that ring. I would be lying to myself.....and God. I'm so sorry, Gage." Arabella dropped her head into her hands, her sobs shaking her entire body.

"Sorry? Why would you be sorry, Arabella? I'm not sorry about what happened! I told you that I love you! There is nothing wrong with what we did last night! This....this God you talk about all the time, if he is angry with you over the love we share, then how can you say He loves you?"

"Gage! Don't talk about Him like that! You have no idea what you're saying. *I'm the one* who messed up, not God. *I'm the one* who turned my back on Him and allowed myself to give in to my emotions and feelings for you."

"Oh, so now what we shared is a mistake?" A wounded expression replaced the anger on Gage's face. "I didn't force you to do anything, Arabella. What happened between us last night was mutual, and it stemmed from our love for one another."

"Gage, I'm not saying anything is *your* fault. I have to deal with this in my own way! I……I'm not…..I am *not* sorry for what happened last night." She choked the words out, but Ari knew with every fiber of her being that it was a lie. She would *always* be sorry for allowing it to go as far as it did. Sorry for breaking the one promise that mattered more than anything, sorry for giving all of herself to a man that she loved but wasn't married to. Anxiety inched its way through her heart. What if Gage never asked her to marry him? What if she was wrong about his love for her, and he *left* her now? The unanswered questions pushed her fear into an all-out panic attack, and she began to sob uncontrollably.

Gage quickly came to her, the anger seemingly replaced by compassion, as he tried to calm her.

"Bella, this is not how I wanted to wake up this morning." Gage pulled her into his arms and hugged her tightly before kissing her on the forehead. "Please, come back to bed with me and let's start over."

Overwhelmed by her feelings, Ari allowed the distraction, when Gage pulled her back into bed and under the covers. He kissed her until she was unable to think of anything but her desire for him.

"Ari, I'm going to love you over and over again until you know in your heart that it isn't wrong. What we have is *love.* You will never be sorry for it, I promise."

And Gage kept his promise. He loved her over and over, until he was all that consumed her thoughts. They never left the loft the entire day, spending all their time wrapped up in the love that they shared. Somewhere amidst their time together, Ari realized she had a choice to make. She could keep Gage happy or keep God happy. And for the life of her, she couldn't turn away from Gage. Even though it meant turning her back on God, the one and only she had *always* been able to count on. She instinctively started to pray for forgiveness, but was unable to complete the thought, as the heavy weight of her sin crept deep into her soul, telling her it was useless.

When Gage finally left Monday morning to pack his belongings for their trip, Ari was left alone with her thoughts for the first time since Saturday night. She made her way to the bathroom, hoping a hot shower would help soothe and comfort her. As she brushed past the bathroom mirror, the reflection she saw was a face she didn't recognize. What stared back at her, was shame and regret.

Damaged. Unworthy. Dirty.

It wasn't until her eyes drifted to the verse she had written out, encouraging her to keep her purity, that Ari lost it. Her body shook with remorse and anger, at the thought of all she had given to Gage.

What have I done? There is no way I can ever go back and change it! How could I be so foolish to toss everything I've ever believed in out the window?

Wait! Couldn't God forgive me, if only I asked? The battle continued to rage. Her mind went from one end of the spectrum to the other. She wanted to believe that everything would be fine. That both Gage and God loved her, and that God would forgive her. Somewhere in the back of her mind, though, she'd already convinced herself that God had no reason to forgive her for such an ugly sin. *Why would He even want to forgive me for such sin?*

Ari's thoughts were driving her crazy, and she knew a decision had to be made or she wouldn't be able to face the day. So, she made the choice right then and there. A choice to love Gage, and not worry about anything or anyone else. Because no matter how hard she tried to deny it, Gage owned her heart. And along with it, all of her self-worth.

By the time they left for the airport that afternoon, Ari had turned her phone off, determined to ignore all of Beth's and Sam's phone calls, blocking everything from her mind but her love for Gage.

Gage tossed his toothbrush into his suitcase, reviewed the mental list he'd made of what to pack, and sighed heavily. Sitting on the edge of the bed, he pushed his fingers through his uncombed hair and tried to figure out what he was feeling. He'd been successful in blocking out the guilt for the past twenty-four hours. But here, alone, his thoughts were beating him up. Torn in a way that he had never been, Gage didn't understand where the guilt came from, only that it bothered him. He'd had plenty of physical relationships in the past, and never once had a women's feelings pulled at his heart like this.

Why now? And why did it suddenly matter to him that Ari had broken a promise to God? God was nothing to him.

Gage stood and walked to the other side of the room where he pulled the window curtain back and took in the scene below. Happiness and joy were what he saw. Tourists enjoying a beautiful sunny day at the beach, laughing and playing as if they didn't have a care in the world. Where had *his* happiness gone? Had he even really been happy with Ari, or just pretending to keep stringing her along until he got what he was truly after?

Shouldn't I be happy, now that I got what I wanted?

Confusion, stronger that Gage had ever felt before, picked at his mind. Stepping backward he glanced at a picture on top of the only dresser in the room. As he held the silver frame in his hands, he realized it was a picture of Ari and her older sister, Maria, as young teenagers. The face that stared back at him, and the smile that he'd come to depend on, gave Gage the answer he was seeking.

He loved Arabella. When he'd said the words to her a couple of days ago, he'd spoken them without thought. But now? Now he was sure. Every word he told her was true. It hadn't been a game to string her along, it was real. The first *real* relationship Gage had ever had, and there was no longer doubt in his mind as to how much she meant to him. So, maybe now the question was, did *she* love him?

He hadn't even entertained that thought until now, but the tears Sunday morning, following their night of passion, and the way she kept talking about this "broken promise," Gage had to wonder. Had he been the foolish one being strung along for the past several weeks? Was it possible that Ari had never meant for their relationship to get to this next level? Gage shook his head in disbelief as he continued to stare at the picture in his hands. She had the face of an angel, a heart so kind, and a mind so very pure. It couldn't be true.

"No!" Gage slammed the picture down and walked back to the bed where the suitcase remained.

"She loves me. I know she does. And I love her. Nothing is going to come between us!" He picked up the suitcase with all the willpower he had and made his way to the door, bound and determined to make the relationship with Ari work. He would make her see that their love for each other was all they needed.

Chapter 13

Nonnie and Max made Ari feel like part of the family from the first minute she met them. Nonnie wrapped her in a warm hug as soon as she set foot in the old, two-story farmhouse. Max's warm smile and welcoming handshake were just as inviting. It was a beautiful home that Nonnie had. There was nothing fancy about it, but it was cozy. Ari could sense that a lot of love had been shared here. She could also see why Gage enjoyed his time here. Nonnie and Max were two of the kindest people she'd ever met. After she and Gage got unpacked and he'd given her the proper tour of the house, he took her out to see the over-sized barns, one where the horses were housed, and the other where the farm equipment and tractors were stored. They climbed onto a four-wheeler next, so he could take her out and show her the property. She saw everything from the horses and cows, to the endless acres of cornstalks and soybeans, and the beautiful pond in the northeast corner of the property. It was a lot bigger than Ari had pictured from Gage's description.

After she and Gage returned to the house, they shared a quiet dinner with Nonnie and Max. It was a simple dinner of fried chicken, mashed potatoes, and roasted vegetables, but Ari was seriously impressed by the taste.

"Nonnie, you are an amazing cook! This is all very delicious."

"Oh, sweetheart, you are too kind." Across the table from her, Nonnie's face lit up and Ari could easily see where Gage inherited his dimpled chin.

"I'm sure this doesn't even *compare* to that fancy food served in your restaurant back home." Nonnie laughed and Ari felt so comfortable with her and Max that it felt like she'd known them her entire life. It was good to see Gage in this environment, surrounded by the people he loved; and she yearned to know even more. He hadn't shared many details of his life with her, only that his mother died when he was seven and that his father became a very angry person afterwards, not loving his only son the way Gage needed him to. Nonnie and Max were the only subjects that ever seemed to bring a smile to his face. And now, she could understand why.

After dinner, Nonnie served them all dishes of fresh strawberry shortcake, the strawberries coming fresh from Nonnie's own garden. Ari was ready to pack Nonnie up and take her back to Francesca's, putting her to work in the kitchen.

"Nonnie, I have seriously never tasted strawberry shortcake this amazing. If you ever get tired of the farm life, you have a job waiting for you in Rock Haven! You would be a welcome addition to our kitchen."

"I told you she was amazing, didn't I?" The twinkle in Gage's eyes spoke volumes about the pride he held in his heart for his grandmother.

They retired to the comfort of the family room for a couple rounds of Uno before Max left for the evening, and Nonnie excused herself to her room. Just as she reached the hallway leading to her room, she turned and explained that Max had left their bags in their *separate* rooms upstairs. Her message was received loud and clear by Ari.

"Goodnight, now. You kids get a good night's rest, and I'll see you at breakfast. Make sure to bring your appetite." Nonnie winked at them before she disappeared down the hall.

Exhausted from the long drive and busy day that they'd had, Ari covered her mouth as she yawned once again, and decided she, too, was ready to turn in for the night.

"Gage, can you show me where my room is, please?"

He made his way across the room to where she was standing and took her hands in his. "Ari, we're sharing a room tonight. Don't worry about Nonnie. We're adults; she will understand."

"Absolutely *not*, Gage!" Her eyes widened with disbelief, mortified at the thought of sharing a bed with him under his grandmother's roof, and against her wishes.

But Gage didn't bother responding to her defiance. He simply took her by the hand and led her up the stairs to the room where her suitcase had been placed. When she turned, expecting to tell him goodnight, Gage pulled her into his arms and kissed her with a hunger she clearly recognized. She pushed against his chest and tried to step back, hoping he would get the hint.

"Gage, we are not doing this! Please, just go to your room for the night, and don't make a big deal about it, okay? I'll see you at breakfast."

"Ari, I can't stand the thought of not *being* with you, not holding you through the night." Gage pleaded with her as his grip grew stronger. "Not after what we've shared. Besides," he leaned in even closer, his breath warm against her cheek, "don't you love me?"

The guilt Gage doled out dueled against her rationale, once again. Ari found that she was unable to say no, even though she was filled with anger at herself for saying yes. Since that first night when she'd allowed herself to indulge in a physical relationship with him, Gage's touch was like a drug her body craved and couldn't resist.

"Promise me you'll go back to your room before morning?"

"I promise, Ari! I'll do whatever it takes to be able to stay with you tonight." The conceited smirk on his face should have been one more indication to how wrong it was, but, she was a goner as soon as she felt his touch, no longer able to make a righteous decision.

She had tried to pray for strength, but it seemed that praying was something she no longer felt comfortable doing. Why would God bother listening to her after she'd turned her back on Him and betrayed Him? She was certain the only thing God felt for her now was disappointment. And so, the cycle continued, Ari giving more and more of herself away and Gage relentlessly taking all that he could. While Ari couldn't deny the fact that she loved the way Gage held her and made her feel, she also couldn't dispute the anger she felt towards herself every time she didn't say no. Gage had a hold on her heart, and he was going to use it to get everything he wanted.

As Ari gave in to his touch again that night, she couldn't help but remember a sermon she'd heard not so long ago. Pastor Ron had talked about the ease of sinning, and how once you made a conscious choice to do it, it got easier and easier to continue, and harder and harder to go back to the truth. It was a slippery slope, and Ari could feel herself sliding faster every time she tried to justify her actions. Her dignity and self-respect? They had taken a nose-dive, and plummeted into a dark and bottomless chasm of sin that first night.

Spending time with the horses quickly became Ari's favorite part of their days on the ranch. Every afternoon she would eagerly follow Gage to the barn where she would help him feed and brush them.

"Gage, they are such beautiful creatures. Strong and powerful…… yet," Ari rested her cheek against Poncho's soft neck and wrapped her arm around him, tangling her fingers in his mane, "yet so peaceful." She had never been around horses before, and there was something about being near the beast that was soothing to her soul.

"Would you like to ride with me today, Ari?"

They'd been on the ranch for three days, and she had yet to agree to it; although he'd asked her every morning. Gage hadn't been shy in telling her why he'd wanted to bring her to the farm. He wanted her to love the things he loved. That's what he'd told her. And she could see it in his eyes, each time he showed her something new. His expressions would come to life, like a kid on Christmas morning, opening the present that they'd been waiting all year for. She had no doubt how much this ranch meant to Gage.

She turned to him with a wide grin on her face. Yes, today was the day she would tuck that last hint of fear away and reach beyond her comfort zone. "I would love to ride with you, Gage."

"Are you serious, Ari? You're really going to ride with me today?" His eyes lit up as he placed his hands on her shoulders, as if questioning her agreement.

"Yes," she giggled, "I will ride with you today, Gage. But," she pointed a finger at him, "you have to promise to take it slow, and remember that I've never been on a horse."

Gage wasted no time. He walked over to the wall where the saddles were hung. "Well, c'mon then. Let's get them saddled up."

He spent the first twenty minutes, teaching her how to control her horse, the different commands to say, and how to use the reins for guiding. She felt awkward at first, but Gage said she looked like a natural, sitting high on Poncho's back, looking prettier than she ever had.

"Bella, you've never looked more beautiful. If only I had a canvas and paints, then maybe you could see yourself through my eyes."

His words sang like a melody to her heart, and once again she questioned herself. If Gage loved her like she felt he did, then what they were doing couldn't possibly be wrong. Wouldn't God agree? It was a battle that she lived with every day. Was it right? Was it wrong? And did she even want to know the truth?

Just as they were getting ready to head out, Nonnie slipped out the back door and surprised them with a lunch that she had prepared for them. She strolled over to Gage, handing the soft-sided cooler to him just as he finished attaching a saddlebag to his mare's side.

"Now you kids go on and enjoy your day together. And don't be in a hurry to get back here. Max and I are going into to town, and we'll be gone for a couple of hours." She winked in Ari's direction.

Relief flooded Ari's mind. She was positive that Nonnie wasn't aware Gage had been staying in her room at night. She was certain the old woman wouldn't have continued being so nice to her otherwise. Ari let a long breath escape and allowed herself to relax just a little more.

The summer day was beautiful. Ari let the warmth of the hot sun, beaming down on her from the brilliant blue sky, soak into her skin and relax her. All of the stress and negative thoughts she'd been trying to ignore were left behind, as she enjoyed her time with Gage. The temperature was near eighty degrees, and there wasn't a hint of humidity in the air; a perfect day in Ari's mind. This, in combination with riding Poncho, was quickly becoming Ari's favorite form of therapy.

After they'd ridden along the perimeter of Nonnie's property for a while, they ventured onto some trails through the woods that separated the property from the neighbors. She and Gage stopped for a break and spread their blanket and picnic lunch next to the pond. Nonnie had made them delicious chicken salad sandwiches and cut up fresh fruit for them to enjoy, along with a piece of freshly baked peach pie for them to share. Gage was unusually quiet during lunch, and it seemed he had a lot on his mind as he leaned back on one elbow, looking up at her while she began to pack the leftovers into the basket.

"Bella, are you happy?"

She leaned back next to him, her eyebrows knit together. "Of course, I'm happy, Gage. Why would you even ask that? I've had a wonderful time here on the ranch this week, and I love your Nonnie. She's very special."

"I guess what I mean is," he paused, and Ari could read the apprehension on his face, "are you happy with me? Not so much as, are you happy on the ranch."

Ari groaned at the thought of replaying the conversation yet again. Every day, since the first night she'd given herself to him, Gage had hounded her with the same questions. Didn't he realize, that no matter how she answered that question, the fact that she had slept with him would never change?

"Gage, why do you constantly insist on bringing this up? I've told you over and over for the past week that I'm fine. I love you, and I'm happy with you. What more do you want me to say?" She couldn't help but feel annoyed.

"I'm sorry, Bella. I know I told you I would drop it but," Gage raised one shoulder, "you just seem different, that's all."

Arabella had no response. She had told him repeatedly that she was fine. And she was tired of playing this game, just so Gage would feel better about her decision to be with him. It was quiet between the two of them for quite a while before Gage finally broke the silence.

"I never meant to hurt you, Bella." He stood up and reached a hand out to her, pulling her to her feet.

"I think we'd better head back to the house now. Nonnie is sure excited about tonight, and I wouldn't want to keep her waiting much longer."

While she was happy that the subject of her feelings for him was closed for now, Ari was certain the topic would be brought up again, long before the sun went down tonight. Until then, she was going to block it out, ignore it, and do whatever she could do, to keep it from seeping into her thoughts and pulling her down into the deep sea of sin she was drowning in. She plastered a smile on her face and turned to Gage, as he approached with the offer to help her into the stirrups.

"I'm excited too! I can't wait to see what Max has in mind." Ari pulled the reins up snug in her hands and before Gage even had a chance to saddle up, she called out to him, "Race you back to the farm."

She nudged Poncho and took off on a fast gallop, leaving Gage standing in a cloud of dust, and mumbling out loud to himself.

"She sure took to riding pretty quickly."

Back at the house, Ari had taken a shower and freshened up before Gage. The four of them were going into town for dinner, although not together. Gage hadn't had any time alone with his grandmother, so Arabella had suggested he take her out to eat. She had spent so much time cooking for them and entertaining them during their visit, that Ari felt she deserved to relax a little and enjoy having her grandson all to herself for a few hours. It was Max's suggestion the day before that surprised her. They had just finished eating supper together and were clearing the table when the old man piped up.

"Arabella, why don't you and I have dinner in town as well? And maybe do a little shopping before you two head back to Michigan?"

"Shopping?" That certainly got her attention. "A girl would have to be crazy to turn that down. What are we shopping for, Max?"

Max just grinned his old lopsided smile, and once again Ari thought about how quickly she'd become comfortable being with him and Nonnie. It felt good to feel like part of a family again. As soon as that thought entered her mind, it was followed by the reality of her "family" back in Michigan who she missed so much. Oh, how she missed the relationship she had with Beth. And Sam? Well, he'd been her substitute father for so long, she couldn't see him as anything less. She had to wonder if things would ever be the same again. Would they ever be able to forgive her for what she'd done and the poor choices she had made?

"How about we keep that a secret for now? Girls like surprises as much as they like shopping, don't they?"

"They most certainly do," Ari replied, Max's comment bringing her attention back to the conversation.

Gage kissed her goodbye at the door before they headed into town in separate vehicles. Gage and Nonnie headed to the local barbeque joint that was her favorite, and Max and Ari drove off in the direction of the large western store that their town was famous for.

Nonnie patiently waited until they'd been seated at the restaurant and placed their order, before she tackled the subject that had been on her mind all week.

"Want to tell your old grandmother what you've been thinking so deeply about? It's obvious that you're smitten with Arabella, and she's a wonderful girl. So, what's got you so upside down, June Bug?"

Gage immediately relaxed. "You know me so well, Nonnie."

"That's my job, Gage. And I take my job very seriously," she smiled.

His response was slow, and she could tell he was wrestling with his thoughts. "Have you ever done something, Nonnie," Gage's eyes dropped to his lap, "that no matter what, you couldn't take it back? No matter how much you tried, or how badly you wanted to, you just couldn't reverse your decision?"

Nonnie placed her hand over Gage's. "Oh Gage, we've all made mistakes that are irreversible, but we can't live with regret. We have to figure out how to learn from our mistakes and move forward, or regret will eat us up inside. Take your father for example," she nodded. "He never could forgive himself for your mama's death. That was not his burden to carry, and look how his failure to forgive himself affected your life."

Gage was quiet for a moment, seemingly thinking on her words, before he spoke again. "I've hurt Ari in a way I can never take back, Nonnie. I can't undo what I've taken from her, and I don't know how to forgive myself for it. The truth is.....I don't know if I'm actually sorry for my actions, or just sorry that she's hurt by them." The words had spilled from Gage's mouth so quickly, she could see that even he was caught by surprise.

"Has she told you she's angry at you for it?"

Gage shook his head and faced her. "No, in fact, she keeps telling me that it's okay.... but it's not, Nonnie. I can see it's not okay. She's different now. The light in her eyes is gone. And I don't know how to make things right for her."

"Oh, Gage, she seems perfectly fine to me. Happy with you, and your life together. Are you sure you aren't just misreading something?"

Gage pulled his hand back and turned away from her, anger and shame contorting his face.

"You don't understand, Nonnie. She was different when I first met her. Confident, sure of herself, and....and so innocent and pure." She could hear the emotion in the words that spilled from his mouth. Her heart ached just knowing something was causing her grandson pain.

"And now, it seems like she questions every decision she makes. She doesn't carry the confidence she used to. And it's all because I made her choose."

"Made her choose? Gage, I don't understand."

"I made her choose *me* over her relationship with God, Nonnie. She gave up on a promise she had made to Him because of my unwillingness to listen. I refused to wait and treat her like she deserved to be treated."

Things were becoming clear as she listened to Gage explain.

"She tells me she made the choice on her own, and Nonnie, I promise I didn't force her, but I still feel like I'm the one responsible for changing her mind and getting her to give in to those desires."

"I see," Nonnie nodded. "Gage, have you talked to God about how you're feeling?"

"*God*, Nonnie? That's the entire problem right there. If she didn't have that stupid purity pledge with Him, then none of this would be an issue!"

She was startled by his abruptness, as well as his words. Nonnie had never heard her grandson raise his voice to her, but what hurt her even more was his negativity towards the Lord.

She leaned in and spoke quietly, hoping her grandson would take the hint. "Gage, you know I'm going to be honest with you, right?" She waited for his response, until he nodded his head in agreement.

"The Lord is the *only* right answer. Every time. I know that you never particularly cared for going to church with me on your visits to the farm, but I also know you've heard me speak of Him time and time again, how He is the only reason I got through losing your mother and your grandfather. God's love is a gift not to be taken for granted, and once you find it, you'll never want to let go."

"That's just it!" He raised his hands in frustration. "I don't know God, or even how to find Him. And if Ari feels so horrible over what she did with me because of her relationship with Him, then I don't think I *want* to know Him."

His words stung her heart. She realized now that she should have been more proactive in making him go to church as a young boy. Instead she'd let him make his choices. And now? Now, her grandson sat across the table from her, angry at a God he didn't even know. Where had she gone wrong? Hadn't her love for the Lord been apparent to him? An example that he'd want to follow?

"Gage, it says in the Bible—"

"Stop, Nonnie. I don't need to know what your book says about my mistakes! I'm living with it every day of my life."

Before she could respond, the waitress had delivered their dinners to the table, and Gage quickly changed the subject. She could only half listen, now that she knew what her grandson was wrestling with. Now that her heart hurt so deeply for him. If only she could get him to understand the truth about the Lord. Surely, he would open his heart to the One that was waiting for him. She wanted nothing more, than for Gage to feel the love that only the Lord could give. But she knew her stubborn grandson well enough to let the subject rest for now. Instead, she made a commitment, then and there, to keep Gage and Arabella at the top of her prayer list, and to revisit the subject before they left the farm.

Chapter 14

A *small blue Honda sat* in the driveway when Arabella and Max arrived back at the farm that evening, ahead of Gage and Nonnie. Before Max could say a word about who the owner was, a pretty young girl with flaming red hair exited the car, and now stood at his window with a giant smile on her face.

Max turned to Ari. "Why don't you go on and take your bags inside?"

"Who is that girl, Max? Is she a friend of yours?" Arabella asked innocently, staring out his window.

The sound of Nonnie's truck barreling up the driveway, caught her attention before Max could answer. Unbuckling her seatbelt, Ari climbed out of the truck, just in time to see the girl run towards Gage and jump into his arms, planting a kiss on his lips.

"Gage, I've missed you so much. Where have you been?" she squealed.

Gage stood stiff, unwelcoming the embrace, his eyes finding Arabella's, as she stood in shock at the scene.

Breathe! Deep breath in. There has to be a reasonable explanation for this. Arabella's stomach plummeted as she watched the stranger claim her boyfriend's mouth a second time.

"Gage?" Arabella prodded.

"Why don't we step inside and give these kids some privacy?" Max reached for Nonnie's hand and all but pulled her towards the back door.

The red head wasted no time in continuing the conversation. She first looked from Gage to Ari, settling back to Gage again, not even a hint of insecurity in her voice. "Gage, who is this? A co-worker?"

Gage spun the girl around to face him, demanding an answer. "Jenna, what are you doing here?"

Fear seized Ari's heart as she watched Gage question the shapely, fair-skinned beauty. Obviously, she was someone he knew well. But just *how* well? Frozen by the unanswered questions, Ari could do nothing but stare.

"What do you mean, Gage?"

Apparently, she too, was caught off guard by Gage's questioning, but Ari couldn't tell if that was a good thing or not.

"Why am I here? I'm here because you're home, silly. Aren't you going to tell me who your friend is?" She pointed in Arabella's direction.

"Jenna, this is Arabella," Gage made his way back to Ari and slipped his arm around her waist, "my girlfriend."

Outrage surfaced on the girl's face as she balled her hands into fists at her side. "*Girl*……friend, Gage? I thought I was your—"

"Jenna, I think it's time for you to go!"

Gage shuffled towards her and grabbed her elbow in an attempt to nudge her into her car, but she was having no part of leaving. The picture was starting to become a little clearer to Ari, and she was certain now that Gage was more than friends with this girl. Fear continued to crawl into her mind until she was consumed by it. She reached a shaky hand out for something to hold onto and found Max' truck. She grabbed on to it as tight as she could, hoping her knees wouldn't buckle and drop her to the ground.

Breathe Arabella! You have to get a grip on your feelings before you make a fool of yourself in front of her.

"I'm not going *anywhere* until you tell me what's going on!" Jenna demanded. She turned her reddened face in Arabella's direction and then back to Gage, waiting for an explanation.

Unsure that she even *wanted* to know the answers to her questions, Ari finally spoke. "Maybe I should step inside, and give you two time to clear up any confusion." She pulled her bags from the backseat of Max's truck and headed towards the house, tears threatening to spill from her eyes as she avoided Gage's stare. Whatever Gage had shared with this girl, it was obvious she still had feelings for him. And why hadn't he told her about it? Did *he* still have feelings for this, Jenna girl? Is that why he'd kept her a secret? Had she been a fool, this entire time, to believe that she alone was enough for Gage? Men like that didn't just change who they were. But after all they'd shared, Ari couldn't entertain the thought that he had feelings for another woman. She had to be wrong. There had to be a logical explanation for everything going on.

Her head was pounding from the thoughts that raced back and forth inside her brain, and the distance from Rock Haven suddenly felt very far. Ari longed for the comfort of her best friend, Beth, and the town she'd grown up in. Beth had always been there for her, even in her darkest days when she lost her mother and sister, and then again when her father died. Rock Haven had always been her safe haven and Beth her protector. Why on earth had she even considered this trip? And why, she wondered, did God allow Gage to bring her all the way out here just to hurt her? Didn't He realize what seeing Gage with another woman would do to her? Or maybe, God just didn't care anymore. Why should He, after she turned her back on Him? That had to be it. God was angry with her for the choices she made, so he was going to punish her, right? And she deserved every bit of pain that came her way. She was a horrible person, a sinner that God would never be able to forgive.

With her head held down in shame, and not speaking a word, Ari quickly and quietly made her way into the house. She brushed past Nonnie and Max, who sat at the kitchen table in silence, and made her way upstairs to the room she'd been secretly sharing with Gage. She felt sick to her stomach as she stared at the bed, where just the night before he, once again, had confessed his love for her.

And surely, he will be a Godly man.

The words from her past, words that she'd spoken to her father so many years ago, found their way into her mind, as quickly as she shut the bedroom door behind her. Defeat and failure threatened her weak, desperate heart as she questioned her relationship with Gage, yet again. Questioned the kind of man he really was and his motives for being in a relationship with her.

How would her family feel about Gage? If they were still alive, would they have welcomed him into her life? Or would they have the same reservations Beth and Sam now had? She knew the answer. She had known it all along. But even as clear as that truth was in her mind, the only thing her heart wanted was for the man she loved to come walking through the door. She wanted him to wrap his strong arms around her and tell her that he loved her, and kiss all of her worries and doubts away.

So, how could she decide? Should she listen to her heart and put Gage's past to rest? Or, should she listen to her head and walk out the door with her suitcase in hand and her head held high?

Quietly she began to weep at her indecision. "I'm so sorry Mama, Daddy. I'm so ashamed at what I've done. I never meant to be such a failure. Never meant to turn out such a mess."

Her tears began to slide down her cheeks in a steady stream. But they didn't last long. With determination she took in a long breath and exhaled deeply. Then, with a new-found strength that came out of nowhere, she realized exactly what she needed to do. And she would do it without crying and making a scene like the other clingy, needy girls that she'd known in her past. She was too strong for that. She pulled out her empty suitcase and laid it open on the bed.

There was just too much about Gage, and the life he lived before her, that she couldn't deal with. She had been crazy to think that a playboy like him could actually fall in love with a simple, small town Christian girl like her. Pain continued to assault her, as the memory of all she had given to Gage resurfaced. How could she have let this happen? *Who was she* anymore? Ari didn't even recognize the woman she had become. Despair tugged at her heart, and her stomach became a large knot of nerves, as she began to fill her suitcase.

Leaving him would be the hardest thing she'd ever done.

Gage waited until he was sure Ari was out of ear shot before he spun around to face Jenna. "Jenna, I *never* promised you anything! What we had was fun while it lasted, but I've met someone that I love and you have no place in my life now. In fact, I don't know why you just showed up here at the farm, anyway."

"Gage, you can't be serious!" Jenna took two steps in his direction, but Gage held out his hand to stop her from getting any closer.

"Don't, Jenna!"

"How can you say you're in love with that girl after everything *we've* shared? Haven't the past three years meant anything to you?"

Tears spilled down her face, but it didn't affect Gage in the slightest bit. The only thing he could think about was getting Jenna in her car and down the drive, so that he could start making amends with Ari.

"I….I," she stared at him with desperate, pleading eyes. "I love you, Gage."

"Jenna, we were never really a couple. Don't you get that? You don't know what love is. Love is what I have with Arabella. What we had doesn't even come close!"

The slap across his face stung, but still, he didn't budge.

"Gage, why are you doing this? I thought by giving you space and time that you would eventually come to realize how serious your feelings were for me." Jenna attempted to place her hand upon his cheek, where the red mark remained, but he pushed her hand away in anger and stepped back.

"Jenna, are you not hearing me? I said I *don't care* about you! I *never* loved you, nor did I ever claim to! I'm in love with Arabella, and you are not going to stand in my way of having her!"

He had never intended for the conversation to turn this bad. But then again, he had never really planned on having the conversation at all. He knew now, that Max had been right. He should've called Jenna and set things straight before he brought Ari to the farm. If only he had listened, he wouldn't be in this mess, fearful of losing the only woman he ever loved.

It wasn't that he hated Jenna. After all, they did share some fun times together. But Arabella was all he wanted, all that he could think about day in and day out, and right now he'd do *anything* to make sure he didn't lose her. Even if that meant hurting Jenna, or anyone else who tried to stand in his way.

Her crying had ceased, and what had been pleading in her voice before, was now replaced by anger.

"Gage, I don't know why you are acting like this. If I've done something wrong, just tell me and we can fix it. You can't honestly tell me you're in love with this," Jenna pointed towards the house, "this other woman. How long have you even known her?"

How many more times or ways could he tell her he was in love with Arabella? "Jenna, I'm not trying to hurt you, but you *have* to understand. Whatever we had is over! I could never love you the way I love Arabella."

"Ugh!" She kicked the tire of her Honda in frustration. "What kind of a name is Arabella, anyway?" Jenna spun around to open her car door, glancing back only long enough to let him have it one more time. "You're making a big mistake, Gage Russell. A mistake you're going to regret the rest of your life!" With that, she turned the key and started her car. Stomping on the gas pedal, Jenna left Gage standing in a cloud of fumes, as she sped down the driveway.

Finally, once he was sure she was really gone, Gage let out the breath that he'd been holding. Thankful that Jenna had left, but fearful of the next confrontation, Gage mumbled, "One down, and one to go."

His eyes locked on the farmhouse, scared of what he would find inside. Reluctantly, after stalling as long as he felt he could, Gage made his way inside to find Nonnie and Max at the kitchen table. Noting that Arabella was nowhere in sight, he approached them, speaking first, before either of them had a chance.

"I suppose you could say 'I told you so,' huh, Max?"

The old man lifted his head and focused on Gage's face. "I was only trying to help you avoid this *exact* situation, Gage. Ignoring your problems will never make them go away."

Gage knew the old man was right and he had no right to be mad at him. It wasn't Max's fault that Jenna had come to the farm. Everything that had taken place was his fault. And his alone.

"Gage, honey," his grandmother began, "I think you'd better head upstairs and see what you can salvage of your relationship with Arabella."

The anger was gone. All Gage felt now was humiliation and remorse for his choices. He'd created a mess. And he could only hope that everyone involved, would forgive him. Especially Ari.

"I'm sorry I didn't listen to you, Max. I should have known you only had my best interest at heart."

Max stood up from the table, his empty coffee cup in one hand, and headed towards the Keurig. He paused briefly to place his other hand on Gage's shoulder.

"It's not about being right or wrong, Gage. We all make choices and have to face the consequences, some harder than others. I have a feeling this is going to be a hard one for you. Just know that Nonnie and I will be praying for you. I think your grandmother is right, though. You'd better head up there," he nodded to the stairs, "and get to work."

It was the longest flight of stairs Gage had climbed in his entire life. All the while, trying to think of excuses to justify his relationship with Jenna. Maybe relationship wasn't a good word to describe what he'd shared with her. He had a feeling that word might imply more to Ari than what Gage intended, and right now, he had to find *just* the right words to get Ari to forgive him. At the same time, his past was his past, and it should have nothing to do with their relationship now. Couldn't she see that? Some how he'd make her understand.

With each step that he took, as he moved closer to the top of the stairwell, his hand gripped the rail a little tighter, his heart beat a little harder, his mind raced a little faster. When, finally, he reached the top of the stairs, he saw that the bedroom door was closed. He leaned back against the wall and hung his head, taking one more moment to get his thoughts in order. What waited on the other side of that door could be anger, tears, yelling, or any combination of those, and he needed to be prepared for the worst.

With one last deep breath, he convinced himself that he was ready. Slowly, he turned the doorknob and opened the door. What he saw, was *nothing* that he had been prepared for. Stunned, he stood in the doorway, his mouth wide open, as he stared at the woman he loved, her suitcase on the bed beside her.

"Arabella, what are you doing? You're not leaving me, are you?" Panic laced his words. What was she thinking? She couldn't leave him. Not now, after everything he'd invested in her. Not after she'd turned his world upside down and inside out. Not after he'd fallen in *love* with her! He had to make her see the truth. They were going to work this out, no matter what. He refused to believe otherwise.

With the calmest, disengaged voice, she responded to him. "Gage, I think maybe it would be best if I head home. It seems like you have some unfinished business here to work through." She stood and turned to pick up the suitcase.

"No! Arabella you can't leave." Gage rushed to her side, pulling her hands away from the suitcase, and spinning her around to face him. "Please, Arabella, that girl means *nothing* to me. She is my past! But you," he cupped her face in his hands, "*you* are my future, Bella!"

He could see she was struggling to keep the tears at bay. She tried to pull away from. "Gage, it's just best if—"

"Arabella, baby, please stay. I can't make it without you! I promise you, there will never be anyone else but you!" Fear grasped at his heart like never before as he clung to her. He had to say something to stop her! She *had* to understand that he would *never* let her go.

"I *need* to go home, Gage. Alone. Can't you see? This won't work between us! We are too different."

"No, I won't let you. You *can't* walk away from us, Ari!"

Ari turned her head away from him, but not before he saw the tears beginning to fill the corner of her eyes. She was struggling with her emotions, and her decision to leave. He could easily see it. He would change her mind. He knew he could.

"Bella, I'm so sorry I hurt you." He pulled her against his chest and kissed the top of her head. "But, you have to believe me about this. Jenna and I were *never* a couple. I admit we had a relation—"

"You had a *physical* relationship with her, didn't you Gage?" Ari pulled back far enough that she could look him in the eye. "Sam warned me about being unequally yoked with you, and now I know exactly why! Gage, it's foolish to think we can continue this game of charades that we've been playing!"

Determined, Gage stood his ground. "Ari, you knew there had been other women in my life. I'm not like you, and I've never hidden that fact."

"No, you didn't. But, I.....I never knew it would hurt this much to see that truth, Gage." She choked back a sob and hung her head in defeat. "I was wrong."

She's starting to cave! You've almost convinced her, Russell. Don't stop know. A small inner voice encouraged Gage to continue.

"Bella, I believe we can work through this! Just give me a chance!"

"Why was she here, Gage? Does she think you are still a couple? Why didn't you warn me before bringing me hundreds of miles away from my home?" She broke loose from his grip and paced to the other side of the room. "I knew coming here was a mistake. You and I," she turned back to face him, "we're a mistake, Gage."

"No, Bella, *we* are not a mistake!" Gage's temper began to flare once again. "You are the best thing that's ever happened to me. I don't know what Jenna was thinking." He turned then, his back to her, as he paced the length of the room, raking his hands through his hair. He had to find a way to fix this mess he'd created. As a last resort, he opted for honesty.

"Fine, you want the truth? Here is the truth, Bella. Yes," he turned back to face her, "I had a physical relationship with Jenna. In fact, we've been together every summer for the past three years. But, I *never* pretended that we were more than friends! And I certainly never told her I wanted a relationship with her! It was just something to past the time while I was here during the summers. That's it."

"That's it? A fun time, Gage, was all you saw in her? For *three years*? How could you *use* her that way? Is that what you're doing with me? *Using* me? Tell me, Gage, is that the kind of man I've fallen in love with?"

She's admitting that she loves you. That's a start. Just keep talking to her. She's not going to walk out on you.

The small voice continued to encourage him, but Gage knew his time was running out. He had to do some smooth talking, and fast, if he was going to convince Ari to stay. Once again, he strode across the room and wrapped his arms around her waist, looking deep into the hidden chambers of her heart. The place he was certain she reserved only for him.

"Bella, I love you. I have never loved another woman, especially not Jenna. I've made a lot of mistakes in my past, but I'm not that person anymore! Please," he kissed her on the cheek, "you have to believe me." He kissed her other cheek, and slowly, his lips made their way to hers. When she didn't resist, and he felt her relax against him, Gage knew her resolve was failing. He was close to winning the battle.

In the end, Gage wasn't exactly sure what he'd said or done to get Arabella to change her mind, but he didn't care. All that mattered was that she emptied out the suitcase, with the promise not to mention leaving him ever again. That, and the fact that she allowed him into her room, and into her bed, that night. And every night after.

"Well, what do you think?" Arabella twirled around in front of Nonnie, lifting her skirt just high enough to show off the new cowboy boots Max had purchased for her.

“I think I like them, Ari. And you make them look even better.” Nonnie smiled and took the girl’s hand in hers pulling her to sit down on the edge of the bed next to her. Gage and Max were loading their suitcases for the long trip back to Michigan.

“Can I ask you something, dear?”

Ari gave a weak smile, nervously wondering what Nonnie had on her mind, as she fumbled for her answer. “Um……. sure, I…...I guess, Nonnie.”

“I know my grandson probably better than anyone else, no offense to you. And I know after spending this week with the two of you, just how much he loves you. My question is, do you love Gage as much as he loves you?”

Arabella didn’t need to think about that answer. That was the one thing she was sure of. Even after all that had transpired over their time in Iowa, including Jenna. She had fought against the passion she felt towards him, but in the end, she couldn’t leave. She would *never* leave him. Not after all that they’d shared. She wanted to be mad at him, hate him even, for the pain that he had caused her. But as soon as his lips found hers, standing in the bedroom that they had shared night after night, she knew no matter what the cost, she would never let him go.

“Absolutely Nonnie! I love Gage more than anything, and I could never love anyone like I love him.”

She was certain that Nonnie didn’t understand the depth of her words.

“Good!” Nonnie smiled. “That was the answer I was expecting to hear.” Nonnie pulled Ari into a hug before standing up and walking towards the door.

“Arabella?” Nonnie turned back towards her quickly, nearly causing Ari to topple into her. “Promise me something.”

“Yes, Nonnie,” her smile was genuine this time, no longer nervous that Nonnie had a hidden agenda.

“Promise me that you’ll be patient with Gage. And,” Nonnie reached out and took Ari’s hand in her own, the tender look in her eye tugging at Ari’s heart, “don’t ever give up on him. He has a really good heart, that boy. He just hasn’t found his way to the Lord yet.” With that, Nonnie turned and walked away, leaving Arabella to her thoughts.

They said goodbye for what felt like the hundredth time, before she and Gage actually got into the car and began their drive back to Michigan. Although she had enjoyed herself immensely, minus the incident with Jenna, Ari was anxious to be back home. She’d never been away from the restaurant like this and was curious to see how things had gone.

For the first half hour, they rode in silence, giving Arabella the time she needed to process the words Nonnie had spoken to her. She’d quit praying after that first night she'd allowed Gage to sleep in her bed. No longer turning to God for guidance, she struggled desperately with her thoughts. She felt more alone than she had in her entire life. She had nobody to talk to, not even Sam or Beth. They would never understand how she felt.

I can't keep doing this to myself. I have to stop making Gage feel guilty about my choices. And I have to stop feeling guilty! They were, and are, my choices. He loves me, and I love him, and we made a choice to be together. There is no reason to pretend I'm not happy when I really am. If God's not happy with my decision, then maybe I don't need God in my life! Gage is enough to make me happy, isn't he? He is all I will ever need and we are going to make this work! He is different than he was before he met me. I can trust him, he loves me.

Arabella had made up her mind. There would be no more moping around, feeling guilty about her decisions. And if God, or Beth, or anybody else had anything negative to say, then she didn't need them! Ari believed Gage when he told her he had no feelings for Jenna, and that she was the only woman he had ever loved. And there was no doubt in her mind that Gage was the only man *she* would ever love.

Ari scooted over to the middle of the seat, where she could be closer to Gage, and turned to kiss him on the cheek.

"I had a wonderful time in Iowa, Gage. Thank you for taking me there and sharing that part of your life with me. Your Nonnie and Max are something special."

Gage tried to focus on the road while still catching a quick glance at Arabella.

"We're good, then?"

"We're good, Gage. I promise I won't bring up your past again. What's done is done."

Gage reached for her hand and intertwined his fingers with hers. "I love you, Bella."

"I love you too, Gage."

Chapter 15

The days turned into weeks, and the weeks continued to fly by, as summer kept Gage busy with all of the jobs he'd been asked to bid on. In fact, as the requests continued to stream in, Gage felt the need to locate and rent an office space in Rock Haven. Arabella had been ecstatic when he secured the place, just two blocks away from Francesca's. And not only did he use the space for an office, he was also using one half of the room to display some of the artwork he'd recently completed. It had been Ari's idea that he put price tags on them and see what kind of offers he would get. Shockingly, the very week he set the easels up, two of his paintings sold. And for a very nice profit! Gage couldn't have been happier, but that was short lived. The following day he spoke to his father and informed him that he was staying in Rock Haven indefinitely.

"What do you mean you're staying in Michigan, Gage? *New York* is your home! Now, I've been patient about you taking an extended leave to visit the farm, but enough is enough!" His father's tone was anything but kind. "You need to come home and run this business the *right* way!"

Gage wasn't backing down this time. He'd spent his entire life running from his father's anger and doing everything he could to please him. But not anymore. His time away from New York had opened his eyes to all sorts of things, and it was time his father respected the man that he'd become.

"Dad, if you'll remember, *you* walked away from the business and left it in *my* hands. That means *I* get to make the decisions now."

"Not when your decisions are this ridiculous, you don't," his father screamed into the phone. "What has gotten into your head, boy? Is it that girl that you've been shacking up with? I'll bet that's what all of this is about, isn't it? I warned you not to fall in love. She's only going to break your heart, and then what good will you be?"

Gage refused to allow his father's words to defeat him any longer; and he absolutely would not let him bring his relationship with Ari into question. His entire life he'd been afraid to stand up to his father. But it wouldn't happen again. Besides, what good would his father's advice on relationships be, when he himself had been nothing but an angry, bitter man for the past twenty years.

"Don't you talk about my relationship with Arabella like that ever again! Just because you were insecure in your relationship with my mother, doesn't mean I'm going to live my life miserable like *you*!"

For a long, uncomfortable moment, a heaviness hung in the air.

This is just great, Gage thought, as a lone chuckle escaped his lips. *The old man wants to give me advice about love. Not going to happen!*

"Tell me dad, what is it that you've done in your life that makes you feel qualified to give me love advice? Let's see, was it the way you loved *me*?" He mocked. "No, it couldn't be that, because I'm not even sure you ever really loved me. You don't show love by blocking someone out of a person's life, pretending they never existed, like you did with my mother. I needed to know who she was and how much she loved me and our family. But, you? You just couldn't do that, could you? No, you just blocked everything out, never giving an ounce of thought to the pain you were inflicting on me! Job well done, Dad!"

The only response he got, was the sound of the other phone slamming in his ear.

Gage set his own phone on the table and released a heavy sigh. He hadn't meant to be that harsh towards his father, but he'd needed to get some of those things off of his chest for years. Ironically, instead of feeling better after his demeaning outburst, he only felt cold and empty. He'd hurt his father; he was certain of that.

"Who am I to judge? I'm no better than my old man," Gage said aloud as he stood up in frustration and shoved his chair against the table. "Maybe *I'm* the one who's got it all wrong." He walked over to the end table that sat next to the couch, and picked up a picture frame that Ari had recently purchased to put her favorite photo in. For someone who'd grown up in a beach town, she hadn't ventured much farther than the end of the pier, overlooking the expansive lake. But that day, she'd let go of her fears and allowed Gage to introduce her to parasailing. It turned out to be a perfect day; everything Gage had hoped it would be. He secretly booked a private charter, just for the two of the them. He'd never forget her reaction when he removed the blindfold from her eyes.

"Gage?" Ari's voice trembled, her green eyes growing wide in trepidation, as she turned to him. "What have you done?"

Reaching towards her, Gage gently squeezed her shoulders and looked her in the eye, a silly lop-sided grin on his face.

"Not what I've *done,* Bella, it's what *we* are *going* to do."

Ari began shaking her head defiantly before he even finished his sentence. "Gage, I can't," she took a step back, pulling herself free of his hold.

"C'mon, Arabella!" Gage closed the distance between them once again, not sure if her googly-eyed expression was exaggerating a slight fear, or if she was truly horrified. "Let go and live a little. I *promise* I will be right next to you the entire time." He pulled Ari's shaking hands to his mouth and kissed them. "Please, Bella, for me?"

He had never seen Arabella laugh so hard or smile so big. The minute they were released from the boat and gently began to ascend into the bright blue summer sky, the fear was gone. The bright yellow canopy of the parasail wing stretched out high above them, their bare feet dangled freely in the wind. She hadn't yet released her tight grip on his hand, as she turned to face him, nearly screaming her words so that he could hear her through the whipping wind.

"I can't believe I'm doing this, Gage! It's so beautiful up here! It feels just like we are flying!"

He squeezed her hand a little tighter, taking in the view all around him. The view right next to him, he'd have to say, was the prettiest thing he'd ever seen. Not only did Arabella's smile warm his heart, but her complete and total trust in him, as she agreed to climb into the harness and face her fears with him by her side, made him tingle from his head to his toes. Nothing had ever felt so good, so complete. So right.

Ari's reactions were all that he had expected and more. Gage couldn't help but stare, enveloped by her laughter, and captivated by her beauty. He smiled as the wind blew her hair in all directions, four hundred feet above solid ground.

Gage knew, as he peered at the picture in his hand of the two of them, their matching blue t-shirts that read "Pete's Parasail—I survived the glide," with their thumbs up and smiles wide, it was a day he would always remember.

The question he couldn't shake from his mind, however, the one that had been plaguing him for weeks, and even more so after the conversation he'd just had with his father, was how authentic his relationship with Ari was. Could she really be happy with him after all of the sacrifices she'd made, or would she some day regret her choices, and leave him as sad and lonely as his father warned? It was because of him, that she had turned her back on the two people she loved the most. And it was also because of him, that she refused to set foot in church. Her church; where she had grown up and been baptized and surrendered her life to the Lord. How many more things would he make her compromise before she began to despise him? He couldn't deny the changes that had already begun to shape the "new" Ari, and how it affected their relationship. How long would it take for her to realize he would never be enough for her? And how long could he pretend that none of this mattered? Pretend that he wasn't head over heels in love with the amazing woman that he'd been spending all of his time with. The beauty that constantly encouraged him to believe in himself, to believe in his abilities as an artist, and motivated him to stand up for himself against his father. The way he saw it, Ari was the one getting the raw end of the deal. The only thing he'd given her was heartache, and he had no doubt that someday soon, she would figure that out and quit wasting her time with him.

Arabella kept pretty busy with the restaurant, and when she wasn't there, she was spending the majority of her free time exclusively with Gage. He had been very excited when, after hours and hours of debate, she had finally agreed to let him renovate the loft, and make a livable space for the two of them. When he presented the final blue print to her one night, she had to admit her excitement for it.

"Gage, this is beautiful. I never dreamed this space could be transformed in such a way. You are amazing!" She flung herself into his arms and planted a giant kiss on his cheek.

"This is all for you, Bella." Gage tugged gently at her waist and eased her feet back to the floor, taking her face in his hands. "You make me so happy. I love you, and I hope you never forget that."

For a moment, Ari thought she sensed something conflicting in Gage's voice, maybe a little too much emotion? She waited quietly, allowing him a chance to continue, but when he released his hold on her and turned to where the blueprints lay on their kitchen table, she assumed she was just overthinking things again.

Gage explained to her, as he showed her the layout, how he planned to build a chef's kitchen with an enormous center island, add two additional bedrooms and bathrooms, along with creating a luxurious master suite for the two of them. The rest of the space would remain an open floor plan, with simple placement of furniture, including the floor to ceiling fireplace that she told him she couldn't live without. That same evening, Ari took a seat on the couch and snuggled up next to Gage, as he flipped on the television just in time for their favorite cooking show. It had become one of their weekly traditions, every Wednesday night. They both left work on time to get home for their favorite take-out food. Ari would bring it home from the restaurant, and they would be ready for the show by seven. Gage thoroughly enjoyed watching the contestants, as they created and cooked recipes, under the pressure of a time limit, and with ingredients that were named at the very last minute. Since Arabella no longer participated in her women's group at church on Wednesday evenings, she got caught up in the hype of the show as well. It had become something they both looked forward to each week. But tonight, Ari couldn't keep her attention on the show to save her life. She hadn't been very eager for Gage to start this remodeling process. It had been a topic that they disagreed on regularly over the past few weeks. Completing the project and making a real 'home' for the two of them together, meant to Ari, that she would be *officially* turning her back on God. She'd been fooling herself for the last few months, that the situation was just temporary. She knew better. But she wouldn't admit to anyone, that what she was doing was wrong, especially to Gage. If she even hinted to him that their living situation was a mistake, Gage would get angry.

Tonight, though, when Gage approached her with the blueprints, Ari had to admit she was thrilled. And now, she was lost in thought about her future, and giving herself permission to think about what it might look like. She pictured the two additional bedrooms being transformed into nurseries for their newborn sons or daughters. She could picture their dark haired, blue-eyed little girls, standing around that beautiful kitchen island that Gage had designed, rolling out dough for sugar cookies. She thought about how their little family would grow, not only in love, but in tiny hands and feet. It was everything she'd ever wanted.

Except, for just one thing. She wouldn't have God's blessing. Ari had to fight that consuming thought, every single day. To think, He would bless the mess she'd created and was living in, was absurd. And she had to wonder, how she could even consider bringing a child into the world, and *not* teach them about God? How could she teach her children about God, when she was living in sin with their father? The heavy weight of her choices, and what they'd cost her, felt like an anchor tied around her neck, pulling her deeper and deeper into a dark and lonely abyss.

And then there were her relationships with Beth and Sam. Ari had always pictured her two close friends playing a big roll in her children's lives. But, how would that be possible, if Ari wasn't on speaking terms with them? Lately, her friendship with Beth seemed more like seminary school than anything. Beth was always speaking scripture to her, and giving an opinion about her living situation. To Ari, it seemed the relationship had become more of a headache than it was worth. She no longer felt she had anything in common with Beth. And Sam? Well, he had been very vocal about his feelings with both Gage and herself. "'Shacking up' was not something the Lord would approve of," he'd told Gage. Sam then went on to tell Gage, that if he loved Ari, he should have already put a ring on her finger.

Even still, Sam and Beth both treated Gage fairly. To discuss any other topic *but* their living arrangement and church, you would think they actually liked him. Gage had definitely done his share of trying to convince them both, that he was the right man for her. Why couldn't they just be happy for her?

"Can you believe she won this round?" Gage cried out. "Even with her steak under-cooked. Man, I didn't see that coming, did you?"

"No, not at all." Ari pretended to pay attention long enough to convince him. But the truth was, her thoughts couldn't be further away. And, apparently, he wasn't buying her story. She should have known; he had always been able to get inside her mind, and figure out when she was upset or sad. He picked up the remote and muted the television, then wrapped an arm around her shoulders.

"You want to talk about what's bugging you?"

"I'm fine, Gage, really." She leaned her head against his chest, trying to avoid making eye contact.

"Bella, c'mon. You think I don't know that this whole birthday party thing is bugging you? I know it has to be upsetting you."

Great! Not this conversation again!

Ever since Gage had found Chloe's first birthday party invitation in the trash, where she had thrown it, he had been hounding her about going.

"Gage, not tonight, please." She rolled her eyes as she sighed and stood up. "I really don't want to have this conversation again. I *don't* want to go to the party!"

Gage's face turned beet red. Ari recognized that he was getting angry, as he also stood and came face to face with her.

"Bella, how do think this makes *me* feel? I know the only reason you aren't going to the party, is *me*. I don't want to be the reason that you don't go. Don't put me in that position, please."

"Gage, your name was on the invitation, too, and Beth made it clear that you were welcome. If you want to go so bad, then go. But as for me, I," she thrust her thumb towards her chest, "will be staying home!" She stormed to the other side of the room, needing to put distance between them. Why couldn't he just leave things alone? Couldn't he see, by bringing up the subject every day, it was only causing arguments between them?

"This is all because your friends don't think I'm good enough for you, and you know it. But I happen to know, you love that little girl. So, why are you letting them stop you from being a part of her celebration? It's her first birthday, Ari; you're her godmother."

"I don't know how many times I have to say it," she threw her hands up in the air. "I don't want to go to the party! Please drop it, okay?" Her resistance was wearing thin. She was tired of the bickering, tired of the fact, that every single day, she had to deal with the fact that the man she loved and her two best friends couldn't put aside their differences, putting her smack dab in the middle of all the friction. Most days she felt like calling it quits and walking away from everybody. This isn't how love should feel. It certainly wasn't how she thought it would be, anyway. Her parents had made it look so easy. Never, did she and her sister, witness a harsh word between them. Their two families always came together in love, without any arguing. Why did it have to be so difficult between she and Gage? It hadn't been like this in the beginning. Everything had been perfect until.......

And that was the answer she didn't want to face. One night had changed it all. And it would never be the same again.

Gage made his way across the room to where she stood. The anger he wore on his face, had morphed into empathy, by the look in his eyes.

"Bella, honey, won't you please reconsider?"

She wasn't strong enough to keep up the fight. At this point, she would do just about anything to avoid having this conversation one more time. When Gage wrapped his arms around her, like always, she found herself under his spell and unable to make her own decisions. Her strong front faded in mere seconds, as she succumbed to his touch. How was it that he could get her to do anything he wanted? When did she become such a weak person, unable to make decisions for herself? She relaxed, melting into his arms, the warmth of his chest against her face. Every last drop of her resistance, once again, slipped away.

"You'll go with me?"

"I don't have to, you know," he said as he kissed the top of her head. "I would be willing to stay home just to avoid a confrontation. I don't want to put you through that."

"Gage, if I go, you go. We are a couple; they have to realize that. So, will you go?"

"For you, I'll go. I love you, Bella." He pulled back, just far enough that he could look her in the eye. "I would do anything for you."

The atmosphere at the party, two weeks later, was strained. From the minute he and Ari rang the doorbell and Beth answered, Gage felt the chill in the air. Ari did her best to appear friendly with Beth through small talk, but it was evident to Gage, and more than likely everyone around them, of the distance between the two friends. A gap existed, that hadn't been there before Gage stepped into the picture.

The party was small, just a few close friends and both sets of Chloe's grandparents, who'd come into town for the occasion. The little girl had them all in stitches with her charming expressions, giggling and laughing with the opening of each gift. After presents, everyone gathered around the kitchen table to watch the birthday girl blow out her candle and attempt to eat her first cake. While the adults continued to cheer Chloe on, each time she stuck her finger in the frosting, Gage excused himself from the chaos to grab another soda from the back room.

"I'm glad I caught you alone, Gage. Could we talk for a minute?" Beth's voice quietly sounded behind him.

He shrugged, his back still to her, neither agreeing or disagreeing. He was unsure if he wanted to hear what Beth had to say to him. He'd known eventually this conversation with her would take place; she hadn't been shy about her dismay regarding his relationship with Ari, or his non-existent relationship with Christ. But today was supposed to be a happy day, celebrating Chloe's birthday. Not a day for confrontation.

Continuing with the forbidding tone, Beth asked, "Gage, what are you doing?" Gage turned from the ice-filled metal tub that held the sodas, popping the top off his drink.

"I'm getting a soda. What does it *look* like I'm doing, Beth?"

"That's not what I meant." She took two steps in his direction, "What are you doing to Arabella?"

Gage had all he could take. He'd been the nice guy, getting Ari to agree to come to the party. And now, Beth wanted to play mind games. He was over it! Refusing to back down, he retorted, "I'm not *doing* anything to her. We are in a relationship, Beth. I know that I don't live up to your standards, but I love Ari and she loves me. Why can't you just be happy for her? When I first came to town you were all crazy happy over the fact that we were dating. I don't get what everyone is making such a fuss about."

"Gage, I don't have a problem with you. I've always liked you. And, I like the thought of Ari being happy. But—"

"But what," Gage interrupted, "you don't think she's happy with me? Is that what this is about?"

Beth closed the gap between them, her words growing quieter, as she continued to speak. "Gage, I've known Ari her entire life. I have no doubt that she loves you. But my question is, are you what's good for her? Gage, she gave all of herself to you, and has now walked away from God. Her *whole life* was wrapped around the promise she'd made to him, then you come along, and all of a sudden she throws everything away."

"*Throws everything away*? Is that what you think, Beth?" Gage felt the anger brewing inside him. This conversation was heading south very quickly, and he no longer wanted to be a part of it. Maybe he'd been wrong, after all, for encouraging Ari to come to the party. He'd surely never understand how people claiming to be Ari's 'friends,' could treat her so unkindly. If that's what following God looked like, then he was right to steer far away from it. "You think Ari is throwing her life away, by choosing to stay with me?"

"What did you just say?"

A pin drop could've been heard in the eerie silence. Gage looked up, at the same time Beth spun around, stunned to see Arabella standing in the doorway.

Ari's fists were clenched at her sides, anger contorted her face. "Beth, I asked you a question!" Ari took one step closer towards the two of them. "*What* did you just say to Gage?"

This was not going like Gage had planned. He had hoped differences could be set aside for Chloe's birthday party, but it didn't seem to be happening. It was the first time he had ever seen Ari this mad, and he felt solely responsible for the scene unfolding around him. He had to get her out of here, and away from Beth's scrutiny. "Bella, maybe we should just go. This obviously wasn't a good idea." Gage took a step in Ari's direction, hoping he could calm her down and usher her out, without a scene. But Ari wouldn't even look at him. Her attention was focused on one thing. Beth.

"You think I threw my life away to be with him? He *is* my life, Beth! And if you insist on treating him this way, then there is no room in my life for *you*! Gage, let's go. *Now*!" Ari turned around and stormed out of the room, leaving Gage to follow behind, and Beth begging and pleading with her to stay.

"Ari, please," Beth cried out, "I didn't mean it like that."

Gage brushed past Beth as he caught up to Ari, who apparently wasn't willing to listen to her best friend any longer. He couldn't blame her one bit. Not after today. It was almost bittersweet for Gage. On the one hand, he didn't like the fact that Ari was being hurt by those claiming to love her. But, on the other hand, it did feel kind of nice that a message was being sent to Beth and Sam that the god they had their lives wrapped around, was not really a fix all. God couldn't hold together one lousy friendship, yet they trusted him to solve all of their problems. He'd been right all along thinking he didn't need God, and now Ari would see that too.

Not willing to give up when Ari didn't respond, Beth continued to plead with her. "Ari, all I'm saying is that your relationship with God should be the most important thing in your life. That's what you've always wanted." Beth's pursuit continued through the house, past all of the party guests staring wide-eyed, but stopped at the front door. Gage continued to follow Ari through the doorway and down the sidewalk towards the car.

Beth yelled out once more, pleading with Ari to listen. "Ari, you can walk away from me, but don't walk away from God! Please!"

The slamming of Gage's car door was the only response Beth got. Gage quickly scooted around to the driver's side and joined Ari. The short ride back to Francesca's was filled with silence, allowing him to process the things that Beth had spoken.

You came along and she threw everything away. Is that what everyone really thinks? That I will never be good enough for Ari? Or any of them for that matter. How can people who claim to be loving, treat others this way?

Gage just couldn't shake Beth's words from his mind. He knew that Ari had made sacrifices to be with him, but wasn't sacrifice a part of every relationship? He'd undeniably sacrificed by staying in Rock Haven, forfeiting his time in Iowa and carrying the burden of running a satellite office for his business back in New York. And why would Beth think that Ari was 'throwing everything away?' Just because she didn't go to church anymore? You didn't need church to have a relationship with someone. All you needed was love. And he and Ari definitely loved each other. Didn't they? Doubt slowly crept in, pushing its way into the empty spaces of his heart, and forming a dark shadow of uncertainty over his mind. Gage pondered another thought. Did *Ari* think she was throwing her life away to be with him? The small sliver of skepticism began to increase, growing deeper and wider until it was impossible to ignore. He had to confront her.

When they arrived home, Gage was expecting Ari to fall apart, to cry in his arms over how her friends had abandoned her, and how they didn't understand her relationship with him. However, they no sooner walked through the door and Ari turned to him, wrapping her arms around his neck and pulling him into a deep and passionate kiss. A kiss that told him *she* was willing to forfeit some things, if that's what it took to be with him.

Breathless and stunned, he held her tight against him, not willing to let go. "Bella, are you sure this is what you want?"

Ari's eyes glistened with tears as she looked into his, and he hoped they were tears of joy. "Gage, you are *all* that I want. If loving you means losing my friends because they are blind to the fact that we are a couple, then that's their loss."

"You don't really believe that you're throwing your life away to be with me, do you?"

Ari didn't respond with words. She simply reached for his hand and pulled him down the hall to the bedroom that they shared, convincing him that she knew exactly what she was doing, and that he was all she needed to be happy.

Chapter 16

As summer slowly gave way to fall, there was a notable change, and not just in the weather. The leaves began to turn from a luscious summer green, to rich shades of red and orange. With the tourist season slowing fading, Ari had much more time on her hands. Especially now that she was no longer participating in her Wednesday bible study group, or volunteering to help with childcare on Thursdays for pastoral staff meetings. Her new favorite way to spend free time, was wedding planning. Her own, of course. She'd Googled every wedding site available online, taking plenty of notes about her favored wedding dress style, theme choice, and bridal party colors. She even looked at wedding venues close to Rock Haven. Her notebook was spilling over with ideas, and those ideas had been scattered throughout the loft. The problem? Gage wanted nothing to do with her notebook, or any talk of marriage. And that, was putting a damper on their relationship, to say the least. He had conveyed to her countless times, his thoughts on marriage. And there was nothing positive about it. Why, he'd ask, couldn't she just relax and live in the moment, enjoying what they had?

"C'mon Ari," he tugged at her arm trying to dissuade her, "let's not have this conversation again tonight!"

They'd just left the movie theatre and were walking home, enjoying, possibly one of the last warm evenings of fall. It had been a fall unlike any Ari had ever experienced. She and Gage had done a lot of the traditional things Ari was used to doing alone. Like going to the apple orchard, for example, and picking bushels of Honey Crisp apples that she would use to serve fresh apple pies and crisps in the restaurant. They also picked out over twenty potted mums, to decorate the exterior and deck of Francesca's. What made this year so much better, was the fact that she was doing it with the love of her life. Getting lost in the cornfield maze after dark, with two strong arms to cling to, didn't seem quite as scary. And nothing could have been more romantic than the hayride they'd gone on. Snuggling under a blanket, with Gage's arm wrapped tight around her. The smell of a bonfire hung in the air, as the rickety wagon made its way through the woods. Yes, it had been one of the best seasons of her life; as long as she avoided that *specific* topic, that Gage wanted nothing to do with. This year, fall had been unseasonably warm, right up until last week. But, even with the slight chill in the air, tonight was a beautiful evening. Just right for a nice, quiet walk home.

Unfortunately, nice and quiet were not going to happen.

Planting herself firmly in place and, refusing to give in to his insistence, she kept her eyes focused on the brilliantly shining ring in the window display. "Why are you so set against looking, Gage? She argued. "It's just a ring."

He stopped and turned towards her, the anger on his face undisputable, as their eyes were drawn to one another's. "Just a ring, Ari? Who are you trying to fool? I'm not buying the 'just a ring' story!"

The icy tone of his words sent a chill down her spine.

"That ring you're dreaming about, comes with the 'perfect wedding' and a 'happily ever after,' that I don't have for you."

"Gage, why—"

"Enough, Ari!" Taken aback by his abruptness, Ari could only stare, wide-eyed, at Gage, as the shards of her broken heart cut deep into her soul.

Gage brought his hand to his forehead and pinched the bridge of his nose, as he paced forward three steps and then back to her again. Ari could see that he was struggling with his frustration. He was mad; and Ari had rarely seen this side of him. The Gage she had fallen in love with, was fun and enjoyable to be around, encouraging and lighthearted. But not angry. And lately, he had been angry a lot.

Without another word, Ari slinked past him and made her way towards home. Alone. Gage pathetically trailed along, a notable distance behind her. Neither one spoke a word until they were home, where Gage broke the silence. Ari heard the front door close behind him.

"Bella, I'm sorry."

Ari didn't want to hear the regret in his words, or the compassion in his tone. All the way home, she had been condemning him for his part in the disagreement. Blaming him was always easier than accepting her own responsibility in the matter. To be fair, she had never even hinted about getting married until a couple of weeks ago. How could Gage have even know how desperately she wanted a family? Their relationship had been contrastive from the very start, and they seemed to be polar opposites no matter what the topic. Now she had to wonder if maybe she was wrong for bringing up the topic of marriage. Maybe she'd pushed him too far. Then again, maybe she *should* push him harder, to get to the heart of the topic. How could they even continue their relationship if he absolutely refused marriage and children?

Ari felt him draw near to her, his strong arms linking around her waist. Gently, he turned her in his arms, tucking a strand of her hair behind her ear.

"It's just, I thought you knew how I felt about marriage. Growing up with my father always talking negatively about it, I think marriage is the scariest thing I'll ever have to face. I don't understand why you want to rush into something, when we're happy with things just the way they are? You are happy with me, *aren't* you?"

Without answering, Ari pulled away. She took a seat on the couch, inviting him to join her as she pulled her legs up into crisscross position and turned to face him. "Of course, I'm happy with you, Gage." She placed her hand on his leg and leaned in closer to him, desperately trying to communicate her feelings. "I love you. You know that. But what's next for us? Don't you ever think about starting a family and settling down?"

"A family? You're seriously going to start adding that to the mix now?" Gage pushed her hand off his leg and stood up. "Ari, we've only been together for five months. Why can't you just relax and slow down a bit? I'm working two jobs and trying to renovate this place into something for us. Isn't that enough on my plate for now?"

He'd been complaining for the past couple of weeks that he felt overwhelmed, trying to keep up with all the bids he'd been receiving in Rock Haven, while still trying to manage the office back in New York. Initially, Ari had encouraged him to keep up with his painting and sketching, but now it felt like all she did was complain that he didn't have enough time for *her*. She wanted to be with him every second of every day. After all, he was all she had to focus on now. She'd given up everything else in her life—for him. Didn't he understand that?

"Slow down? That sounds funny coming from you, Gage. Mister 'I'm ready to take our relationship to the next level,' after knowing me less than two months! After all I've given to you, and *for* you, how dare you ask *me* to slow down!"

She could tell by the flash of anger across his face that she'd done it. She'd pushed too far.

"When are you ever going to let that die, Ari? You were in that bed right along with me, making your own choice to sleep with me, and you continue to do so! I *never* forced myself on you! And you've told me that over and over! So, how dare you change your attitude about it now! Just to try and get me to give in to what you want! I've had all I can take from you about this subject! If you want me out of your life, just say the words, and I'm gone! That way, you don't have to live with the shame and regret that you apparently feel every time you look in my eyes!"

Gage stormed towards the front door and Ari's heart leaped inside her chest. What had she done? Why had she pushed him when she knew he didn't want to discuss it? Would he really walk away from her so easily? She couldn't take that chance. Couldn't let him leave her after all that she had given. He was her entire world now.

"Gage! Please, don't," she begged through her tears, "I'm sorry." She stood up and made her way to him, but he refused to turn away from the door, even as she placed her arms around his waist, and leaned against his back, her tears soaking through his shirt. "You're right about everything," her voice shook. "I........I didn't mean to say those things. I'll never bring it up again. I promise."

She felt the muscles in his arm tighten as he continued to grip the door handle. He inhaled a deep breath as she clung to him, paralyzed with fear. "Gage, please don't leave me. I'm begging you. I love you so much."

Gage spun around and wrapped his arm around the back of her neck, pulling her into a deep kiss with a possessiveness like she had never felt from him. When he finally released his grip on her and pulled back, he simply stared at her. Stared at the tears sliding down her cheeks, and her lips, rosy and swollen from his kiss. His steely-eyed look said everything that he was thinking. She was his and only his.

"I need to know, Ari, once and for all, that you love me, and that you don't regret being with me. I need you to show me."

Ari knew, when it came right down to it, that she would do anything, *and* everything, to make Gage stay. Even if that meant giving up on her dream of a marriage and children. Gage owned her heart.

Reaching for his hand, Ari silently pulled Gage down the hall to the bedroom, where she showed him everything he needed to know. She loved Gage. And Gage loved her. And neither one of them was strong enough to say no to having each other. No matter what the cost.

His mind was definitely not on work. Gage shuffled the invoices on his desk one more time before pushing them aside. He'd been unable to concentrate on anything this morning. Anything besides his relationship with Ari. He pushed his chair back and stood up from behind his desk, pacing the floor for the third time this morning. He'd asked himself the same question a thousand times.

How did this relationship with Ari spiral out of control so quickly? Talk of marriage and children? That isn't for me. But, how can I walk away from her? She controls my every thought, every desire.

Gage had never known feelings like this even existed. Feelings so strong, so raw and powerful, that they controlled your thought.

Last night, in the heat of their argument, he had every intention of walking out on Ari. Certainly, he was strong enough to get through the break up and get his life back on track. Yet, when she'd wrapped her arms around him, and he'd felt her tears through his shirt, something inside of him snapped. How could he leave her when he loved her so much?

Gage was trying his hardest not to do one more thing he'd regret. But what would he regret more? Walking away from the only woman he'd ever loved, and going back to his old ways? Spending life single and miserable, using women like he had before? Working day in and day out and not taking time to enjoy the passing time? Or, would he regret embracing Ari's request for marriage and children? It seemed no matter what his decision, there was bound to be a lot of pain involved.

When Ari pulled him into their bedroom last night, he was confident that she was finished second-guessing their relationship. They'd shared something strong and powerful, and Gage knew then, that his heart would always belong to Arabella. He continued to wonder, though, could she ever really forgive herself for loving him? And could he live with what he'd taken from her? Would their relationship ever be able to withstand the turmoil their decisions had brought to it? He thought about what his life had been like before he met her. How empty and lonely it had been. If only they could get back to how it was when they first met. Before he asked her to go against everything she'd ever stood for.

All talk of marriage and babies disappeared. Once again, Arabella found herself settling into a comfortable routine. She'd all but given up on her dreams of marrying Gage and having a large family, and had begun to accept the fact that she would never find her way back to the woman she used to be. She'd made her choices, and this was who she was. She belonged to Gage. Heart, mind, body and soul. It seemed there was no room for anyone or anything else, even those she loved the most. Ironically, she was the happiest she'd ever been, and the saddest she'd ever been. All at the same time, if that made any sense.

The holiday season was upon them. Arabella was happy to focus her attention on that, while Gage completed the loft renovations and small jobs in town. All while he still managed to run his New York office.

She and Gage spent their first Thanksgiving alone in the loft, filling up on the turkey and fixings they had prepared together in their new kitchen. They watched the Macy's day parade in the morning, and later settled in to watch the Detroit Lions square off with the Chicago Bears. She was shocked to hear Gage's confession about how he and his father usually spent the holiday.

"I can't believe you've never made a turkey dinner! What did you and your father eat on Thanksgiving?" Ari asked as she shoved the ten-pound turkey into the oven.

"It was nothing big for us to celebrate," he shrugged as walked past her and towards the refrigerator. "Just a day that my old man didn't go to the office. We usually bought a pre-cooked dinner and had it delivered. But—," he pulled the small plate of deviled eggs from the second shelf of the refrigerator and snagged one from the plate before she could stop him, "once in a while, when I got lucky, dad would forget to order it in time and we'd have to eat Chinese." He stuffed the entire egg in his mouth without an ounce of shame.

Ari shook her head in disbelief. "Gage, you can't be serious. *Chinese* for Thanksgiving? That's un-American."

Past Thanksgivings, and the wonderful memories they held, pushed their way into Ari's mind. It had been her mother's favorite holiday. Ari could still remember how excited she and her sister would get the evening before the holiday, as they were allowed to stay up late to help with the preparations. She and Maria would assist their mother with making the deviled eggs, and baking fresh pumpkin and apple pies. Then, they would rise very early the next morning, in time to enjoy Mama's homemade cinnamon rolls, and help prepare the dressing to stuff the turkey, which was always a much bigger bird than their small family needed. Mama always fixed enough for an army. "Just in case," she'd say, with that sparkle in her eye. She made sure that nobody in Rock Haven spent the holiday alone, or without a good warm meal. It was the memory of what happened *after* the big dinner, and the dishes washed and put away, that brought a bigger smile to Ari's face. Tradition in their home, was game night. Anything from Dominoes to Checkers, to Phase 10, and even Yahtzee. Whether it was just the four of them, or a houseful of guests, it was always a deep-belly laughing, knee-slapping, good time for everyone.

After her mother and sister were killed, traditions changed. She and her father began celebrating the holidays with Sam and Karen's family, along with Beth and Anthony. It was different and new, but it was what held she and her father together through those first few, very rough, years. As Sam's children grew up and began to have kids of their own, the small gathering grew into a much bigger one, and with it, a lot of laughter and chaos.

This year was definitely going to be different. Although Ari was happy to be sharing a quiet dinner with Gage, she did miss the excitement and pandemonium that went hand in hand with Sam's large family. More than anything, she missed her best friend, and the memories they shared of past holidays. Ari only hoped that someday again, she'd have a houseful of family and friends to share her special times with.

Gage responded to her nonchalantly, "When you grow up doing it, it seems normal. You just accept it for what it is. When my mom was alive, she always made a big dinner. I think."

"Oh, Gage, I'm so sorry." Ari walked the length of the kitchen and wrapped her arms around his waist in a hug. "I hope from this year forward, you will have better memories of the holidays." She stepped back to look into his eyes. Suddenly, her memories of past Thanksgiving dinners were once again filed away. Recognizing how lucky she was to have them, she knew how much this Thanksgiving would mean to Gage. If it meant not being with the rest of those she loved, then so be it. She was going to make sure, in the future, that Gage always had holiday memories to reflect on.

"Ari, I've already made so many happy memories with you! Many more than I had ever made in my life *before* I came to Rock Haven."

After a quick kiss on her nose from Gage, Ari busied herself with kitchen clean up as he disappeared into the living room.

"I was at that parade last year," she heard him call out. Drying her hands on a kitchen towel, Ari walked into the living room, where Gage sat staring at the television, and took a seat on the arm of the couch.

"Do you miss New York, Gage? You never really talk much about it. Or about your life there." Ari had been relieved to find out last week, that he wasn't going to renew the lease on his condo out east when it expired. He'd had a few things shipped out to Michigan, but the majority of his belongings had been packed and put into storage by the moving company he'd hired.

Gage leaned back, crossing one leg over the other. "I think I miss what I had in New York at one time, when my mom was still alive, and the three of us were happy. But after I lost her, it didn't feel much like a home. I know my dad did the best he could, and I love him; but the farm almost seemed more like home to me. Even though I only stayed there during the summers. There's just something about that place."

Ari was struck, once again, by what a sad and lonely life Gage must have had growing up. They hadn't talked much about it before now; and Ari's heart broke at the thought. The holidays had always been a favorite time for her family. Living in the small town that they did, everyone looked out for one another. So more often than not, there were extra guests around their large dining table. Her parents had always taught her and Maria to love the lost and broken, just like Jesus. And they definitely led by example. It was what made their house a home, and their restaurant a success. They loved everyone and anyone. Ari couldn't imagine growing up without an entire town that loved her, and that she loved back.

It was then, that Ari was struck with the idea of what to give Gage for Christmas. She was going to make sure this was the happiest Christmas he'd ever had. She only hoped no other "issues" came out of the woodwork in the midst of it all. The wheels began to turn in her mind as she formulated a plan.

Later that afternoon, she asked Gage to carve the turkey while she set out the rest of the side dishes. As they stood back and looked at their table full of food, they realized they had prepared more food than the two of them could eat in a week.

"Well, better too much than not enough, right?" Gage laughed. "I've got a few years to make up for!"

"I wanted everything to be perfect for you, Gage." She reached for his hand as they stood side by side staring at the feast.

"Ari, you have outdone yourself. Everything looks so delicious! I can't wait to dig in. C'mon!" He pulled her to the table, and held out her chair before seating himself directly across from her. They enjoyed a quiet dinner by candlelight, loaded the dishwasher, put leftovers away, and eventually found their way back to the couch, stuffed beyond a comfortable amount.

"I think I will skip the pumpkin pie tonight," Ari patted her too full tummy.

"You can't skip *dessert,* Ari. That's the best part of the meal!" But long before Gage went back to the kitchen for pie, Ari had fallen fast asleep. She had curled up on the couch in an afghan, dreaming about the Christmas present she was going to give Gage.

Five blocks away, as they cleaned up from another fantastic Thanksgiving dinner at Sam's, Beth and Anthony were elbow-deep in conversation over a sink full of dirty dishes.

"She's just pretending to be happy, you know." Beth scrubbed the dinner plate in her hand a little harder than necessary. Ari's absence from their "family" Thanksgiving dinner had weighed on her mind all day.

As tears threatened to spill from her eyes, Anthony laid the dish towel on the counter and turned to her, taking her wet and soapy hands into his. "Honey, I know this hurts you, but Ari is a big girl. She has to find her way on her own."

"She hasn't missed a Thanksgiving meal with her 'family,'" Beth motioned to their beloved friends gathered around the table, playing a game of cards, "since her mom and sister passed away."

Anthony pulled his wife into a hug and whispered into her ear. "You have to let this go, Beth, or it's going to drive you crazy! You can't control her decisions." Anthony released her from his grip and took a step back. "Besides, maybe she's happy with her choices. And you do want her to be happy, *don't* you?"

"How can you say that, Anthony? You know as well as I do, that Ari can't possibly be happy living her life this way!" Beth didn't realize how escalated her voice had become, until she saw a tableful of stares aimed in her direction.

"Sorry!" She called out to them, and then took a couple of steps deeper into the kitchen, hoping nobody but Anthony would hear.

"I don't know why she's continuing with this farce," she mumbled, turning back towards the sink.

"People change, Beth. I never thought Ari would be one to do it, but she's definitely not who she used to be."

Beth reached back into the sudsy water, thinking on that for a moment. It didn't sit well with her. And it didn't take long for her to figure that out.

"No! You're wrong," she shook her head. "Ari's the same person deep down inside. She's just choosing to walk a different path right now. A path God wouldn't have chosen for her. A path that's going to lead her right into heartache."

"Never the less, you don't have a say in the matter, honey. I know you miss her and want the best for her, but this situation is in her hands."

"Ugh," Beth grumbled as she scrubbed another dirty plate. "I wish that man had never set foot in this town! He is nothing like the man Ari dreamed of marrying someday."

"He must be something like she wanted or she wouldn't be with him, Beth."

"I have to disagree." Beth dropped a dirty fork back into the sink and turned to Anthony again. "She's just settling! She was tired of being alone. That's what all of this is about."

"Beth—"

"Anthony," she interrupted, her voice an angry whisper, "since we were old enough to know what being married was about, Ari wanted a man like her father. A godly man! *And,* she has always dreamed of getting married on the beach, with me as her maid of honor, and having an entire house full of children." Beth shifted her weight and put a hand to her hip. With a smirk on her face, she asked, "I don't see that dream coming true anytime soon, do you?"

"Probably not so much the maid of honor thing," Anthony smiled.

"You're impossible, you know that?" Beth grinned in her husband's direction. Then, rolling up the dishtowel in her hands, swatted him on the behind.

"It made you laugh, didn't it?" He caught her by the wrist, just as she was about to flick the towel on him again, and pulled her into a hug.

"What did I ever do to deserve you? You always know just what I need." Beth leaned her forehead against her husbands and sighed, knowing somehow, someday, that everything would work out. Because there was no doubt in her mind that God was ultimately in control. It just might not unfold in the time frame she would like.

Chapter 17

G*age and Ari landed in* Des Moines three weeks later. He had been completely caught off guard when, two days after Thanksgiving, Ari handed him a beautifully wrapped gift box. He'd barely had time to wake up that morning, lounging on the couch with his morning coffee. But the minute he realized what he was holding, he jumped up and went to her, pulling her into a hug and lifting her off the ground.

"Bella, I can't believe you thought of this for me!" His voice crackled with emotion. It was more than anyone had ever done for him. This was a gift that came straight from her heart. As he looked into her eyes, the happiness he felt seeped deep into his soul.

"Are you *sure* you want to spend our first Christmas together in Iowa? We don't have to, you know. We can spend it alone, just the two of us, right here." He'd set her back on the ground, but his enthusiasm hadn't dwindled. Being at the farm for Christmas would be, well it would be, the *best* thing in the world. To share it with the woman he loved, was even better. Things had been strained between them lately, although Ari would never admit that anything was wrong when he asked. Gage knew that the distance between them was partly his fault, with Ari's talk of marriage and babies scaring him half to death. Maybe this trip would be just what they needed to help get their focus back on each other, and *only* each other.

Ari nodded and took his hand in hers, drawing his attention back to their conversation.

"Gage, I love you and I know how much you long to be on the farm. Of course, I want to spend our first Christmas there."

Once again, he was astounded by Ari's generosity. Especially after he'd been so cold to her lately. Her talk of marriage and babies had really thrown him for a loop, and he knew he was handling the topic less than ideally.

"Why, Bella?" He saw the confusion in her beautiful green eyes, so he continued. "Why," he placed the palm of his hand gently against her cheek, "do you love me so much? I don't deserve you."

And he knew that was the truth. As much as he wanted to, Gage couldn't convince himself that he would ever be deserving of her love, or enough of a man to keep her happy. From the minute he'd shown up in Rock Haven, he'd done nothing but greedily take from her, and she had so willingly given. She deserved a man that could give in return, and he wasn't foolish enough to think he was the one to do it.

"Oh, Gage," she placed her hand over his, "why would you ask such a silly question? I love you for so many reasons."

He'd been wise enough to leave it at that and not press any harder, fearing the real truth would be exposed. The truth that he knew without a doubt, but Arabella had locked away and refused to acknowledge. The simple truth that she deserved a man that could, and would, give her so much more.

It had been a long three weeks, full of anticipation. And, even now, as they made their way into the airport terminal, his excitement grew once again at thought of Nonnie's reaction. Yes, this was definitely going to be the best Christmas he ever had!

Max picked the two of them up from the airport that afternoon, and they rushed back to the farm to get everything in place for the big surprise. Gage was getting more excited as he watched Ari go over all the last-minute details. With her coaching, and a little help from some of Nonnie's friends, they all had convinced Nonnie to spend the day in town, doing some Christmas shopping with the girls. Gage had made dinner reservations for four at one of the nicer restaurants in town, unbeknownst to Nonnie, who thought it was going to be a quiet dinner for two. Just she and Max. Nonnie's friends had been kind enough to agree, and keep her busy until they would drop her off to meet Max for dinner at six.

Once they arrived back at the ranch, Gage suggested Ari quickly jump into the shower to freshen up while he got the luggage unloaded. Ari had been telling him all day that she couldn't wait to finally wear the cowboy boots Max had purchased for her on their last trip out to the farm. She'd found the perfect skirt and blouse to match, and was thrilled about going out tonight.

Standing just outside of the bedroom doorway, with the last of the luggage, Gage stopped for a moment and took the opportunity to watch Ari, as she sat at the vanity applying her makeup, her wet hair twisted up in a towel. She was the prettiest woman he'd ever known. He still couldn't get over the fact that she'd planned this trip for he and his Nonnie. Never, had he met a woman with such a kind heart. Knowing they would be late for dinner if they didn't get moving, Gage broke from his reverie, and made his way into the room.

"Well, aren't you going to be the cutest cowgirl in the world tonight?" Ari jumped, as Gage snuck up behind her and bent to nuzzle her neck. "Mmmm, you certainly *smell* better than a real cowgirl who's been out wrangling horses all day. Maybe we have enough time to—"

"Gage, you better hurry up and get your shower." She playfully swatted him on the arm. "We can't be late getting to the restaurant, or we'll blow Nonnie's surprise!"

He raised his eyebrows at her teasingly. "What if I said I changed my mind, and I want to stay home with you instead?" He flirted with her in his typical playful way, and for a moment, judging by the dreamy look in her eyes, thought she would give in.

Okay, maybe not! Ari's beautiful face quickly morphed into that of a drill sergeant.

"Gage, you get in that shower right now! We'll have plenty of time alone tonight *after* dinner." Ari swatted him on the behind and nudged him a little less than gently.

"Your clean towel is on the sink!" she informed him, as he grudgingly dragged his feet in the direction of the shower.

"Can't blame a guy for trying!" He called out over his shoulder. He heard Ari's giggle in response just as he stepped under the hot spray of the shower.

Nonnie and Max had just been seated and given their refreshments, when Gage and Arabella made their appearance. His Nonnie couldn't have been more surprised, or happy, judging by the gleam in her eyes.

"Could we interest you in one of the specials tonight, ma'am?"

"Oh, young man, you don't have to call me ma—" she froze in her seat as she looked up to see her grandson, holding a menu in his hand.

"June Bug, what are you doing here?" She stood up from her seat, immediately wrapping her arms around his neck, as tears streamed down her face.

"Arabella wanted us to spend Christmas together, Nonnie. Isn't this the best present ever?"

Nonnie released him from her embrace and looked over his shoulder at the woman behind him. "Oh, Arabella, what an amazing gift for us all. Thank you so much, dear."

"And *you*," she turned back towards the table, her wrinkled finger pointing directly at her best friend and ranch hand, "Maxwell! You were in on this surprise all along, weren't you?" She might have pretended to be upset, but she couldn't fool a one of them. Gage had never seen his grandmother look so happy.

Slowly, Max raised his hand in acknowledgement. "But I can tell from that smile you gave your grandson just now, that I am already forgiven."

They had a wonderful evening, the four of them. Gage excitedly shared all the details of the loft that he was renovating into a home for he and Ari, and he let Nonnie and Max in on the secret that he was painting and enjoying photography as much as he could in the little spare time that he had.

"Gage, it does my heart good to see you this happy. To hear that you're painting," her hand went over her heart as she turned from him to look at Arabella. "Oh, sweetie, you have made my grandson so happy. Thank you for sharing your life with him." Gage recognized the tears that were forming in Ari's eyes. He reached for her hand underneath the table, and gave it a gentle squeeze of encouragement.

"Nonnie, Gage has made me happier than I ever thought possible. And to have you and Max in my life, well, that is just an extra blessing."

Gage had to wonder if he was the only one seeing the holes in that statement, or if Nonnie and Max were sensitive to the change between he and Ari as well. He'd never been able to hide anything from the two of them. Gage finally relaxed in his seat as Max and Nonnie gave updates about the farm and all that was happening in their small community. Back at the farm later, long after Max went home and Nonnie had turned in for the evening, Gage and Ari sat by the fire in the family room. Gage pulled her close and draped his arm around her shoulder, as she rested her head against his chest.

"Arabella, thank you again for this Christmas gift." He leaned down and placed a kiss on the top of her head.

"You're welcome, Gage. I'm just glad we could pull off the surprise for Nonnie." Ari sat up straight and turned to him, wearing a huge smile. "Did you see the look on her face when she realized it was you asking to take her order and not a waiter?"

"Yeah, that was priceless," he shook his head. "And it was all possible because of you." He turned sideways and gently held Ari's soft cheek in his hand. "I don't know what I ever did to deserve you Bella, but I love you. I hope you know that."

"Are you okay, Gage? You've seemed a little distracted ever since we got off the plane this afternoon."

Gage turned away from her and leaned back against the couch, staring at the wall across the room as he took in a deep breath and exhaled, barely able to speak around the thick emotion in his throat.

"I'm fine, Arabella. I guess I'm just sentimental about this old place. It just feels so good to be here. To be home."

How did he tell her what had really been running through his mind from the minute the plane had touched down?

Home. The way he said the word caused a stirring in Arabella's soul. And not in a good way. She had known from the day they met, what the farm meant to Gage; and she was quite aware that he felt more at home here than in New York. But for the first time, she had to wonder if maybe the farm was more of a home to him than the loft back in Michigan, too. The doubts that she'd been trying to ignore for the past several weeks, crept into her thoughts once again. She'd had this talk with herself more than one time. The talk where she tried to convince herself that she and the little town of Rock Haven could hold onto a man like Gage. He was used to women with a lot more experience, and so much more to offer than she could ever dream of. He was used to the fast pace of New York City, and all that came with it. Some days, it took all the strength she had just to convince herself she was good enough for him. Then, there were the days when she tried to tell herself that she wanted more than him. She wanted a man that was ready to settle down and get married, raise a family together, and Gage was definitely not that kind of man. But those silly conversations she carried on in her head, were quickly squashed by the absolute love that she felt for the man she had given so much to.

Ready to focus on her current surroundings and not the past, Ari leaned back against the couch, once again leaning her head on Gage's shoulder. "I could sit by this warm fire all night long," she sighed happily.

"Well," Gage chuckled quietly, "don't get too comfortable. We have to get bed soon. We've got a big day ahead of us tomorrow."

Ari sat up and turned to face him, unaware of any plans that had been made. "We do, huh? Mind filling me in on that?"

"Nope. You're going to have to wait until tomorrow." When he stood up, he reached for her hand. "C'mon, let's head upstairs."

Ari wouldn't budge. Planting herself in place, she waited for Gage to realize she wasn't following him. Finally, after he'd made it all the way to the stairs, Gage turned to her. "Are you coming or not?"

"Not until you tell me what our plans are for tomorrow."

"Ari, it's late. I don't have time for this." He reached out his hand again, beckoning her to follow. "I promise it will be worth the wait."

The sly grin he gave her was all it took. In seconds, she was right behind him as they made their way to their room.

The next afternoon, following lunch, she and Gage set out to find the perfect Christmas tree for Nonnie's. She hadn't been surprised to learn that Gage, like herself, had always had an artificial tree growing up. It looked to be a milestone event for both of them. The temperature was brutally cold, but with the sun shining brightly in the sky and glistening on the snow, it was a picture-perfect day. She and Gage trekked through the snow in their boots, hats, and gloves, that they'd purchased in town that morning, along with the handsaw Gage carried to cut the tree with. For over thirty minutes, they had been searching for just the right one, when Gage called out.

"This is it! Ari come quick, I've found it!"

Ari scrambled through the maze of trees between them, until she came to a stop next to Gage, who stood admiring a beautiful, eight-foot, Douglas Fir. Ari inspected its fullness from all angles, carefully checking for any uneven spots or broken branches, and gave her two thumbs up approval before Gage took the saw to the trunk of it. By the time they hauled the eight-foot beast with its thick, full branches back to Max's truck, she was exhausted. Bent over, with her hands on her knees, and trying to catch her breath, Ari heard Gage's laughter. She stood up and looked at him in wonder.

"What....is...so....funny?" She finally choked out the last word in between gasps for air.

"You! You're what's funny. I figured with all the jogging on the beach that you do, this little hike would be nothing."

"*Little hike*?" She glared at him, slightly irritated by his words. "Are you kidding me, Gage? That was more than a little hike. I can't believe you're not out of breath."

Gage closed the distance between them, removing his gloves in the process, and stood mere inches from her.

"Do you have any idea how beautiful you are right now?"

"Beautiful?" Now it was her turn to chuckle. "Has the cold air gotten to your brain, Gage? You can't possibly think that red-faced, out of breath, hat hair is beautiful."

"Your eyes are brighter in the cold. And your cheeks," he brushed his thumb against one side of her face, "are rosy pink from the chill in the air. You are so beautiful, Ari."

She felt the warmth of embarrassment rush to her cheeks, but remained silent, savoring his touch.

"Arabella, I don't think you will ever realize just how happy you make me."

"It's just a tree, Gage. Why so sentimental all of a sudden?" Ari looked at him in wonder.

"It's more than a tree, Bella. It's the fact that we're doing it, *together*. You and me. I've never shared so much with anyone."

The smile on Ari's face grew until it reached her eyes. And did she ever need to smile. This trip, although exactly what she wanted, was more nerve racking than she thought it would be. Her mind was constantly being pulled back to the day she'd encountered Jenna at the ranch. Because of that, just being in Iowa left a bittersweet taste in Ari's mouth. It was one of the most painful days she could pull from her file of memories. Everything from the girl's stunning, flaming red hair, to her trim figure, and pretty face, Jenna seemed to find her way into Ari's thoughts more often than not. She could remember every minute detail of that day, beginning with the perfect weather she and Gage had enjoyed while eating their picnic lunch out in the open field, and ending with Gage begging and pleading with her to stay at the ranch with him. Ari would never be able to erase from her mind, the sadness on the faces of Nonnie and Max as they sat at the kitchen table, waiting for the verdict. Even though Gage vehemently denied that there was ever real feelings on his part, Ari couldn't help but wonder if being back in Iowa affected Gage the way it was affecting her. Did he long to see Jenna again? Did he think of Jenna as often as she did? Had he taken it a step further and called Jenna since they'd been back in town?

She had to stop thinking like this or it would drive her crazy. Forcing herself to once again forget the past and think only of the moment she currently shared with Gage, Ari responded to his comment.

"Gage, I love sharing my life with you. I wouldn't have it any other way. Don't you know that by now?" Ari reached over to wipe the sweat running down the side of his face, but Gage grabbed her wrist in his hand and brought it to his mouth.

Looking deep into her eyes with a seriousness that Ari had rarely seen in him, Gage replied. "I get scared sometimes, Ari, that you're going to stop loving me. That this is just a dream, and one day you're going to change your mind. I don't think I could go on without your love. Promise me, Ari, no matter what happens between us, you will *never* stop loving me."

Ari chuckled at his absurd request. When would he ever realize she wasn't going anywhere. She was in it for life. "Gage, I could never stop loving you. Until I breathe my last breath, my heart will always belong to you."

Her answer seemed to satisfy him. He drew her in and kissed her gently on the lips, then walked to the front of the truck and opened the door for her. Gage held her hand the entire drive home, and Ari noticed that this time, he held it with a stronger grip, as if to let her know she could never escape him. Instead of it bothering her, that he seemed so possessive, Ari couldn't have been happier for this symbol of validation, as she leaned her head on his shoulder, thinking they had a love that would last forever.

Later that evening, with mugs of hot chocolate and marshmallows already gone, Nonnie and Max joined her and Gage to decorate the tree. Stringing lights and hanging tinsel had never been so fun, as Michel Buble`s 'Winter Wonderland' echoed in the background. When the last of the ornaments were hung, Gage whisked Ari into his arms and danced with her across Nonnie's hardwood floor. Before they knew it, Max had extended his hand to Nonnie, and the dancing and laughter continued late into the night. When Max finally decided to say his goodbyes and bid them all a good evening, Nonnie excused herself to her room. Gage and Arabella sat alone by the fire reflecting on the day's events, until they too, were barely able to keep their eyes open, and made their way to bed.

The following week, on Christmas Eve, the boys worked outside from sun up to sun down, much like they did every day. It was obvious to everyone, that Max was enjoying the extra time he had with Gage this year. Every day, he was eager to fill Gage's mind with information about the farm and how it ran. Mending fences, repairing the barns, and feeding the animals was a never-ending job, Ari quickly realized, as Gage shared each evening, all that he had learned.

Ari felt bad as she stared out the window, watching the two men work in the cold. Especially, since she was inside where it was warm. She was helping Nonnie to prepare a ham and all the fixings for dinner. And, more importantly, baking Gage's favorite chocolate cake.

"It's always been tradition to have this cake on Gage's birthday, but I think we'll start a new tradition for Christmas too," Nonnie winked. "What do you think, Ari?"

"I think it's a wonderful idea, Nonnie! And Gage will love it, I'm sure."

Nonnie was becoming very dear to Ari's heart. They'd spent many hours together over the last week, Nonnie sharing all of her secret recipes, and teaching Ari how to cook Gage's favorite childhood meals. They'd looked through old photo albums of Gage when he was a child. They'd even come across photos of his mother that were found in the bottom of Nonnie's old shoebox in the back of her closet. They'd laughed together and cried together, as they shared their life stories. Besides Beth, Sam, and now Gage, Nonnie was the only person Ari had really opened up to about the loss of her sister Maria, and her mother. And Nonnie, according to her, had never had another female around the house to talk with about her daughter's loss. Ari felt sorry for the pain she had endured, but also honored that the older woman would share her burden with her. Both women confided in the other, their bond growing stronger with each passing day.

It became one of the happiest Christmas days that Arabella would remember. Max had joined them for fresh, homemade pecan rolls for breakfast, and then the opening of the presents that filled the space under the beautiful tree. She and Gage had spent two entire afternoons shopping in town, buying all sorts of gifts he thought Nonnie and Max would like.

Wrapping the presents, was a story all in itself. Apparently, Gage had not been taught how to do that. The first gift she'd given him to wrap, ended up looking more like a large ball of tape.

"What are you doing?" She chuckled, pulling the oddly-shaped package from his hands.

"Did I do it wrong?" His face told the story. He really didn't have a clue what he was doing.

"Ummmm....how did you wrap the presents you gave to your father when you were a child?"

Gage ducked his head, and Ari was afraid maybe this had been a poor subject to bring up. Maybe she should just offer to wrap the gifts herself, and let him off the hook. She barely finished her thought when he responded.

"When I was old enough, and able to save a meager amount of cash I'd earned from mowing lawns or raking leaves, I would usually just hand the presents I bought to my dad. Once in a while, if he got lucky, I would put it in a gift bag."

Although she was used to his confessions about his life as a boy, it didn't take away the sting of his latest recollection. She would never be able to understand why James Russell cared so little for his only son.

Arabella knew what she had to do. She moved behind him, facing the table, and the gift still in his hands. Gently and slowly she placed her hands over his, and unwrapped the taped mess. Then, with loving guidance, Ari taught the man she loved, the man who had withstood so much pain growing up, how to wrap a gift. It was a simple gesture that made a huge impact, and by the end of the hour-long 'giggling at each other through it all' session, you couldn't tell which gifts were wrapped by her and which had been wrapped by Gage. You *could* tell, however, how much of an impression it made on the man's heart.

Since they'd shared their holiday dinner on Christmas Eve, they spent the rest of Christmas day quietly enjoying each other's company, each of them reflecting on their pasts and sharing holiday stories. Ari had done most of the sharing, as the others listened and laughed along at her funny stories of holiday dinners. It seemed Christmas, for Gage, was no different than Thanksgiving. A pre-cooked packaged meal, no decorations, and no family or happy memories. It all sounded very lonely to her.

As the sun went down and stars came out, with the evening drawing to a close, Ari pulled on a coat and joined Gage out back on the old porch swing. It had become one of her favorite places on the farm. It was peaceful and quiet at night, a place where she could reflect on her decisions and her current situation. Wrapped up together in a blanket, the glow of hundreds of twinkling lights, cast a soft glow upon them. Gage turned to her, a look of uncertainty on his face.

"Bella, do you really believe that you can make any place a home as long as you are with the people that you love?"

The unexpected question seemed to fit the 'on again-off again,' somber mood, Gage had been in for the past couple of days. One minute he was laughing and talking about his future with Ari, and the next minute he'd drift off to some far away place in his mind, where he seemed to be wrestling with deep, and possibly troubling, thoughts. What those deep thoughts were all about, was what had Arabella concerned.

"I'm not really sure, Gage," she shrugged. "I mean, it was never something I had to think about. I've only lived in Rock Haven, with the people that I love and have grown up knowing. That is the only home I've ever had. I understand it's been different for you, but I'm not sure that my thoughts are of much help to you."

Gage continued his line of odd questioning.

"Do you believe forgiveness is real, Ari, or do people just *say* they forgive to make others feel better about something horrible that they've done?"

Ari turned towards Gage's silhouette, as he continued to stare out into the dark night surrounding them. "Gage, where are these questions coming from?"

"Just some things from my past that have been on my mind, that's all."

"Gage," she placed her hand on his knee, "forgiveness is very real and when forgiveness is truly extended and received, it can make a relationship like ours, that was once struggling, or even good for that matter, turn into something strong and wonderful. The Bible tells us we should all be forgiving just as the Lord has forgiven us for our sins."

Where did that come from? She hadn't bothered to think about the words of the Bible in quite a while. Honestly, if Gage called her a hypocrite right now and walked away, he'd have every right. She was walking in constant sin, and in no position to be offering Godly advice.

Gage turned to face her, an uncomfortable look on his face. "Bella, I don't want to talk about God tonight."

"Well, what is it that you're struggling with?"

"It doesn't matter anymore, Bella." He kissed her on the top of her head and stood up, offering his hand to her. "Let's call it a night, shall we?"

They made their way up the stairs and got ready for bed. Sometime after the light was turned off, Gage held her in his arms, and began to question her once again.

"Arabella, you know that I love you. Don't you?"

"Yes, I know, Gage. And you know that I love you, right?" Ari questioned back.

"Just promise me, that no matter where our lives take us, you will never forget how much I love you."

"Gage, wha—"

"Just promise me."

"I promise."

As Ari drifted off to sleep in Gage' arms, she was certain she felt his tear drops fall upon her shoulder.

It seemed Nonnie wasn't feeling quite herself, the day before Ari and Gage were set to leave. She'd been quiet all afternoon and had gone to rest in her room rather early. Arabella had fixed supper for the boys and they were sitting by the fire playing chess, as they ate dinner and enjoyed each other's company. It was the perfect opportunity for Ari to sneak away and spend a little more time with Nonnie before their departure in the morning. She ladled up some chicken noodle soup into a bowl and made her way towards Nonnie's room, stopping to knock quietly before entering.

"Nonnie, I've got some hot chicken soup here for you. Are you hungry?" Ari stood in the doorway waiting for her response.

"Come in, dear," Nonnie replied.

Ari carried the tray in and sat it on the dresser. Nonnie motioned for her to join her on the bed.

"Come sit with me a while, Ari."

"What are you working on?" Ari noticed that Nonnie was working on another crochet project. Crocheting was another one of the many things Nonnie had taught Arabella over the past two weeks.

"Take a look for yourself." Nonnie held up a tiny blue bootie for Arabella to see.

"You're making baby booties? Who are they for, Nonnie?"

"They're for you and Gage, dear." Nonnie smiled at Arabella, like she should know what she was talking about.

"But Nonn—"

"Someday, Arabella." Nonnie placed her hand on Ari's. "My hope is that someday you and my June Bug will fill have a home full of tiny little toes who will wear these booties." Nonnie pulled open a little tote that sat next to her on the bed. It was filled with little pink and blue booties and matching hats.

Tears sprang to Arabella's eyes as she reached in to pick up a tiny pair and hold them in her hands. She could easily picture a baby in her arms looking just like Gage. It was something she'd thought of often, and desperately wanted for the both of them.

"They're beautiful, Nonnie," Ari sighed. "I just wish I was as confident about my future with Gage as you are. I would love nothing more than to marry him, and have a dozen of his babies. But—"

"He'll come around, Arabella."

Ari's discouragement was obviously not hidden from Nonnie.

"He has some things he's still trying to work through. But I know my June Bug's heart, and I believe with all that I have, he will find his way home."

"Home, Nonnie? I don't think Gage has any idea where his home is. I'm beginning to think this farm is more of a home to him than our loft will ever be."

"Sweetie, that's not the home I was talking about. Gage's home on earth is wherever his heart is. And that is with you. But the home I'm talking about, is his eternal home. With God. And speaking of Him, have you made peace with the Lord?"

Arabella turned away from Nonnie. The ever-present shame she was constantly trying to bury, quickly worked its way to the surface of her mind. She wondered to herself, if this was the way she would always feel. Could she *ever* forgive herself? Was there ever going to be a day in her future, when she would feel whole again, not ripped apart by guilt and self-reproach? Then again, why did she feel she deserved to be forgiven? She'd been the one who'd made the mistake that changed the course of her life. She had made her bed, so to say, and she would lie in it the rest of her life. That's exactly what she had coming. She deserved whatever came her way. There was nothing left to do but embrace it, and never let the pain she felt, be a burden to anybody else. Finally, after a moment to collect her thoughts and take a deep breath, Ari answered.

"Nonnie, I've made peace about my decision to love Gage, and to continue our relationship. I don't have any room in my life for anyone, or anything, that doesn't support my choice."

Nonnie's old wrinkled hand reached up to gently brush Ari's cheek. "I didn't mean to upset you, dear. But Ari," she paused briefly, "take some advice from an old woman who's lived a very long life. You don't need to give up your relationship with the Lord to love Gage. You might need to make a few changes, and Gage might not like those at first, but I believe eventually, he'll come around. Just always remember that the Lord should come first, and everything else will fall into place."

"Nonnie, I've made so many wrong choices, I fear there's no going back."

"Nothing is impossible with the Lord on your side, dear."

Ari stood up from the bed, smoothing the wrinkles on her shirt. Then, looking into the eyes of the women that held a very special place in her heart, she bent down and placed a soft kiss on Nonnie's forehead. "I know you are trying to help, and I love you for that. But, I need to do this my way. Please respect my decision, Nonnie."

Without another word, Nonnie nodded in agreement before Ari made her way to the door.

Chapter 18

Things seemed strained with Gage when the two of them returned from Iowa. Ari couldn't quite put her finger on it, but it was something she first noticed their last night at Nonnie's farm. He was slightly distant, or maybe just pre-occupied. Whatever it was, Ari sensed that it wasn't good. Gage continued to assure her that everything was fine, but it seemed like something heavy was weighing on his mind. Ari definitely felt a chill in their relationship, as if an icy wind had blown in and settled between them. After a few days of trying to drag the truth out of him, Ari dropped the subject all together. She hadn't been feeling well herself. Maybe Gage was right, and her illness was just making her paranoid.

They'd been back in Michigan for three weeks when they received the call one early morning, interrupting the disagreement that they were having about Ari making a doctor's appointment. Ari was certain she had a simple case of the flu. She'd been extremely tired, and had little appetite for the past ten days. Gage was insisting she schedule a visit with her family doctor. His cell phone ringing was a distraction that she was thankful for.

"Hello? *Max*?"

Ari glanced at the clock, noting it was much too early for Max to be calling. Initially deciding to climb out of bed and head into the bathroom for a quick shower, she now leaned back against her pillow and anxiously waited.

"Is everything okay? What's going on?"

She watched in fear, as trepidation slowly spread across Gage's face.

"I don't understand how this could happen! We were just with her three weeks ago!"

Ari bolted upright. Something was wrong. Very wrong. She hung on Gage's every word.

"No, don't worry, Max. I will be on the first flight out this morning."

Gage finally disconnected the call. Before Ari had a chance to ask for further details of the conversation, he tossed back the covers, jumped out of bed and rushed to the closet where he located his suitcase. After hoisting it onto the bed, Gage quickly began pulling clothes from hangers and haphazardly tossing them in.

"Gage, what is going on?" She reached out for his hand. "Please, tell me what happened!"

He made no effort to slow down, pulling out of her grip, as he answered.

"It's Nonnie. She's had a heart attack. They don't know if she is going to survive."

She was certain that she saw moisture pooling in his eyes, as he frantically continued to shove clothes into his bag.

"No!" She cried. "Not Nonnie!" Ari climbed from her side of the bed and ran to his side. She tried to pull him into a hug, but Gage flippantly brushed her aside. Although stunned by his resistance, Ari waved it off to the hurt she knew he must be feeling, and took a small step back. "What all did Max tell you?"

"There isn't much to tell. She's in the hospital now, but," his voice crackled with emotion as a tear slid down his cheek, "things don't look good." He stopped packing and turned towards her, watching as she pulled her suitcase from the closet. "What are you doing?"

"What do you mean, what am I doing? I'm packing, Gage. I wouldn't let you go to Iowa alone like this. They will just have to run the restaurant without me a few days." Ari continued to pull clothing from the closet.

"Ari, I think it's best if I go alone."

She stopped mid-stride, dropping the blouse she held in her hands, frozen by his cold words.

Obviously recognizing the shock on her face, Gage quietly added, "I mean, with you being sick and all. I just think it will be better this way."

Ari struggled to catch her breath, feeling as if the wind had been forced from her lungs. "I don't understand, Gage," she whispered with much effort. "Why wouldn't you want me to go with you? I love Nonnie, too!"

"Bella, please don't make a fuss about this now. You stay here; get an appointment with the doctor. I need to get home to Nonnie, and I can't be worrying about you being sick at the same time."

"Home, Gage? I thought *this* was your home?" Ari felt dizzy. Nausea rolled across her stomach, forcing her to take a seat on the edge of the bed to steady herself, and make sense of what Gage was saying at the same time.

How could he possibly make this trip without me? Doesn't he know how much I love his grandmother?

Panic seized Ari, as she stared in disbelief at the man her entire life now revolved around. And then it hit her. He wasn't coming back! The cold shoulder she'd been feeling lately, now made sense. Her relationship with Gage was over.

"You know what I mean, Ari. Stop making a big deal about nothing."

"Except, I don't think it's *nothing*, Gage. You've never felt like this was your home, have you? We've just been playing house until you decided you were ready to move on!"

Ari's eyes pleaded with Gage to tell her she was wrong. But in her heart, she'd suspected that this might happen. He'd never had any intention of marrying her, of making Rock Haven his permanent home.

"This is ridiculous, Arabella! I love you, and I love our place together here. Now *please*, let me finish packing. I need to get to the airport and secure a flight to Iowa before it's too late."

Our 'place'? Not our 'home'.

Arabella no longer had the strength to fight it. She'd come to realize, her dream of having Gage and the relationship she'd fought so hard for, wasn't going to be. With her head hung in defeat, and no more tears to cry, Arabella left Gage alone to do what he needed to do. She found her way to the couch, where she curled up into an emotionless ball, and waited for him to leave.

Gage set his suitcase by the door ten minutes later, and walked over to her. He bent down to her level, but never made eye contact. "Ari, you're over thinking things. I will call you when I land and let you know what's happening, okay?" He kissed her on the head one last time and, without saying goodbye, turned and made his way to the door.

Shortly after Gage's departure, Arabella made her way from the couch to her bed, where she stayed the rest of the day. Her mind numbly went over the last year of her life, as she drifted in and out of sleep. When the phone rang much later that night, Arabella was startled. She reached over to the bed stand, anxiously reaching for the ringing device. The number displayed was one she didn't recognize.

"Hello?"

"Arabella, dear? This is Max."

"Oh, thank goodness," Ari released the breath that she'd been holding. "Please tell me how Nonnie is. And did Gage get there safely?"

"Ummm, yes. Gage arrived a few hours ago."

Ari felt the sadness that hung in the silence of the air.

"I'm sorry, honey. There is no easy way to tell you this, and I hate that you're there alone Ari, but," the sudden pause and Max's silence that filled the line between them, caused fear to course through her veins, "Nonnie passed away before Gage arrived. He is beside himself with anger right now."

"No!" Her cry rang out loudly across her bedroom.

It was the only word Arabella could manage to utter before the sobbing over took her. She hung up the phone and cried uncontrollably. Nonnie was gone. She knew from experience the pain that Gage must be feeling, and she felt helpless lying in bed hundreds of miles away. She attempted to call Gage, hoping to convince him to let her come to Iowa, but her calls when straight to voicemail. After a couple of hours, and dozens of attempts, she simply gave up.

She was still in bed the next day, her eyes swollen and puffy from crying through the night, when her phone rang again. This time, it was Gage's picture that illuminated her screen. Fearful of the conversation that awaited, she answered hesitantly, her word a mere whisper. "Gage?"

"She's gone, Bella. My Nonnie is gone." Gage had never openly cried in all the time Ari had known him. Until now. The sobs coming from the other end of the phone shattered her heart. She wanted to be there for him, to hold him in her arms and comfort him.

"Please, Gage. Won't you let me come to you? I want to be there for you."

When he didn't answer immediately, the silence spoke volumes to Ari's bruised and battered heart.

"Bella, I'm sorry. I…I just can't……please, don't come. Not now. I need time."

With nothing left to say, Ari disconnected the call with a heaviness in her heart. Gage didn't need her. Not like she needed him.

He called her every day for the first week, sharing details of the funeral, how he was spending his time, and the people he'd met. Some were old friends of Nonnie's that he'd known from his childhood, but others, many from church, he was meeting for the first time. Their conversations seemed normal again. And at first, Ari thought maybe Gage had been right. She was just overreacting with her thoughts about his homecoming. But slowly, their conversations began to feel more friendly than intimate. The calls became more sporadic over the next month, with no mention of Gage returning to Rock Haven. He continued to tell her that he had things to take care of, but never really explained in detail what he meant. He stopped talking about the farm, didn't mentioned his business in New York, and never once did he tell her he missed her. Or loved her. Soon, the phone calls stopped altogether, and Ari was forced to face the truth she didn't want to see.

She'd made the appointment with her doctor two weeks after Gage had left. No one could have been more surprised that it wasn't the stomach flu she had. She was pregnant. Pregnant by the man she had given her body, heart, and soul to. Their child had been conceived at the ranch, on Christmas night. The place Gage considered home. The place Ari was sure she would never see again. How had her life spiraled so far out of control? The weight of her decisions pressed heavily on her mind.

The very day she found out the news from the doctor, Arabella made her decision. Sitting on her bed with her hand resting on her stomach, the past year of her life played out, once again, in her mind. She was in no condition to raise a child! And what's more, the man she loved and had given so much of herself to, had left the state and all but forgotten her. Leaving her with no choice but to bring this new baby into a fragmented home, fatherless. Pain coursed through her as she debated her options. An army of darkness had all but encamped itself around her thoughts of the future, until suddenly, quietly, her eyes were drawn to the drawer of her bedside night stand. Reaching inside, Ari pulled out the familiar book that she had tucked away, and unsuccessfully tried to forget about, so many months ago. As she clutched the tattered, high-lighted pages in her hands, she realized then, that the one thing she had always needed, was the one thing she'd been running away from.

God.

A wave of emotion rolled over Ari, and she began to sob.

"I'm so sorry, Lord," she cried out.

Ari climbed down and knelt next to her bed, her hands folded in front of her as she began her plea.

"I've made *so* many mistakes, Father. I turned my back on you. I made choices that will bring lifelong consequences. I've judged others unfairly. I've criticized others for their actions. And here I am. Pregnant and not married. About to become a single mother! Oh, Lord, can you ever forgive me?" Tears began to flow effortlessly down her face. She couldn't help but wonder if God would forgive her. And why would he want to? He didn't need her. She needed him! Desperate for an answer, a promise to cling to, Ari opened the bible that lie on the bed in front of her. She flipped through the pages seeking out any passage she could recall on redemption and forgiveness. Her hand rested at Ephesians 1:7.

"In him we have redemption through his blood, the forgiveness of sins, in accordance with the riches of God's grace."

"Oh, Lord, can you ever forgive me?" she whispered.

Next, she found Psalm 32:5.

"Then I acknowledged my sin to you and did not cover up my iniquity. I said, 'I will confess my transgressions to the Lord.' And you forgave the guilt of my sin."

"I'm so sorry for what I've done, Father." Her voice began to grow stronger, simultaneously with the hope that began an assault on the darkness surrounding her heart.

Ari stayed on her knees, crying out to Christ until her aching back and legs forced her to give in. She climbed into bed a few hours later, her body completely and utterly exhausted, but her heart filled with the peace she had been missing. Ari knew she would face many struggles in the days to come because of her choices. But now, with the Lord's guidance and forgiveness, she had no doubt that she and her child would be okay.

Even without the man she loved. The father her child would never know.

The following Friday, Ari pushed past her morning sickness to get ready early, and go down to the restaurant. She was hoping to catch Sam before the rest of the staff came in. It was the first time she'd left the loft since finding out the news of her pregnancy. The shame and embarrassment she felt was overwhelming, but she knew it had been long enough. She needed to make amends. There was no doubt that she'd hurt Sam; and it was time to set the record straight.

"Hey, Sam. Mind if I sit down for a minute?" Ari stood next to the table where Sam sat, thumbing through paperwork. Without looking up, Sam motioned towards the chair opposite of him, and shuffled the weekly stock order into a pile.

"Good morning, Arabella. It's good to see you up and about."

"Sam, there's something I need to talk to you about."

Sam pushed aside his paperwork and focused on Arabella's face. "Sure, honey, what's on your mind?"

Honey? The kindness in his voice was like a knife to Ari's heart. She'd treated him horribly, unnecessarily. Arabella took a deep breath and exhaled, as she picked at a napkin lying on the table, nervous and unsure of what to do with her shaking hands.

Sam reached over and covered her hands with his. The loving gesture comforted her more than Sam would ever know.

"Whatever it is Ari, you can talk to me." His voice was soothing and full of love, filling Ari with the confidence she needed to proceed with her confession.

"I'm sorry for the way I've acted, and how poorly I've treated you lately, Sam. You," she sniffled and tried to hold back the tears, "you have been like a father to me, and I should have known you were only looking out for me. I....I," she choked out the words, "never meant to hurt you." Ari shoulders shook with emotion as the tears found their way down her cheeks. Although she felt relieved to have the confession off her chest, the overwhelming pain that came from knowing she'd hurt those who loved her, continued to tug at her heart.

Sam pushed out his chair and came to her, wrapping his arm around her shoulder and bending slightly to kiss her on the top of her head. "Arabella, I forgive you. I'm sorry things have worked out the way they have," Sam lifted her chin, forcing her to look in his eyes, "but I love you like a daughter, and no matter what you say or do, I will never stop loving you. Or praying for you." He paused momentarily, his expression changing like a chameleon adapting to its environment, then chuckled. "Besides, I know love can make people crazy."

Ari felt a huge weight lift from her shoulders at Sam's lighthearted comment. She managed a half smile as she stood, and wrapped her arms around his neck, giving him a squeeze.

"Thank you, Sam. I love you, too."

Sam turned and walked back to take his seat. "Now that that is out of the way, I have two questions for you."

Ari's smile increased. "Only two? I think I can handle two, Sam." It felt so good to talk to him again.

"When are you coming back to church, and does Gage know about his baby?"

Ari's eyes grew large. "Sam, how did you find out? I haven't told *any*body else! In fact, I only just found out the news myself."

That made Sam laugh. "Honey, you forget that I'm married with five children. I know the signs. And besides that," Sam leaned in to whisper, "Dr. Halstead and I go way back."

"He didn't!" Ari shook her head back forth. "Oh, Sam, what are people going to be *saying* about me?"

"Don't worry, Ari, he won't say anything to anybody else. And neither will I. I just need to know that you are going to be okay. You know Karen and

I will help you in any way that we can," he paused briefly and his expression turned serious, "but Gage needs to know the truth."

"I can't, Sam," Ari's gaze fell to the floor. "He's gone."

"I kind of figured something like that, since he hasn't been around for a couple of weeks. But still—"

Ari looked up, crossing her arms over her chest defiantly. This was the *one* thing she'd already made up her mind about. And would *not* negotiate! It was best she let that be known, right now!

"I don't want him to come back just because I'm pregnant. I mean, it's not that I don't want him to be a part of our child's life. But if he doesn't love me now, this child won't make it any better. It would never work out between us. I would constantly question his love for me, and why he was really with me. I don't want our child to have to endure that. *I* can't endure that!"

Our child.

That one small word cut away at Ari's heart like shards of glass, one sharp piece at a time. Did she have a right to keep Gage from knowing about the pregnancy?

Lord, is this what You want for my baby?

Overwhelming emotions wreaked havoc in her mind as she thought about all that Gage would miss out on. Ari could love this baby with all of her heart and soul, but wouldn't the absence of a father cause pain and heartache far too great for her son or daughter? She wanted to make the right decision. But, how could she? Especially considering the fact that she and Gage weren't even on speaking terms.

"Ari, if you were completely honest, would you say you are angrier at Gage over what happened, or yourself?"

Still lost in her own thoughts about Gage's absence in their child's life, Ari didn't even bother to absorb the real question posed by Sam's words. She responded without thought or hesitation.

"Why would I be mad at myself? If it weren't for Gage pushing me to get his own way, none of this would have happened! I know I made a mistake, Sam, but *he's* the reason I made that mistake!"

Sam was quiet for some time. Long enough for Ari to become uncomfortable and shift in her seat.

"Sam?"

Sam's eyes locked with hers. "Arabella, I don't think you're being honest with yourself. I've known you far too long to think you don't feel responsible for your part in this. Unless—"

"Unless what, Sam?"

"Is there more to the story that you're not sharing?"

"Hmm? I'm not sure where you're heading with this, Sam?"

"Ari, Gage didn't force you to do anything against your will, did he?" Sam's eyes narrowed in her direction.

"Well.....I mean...it....it...wasn't what I would have *chosen*."

"But you did choose it, didn't you? If Gage didn't *force* you to do anything, then despite you saying you wouldn't have chosen it, *you* ultimately were responsible for your actions. Right?"

The anger and disgust towards herself that Ari thought she had relinquished to God, resurfaced in a matter of seconds, bringing with it another wave of tears.

"You're right, Sam," she whispered. "I asked the Lord to forgive me, but I'm still holding onto the thought that Gage is to blame. I need to take responsibility for my own actions, and stop pointing the finger at him."

"Maybe you should speak to the pastor about working through your own forgiveness, Ari. Maybe then, with your heart a little less inclined to feel so much anger towards Gage, true healing can begin.

This was going to be a tall order to fill. Although Ari knew Sam was right, she wasn't about to tear down her defenses when it came to Gage being a part of her life again. The wounds were just too fresh.

"Sam, I agree with you about needing to work on forgiving myself. And I even agree that talking to the pastor would be helpful. But....," she looked down at the table, unable to keep eye contact with him, "it doesn't change how I feel about telling Gage the news of my pregnancy. He walked away from me, and I won't beg him to be a part of my life."

"Well, you know how I feel about this, Ari. *But,* I will support your decision, and keep my mouth closed about it until you're ready to talk." There was an uncomfortable moment of silence between them before Sam continued. "However, I *won't* stop asking you about church. So, can I expect to see you there on Sunday?"

Arabella smiled. Really smiled. She could feel the happiness clear to her toes. For the first time in so long, she felt at peace again with her life. She clung to that peace with everything she had. The heavy burden she had carried around her heart since that first passionate night she'd shared with Gage, was finally lifted.

"Yes, Sam. I will be at church on Sunday. Scouts honor!"

Chapter 19

Ari spent more time in the restaurant that week than she had in a while; happy to get out of the loft and get her mind on anything other than Gage. She worked in the kitchen alongside the staff she loved, and had even made an appearance at dinner time, talking with her guests like she used to. She was finally starting to feel back to her old self. She still hadn't seen or talked to Beth, though, and the weight of that felt like a pile of heavy sandbags on Ari's heart.

By the time Sunday rolled around, Ari had begun to second-guess her decision to attend service. That was, until Sam called her out on it that morning. It was nine o'clock and she'd just been thinking to herself that she should stay home, when her phone rang with an incoming call.

"You're not thinking of backing out, are you?"

How Sam could read her thoughts, she would never understand.

"I'm a little nervous, Sam. What if people think I shouldn't be there because of what I've done? How are they going to react when they find out?"

"Arabella, the only one you need to worry about is God and what He wants from you. Do you believe God wants you to be there?"

"Well, when you put it like that, yes. I *know* I should go."

"Great. See you in two hours then. Karen and I will save a seat for you."

Sam's pep talk had been just the inspiration Arabella needed. She took a warm shower and got dressed before grabbing a bite to eat and heading out the door.

Moments later, she found herself standing at the church entrance. Her fingers trembled as she gripped the door handle, trying to convince herself she was strong enough, and that her mistakes *could* be forgiven. She nearly jumped out of her skin when she heard Beth's voice behind her.

"Those doors aren't going to open themselves, you know." Beth reached up to pull one door open, motioning for Anthony to take Chloe inside. An awkward silence filled the space between them, causing Ari to wonder if the cold chill she was feeling was from Beth, or the weather outside.

Ari slowly looked up, finding her friends eyes. They held not an ounce of condemnation, only the love Ari had always known. "Hi, Beth," she spoke quietly. She knew this conversation was going to be difficult, but she was suddenly ambushed with a flood of emotions.

"It's good to see you, Arabella." Beth's words, surprisingly, held no anger. Only the warmth of kindness and forgiveness.

"Beth, I'm really—"

Beth held up her hand to stop Ari from continuing.

"Arabella, would you like to join me for lunch after church today? Just me and you," she asked. "I'm pretty sure Chloe would love an afternoon alone with her daddy."

Ari smiled weakly, thankful for her best friend's generosity. "I think I would really like that, Beth."

"Great!" Beth turned her cheery face towards the group of people pooling at the bottom of the stairs. "I think we'd better get moving before we get trampled!" She nodded towards the door.

The girls made their way down to the front pew where Sam and his wife Karen had saved them all seats. Anthony had just returned from dropping Chloe off at the nursery, and was joining them.

"It's nice to see you, Ari." Anthony pulled her into a hug.

"It's good to see all of you too." Ari waved to everyone sitting in their row before taking a seat.

As the praise team began with one of Ari's favorite Elevation Worship songs, "I Have Decided," all of the negative thoughts that had been circling in her mind were quickly washed away. She felt the words of the song renew her heart with encouragement. The Lord's love for her pushed all other thoughts aside. She had missed this. She missed Him and the relationship she had with Him. As the pastor began his sermon, which, by no coincidence she was sure, was on forgiveness, Ari relished in the feeling of being truly at home. She knew right then, that no matter which direction life took her in the future, she would never leave her God again.

Pastor Ron invited the church to join him, as he shared bits and pieces of the story of Saul with the congregation. He spoke of the man's upbringing, his grooming that trained him to be a Pharisee doctor of Jewish

Law, held in great esteem by all Jews. Pastor Ron continued sharing how Saul stood by as, Stephen, one of Christianity's earliest messengers, was killed for his beliefs that were so different than Saul's. And then, how Saul, a devoutly religious man, bent on the destruction of the believers in Jesus, was transformed. Pastor Ron moved from behind the pulpit, energized as he began to talk about Saul's blindness, and how he regained his sight, now filled with the Holy Spirit.

"After being baptized, this man that had now become known as Paul, the one that once sought out and persecuted Christ followers, became, perhaps, the most recognized follower and believer of Christ, whose writings still greatly influence the world today."

"So, I ask you, the congregation before me, those that may be feeling burdened or ashamed by choices you have made, are your sins too great to be forgiven when you look at the sins of one of the most influential men of the Bible? Christ, who took His place on that cross some two thousand plus years ago, took the burden of your sin *with him* to the cross, carried it to the tomb, where he was raised again three days later. The promise of a hope we are all graciously given. I say to you today, beloved children of the Lord, isn't it time for you to let go? Embrace the forgiveness of the good Lord and come home!"

Tears streamed down Arabella's face, certain the sermon had been directed specifically at her, as God's unending grace and mercy filled her heart. She vowed to not let the mistakes of her past control her life or pull her away from her relationship with the Lord. She'd certainly made more than a few poor choices, but if God didn't look back at those choices, why should she?

Ari soon found herself making the walk towards the front of the congregation. As the altar call was opened, she found her best friend Beth, right alongside of her. With every ounce of faith that she could muster, Ari surrendered her hands above her and embraced His forgiveness, pledging her love and faithfulness to Him once again. She was determined, more than ever before, to start fresh. She would be the person God wanted her to be, and the mother that her unborn child *needed* her to be.

"You doing okay?" Beth asked as she filled their bowls with steaming hot soup and placed them on the table. "You seem....I don't know.... different. Quieter I guess. Like you have a lot on your mind.

Arabella's solemn expression slowly changed, as she began to speak. "I'm probably better than I have been in months, Beth." She turned her face up to look at her friend. "That was quite a sermon today, huh?"

"Yes, it was a good sermon."

Beth reached for Ari's hand and led them in blessing their meal, before continuing the conversation.

"Was there something in particular about the sermon that spoke to you today?" Beth opened her napkin and spread it across her lap.

Arabella swallowed a bite of soup and allowed a slow smile to creep across her lips. "How about the entire sermon? I felt like it was aimed directly at me."

Beth gave a half-hearted laugh. "I know what you mean. There've been plenty of times when I felt Pastor Ron must have had a window right into my heart and knew exactly what was going on in my life when he wrote his weekly sermon. Strange, huh?"

"You could say that." Ari bent forward and took another bite of the hot soup Beth had prepared, savoring the taste and allowing the warm broth to soothe her.

"Okay, Ari. You know I've never been good at biting my tongue and holding back. Maybe I'm way out of line by bringing it up, but I can't stand it any longer!"

Ari laughed harder than she had in a long time. She had wondered how long it would take her friend to cut to the chase.

"So, is it okay for me to bring up the subject? Or would you rather I didn't?"

"And what might that subject be?" Ari grinned teasingly. She had wondered how long it would take her nosy friend to ask.

"If you don't want to talk about it, I understand, Ari."

"No, it's okay Beth," she shrugged one shoulder. "It will actually be nice to have someone to talk about it with. I've missed your friendship."

Beth sighed, and Ari could see the relief on her face.

"So, where is he?" Beth questioned with a slight scowl on her face. "I mean, what happened? One day he was here, adamantly professing his love for you, and then he was just... gone." Beth bent to slurp a spoonful of noodles, giving Ari a chance to respond.

"Gage is no different than me, I guess, in the sense that he's running. The only difference is, I'm not sure he even *realizes* he's running. The last I heard, he was back at his grandmother's ranch in Iowa." Ari turned away from the table as tears threatened to spill from her eyes. She'd promised herself she was done crying over Gage and what she'd lost, but the very sound of his name had her heart in tangles.

"I feel like there's more going on here. Are you really okay?" Beth placed her hand on Ari's, offering comfort.

"Nonnie," Ari's voiced crackled, "she passed away, Beth."

Beth immediately went to Ari, wrapping her arms around her in a hug. "Oh sweetie, I am so sorry." They stayed that way for a few minutes, allowing Ari to cry over the loss of the woman she had grown to love so much.

"Is Gage planning on *staying* at the farm, then?" Beth returned to her seat and faced Ari as they continued their conversation.

"I'm really not sure what his plans are," Ari shrugged. "We haven't talked in weeks." The sadness she felt just would not release its hold on her, no matter how hard she tried. "I really don't know what to think about any of it."

"I know this is painful, Ari, but if he can walk away from you that easily, then maybe it was never meant to be. You have to admit, the relationship you shared with Gage wasn't one *God* would have chosen."

There was *no way* Ari was going to share her news of the pregnancy with Beth today. Not after that comment! Ari reminded herself that her best friend was only looking out for her, as she forced herself to take a deep breath in and slowly exhale.

"Beth," she said pointedly, while trying to remain calm, "I love Gage. I know you mean well, but after what I shared with him, there will *never* be another man for me. I can only pray that through his struggles he might come to know the Lord and allow Him to work in his life. Gage is lost. Like we've *all* been at one point or another in our lives. I don't doubt that he loved me. For a fraction in time, anyway."

Beth didn't respond immediately, seemingly taking time to process Ari's words as she took another bite of hot soup.

"Well, no matter what happens, Arabella, know that Anthony and I are here for you."

The words were music to Ari's heart.

"You have no idea how much I appreciate that, Beth."

She and Beth could have their differences of opinions. But it felt like they'd mended their relationship. That was most important! Ari felt confident that, with the Lord on her side, and Beth and Sam to help her through her pregnancy, she and her child could overcome any obstacle life may present.

"With that being said, there is one thing I could use your help with."

"Sure," Beth's face lit up. "Whatever you need! Just ask it!"

"I'm glad you feel that way. Umm," Ari paused, looking down at the table as she searched for the words she needed.

Finally looking up, she found Beth's eyes and continued. "I know that what I'm about to ask is big, but—"

"Don't beat around the bush, Ari! Out with it already."

"Could you and Anthony please pray for Gage?" The words poured from her mouth at the speed of lightning. Then, as a look of shock registered on Beth's face, Ari's heart plummeted. Maybe she was asking to much of her friend. When Beth remained silent, longer than Ari was comfortable with, she withdrew her request. "Never mind. I shouldn't have asked."

Ari made to get up from the table, but Beth reached out, holding her by the wrist. "I'm sorry, Ari. That just took me by surprise. Of course, we will pray for Gage. It won't be the easiest thing, I admit. But we will do it because it's the right thing to do.

This time, the tears that flowed from Ari's eyes were of happiness. Although she hadn't quite gotten to the point where she could pray for Gage herself, at least her friends would be. After all, she knew that the Lord loved Gage as much as He loved her.

"Alright!" Beth stood up and reached for Ari's empty bowl. "Now that we got that out of the way, let's discuss something fun!"

Ari made a conscious decision to hold off on sharing the news of her pregnancy with Beth. For now, at least. It had already been an emotionally draining day, and Ari knew her friend well enough to realize she would have quite an opinion about the subject! Ari wasn't sure she was ready to tackle that quite yet.

The sound of the backdoor slamming caused Gage to look up from his seat at the kitchen table. It had been four weeks since Nonnie's funeral, and it was all he could do to get out of bed each morning. He'd been sitting at the table thinking of Arabella, as he often did, wondering where she may be and what she was doing without him. Wherever she was, he was certain her heart was broken. The last day they'd spent together began to play out like a movie in his head. She had been so sick. And yet, when he got the call about Nonnie, her first response was to go to Iowa with him. No hesitation. She continuously was good to him, pretending every time he held her that she didn't regret her mistake. But he knew better. Gage knew what he'd cost her, and he couldn't keep rubbing her nose in it, pretending everything would be okay. Nonnie's death had given him the perfect opportunity to act on what he already knew. Arabella deserved better. He only hoped, that with time, she would forgive him. Maybe even move forward with a man that was better suited for her.

The thought of her with another man was enough to make Gage sick to his stomach. The jealousy of his human nature reared its ugly head. Gage never wanted another man to touch Ari. Not like he had. He wanted to be her only one. But this was about Ari, and what she deserved. And she certainly deserved a whole lot better than him. In time, she would see it too.

Max's shadow filled the doorway, causing Gage to look up.

"Son, don't you think it's time to make some decisions? You can't keep hiding out here you know."

"I'm not hiding from anything, Max!" Gage straightened in his chair. Still unwilling to openly admit his mistakes to anyone, his new-found, short temper started to flare.

How dare he say that to me. The old man could never understand how much my heart hurts.

"Anything or anyone? Gage, you're going to wait until it's too late and she's going to move on. Why are you pushing her away?"

Gage slammed his fist onto the table. "Maybe moving on is the best thing for her, Max! I'm certainly no good for her!" Gage stood, shoved his chair against the table and began to pace the kitchen floor. Couldn't the old man see, he too, was suffering? He'd done nothing but mope around the house for weeks now, pain tearing at his heart.

"Are you really that much of a fool, Gage? That woman loves you more than life itself. You can see it in her eyes every time she looks at you. Why would you go and throw something like that away? Quit feeling sorry for yourself, and do something to get her back before it's too late!"

Gage turned around to face Max, pain and anger filling his eyes. "You really think you have all the answers, old man? You don't have a *clue* what you're talking about!"

Max was quiet, staring down at the table for the longest time. Gage began to feel the weight of his outburst. He watched the old man, who was like a father to him, struggle for words. How had his life slipped so far out of control? It seemed that all he did anymore was hurt those that he loved. It had to stop!

"Gage, I've never bragged about having all the answers. In fact, I struggle for answers every day of my life. But if there's one thing I am certain of, you won't find the answers in any of the places you've been looking."

Gage rolled his eyes and shoved his fingers through his hair. He wanted nothing to do with this silly game Max was playing.

"Son, I think it's time for you to see something. Come with me." Max brushed past him and out of the kitchen towards Nonnie's bedroom. Gage followed, but stopped before his feet crossed the threshold of her room. He hadn't set foot in there since the day he'd come home. It felt wrong. Like an invasion of her privacy.

"Max, I don't think you should be in here," Gage called out. But Max's back was turned to Gage as he stood at Nonnie's dresser. Slowly he turned, a thick, well-worn, black book in his hands.

Gage gasped when he realized he was holding Nonnie's bible. "Max, put that down! You have no right to touch her things!" Gage stormed into the room and grabbed the book from the old man's hands.

Max just reached out and patted Gage on the shoulder. "Sit down, Gage. Sit down and spend some time with the gift your grandmother left for you." Max didn't say another word, just silently slipped from the room, closing the door behind him.

Gage stood for several minutes, his hands running over the cracked leather that had been Nonnie's most loved possession, before the tears began to slip. Before long, he found himself sitting in her old rocker, the same wooden rocker she had rocked and comforted him in as a child. It felt surreal. He still couldn't believe that the woman he thought was larger than life, was really gone. He must have sat rocking for at least half an hour, reliving old memories, before he gently pulled the cover back on the book, a photograph falling to the floor as he did.

Gage bent to pick it up, turning it over tenderly with his fingers, curious as to what he held. He was not ready for the emotions that sucker punched him in the gut the moment he saw his infant self in his mother's arms, Nonnie standing next to them. A flood that he'd been holding onto for so many years, finally broke like a dam, and Gage found himself on the floor, his body racked with sobs.

A short time later, he steadied himself, long enough to notice a bookmark sticking out from the tattered pages. Nonnie must have thought it important enough to mark it. What if it was the last thing she had read? The unanswered question provoked his heart to open the page. His trembling hands followed his eyes to the margin where, in red, he saw his name written in Nonnie's beautiful handwriting.

Gage my little prodigal. My prayer is that you find your way home.

The words were written next to Luke 15: 11. Gage wiped the tears from his eyes and focused on the words that Nonnie had highlighted. It was the first time he'd ever read from the book that Nonnie loved so much. As he read a parable about two sons and the different choices they made with their father's inheritance, Gage began to see similarities in his actions and choices with that of the younger son. Gage recognized his greed and desires to please himself, not caring what he took from others. He could easily compare it to his relationship with Arabella.

He continued to pore over the words, reading of how the youngest son foolishly squandered away everything he had been given. He ended up penniless and hungry, alone in a foreign land. Eventually, the son came to his senses, and set out on a journey back home to his father. He hoped and prayed for any morsel of forgiveness his father might bestow upon him. As the story continued on, Gage was shocked to read how the father took his youngest son back in, without a second thought, forgetting all the terrible things he had done. He was forgiven without question, and the father readily gave his son all that he had available.

Gage began to wonder if this was what the Lord's love could look like for him. Curious, and hungry for more answers, he continued to read, turning page after page. He finally stopped when he could no longer see the words through the darkness of the room. Standing, he turned his attention to the clock on Nonnie's dresser, surprised that so much time had passed. He wasn't ready to stop. Desperate for answers, Gage raced to the kitchen. Not finding what he was looking for, he then made his way to the living room where he found Max sitting on the couch in front of a roaring fire.

"Will you take me to church with you tomorrow, Max?"

The ranch hand turned and nodded with a smile. "I would love nothing more, Gage."

Gage had been in church several times with Nonnie as a child. He had even gone with Ari, before the night that changed everything in their relationship. But when he walked through the doors this time, something was different. There was a feeling of peace and belonging that filled him, as he took a seat in the pew next to Max. He listened intently as the pastor began his sermon. This time, Gage didn't feel as if the words were attacking him. This time, the words were soothing and calming to Gage's soul. He began to wonder, as the pastor spoke about forgiveness, if being forgiven was really something in the cards for him. Mentally, he began to make a list of the things he regretted and the people he'd hurt. As he played out the past six months of his life, his heart ached with longing and remorse. The brilliant light in Ari's eyes had been dull for some time. And the warm smile that initially drew him to her, just hadn't been the same after that night. He loved her. He was certain of that. And in this moment, Gage felt a stirring of hope that just maybe, those things could be regained. Maybe he *could* be a man entrusted again with Ari's love. If given the chance to try a new way. God's way.

At the end of service, Gage introduced himself to the senior pastor, who easily remembered him from his days of visiting as a younger boy.

"It's good to see you again, Gage!" The pastor shook his hand. "We were all so saddened by your grandmother's passing. Please accept my condolences on behalf of the congregation."

"Thank you, sir, I appreciate that. One thing's for sure, my Nonnie loved this church and the people in it," Gage smiled.

"I wasn't aware that you were still in town. Does this mean you'll be making the farm your permanent residence?" the pastor queried.

"That is still somewhat up in the air. I've been reflecting on things, trying to make a decision on what's next in my life," Gage looked down at his feet.

The pastor patted his arm. "Well, if there's anything I can do for you before you leave town, you just let me know, okay?" The pastor started to walk away.

"Sir, um....Mr.....um...Pastor?" Gage stumbled over his words nervously. The pastor stopped and turned towards him with a warm smile.

"Yes, Gage?"

"Do you think you could sit down and talk with me some about this God thing?"

The pastor's smile widened. "Gage, I would love nothing more than to sit down and talk with you. Could you meet me here tomorrow morning? Say nine o'clock?"

Gage nodded his head in agreement, feeling a burden of weight lifted from his heart. "That would be perfect. Thank you."

"See you tomorrow, Gage."

Max approached Gage as the pastor walked away. "Are we all set to go?"

Gage couldn't contain his smile. "Readier than I've ever been, Max."

Chapter 20

After lunch at the farm, and a long talk about the morning sermon, Gage changed into his work clothes and joined Max to help with the afternoon chores. Max approached him about his plans once again, as he was cleaning out Poncho's stall.

"Gage, what are your thoughts about the ranch? I've tried not to bother you about it, all things considered, but you need to make a decision. And fairly quickly. The staff would really like to know whether they will have jobs in their near future. Spring time isn't that far off. They will need to find work elsewhere, *if* you decide to sell the ranch."

Gage turned towards the old man and leaned his pitchfork against the stall, baffled by his statement. "Max, I could never sell Nonnie's farm. I just assumed that *you* would take care of all those details. You are more than welcome to live here now, if that will make things easier for you."

"Gage, that's very kind of you but—" Max hesitated, not wanting to upset him anymore. "I think it's time for me to slow down a bit and think about retirement. And," his voice was filled with emotion, "now that your grandmother is gone, I could never stay in this house. Too many memories." Max exited the barn. Gage followed and leaned back against Max's old Ford pick-up truck that sat in the driveway. He stared out over the open field, covered in snow. The cows were huddled near the big red barn and the pond was nearly frozen solid. It sure didn't look like much in the winter, but three months from now, with the first signs of spring, all of that would change. His Nonnie had loved this farm, and so had his mother. There was no possibility of him ever letting it go. But, what would he do with over three hundred acres of land and crops? That didn't even include the herd of milk cows that were raised here! Then, there were the horses to think about. Gage wouldn't have a clue where to start.

"I know that losing Nonnie has been hard on you too, Max. But, retirement? What will happen to the farm? You can't walk away from Nonnie's dream." Gage's heart ached just thinking about it.

"Gage, this farm is *yours* now. *That's* what your Nonnie wanted. I thought you understood that? Have you made up your mind about where *you're* going to put down roots? I'd hoped that you'd be back in Michigan by now. Or possibly that you would bring Arabella here to live. My decision is going to greatly depend on your choices."

Gage turned away from him as he mumbled a response. "I don't think I can go back to Michigan, Max. How could Arabella ever forgive me for walking away from her like I did?" Even after the church service had opened his eyes to the possibility of forgiveness, Gage was hesitant to believe that Arabella would ever be able to get over what he did to her.

Max kicked the snow from his boots before looking up. His eyes were full of compassion for Gage. "She loves you, Gage. I think you'd be surprised at how that love can extend further than any miles you've put between you. You know, I've heard it said that love has no memory. Why don't you at least give her a call and let her know how you are doing? I'm sure she's worried about you."

"I'm meeting with the pastor tomorrow morning, Max. I've got some questions I think only he can answer. I think I need just a little more time to process things. Can you give me that?"

Max nodded. "I don't think you'll be sorry for meeting with Pastor Dave, Gage. I will let the staff know to continue with things the way they are currently, with the promise that within the next thirty days they will have a definite answer about the farm and its future. Now……about that phone call back to Michigan," Max prodded.

It took Gage the full thirty days promised to the staff, and then an additional thirty days they graciously extended to him, before he'd made his decision. During those two months, he spent every day alongside of Max, learning all that he could about the ranch. Every afternoon, he'd head up to the church to learn from the pastor. He spent his evenings diving into the Bible, and re-visiting the information he'd learned during their conversations, absorbing everything his mind could hold. For the first time in his life, Gage felt content with himself in a way that he'd never known possible. Prayer had become something that he did, not only in the morning and evening, but all day long, sharing his hopes and dreams with

God. It became an ongoing conversation, with the One he had come to know and love.

During one particular meeting, Gage had been consumed with guilt and anger for the way he'd hurt Ari.

"Pastor Dave, I'm afraid I don't know how to forgive myself for what I took away from her."

"Gage, do you feel like you're the same man today that you were then?"

Gage looked down at his feet, thinking about the depth of the pastor's words. He *wasn't* the same man anymore. He refused to ever be that ugly man again.

"No, sir." Gage looked up to the pastor. "I'm not that same guy."

"Failing to forgive yourself will put blinders on your spiritual eyesight quickly, Gage. It causes you to see things through the eyes of guilt and shame. You have to let go of it. It says in 2 Corinthians 5:17: '*Therefore, if any man be in Christ, he is a new creature: old things are passed away; behold all things are new."*

The pastor continued. "If you believe you are a new creation because Christ now lives in you, then you can forgive yourself, Gage. But, don't be mistaken. We all have to face consequences because of our choices."

"I'm not sure I follow. If the Lord forgives me, doesn't that wipe the slate clean for me?"

"Let's look at your situation with Ari, Gage. The Lord can and will forgive the sins you committed when you ask, but you will still suffer the consequence of that broken relationship. Do you understand the difference?"

"So, forgiveness is just a process towards happiness. Is that what you're saying?"

"Exactly, Gage. The Lord allows us to have free will and make our own choices. Some of those choices may not be the wisest. Because of those choices, we have consequences. Be it good *or* bad. It doesn't change the fact that the Lord loves us. And if we trust in Him, he will walk with us through our trials. But he will not *wipe out* those trials. That's how we learn and grow."

"So, even if I'm a changed man, I may never win Arabella back, I guess?"

"I think focusing on your changes is the first step, Gage. Why don't we pray about it?"

The pastor placed his hand on Gage's shoulder and began to pray over him.

But it wasn't the words of the pastor that gained his attention. It was the small voice that called out in his head.

Leave behind your regrets and mistakes. My arms are wide open. Come to me.

Gage shook his head, trying to focus on the pastor as he spoke, but the words wouldn't go away.

I'm calling for you, Gage. Come to me.

With his heart assaulted from all sides by God's love, Gage stood up and slowly made his way to the altar. There, he fell to his knees, as he felt grace and mercy begin to wash over him.

"Forgive me for the horrible mistakes I've made. For hurting so many people." Gage's voice shook as he continued, "I want to be a different man. Please," he begged, "*help* me to be a better man. I don't know how to do this, and I'm scared, Lord. Please don't leave me. And if it's at all possible, could you please help me win back the woman I love?"

Gage knew as he stood from the altar that day, his life would never be the same. As he walked out of the church doors, his head held slightly higher than before, due to a newfound confidence, the only thing on his mind was becoming a better man. He only hoped in figuring that out, he might find out how to get Ari to forgive him, too. That process, he declared to himself, was going to start right now!

Gage was making some big changes at the farm. Max had agreed to stay on staff to oversee things, without having to mess with the daily physical demands. Gage had left it up to him, and encouraged Max to hire all the help he needed. Gage planned on expanding the ranch, and after tying up a few loose ends in New York and Rock Haven, making it his permanent residence.

He'd been on the phone all morning, trying to get things in place before his trip back to his father's in New York. Nearing the bottom of the list, Gage felt the anxiety set in, trying to control his heart. The last few calls were going to be more difficult, and had caused Gage a lot of stress in the past few days. But he knew the time had come. He had been in Iowa a few months now, and it was time to make peace with his past, and put some issues to rest.

"Good afternoon, Francesca's."

Hearing Sam's voice on the other end of the line, instantly brought back a flash of memories, especially of the last time they'd talked.

"Hello? Anybody there?"

"Sam? It's Gage." He spoke quietly and was met with silence.

"There's some things I need to say to you, but I would like the chance to say them in person. I'm going to be coming through Rock Haven on my way back from New York, and was wondering if you could take time out of your schedule to meet with me?"

"On your way back from New York, Gage? Is that where you've been hiding all this time?"

Gage bit his lip to keep himself from responding negatively. "I guess I deserve that."

"Gage, I'm sorry, but I don't have much to say to you after you walked out on Arabella like you did. It was wrong of you, no matter how you look at it."

It didn't take long for Gage to respond. He only wished he could see Sam's expression when he did. "You're right, Sam. What I did was wrong. And I'm trying to—" His apology was interrupted by a long sigh.

"It wasn't right for me to speak to you that way, Gage. I'm sorry. You know, no matter what choices you made, whether I agree with them or not, you deserve to be treated with respect. If you want to still meet with me, I will make the time for you. But let me ask you this. Does Arabella know that you're coming to town?"

"No, sir." Gage waited for Sam's outburst. When the bartender was silent, he continued. "I'd like to keep it that way for now, please."

"I've got to be honest, Gage. You are asking a lot from me. I don't keep secrets from the people I love."

"Sam, I know that I've caused doubt in your mind as to the kind of man I am. But I'm asking, just this once, if you could please trust me. I promise it will all make more sense when I get the chance to sit down and explain things to you."

"One time, Gage. I will do this thing you are asking of me, one time. You'd better be prepared to shed some light on a lot of things when you get here!"

Sam hung up on him before Gage had a chance to respond. Nevertheless, he'd completed what he set out to accomplish. Meeting with Sam was the first place he'd start, and he couldn't wait to tell the old bartender the good news. This would change everything! He used his newfound enthusiasm to propel him into the last and final call on his list. This one would be the most difficult.

Hearing Gage's voice was the last thing Beth expected to hear when she answered the phone. The last time they had been in the same room together, it hadn't ended well. She'd made Gage perfectly aware of her feelings towards him, surrounding the poor choices he'd made. She hadn't held back, reminding Gage of all Ari had given up for him. She'd been brutally honest. And even now, the weight of Gage's actions still bore a tender wound in her heart.

"Gage?"

"I know you're surprised to hear from me, Beth, but I have a lot I need to say to you."

Matthew 6:14-15 rang clear as a bell through Beth's mind as she contemplated hanging up the phone.

For if you forgive other people when they sin against you, your heavenly Father will also forgive you. But if you do not forgive others their sins, your Father will not forgive your sins.

Beth didn't want to hear that.

"I don't think I have it in me today, Lord," she thought to herself, "to stand here and listen to his excuses."

Beth, are you without sin?

"What he's done is horrible, Father! He's hurt someone I care greatly about!"

Again, I ask. Are you without sin, Beth? Have your mistakes been forgiven?

Pastor Ron's recent sermon about judgement, was still fresh in her mind. He had been clear about the topic, how it wasn't our place to be passing judgement onto others. How there are personal consequences we reap from when we practice such behavior. Beth's words were laced with reluctancy as she responded. She may not feel like it, but she knew extending forgiveness to Gage was the right thing to do.

"I'm listening, Gage."

Gage cleared his throat as he began. "Beth, first I want to say that I'm sorry for anything I did to hurt you. And to ask for your forgiveness." He paused but Beth didn't comment. She just couldn't bring herself to say the words 'forgiven' and 'Gage' in the same sentence. Did he even know what forgiveness was? And why, all of a sudden, did he want *her* forgiveness? Certainly, if he had talked with Ari, she would have relayed that information. What exactly was going on here?

"Second, I want you to know that I'm a changed man."

"Oh please, Gage, I don't want to hear your excus—"

"Beth, I've given my life to the Lord."

No words could have been more shocking or more intriguing to Beth's ears. Once she was able to pick her jaw up off the floor, she responded. "I'm listening, Gage."

They spent the next forty-five minutes talking about Gage's transformation, and all that he'd been doing in Iowa, before Beth broke down in tears and prayed with him.

"There is something I need your help with, Beth. Aaaand," he said slowly, "Ari must not know *anything* about it, okay?"

Beth grinned into the phone. "Do I get to hear what it is before I promise not to tell her?"

"Not this time, Beth. This is too important. I want to make sure it goes off without a hitch. Can I count on you?"

"I'll help you on one condition, Gage."

"And that is?" Gage sounded nervous.

"Gage, promise me you'll talk to Ari soon. Tell her everything you just shared with me. She's so miserable without you."

"Don't worry, Beth, I have just a few more things to finish up with here in Iowa before I can head that way. But believe me, I want to tell her as quickly as possible. Do you think I have a chance at winning her back?"

For the first time in nearly a year, Beth was excited about the direction of Ari's life. She smiled as she said as much to Gage. Now, with the changes Gage had made, maybe he and Ari could begin their life together, as it should be.

"Well, there's no doubt about how much you hurt her. But I have to say, after hearing what you've shared with me, I'm thinking it's a good possibility, Gage. Just don't push her. It's going to take time, and lots of work on your end before she trusts you again."

"I've got the rest of my life to wait for her, Beth. And if that's what it takes, then I'll do it."

Chapter 21

Arabella was more nervous than she could ever remember as she sat in the waiting room of the obstetrician's office. After finding out the news that she was pregnant, Ari hadn't wanted to continue seeing her family doctor in her small home town, fearful that residents would find out her news sooner than she was ready to share it. She had decided early on that she would find a specialist in the nearby town, of Burlington. The office she had chosen was conveniently located in the hospital, where she would deliver.

The bubbly blond seated next to her, had been chattering to everyone in the office. It seemed now, that it was Ari's turn to listen.

"So, sweetie, how far along are you? You can barely tell you've got a little bump there," she giggled.

"Just fourteen weeks. How about you?" Ari's hand instinctively went to her belly as she waited for the girl to answer.

"Oh, this is my very first appointment. I'm not exactly sure how far along we are," she laughed, reaching her hand out to Ari. "I'm Stephanie by the way. Is this your first?"

Still somewhat uncomfortable talking about the pregnancy, Ari answered hesitantly. "Ummmm....yes. How about you? Is this your first?"

"Yes, and we couldn't be more excited! We just moved here from the mid-west. Well, here being Rock Haven. My husband just happened to stumble across the little town not too long ago, and he thought it was the perfect place to raise our little one."

Ari looked around the room in search of the woman's husband.

"Oh, he's not here. We just recently purchased a small storefront downtown in Rock Haven for my event planning business. And we have too many things to get in order before opening day. He will be here for the next appointment, though, guaranteed. That's when we get to hear the heartbeat, I think."

The woman was obviously thrilled with her pregnancy. "Well, you are going to love Rock Haven. That's where I'm from too. It's a beautiful little town."

"Is your husband joining you today?" The woman's question caught Ari off guard.

"No, I'm not…I'm, um……," guilt and shame consumed her.

Without missing a beat, the woman continued.

"Sorry, I wasn't trying to be nosy. It's just that, being new to the town, we are looking forward to meeting some friends. And don't worry, I completely understand. We just got married ourselves. We were a little shocked with the pregnancy news, being that we only met a couple of months ago. We'd only been married three weeks when I found out the news. But—," Stephanie sighed and a dreamy grin soon covered her face. "It was love at first site," she clapped her hands together in front of her, "and we couldn't be happier!"

Luckily, at just that moment, the nurse called out for Stephanie and she stood to leave. "Maybe we'll run into each other again at another appointment? Or who knows," she shrugged, "maybe we will even see you in Rock Haven. I would love it if you stopped by my store sometime."

"Sure, maybe I'll do that," Ari agreed half-heartedly, not putting too much thought behind it. "It was nice to meet you."

Great, just what I need. Happy couples having babies. Lord, I need you now more than ever. I'm feeling ashamed of my choices, again. I know that I have your forgiveness, Father, but what if my child won't be able to forgive me? What have I done? If I had only kept my promise to you……..

Arabella felt the tears pooling in the corner of her eyes as the nurse called out her name. Quickly, her focus was back on the reason for her appointment, and her worries were pushed to the back of her mind.

In the room, the nurse took Ari's vitals and asked her a series of questions before handing her a gown. She let her know the doctor would be in soon, and quietly excused herself so Ari could change. The entire time Ari's emotions were working overtime, and she soon found herself unable to control her tears. She'd been crying a lot the last couple of weeks. It seemed everything made her cry these days— happy tears, sad tears, it didn't matter. She was an emotional train wreck.

Ari attempted to brush the tears away when Dr. Collins entered the room and shook her hand.

"Good morning, Arabella. How have you been feeling?"

Arabella received her handshake. "Hi, Dr. Collins. I have been feeling pretty good. About the only thing I have to complain about are my unstable emotions."

The doctor smiled knowingly. "I wish I could tell you it gets easier, but I won't lie to you." She walked over to the ultrasound machine. "Well, shall we get started? I'll bet you're anxious to hear and see this little one!"

Arabella took her place on the exam table and lay back on the paper covered pillow. Her entire body was shaking from nerves. But the minute the doctor placed the warm gel and ultrasound wand on her growing belly and she heard what sounded like the galloping of little horses, all was right in Ari's world.

"Do you hear that, Arabella? *That* is your baby's heartbeat. It sure sounds strong and healthy."

Ari turned to face the small screen, and instantly fell in love. She watched the movement of her child, listened as its heartbeat continued. This time, she didn't even try to hold back the emotion.

I wonder if our child will have Gage's blue eyes. I wonder if he or she will have my nose or my ears and oh, I hope our baby has his daddy's smile.

The feeling of guilt, knowing that she'd kept the news of her pregnancy from Gage, weighed on Ari like a lead ball and she wrestled with her thoughts.

How could I ever tell him the news? I don't want him back if he doesn't love me. Maybe he wouldn't even want to come back. Maybe a child would mean nothing to him. After all, he never liked it when I wanted to talk about the future. Weddings and children were his least favorite subject! And, he's the one that left me. Doesn't he forfeit being a part of my life by walking out? But then again, he does have the right to be a father if he chooses, doesn't he? Whether he loves me or not? How can I keep this secret from him?

"And this is the baby's spine," the doctor continued speaking, as she moved the ultrasound wand back and forth across Ari's baby bump.

"He's healthy then? Can you see his little fingers and toes? He's growing like he should?" Ari was suddenly full of questions, as she realized just how *real* the little life inside of her was.

"Everything looks and sounds perfectly normal. Although, whether it's a 'he' or 'she,' cannot be determined for another couple of weeks. Were you wanting to know the gender? You seemed pretty confident it was a boy," the doctor questioned.

Ari shook her head. "No, I don't want to know," she smiled. "I want to be surprised. As long as he or she is healthy, that's *all* I care about."

When the doctor ended the ultrasound and began to clean the equipment, Ari felt a little sad. Seeing the images on the screen today had changed everything. Suddenly her pregnancy took on an entirely new feeling, and she was determined that no matter what happened, she and her child were a team. And together, they would get through anything and everything life brought their way. She had God's forgiveness. She had gotten her life back on track. She was going to make things right and raise this child with all the love and devotion she could. With or without its father. And at this point, Ari had given up all hope that she and Gage would ever be a family.

As Ari scheduled her next appointment and made her way towards the parking lot, she knew that the time had come to open up and be honest with those closest to her. She couldn't keep the news any longer. And frankly, she didn't want to keep it a secret now. Everything had changed with the sound of that little heartbeat. She would no longer let embarrassment hold her back. Her true friends would still love her for who she was. And speaking of true friends, the first place she needed to start was at Beth's.

"Ari, what a nice surprise! Come on in." Beth held the door open for her friend. "Sorry," she cringed slightly, "but your beautiful goddaughter is taking a nap."

Ari stepped into the house and closed the door behind her. "Actually Beth, that's probably best. I really need to talk with you alone, if you have a few moments."

Beth could sense that whatever Ari needed to share was serious by the dark look on her face. She had to wonder if Gage had decided to call her after their talk last week. Maybe they had talked and decided to give their relationship another chance and she was planning on breaking the news to her. Excitedly, Beth waved her towards the kitchen.

"Chloe just laid down so we should be good for at least an hour," Beth smiled. "How about some hot tea?"

"Tea would be wonderful!" Ari agreed.

Once they were settled on the couch with warm tea in their mugs, Arabella turned to her, a look of uneasiness on her face.

"Beth, I know this is going to come as a surprise, but—"

"But—"

Beth encouraged her friend to continue, hoping Gage had called her and Ari was here to share the news with her that they were getting back together! "Ari," she placed her hand on Ari's knee, "whatever it is, you can tell me."

"I'm three and a half months pregnant, Beth."

The words flew from Ari's mouth, hitting Beth like a freight train at high speed. She could feel the blood drain from her face as the shock set in. "*Pregnant*, Ari?" Beth's thoughts went back to the conversation she'd had with Gage. Did he know this news and didn't tell her? Is this what prompted him to change his life? She had to find out! "Does Gage know this?"

Immediately, Beth watched Ari's defenses go up. She sat back against the couch, arms folded across her chest. "No, and I have no intention of telling him, Beth."

Beth's frustration grew stronger. Her best friend had not only made a huge mistake by walking away from God and breaking her purity promise, but now, when she thought Ari had finally come to her senses, she decides to keep this life changing secret from her child's father. Someone had to get through to her, especially with what Beth had just learned from Gage.

"How can you even *think* to keep this from Gage? This is his child, Ari, and no matter how things ended between the two of you, he has every right to know he is going to be a father! Don't wait until it's too late, Ari, *please.*"

Ari took a deep breath and exhaled slowly, but Beth could still see the tension on her face. Now that she knew Ari was expecting, Beth didn't want to be a source of stress to her in any way.

"I'm sorry, Ari. I just feel very strongly that children need to have both parents in their life."

"I'm really surprised by your reaction," Ari's face had confusion written all over it. "Aren't *you* the one that said I'd thrown my life away by allowing Gage into it?" Ari stood up and walked across the room to the large bay window. She stared outside for what felt like an eternity before she returned to the coach. "Why the sudden change of heart where Gage is concerned, Beth?"

Beth didn't want to give away the secret Gage had entrusted her with. "It's not about Gage, so much, Ari. I just don't think keeping this kind of information is beneficial to any party involved; especially the child that can't speak for itself."

"Beth, please try to understand my position here," Ari pleaded. I would *never* intentionally keep Gage away from his child if he chose to come back to Rock Haven on his own. But—"

She paused briefly, and Beth could see she was struggling to keep her emotions intact.

"He's proven that he doesn't love me. I don't see him beating down my door trying to save his relationship with me. How would it benefit our child in the slightest bit if I tried to force Gage to be a father? I certainly don't want Gage coming back to me out of obligation. I can raise this child on my own, and he or she will never have to feel the rejection I've felt from Gage, when he decides to walk away from their life like he did mine. Don't you understand?"

The tears that fell from Beth's face matched those of Ari's. Her heart hurt so deeply for the friend she loved like a sister. She couldn't walk away from Ari in her greatest time of need, whether she agreed with her decision or not. She and Anthony, along with Sam and his wife Karen, would all have to rally around Arabella and be the strength she needed, whether she included Gage or not. Beth pulled her best friend into her arms and hugged her tight, silently praying that Gage would do and say whatever he had to, to win Ari back and be a part of his child's life. Soon!

"Ari, we will all stand beside you and help you the best we can. But as your best friend, I have to be honest with you and tell you that I think your decision to keep this from Gage is wrong. I promise you that I won't be the one to tell him the news, but please Ari, consider sharing this with him before it's too late, won't you?"

"My decision has been made, Beth. We will just have to agree to disagree on this one for now."

Even though Beth nodded in agreement, she couldn't help but wonder how this information would affect Gage's visit to Rock Haven.

Ari continued. "I need your help with one more thing, Beth."

Beth turned to face her, scared of what else might be coming.

"I'm moving into the cottage. I can't stay in the loft any longer," Ari said, clearly and defiantly stating her plan. "There are just too many memories of Gage there and I need to focus on the future. I can't continue to live in the past with 'what could have been'. The truth is, Gage made his choice and he doesn't want to be with me," Ari's voice caught as she spoke the last, very emotional words. "Anyway, the cottage will be the perfect size for me and the baby, and I've already got plans for painting and furnishings. What do you say? Will you help me?"

Relieved that the worst of the conversation was over, Beth readily agreed. "I would love to help you, Ari. Chloe is going to be so excited to have a cousin to play with!" Beth couldn't help to feel somewhat excited about the baby, even though she knew the struggle that lie ahead for Ari.

Long after Ari had left and Anthony made it home from the office, Beth finally had the opportunity to ask her husband's opinion on all that had transpired. They were sitting on the floor of the bathroom sharing the job of bathing Chloe before putting her down for the night.

"I really feel like I need to call him, Anthony. Give him some kind of warning."

"I think you'd be making a huge mistake, Beth." Anthony poured a glass of bath water over Chloe's head, and they watched her giggle and splash about. Bath time was her favorite part of the day. "You swore to Ari that you'd keep her pregnancy a secret."

"But—"

"Honey," Anthony placed his hand over his wife's where it rested on the edge of the bath tub, "he's going to find out when he gets to Rock Haven. Just let them work it out for themselves."

Beth shook her head. "I don't think I can. She's going to freak out when he gets here, Anthony! And I don't mean in a good way! I know she still loves him, but she has hardened her heart to the topic of him being a part of her life *and* the baby's." Beth stood up and walked over to the sink, grabbing a towel and giving her husband room to pull a soaking wet, and very happy Chloe, from the tub. She helped him wrap their daughter in her hooded duck towel and the three of them headed into the nursery. In the midst of drying and smothering Chloe in sweet smelling lotion, Anthony continued to share his thoughts.

"Honey," he placed their daughter in her arms, "everything is going to be okay. You have to let go and give it to God. What did Pastor Ron say just last week during service? 'You can worry, or you can trust God. But not both! By choosing to worry, you are telling God that you don't trust him to work this out."

Feeling defeated, Beth pulled Chloe tight against her chest and sighed.

"How about you just sit down here and spend some time singing and cuddling this sweet little girl that wants her mommy's attention."

Beth would never understand how her husband *always* knew exactly what she needed, at just the right time. She took a seat in the white glider rocker that sat next to Chloe's crib and snuggled their daughter close, as Chloe reached up and patted her cheek. This had always been Beth's favorite part of their evening routine. Nothing could compete, with the scent of a freshly bathed baby smothered in lotion, to make the worries of the day disappear.

"*Mama.*"

"Anthony, did you hear that?" Beth called out to her husband who'd just started down the hallway. He came rushing back into the nursery just as Chloe said the word again.

"Mama."

"She did it, honey! She said her first word; and it was mama!"

"Mama," Chloe mimicked her mother in a sweet baby voice and Beth squealed with joy.

"See honey, I told you everything was going to be alright. How could you have a worry in the world when you've got Chloe in your arms calling out to you. What a beautiful sight you two are."

Anthony placed a kiss, first on Chloe's head and then on Beth's. "Don't take too long getting her to sleep. I'll be waiting for you."

He flashed the grin that had melted Beth's heart for over fifteen years, and she couldn't miss his suggestion. She sang two rounds of "Puff the Magic Dragon" before Chloe's heavy lids finally closed for the night. Beth wasted no time placing her in bed and heading towards the master suite. Anthony was in bed, reading his Bible, by the soft light of his lamp.

"How do you do it?" Beth grinned.

"What's that? How do I do what?" Anthony teased.

Beth made her way to the other side of the bed, pulled the covers back and climbed in, facing him. "Oh, you know *exactly* what I mean! You never cease to amaze me, Anthony. You always know how to keep me together and calm when I feel like I'm spiraling out of control. You know just what to say to keep me grounded."

"So, what you're saying," he grinned, "is that you'd like to thank me?"

Beth swatted him playfully on the arm. "I don't know. You look awfully engrossed in your reading."

"Come here, silly girl. I will show you how engrossed I can be."

The next morning at breakfast, Beth was a different woman. Between her husband's affection, and the time she'd spent in the Word, her outlook on Ari's situation had taken a complete turn for the better. Beth felt nothing but hope for her friend's future.

Chapter 22

"*Son! It's nice to see* you could finally make the trip. Come in." James stepped aside to allow his son to enter through the doorway. His cool tone made it clear to Gage, that he'd hadn't forgotten their last conversation.

James peeked his head out into the hallway as he kept talking. "How long are you in town? I'm expecting that this might be a permanent move for you?" He craned his neck one way and then the other. "The office hasn't been the same without you."

"Whoa, slow down, Dad. Let me get my coat off and get settled in before we get too deep into this conversation, okay? And, you can close the door and stop worrying. I didn't bring her with me."

James nodded. "Sorry, Gage, it's just—", his father paused as if unsure whether he should be transparent with his son about his feelings. "Well……. it's just been a while. Seems your life has changed quite a bit since you left here." He patted Gage on the shoulder and for a brief moment, Gage thought his father was actually happy to see him.

Gage pulled his suitcase through the doorway and set it against the wall, while he removed his coat and shoes.

"Are you planning on staying *here* tonight?"

"Actually dad, I was planning on staying a couple of days. If that's not a problem?" Not waiting for his father's response, Gage headed towards the kitchen to grab a glass of water. It had been a long, emotional week already. He knew the next couple of days were going to be even worse.

James waited to speak until his son to returned to the living room and settled into the recliner, opposite of where he was sitting.

"Am I missing something, Gage? It's not that I *mind* you staying here. You're always welcome. But why on earth would you *want* to stay here? All of your belongings are at your place five miles down the road."

"Dad," Gage looked straight into his father's eyes with more confidence than he'd had in his entire life, "I've actually been back in New York for a week now. The condo has been sold, but I haven't been to the office yet. That's probably why you weren't aware." His father still kept in close contact with many of the employees at their firm. Another one of the reasons Gage had kept his visit a secret.

James' puzzled gaze lingered on his son. "A *week*, Gage? Well, why haven't I seen you before now? What in the world is going on with you?" Something seemed to click in his father's mind. Gage watched his father's expression change from confused to enlightened. "Does this have something to do with that girl you've been playing house with out there in Michigan?"

Gage just shook his head at his father's description. Could he even begin to understand what Gage had been through, or just how much he'd changed in the past several months? And would he ever truly understand his relationship with Arabella? The scale weighed heavy with doubt in Gage's mind.

"I came back long enough to sign on the closing of the condo. I want to empty out my storage unit and make arrangements to have my belongings shipped to Iowa." Gage bravely waited for the outburst surely to follow.

James stood and turned his back to Gage as he walked across the room. After a moment, he turned back to face his son, anger stretched across his face. "*Iowa,* Gage? Really? Are you *purposely* trying to hurt me?"

"Dad, I know you don't want to hear this, but I want to live my life in Iowa. It's where I've always loved to be! And one thing that I've learned recently, is that life is too short to be unhappy. Being on the farm makes me happy, Dad; and I'm sorry if that hurts you. I'm taking over Nonnie's ranch now that she's gone."

His father stormed back across the room, stopping directly in front of him and glaring down at him as he began his verbal attack. "Gage, this is absurd! *Why on earth* would you want to throw away the life you have here in New York for that *silly farm*? You sound more like your mother every day, you know that?"

Gage steadied his elbows on his knees and dropped his head into his hands. He had suspected this would be his father's reaction. When he looked up again, he questioned his father with the thought he hadn't been able to get off his mind for some time. "Dad, did you even love my mother?"

James drew in a sharp breath and stared at Gage, clearly shocked. When he finally spoke, moments later, his voice crackled with emotion.

"How could you *ever* doubt my love for your mother, Gage? She was my entire world, from the moment I first laid eyes on her. And then, when you came along.......well, we were happier than two people could ever dream of being."

Gage continued to stare his father in the eye as he shoved his hands into his pockets. "She loved the farm, Dad. And you made her choose. Why would you do that to someone you claim to love?" The minute the words left his mouth, Gage thought of Arabella. How he had made her choose between himself and God. He realized in that moment that he was no better than his father. And he certainly, had no right to judge.

"Gage, your mother chose to come to New York because she loved me. We built a life here together. I knew she had a happy childhood on the farm. But that was her childhood, her past; and I was her future! You and I were her life!"

"It didn't have to be that way, Dad! You could've attempted to visit the farm with her! We could have gone as a family during the summers. Just imagine how happy that would've made her." Gage looked down at the floor before he continued. This conversation with his father was difficult, but Gage had promised himself he would be honest and tell his dad *exactly* how he felt this time. "How happy that would've made *me*."

"Gage, this is all part of the past. I don't know why you insist on bringing it up again! It serves no purpose."

Gage had expected his father to put an end to their talk as soon as he felt uncomfortable, but Gage wasn't quit finished with him. "Why didn't you ever tell me that my mother was an artist?" Another question that had been sitting on Gage's heart since his Junior year Art Expo.

"Why do you insist on bringing up the past, Gage? It's over! It does no good to dwell on it!"

Gage couldn't believe how sheltered his father had kept him. "Dad, you're talking about my *mother*. I had a right to know about her! I wanted to know what she liked and what she didn't like! Her favorite color, favorite food, everything there was to know. Don't you get that?"

"But *why*, Gage? I don't understand the difference it will make. It only hurts to talk about her."

Gage had spent the last several weeks, growing in his relationship with the Lord. He wanted more than ever, for his father to have that too. To let go of the anger and resentment he had towards God for taking his wife away.

Gage stood up, toe to toe with his father. His voice was soft and gentle as he spoke to the man he once adored. The man he longed to have a relationship with. "Dad, I've been at the farm for the past two months, trying to get my head on straight and to figure out what I want with my life. The only thing I've found that matters is the Lord. Dad, I wish you could see how much your anger and resentment have taken a toll on your life……and mine. It's driven a wedge between us since mom died. And I'm begging you to let it go."

"That right there, is your Nonnie talking," James' voice escalated as he shook his finger at Gage. "Just like when your mother first came to New York with me! All her talk about God, and how loving and kind He is. Let me ask you something, Gage. If God was so kind and loving, then why did He take your mother away from us? Can you answer that?" His father's voice had escalated to a point Gage wasn't comfortable with.

Gage pushed his fingers through his hair. He'd hoped to have one good night's rest and a hot breakfast before tackling this conversation, but there was no turning back now. "Dad, things happen in life that we don't understand. But God is real. And He loves you, and He loves me. He desires to have a relationship with you. Of that I'm positive."

"I think I'm going to step out for a while, Gage." His father stormed to the closet and grabbed his jacket, exiting the front door before he even took the time to put in on.

"I guess I should've been more prepared for this," Gage muttered and shook his head. He gathered his suitcase and made his way down the hall to the guest room. He'd give his father the rest of the night to think things through, before he addressed the issue again in the morning.

As could be expected, Gage didn't sleep well that night. He tossed and turned as he thought back to his many conversations with Pastor Dave in Iowa. Then he'd think again about the talk he'd just had with his father. Of course, interwoven in all of that, were thoughts of Arabella. She always found her way into both his thoughts and dreams, just as she'd done every night since the he'd left her back in Michigan. He longed to talk with her. To hold her and tell her how much he loved her. But would she ever be able to forgive him for leaving her and turning his back on their relationship? Gage had been working through forgiveness with the Lord for the mistakes he'd made with Ari. But would *Ari* ever be able to forgive him, or trust him again?

Eventually, Gage must have drifted off for a couple hours of sleep. When he woke, it was half past seven. After a hot shower, bowl of oatmeal, and some time alone in the Word, Gage approached his father once again. He was hoping to continue their conversation, and praying it ended better this time.

"Good morning, Dad." Gage found his father sitting in his favorite leather chair in the den, holding a book in his hand. As Gage drew closer, he realized that is wasn't just *a* book, but a photo album that Gage had never seen before.

"What have you got there?" Gage pointed to the blue book as his father closed the cover.

James looked up, emotion filling his eyes. "I thought I was doing the right thing for us, Gage. I thought if your mother broke all ties to the farm, then she wouldn't be tempted to leave me and return there."

Taken aback by his father's words, Gage moved towards him and took a seat on the ottoman near his feet.

"Dad, why did you think she would leave you? Mom loved you. Don't you realize it's possible to love more than one person at a time?"

"Gage," he sniffled, "I never had a family growing up and it was all I ever dreamed of. When I met your mother, we fell in love. It was as if every dream I ever had was coming true. But then I made my first, and only, trip to the farm." His father sat back in his chair, placing the album on the end table next to him. "Your mother was a different person there. I felt like she loved that place more than she loved me. It was all she ever talked about, her happy years there growing up. It seemed to be the only place she wanted to be. But I wanted to build a life for us here, in New York, just the two of us. So, I made her choose. Don't you see, I was doing it for all of us, Gage! For our *family*."

Gage felt overwhelming sadness for his father and the years that he'd lost by refusing to let go of his insecurities, his anger. At that moment, he didn't want to talk anymore about loss and pain, he only wanted to be the son that his father needed.

"Dad, what do you say we head over to the office for a little bit and grab some lunch together after that?"

Conscious of where his father had placed the photo album, Gage made a mental note to look at it later.

Relief flooded James' face at the offer. "I would really like that, Gage." James stood, and together they made their way to Gage's car. They headed downtown to the office, where Gage made his official resignation announcement. He could tell his father was still angry about it, but in the end he had no say in the matter. He had signed the business over to Gage nearly four years ago and, it was, by all rights, Gage's company now.

Gage spent the next couple of hours talking with his manager and operations director, about how the office would continue to run under their control until he found a buyer for the business. With the employees gathered together, he promised he would do all he could to keep their jobs secured. There were a lot of goodbyes and well wishes before Gage cleaned out what used to be his office. Even though Gage was certain his decision to give up the business and make a life in Iowa was the right choice, it was still bittersweet as he said goodbye to each and every one of the employees that he had worked beside of, and had been in charge of, for so many years. He and his father were at the office for nearly three hours before they made their way downtown for lunch.

Conversation was a struggle once they were seated at the restaurant, and Gage quickly realized that work was the only thing they had in common. It was a sad realization. He desperately desired to have the type of relationship with his father that would allow him to be open about his dreams, goals, and even the struggles he encountered along his path. He wanted more than anything to share with his father, the love that he had found in Arabella, and the life he was planning on building in Iowa. But he knew that his father was struggling with everything he'd thrown at him already. So, he chose to let it rest for the time being, promising himself that he would make another trip to the city sooner than later.

That evening, Gage explained that he would be leaving New York in the morning. Although he could sense his father's disappointment, he didn't argue with Gage or ask him to change his mind. After his father turned in for the night, Gage made his way back to the den, curious to find the photo album he'd seen earlier that morning.

He found the book right where his father had left it. Taking a seat in the well-worn, brown leather chair, Gage ran his rough hand over the soft, velvet exterior, preparing his mind and heart for whatever the pages held. As he turned back the cover, Gage discovered it was more than just a photo book; it was *his* baby album. An album he'd never even seen. It contained pictures of him, both alone and with his parents, from birth up to the time his mother had been killed. For his entire life, Gage had wondered why he never had any pictures of himself in their home. Why his father refused to hang pictures up of he or his mother. The house remained cold and lonely, even though Gage had pleaded with his father numerous times to hang pictures of the mother he missed and loved so much, to no avail.

Turning the page, Gage found a lock of hair from his first trip to the barber, tucked into a photo pocket along with his newborn hospital bracelets. Gage fought against the anger growing deep inside of him, questioning why the old man would have kept this from him all these years.

"I was only trying to protect you, Gage. I can see now what a mistake it was." Gage turned to see his father standing in the doorway.

"I thought you'd gone to bed." Turning, Gage wiped a stray tear that had slid down his face, and focused his attention on the book. "I just wanted to see what was in the album." Gage closed the cover.

"It's yours, Gage, and you have a right to it. I'm just sorry it took me so long to realize how much I was hurting you."

This time it was his father that took a seat on the ottoman and faced Gage as he continued. "I wish I could take back all the years that I hurt you and change the way I did things. I was so distraught over your mother's death, and so angry at Nonnie and that stupid farm, that I let it cloud my judgement. I would have done anything to protect you and keep you in New York with me."

The only time Gage had ever seen his father cry was at his mother's funeral.

Until this moment.

Torn between his anger at the situation and compassion for his father, Gage remained silent.

"Gage—"

"Dad," Gage interrupted, "why did you think I would be anywhere but New York? This was our home. Nonnie never had any intention of keeping me in Iowa." Gage just couldn't wrap his head around his father's thinking.

His father refused to look him in the eye as he spoke. "Gage, I couldn't think clearly when I lost your mother. My first instinct was fear. Over time I let that fear turn into anger. In the end, I just allowed it to consume me." When James finally lifted his head and made eye contact with his son, the hurt he'd kept bottled up for all those years streamed down his face. "I'm so sorry for the pain I've caused you, Gage. If I could go back and change things I would, but we both know I can't. I have to live with that decision. My only hope is that someday you will be able to forgive me."

"Dad, I forgive you. And—-I love you." Gage shrugged and shook his head, "I may not understand your choices, but they weren't mine to make. I've made plenty of mistakes in my life that I wish I could change, so I'm not judging you. But—" Gage laid his hand upon his father's and took a deep breath, contemplating the depth of his next words. "Dad, it's not *my* forgiveness you need to worry about. You need to learn to forgive yourself. And that won't happen until you connect with the Lord."

Gage silently prayed that he and his father had broken through a barrier. Maybe, just maybe, now would be the time for his father to begin the journey Gage too had started. The journey that only pointed in one direction. And that was toward the Lord. When his father abruptly pulled his hand away and stood up, Gage could do nothing but stare up at him and watch, as anger and rage overtook him. The tenderness that had gently emerged from his father's eyes just moments ago, was squandered abruptly.

"*Your* forgiveness is all I need, Gage. I refuse to believe in a God that took the only woman I *ever loved* away from me!" His father turned and stormed out of the room once again.

James never came out of his room before Gage left the next morning. Feeling completely devastated, Gage did not try to speak with him. Before he left the house, Gage set the pile of letters that Nonnie had shared with him, on his father's kitchen table. Maybe the letters, along with some time to think, and lots of prayers on Gage's part, would be the best thing for his father. Gage forced himself to look forward, not at the past, as he made his way towards the airport.

Chapter 23

Ari stood sideways in front of the full-length mirror in her bedroom, admiring her growing figure. Her hand gently rubbed the baby bump that she could no longer hide, and no longer felt that she needed to hide. She was nearing her fifth month of pregnancy and had *finally,* with Beth's encouragement of course, purchased some maternity clothes. She had to admit, as she continued to stare at her expanding waist line with unexplainable joy in her heart, it couldn't be for a better cause. She fell in love with her child more and more each day. And she was now beginning to feel the first flutters of movement.

"Your Auntie Beth will be happy that I'm dressed to her standards for our little shopping trip today. Don't you think, little one?" Ari ran her hands over the soft pink maternity top that Beth had given her earlier in the week. "Oh!" she exclaimed at the slight movement she felt where her hand rested. "I guess you agree," Ari giggled. She continued talking out loud as if the baby could hear and understand what she was saying. "Time to refocus our attention! We've got some important business to take care of today." Ari's bright smile grew wider as she thought about what the day held in store for them. Struck once again by the depth of love for the unborn child she was carrying, Ari looked at her reflection one more time. Cradling her round belly between her hands, she felt an overwhelming peace wash over her. "It's going to be a great day!" she announced. "No more crying for what could've been," her voice quieted to a whisper, as if it wouldn't affect the baby. "Today's a new day and a fresh start."

The girls had a shopping trip planned for the afternoon, but this time it wasn't for maternity items. Ari's birthday was just two weeks away; and Beth was treating her to lunch and shopping. Between finishing the nursery and preparing the cottage, the girls thought this might be the only time they had to get together outside of work to celebrate.

Beth's knock sounded at her door. Turning away from the mirror, Ari called out to Beth as she headed that way. "C'mon in!"

"Oh Ari, look at you! You are simply glowing today." They met in the living room, and at Beth's compliment, Ari twirled around in front of her.

"Don't you mean I look good because of the pretty shirt that *you* picked out for me?" Ari teased.

Beth grinned and audibly sighed, no doubt feeling more relaxed since they'd had their talk. "Well, you know, I do have impeccable taste!" She teased Ari back. "Better grab a sweater, it's still a little chilly out there."

Ari slipped her arms into her white sweater sleeves and the girls made their way to Beth's car. Before she pulled away, Beth wanted to discuss lunch plans and formulate their list of "must go to" stores.

"Let's just stay in town today, if you don't mind," Ari answered, thinking how nice it would be to eat somewhere other than her own restaurant. As big as their menu was, it still got boring after a while. "I've really been craving tacos from Nina's, if that's okay with you. And you should already know we have to eat first, silly!" Ari patted her tummy.

Beth laughed as she put the car in drive and headed downtown.

"I was secretly hoping you'd pick Nina's place! It's been *three* weeks since Anthony and I have been there."

The girls both giggled. Less than five minutes later, they were parked outside Nina's bright orange building, that boasted red and green accents and several Mexican flags. It was the one place in their town, besides Francesca's, that everybody was aware of. Towns people and travelers alike were drawn in by the sight of place. Inside, was nothing less. Brightly painted chairs, colorful table runners and wall hangings made everyone feel right at home. Additionally, there was always music that sang out from the speakers, and the owner danced around tables and straight into your heart. Nina was loved by all who knew her.

Once the girls had been welcomed warmly by Nina, they were seated at their table and began placing their orders.

Beth was eager to fill Arabella in on Chloe's latest baby antics.

"Just you wait, Ari. Your time is coming. That precious little thing you're going to deliver will have you running non-stop by the time she's two!"

"I can't believe Chloe gave her baby doll a bath in your toilet! You've really got your hands full with her, Beth."

"Can't take my eyes off of her for a second," Beth's face lit up, even as she discussed the trials that motherhood brought with it. "I thought I was safe, keeping her in the bathroom with me while I showered." Beth rolled her eyes and grinned. "I certainly learned my lesson with that one!"

"And trying to use your pizza pan for a slide on the stairs," Ari raised her hands in the air, a large grin spread from ear to ear, "that girl has *quite* the imagination."

"She did have a *little* help from her daddy with that one," Beth admitted, then leaned in close and continued. "Seriously Ari, if I knew how much fun having kids was going to be, I wouldn't have made Anthony wait as long as we did. I'm ready to hear a houseful of little pitter patters!"

"*Really*?" Ari questioned her with surprise. Beth had been an only child and uncertain if she even *wanted* children, before she married her husband. But Anthony had been adamant that they have kids. It made Ari happy to see her friend so excited about motherhood. "Should I be expecting some news of another pregnancy anytime soon, then?"

"Wellllllll," Beth gushed.

"No way!" Ari's eyes grew wide in suspense. "Beth, are you pregnant?"

Beth nodded in answer to Ari's question and both girls squealed with delight. "The doctor confirmed it a few weeks ago, but it's still a secret to everybody but you! You have to know my husband adores you. You are the *only* one he's letting me share the news with!" Beth's face radiated with joy. "My first ultrasound is next week and then we will share it with our families. Anthony is over the moon excited!"

"This is wonderful news, Beth. I can't believe our little ones are going to grow up together just like you and I did," Ari exclaimed. "I couldn't be happier for you guys. You are two of the best parents I know, and your kids are lucky to have you! Congrats."

"Thanks, Ari. I can't *believe* how happy I am. It seems like all of the dreams I ever had, and some I didn't even realize I had, have come true with Anthony. I feel so blessed."

Inside, Ari's emotion retreated. The overwhelming thought that she and Gage would *never* have a life together like that with their baby, pressed against her heart from all sides. She was certain all the blood had drained from her face.

"I'm sorry, Ari. I didn't mean to go on like that." It was quiet for a moment before Beth continued. "But you know— maybe it's not too late for you?" Beth reached out and placed a hand over her friend's, when Ari rolled her eyes in response to that comment. "Won't you even consider telling Gage about his child?"

"We agreed this topic was not up for discussion, Beth, and I haven't changed my mind." Ari crossed her arms defiantly, hoping that Beth would get the hint and leave it alone.

The waitress appeared with their lunch and Ari couldn't have been more relieved for the distraction. So far, Beth had respected her wishes about *not* discussing Gage, and Ari certainly wasn't going to change her mind on that topic anytime soon.

After dabbling in her rice and nudging her taco around her plate, Ari finally took a bite of her food, allowing herself to savor the taste. "Oh, man! I have been waiting all morning for this. Seriously, Nina has to be the best cook in the entire world! If only I could convince her to come work for me. I would love to expand the menu and add some Mexican options." Ari laughed. She had been trying to talk Nina into that for over ten years; it was now just a joke between them. Ari knew that Nina would never leave the restaurant that she considered home. Truthfully, it was a nice treat for Ari when she could find time away from her own place.

"I couldn't agree more. This is the best burrito I've ever tasted!" In between bites, Beth managed to ask Ari if she intended to find out the baby's gender.

Ari shook her head and took a drink of her water before responding. "No, I want to be completely surprised. I mean," Ari pointed towards her bump, "this is it. The only baby I'm ever going to have and I want to do it right."

"Ari stop talking like that. You're twenty-six years old, for Pete's sake. You act like your life is over."

Ari rolled her eyes. "Right, Beth. Because I'm sure there will be a line of guys *dying* to go out with me when I've made the mistakes I've made. And not only that," she took another sip of her water, "but what man in his right mind wants to raise someone else's child? No," she shook her head defiantly, "we will be just fine on our own. Just the two of us, thank you."

"I assume since you have now re-opened the topic for discussion, that you are ready for a little more of my opinion! Maybe you're just thinking about it all wrong, Ari. If you would only share the truth with Gage and let God work things out, you might have the future you've always dreamed about!"

"Beth, please, I can't discuss this with you right now, okay? My heart is still trying to fight through the hurt of losing him."

Beth simply nodded in agreement, biting her tongue to keep the secret that Gage had shared with her.

The girls finished their meals, talking about Chloe, and sharing pregnancies stories. They were both ecstatic to know that their due dates would be weeks apart!

When they were done with lunch, Ari decided they should walk a few blocks as they shopped, determined to burn off at least *some* of the calories they had just consumed. The sun was shining brightly, and even though the spring breeze was still a little chilly, the promise of summer was near. The scent of lilacs filled the air and bright tulips filled the flower boxes along the main street.

"Hey, have you seen that new store that opened on the corner of Fifth and Washington? It's supposed to be some event planner from what I hear. Maybe we should stop by and check it out." Ari tried to pick Beth's mind for any information she might have about Stephanie's store front. She hadn't made it over there yet, but maybe this was the perfect time. Maybe she would invite the couple to church on Sunday, and that way Ari could meet Stephanie's husband.

"I haven't heard anything about it. Oh," Beth stopped abruptly, "let's run into here!"

Ari found it odd that Beth quickly changed the subject, but before she could think twice about it, Beth had linked arms with her and was dragging her into Hemmings children's store to look at a pair of very tiny cowboy boots that were displayed in the window.

"We *have* to buy those. Between the two of us, we're bound to have one boy, right?" Beth bubbled over with excitement.

The girls exited the store some time later, with multiple bags full of infant clothing and toys. They also purchased not one, but two, very cute pairs of infant cowboy boots. Ari hadn't been able to argue the fact that brown was a color both boys and girls could wear. As they strolled down the sidewalk, arm in arm, the spring sun warmed their faces. Ari realized just how good it felt to be getting out of the house and spending an afternoon with her best friend. The news of Beth's pregnancy had been the highlight of Ari's day. Though the thought of going through this special time without Gage was depressing, at least now she had Beth to swap stories and share it with.

As they made their way down Main Street, Ari turned to Beth with an infectious grin on her face. "I know it's chilly out, but I'm craving Butter Pecan ice cream. Let's run over to Kilwin's!"

"One thing I've learned, is that you *never* argue with a pregnant woman when she has a craving! And besides that, Kilwin's sounds wonderful. But, can you hang on just a minute? I promised Anthony I would pick up his prescription." Beth pointed at the pharmacy three doors down. "And then after ice cream we are going to shop for your birthday, okay?"

"Sounds like a perfect plan," Ari smiled. "I'm just going to wait outside and soak up some more sun. Take your time." Ari made her way to the book store window while Beth headed down to Miller's.

A few minutes passed before Ari moved on to Clara's boutique where she stood at the window, taking in the fashionably dressed mannequins.

"Very cute. Too bad they don't carry maternity clothes," she chuckled to herself.

The thought of losing her figure hadn't crossed her mind until a few weeks ago. When Ari couldn't zip her "normal" jeans, as of that morning, she had a slight meltdown. Kindly, Beth reminded her that the sacrifice would be well worth it, as they scrolled through Chloe's newborn photo album. Ari had been in tears by the time they closed the book. She no longer cared about her figure, only the health and well-being of her child mattered. Beth's pregnancy news this afternoon had been both exciting and bittersweet for Ari. Sweet because she would get to share her pregnancy and all of the up and downs that went with it. Bittersweet because Beth had Anthony, they were a family. Ari's mind began to wander back to the discussion she'd had at lunch, and Beth's declaration that it wasn't too late for her and Gage. He had *relentlessly* filled her thoughts over the past couple of weeks, but Ari was determined not to give in and call him. As much as she wanted him to be a part of their lives, she wasn't strong enough to place that call and take a chance that he would reject her. With her head down, lost in thought, Ari turned to walk away, stumbling right into another pair of feet. Her head jerked up as she instinctively began to apologize.

"Oh, I'm so sor—" The tumbling words that spilled from her lips stopped abruptly as she looked up into the bluest eyes she'd ever seen.

"Arabella, right?"

Stephanie's words didn't register, because the blue eyes that stared back at her belonged to the man that owned her heart. The father of her unborn child was *here,* in Rock Haven! It was enough to knock the wind from her lungs. She continued to stare, trying to comprehend what Gage was doing back in town and why he was with this pregnant woman.

"It's me, Stephanie. We met at the obstetrician's office a few weeks ago." She continued, barely taking time to breathe. "Gage, this is Arabella." The woman looked from Gage to Ari as she introduced them. "I met her when I was in for my first baby appointment. She's expecting too." She seemed way too excited, which irritated Ari. "Arabella, this is Gage, my—"

"You're *pregnant*, Bella?" Gage's blazing eyes pierced her soul as he took a step closer.

Ari's hands quickly moved to cover her growing baby bump, trying to hide the truth from him. But Gage's knowing eyes followed her hands and rested on her belly. Seemingly in shock from the news, his face lost all color as he stared at her mid-section, waiting for her response.

"Wait, you two know each other?" Stephanie's confused look mirrored Gage's.

"*Bella, why didn't you tell me about the baby?*"

"Is somebody going to tell me what's going on here?" Stephanie questioned.

It felt as if quick sand was slowly sucking Ari under. She couldn't move her shaking legs. Was Gage the husband that Stephanie had talked about? She tried to put the pieces together in her head. Stephanie had mentioned that she and her new husband had just recently met and that they lived out west. Could it possibly be?

Please God, don't let it be true. Is she the reason he stayed in Iowa? Tears stung her eyes.

"*Gage*, is that you? I thought you weren't coming until next week!" Beth's voice called from down the sidewalk.

Ari struggled to catch her breath, as she turned towards her friend, confusion in her eyes. When Beth caught up to the trio, Ari wasted no time. "You *knew*? But how? How did you know he was coming back to Rock Haven? Why didn't you—" Ari accused, unable to complete her thought as she tried to wrap her mind around what was unfolding in front of her. "Weren't you the one *just* saying I should try to work things out with him! You are unbelievable! How could you?"

"Get back *together?* Okay, I'm really confused. Gage, I thought your ex's name was Ari, not *Bella*?" Stephanie's outburst only made the tears come faster.

"Ari, it's not what you think." Beth's pleading eyes bore into her. "Please give us a chance to explain."

Us? When did Beth and Gage become an 'us'? Ari didn't understand what was going on, but she refused to stand around and listen to one more word of deception. The two people she loved most in her life had betrayed her. Her fractured and splintered heart couldn't take one more lie. Slowly, she took a step backwards, but Gage wasn't going to let her go. He reached out to her, trying to grasp her hand.

"Bella, look at me. I need to know the truth. Are you carrying *my* child?"

Ari's hands were shaking so hard, the packages fell from her grip. Fighting desperately to not fall apart in front of him, Ari turned and began to walk away, as fast as her trembling legs could move.

"Bella, stop! We need to talk. Please," he begged.

She'd waited *so long* to hear his voice again. But not like this. No, she had to get away! Their betrayal continued to pound in her head and everything began to blur.

"So, this woman, *Bella*, is carrying your child, but...... you're in love with someone named *Ari*? Stephanie's blaring words found their way to Ari's ears before she could pull herself far enough away.

Love me? He doesn't even know what love is! Suddenly, nausea and dizziness grabbed at Ari, her heart thumping so violently, she was certain it would beat right out of her chest. A darkness began to close in around her. Feeling as if she were falling through a dark tunnel, Ari reached out grasping at anything she could to keep her balance. She heard Beth and Gage both calling out to her frantically, one last time, before all sounds disappeared, and everything went black.

"*Why didn't you tell me* she was pregnant, Beth?"

Beth got up from the tattered vinyl chair in the hospital waiting room, and closed the distance to where Gage stood, staring out the window. "Gage, it wasn't my place to tell you that. That decision was Ari's alone."

Gage turned to her, a flash of anger covering his face. "Beth, it's not like she was deciding on a new car or something! She's carrying *my child* for crying out loud. You didn't think that was important enough to tell me?"

Pulling her nervous hands apart, Beth reached out and placed one gently on Gage's arm. "I know your hurt and confused, Gage, and I really am sorry this is how you found out. But this is between *you* and *Ari*."

"I would've come back sooner if she had only told me." It was no longer anger that he expressed, but regret, as he dropped his head and stared at the floor. "I can't believe I'm going to be a father, and I didn't even know."

"It's a lot to take in, huh?" Beth easily remembered the day she and Anthony found out they were expecting for the first time. How exciting, but overwhelming, the news had been. But they had also planned their pregnancy. She couldn't imagine the pain Gage was feeling. And Ari? Well, Beth knew her friend had to be confused right now. All Beth wanted, was for the two of them to sit down and hear each other out.

"Beth, she has to forgive me." Gage looked up into her eyes, the pain in them nearly ripping Beth's heart in two. "I will do whatever I need to. But, she *has* to realize we are going to be a family. There's no other option!"

"Gage, I think you'd better prepare yourself. Ari is hurting. It might be wise to back off for a few days and let her absorb everything."

"No *way*, Beth! One look at the ultrasound monitor this morning, seeing our child suck its thumb and move around, and I knew. There is not a chance that I will let her shut me out of my child's life. Or hers! We are *going* to be a family!" Gage stepped back and took in a deep breath. "I didn't mean to raise my voice to you, Beth. I'm just—I don't even know how to express what I'm feeling right now."

"I understand, Gage. This is a delicate situation."

"I'll tell you one thing. Whatever questions I had before, about God's existence, were *gone* when I saw our baby. The minute I realized I was going to be a father, I made a promise to myself and God, Beth, that I would be the father He created me to be! My future has never been clearer, than in that single moment, hearing our child's heartbeat. In that one quick second, every fiber of my being was lost to the joy of this little miracle."

Beth watched as Gage strode across the room. With every step he took, confidence oozed from him. The self-assurance, evidenced in his step, and the way he held his head just a notch higher, scared Beth. She knew Ari well enough to know that there was going to be a fight on their hands. How long she held out before forgiving them, that was something Beth didn't care to guess at. All she could do was pray. And she'd be doing a *lot* of that!

Arabella squeezed her fist and forced her heavy eyelids open. Taking in the site of the IV running into her arm, she realized quickly the she was in the hospital. It took only a few moments, before the reality of what had happened caught up with her, and she began to panic. Tears spilled down her face as worry for her unborn child set in. Her hands found their way to her round shape, as she silently prayed that her child was okay. Caught up in her thoughts, Ari was completely unaware that she wasn't alone in the room.

"Bella, you and the baby are going to be fine. You got dizzy and blacked out, but fortunately, neither one of you were hurt in the fall. The doctor says you can go home tomorrow once you've rested and gotten plenty of fluids in you." She heard his voice growing closer as he moved slowly towards her bed, but she didn't understand a word he was saying. All her mind could think to do was pray for her baby as her eyes settled on her mid-section.

Thank you, Lord, for keeping my child safe. Relief was hers only for a moment, before the anxiety took over once again. *Oh, Lord, how am I going to get through this? Gage is married to another woman and now he knows about our child. Why would he bring his wife to Rock Haven? How could he do this to me?*

She could barely choke out the words through her emotion-filled throat. "Gage, you shouldn't be here. You need to leave."

"Leave? Are you kidding me, Ari?" Gage stared at her in disbelief.

"Ari, you're awake!" Beth's way-too-chipper voice preceded her entry into the room. "We were so worried about you!"

"Bella, I'm not going anywhere, now that I know you're carrying my child. I have a *right* to be here!" Gage's voice became slightly elevated, which only made Ari more upset.

The tension in the room grew thicker by the second. Ari looked from Gage to Beth in frustration.

"Neither of you has a *right* to be here, and I want you both to *leave*!" Arabella pushed the call button for the nurse.

Beth's eyes narrowed, her stern gaze directed towards Ari. "What is wrong with you?" she asked. "Why can't you just listen to what Gage has to say to you?"

The nurse walked into the room and addressed Ari. "Is there something I can get for you, dear?"

"I want these two to leave immediately. I don't want either of them in my room again, do you understand me?"

Obviously shaken by the tone of Ari's outburst, the nurse looked from Gage to Beth and then back to Ari. She quickly brushed past Beth and went to the head of Ari's bed where she tried to comfort her. "Honey, you just need a little rest." She attempted to fluff Ari's pillow. "You took quite a fall today. No worries though, the baby is fine. Would you like to see the ultrasound pictures?"

Gage closed the last bit of distance between he and her bed and displayed an accordion strip of black and white ultrasound images for Ari to see. "Our baby is perfectly healthy, Ari. Isn't he beautiful?" Gage beamed with pride as he attempted to brush the hair from Ari's eyes.

Filled with anger, Ari shoved his hand away. "You allowed this man to be present during my ultrasound! How dare you! He has no right to be near me or my child—I want them both removed *now!*"

Seemingly nervous that the situation was continuing to escalate, the nurse spoke up as she turned to Beth. "Maybe it would be best for the two of you to step outside for a few moments?"

"I can't believe you, Ari," Beth glared at her. "Do you realize how unreasonable you are being right now? Gage has every right to be a part of his child's life. If you'd only give him a chance, you might see how much he wants to be a part of yours!" Beth turned and left the room, but Gage lagged behind, much to Ari's dismay.

"Arabella, you can't keep me from our child. Please," he pleaded, "won't you just let me explain what I came here to tell you?"

Ari responded with a cold, steely-eyed glare as venom dripped from her lips. "I have nothing to say to you Gage. You made your choice months ago. If you care for me or this child at all, you will walk away from us both right now and *never* come back!" She felt the pain so sharp in her heart, as she uttered the words. After all, wasn't this exactly what she wanted? Gage. Their child. And her. *Together* as a family? But the ugly truth was, Gage already had a family. And it didn't include her.

Lord, this isn't how it was supposed to be. I love him so much and now we share a child. Why, Lord? Why did he have to leave me? Why did he have to fall in love with somebody else? Why was I so foolish to believe in him? Ari continued to wrestle with her thoughts.

"Sir?" The nurse moved closer to Gage, extending her arm towards the exit, encouraging him to leave.

Maybe realizing he was defeated, or maybe that he really didn't want to upset her, Gage spoke his next words very calmly before finding his way to the door. "Ari, I refuse to ever give up on you, on us, or our child. And there's nothing you can say or do to change that. You might kick me out of your room, but that will never change my love for you, or the fact that we have a future together. And it's growing stronger and bigger within you each and every day."

"Gage, I'm so sorry."

"It's not your fault, Beth." Gage took a seat next to her in the waiting room. "I should have told you my plans had changed and that I was in town. If only I could've talked with Ari *before* she saw me with Stephanie." Gage shook his head.

"I'm not sure it would have made a difference, Gage. She's determined to keep you out of her life." Beth's expression clearly showed how defeated she felt. "How are we ever going to pull this off? Or maybe the question I should be asking is, are you sure this is how you want to proceed?"

"Don't you worry, Beth, I have faith that this is all going to work out." Gage stood up to leave. "Listen, I've got to go see Stephanie and explain some things to her. Are you going to hang out here for a while until I can get back? I don't want Ari to be alone, even if that means we sit in the waiting room until she's ready to speak to us."

Again, Beth was struck my Gage's devotion. She could easily see the changes the man had made in Iowa, which gave her hope.

"I'm not going anywhere. Ari might not realize it right now, but she is going to need us both in the very near future. No matter how hard she tries to push me away, I will never abandon her." Gage leaned down to hug her. "You're a good friend, Beth. I'm sorry I put you in this position. But I'm going to do all I can to fix it. I promise you that."

Beth smiled at Gage as he stood back up. "Well, I'm confident you're the only one for the job, Gage. I will keep praying for you both."

After Gage left the hospital, Beth pulled out her phone and dialed Sam's number. Ari was going to need someone to drive her home tomorrow; and Beth doubted that she would be calmed down enough by then to let Gage or her do it.

"Hey, Sam. It's Beth. Have you got a few minutes? Ari needs some help."

"Sure, Beth, whatever my girl needs. I can assemble a cribs or dresser in no time! I don't even mind changing diapers. But I figure we've got a *little* time before that happens," he chuckled.

Beth groaned inside her head. She didn't want to burst Sam's bubble, yet here she was, stuck in the middle again. Hesitantly, she explained the entire story to him, as well as including the fact that she and Gage had been talking regularly over the past couple of weeks.

"Well, first things first. Is my girl okay? And what about the baby?"

"Oh, yes! I'm sorry, Sam," Beth sputtered. "I should have told you that first! Ari and the little one, are perfectly *fine*. They did an ultrasound and gave her fluids from an IV. They plan on releasing her in the morning."

"Good. Now that I know they are both okay, we can move on to the next subject. I figured he was going to call you too."

Now Beth was the confused one. "What do you mean, Sam?"

"Gage contacted me a couple of weeks ago, told me a little about what happened out in Iowa. We were supposed to finish that conversation when he got to town." Sam paused. "I didn't have any idea about Stephanie's shop downtown though. I'll bet seeing the two of them together was a very unpleasant sight for Ari."

"Unpleasant doesn't even begin to describe it, Sam. And the worst part is, I'm stuck in the middle and she's angry with *me* now. Not that I'm blaming Gage or anything. This whole situation just stinks. That's all I can say."

"I will do what I can to help the situation, Beth. Karen and I will head over to the hospital in the morning to pick her up. We'll plan for Karen to stay the night at the cottage with her. That is, of course, if Ari will let her. Stubborn girl."

For the first time all afternoon, Beth thought maybe she saw the slightest bit of light at the end of a very long, dark tunnel. "Thanks, Sam, and I say that from Gage too." She paused for a moment, unsure how onboard Sam really was with the current decisions Gage was making. "You know, Sam, I think maybe this really is going to work out."

"I hope so, for Arabella *and* the baby's sake. It seems on the up and up and I've always liked that boy. But," Sam paused again, "they sure have an uphill battle in front of them, don't they? We will put them all at the top of our prayer list."

"Well, I know one thing. Now that Gage knows about his baby, he isn't going anywhere!"

Chapter 24

The minute he walked in, she began her verbal assault.

"Why didn't you tell me she was pregnant, Gage? I *can't believe* you didn't tell me!" She stood facing him, hand on her hip, looking like she was ready to rumble. Obviously, she was upset over what had taken place this afternoon.

"I honestly did not know until this afternoon. Besides, it doesn't change anything. We are still moving through as planned, aren't we?" Gage moved closer to her as he talked.

"Seriously, Gage? You really want us to continue as planned, after the way she reacted today? Do you think we should proceed at all?"

"Oh, we are going to proceed, alright! But I do think we need to work faster, and move the date up. Don't you agree?"

"I never meant to hurt her, Gage!" Stephanie turned away from him, her head bent slightly toward the ground. "This isn't the way it was supposed to happen."

"Listen," he reached out touching her arm, "I don't want you getting upset. It can't be good for the baby."

"What about *her* baby, Gage? It is *yours*, isn't it?"

Although he'd had the last few hours for the news to sink in, it still took his breath away to hear it said aloud. "Yes," he nodded, "there's no doubt in my mind, that it's my child she's carrying."

"Wow. This really changes everything, doesn't it?"

"It certainly does. I just can't believe that, in all this time, she never picked the phone up to tell me I was going to be a father."

"Welllll," she said slowly, "you can't really judge her for keeping a secret when you've been hiding things as well, Gage."

"It's not the same," he snapped. "There is no comparison what so ever."

"Whoa, there." She lifted her hands in defense. "Back down, Gage."

"I'm sorry," he attempted to smile at her. "You didn't deserve that. You just can't imagine the thoughts running through my mind right now. I never expected to come back to Rock Haven and find her pregnant."

"What was her reaction at the hospital? Did you tell her *anything* about why we were together?"

"I couldn't do that. It would only make her more upset at this point."

"Gage, don't you think you should reconsider? Now that you know she's having your baby, doesn't that come first?"

"I can make my own decisions. I appreciate your input, but I'm moving forward as planned."

"Alright, Gage, if you're sure this is what you want, then I promise I will stand by you, and follow through with our plans."

"Good." Gage breathed a sigh of relief. "Now, I've talked with Sam and Beth, and it would appear that at least Beth is still on board. Sam, I may have to work on a bit longer, especially after today. I think we need to agree on a new date before I leave. Wouldn't you agree?"

"How soon are you thinking?"

They talked for another twenty minutes trying to iron out the plans they had been working on, and decided on a new date. It was only going to be a few days sooner than originally planned, and Gage was certain it would still be a surprise. A big surprise!

"This is going to be perfect!" Gage grinned and leaned forward to press a kiss on her cheek. "It's not exactly how I intended for it to go," he shook his head, his grin replaced with a look of pure determination, "but it's going to turn out just fine." Gage hesitated, looking down at the floor and then towards the window. In a small, desperate voice he added, "It has to work."

The tears began the minute Gage left her room, continuing until Sam arrived the next morning to pick her up. Ari felt like she hadn't slept at all. She was extremely tired. All she wanted, was to go home and sit in the baby's nursery. Alone! Maybe then, she could try and process everything that had happened in the past twenty-four hours, and figure out how she planned to proceed.

Is this really what I signed up for, God? I know I made a mistake, but.......okay a lot of mistakes when it comes to Gage, but is this really how my life is going to turn out? This certainly doesn't feel like I'm getting my life back on track. I don't know if I can do this!

There was a soft tap at her door and Sam opened it just wide enough to stick his head in the room. "Good morning, angel."

"Hi, Sam. You can come in." Ari sat up a little straighter in bed and smiled weakly.

"It looks like you've had a pretty rough night, kid." Sam came to Ari's bed side and kissed her on the forehead before taking a seat in the chair next to her.

"I'm fine, Sam. I suppose Beth was the one that called you?" Ari's words were filled with sarcasm. "I guess I should be thankful for that. But right now, I can't stand the thought of how she lied to me!"

"Ari," Sam picked her hand up in his, "you know that I love you. And that I'm going to be completely honest with you, right?"

Ari turned her head away from him. "Sam, I really don't need a lecture right now, please."

"Honey, I'm not going to lecture you. But you know that Beth loves you. If she has done something, it was probably for your own good. You may not like the way she handled it, but can't you at least talk to her about it? She is your best friend."

"I'm hoping someday I can think of her as my best friend again, Sam, but not now." Ari turned back to face him. "How could she keep a secret like that from me? What possible reason could she have for talking to Gage? Did she bring him back to Rock Haven just so he would find out about our child? That was *my* information to share! When and *if* I was ready. What's going to happen now that he knows? I can't do this, Sam." Tears began to spill down her cheeks again.

Sam moved from the chair, sitting on the edge of her bed and pulling her into a hug. Ari felt like she had been riding an emotional roller coaster these past few weeks as she cried about everything and anything. Her pregnancy hormones were definitely giving her a run for her money.

"Oh, Ari. It hurts me to see you this way," Sam gently rubbed her back. "Let's just not talk about it right now. We'll get you home and rested up for the next couple of days. Then, maybe we can revisit the topic. Okay? You need to take care of this little one." Sam pointed to Ari's tummy and grinned.

Ari relaxed against her pillow, a smile working its way across her face. "*Yes,* please get me out of this hospital. I want nothing more than to go home and be alone with my baby." Ari called for the nurse, who helped her get dressed and discharged, as Sam waited just outside the door.

Back at the cottage, Sam and Karen got her settled in before leaving for the evening. She absolutely refused for Karen to stay with her, assuring them both that she would do nothing but rest. She promised if anything happened, she would call them immediately.

For the next two days, all Ari did was sleep and cry. And eat and cry. And pray and cry.

Lord, how did my life end up such a mess? Please help me to sort through the truth and lies and make the right choices. Gage does have a right to be a part of this little one's life, but the thought of him with Stephanie and the two of them with my child.....that's too much to bear, Father. How do I make the right choice? What Ari couldn't understand, was why Gage had sent her flowers for the past couple of days, and continued to leave her voice mails telling her that he loved her. Eventually she had just turned her phone of completely. *It's only because of the baby, right? Why would he want anything to do with me when he's married to Stephanie? None of this makes sense to me! And why would Beth not tell me that he's married to another woman? Best friends don't keep secrets like that from each other. I thought I could trust her.* Their betrayal burned inside her chest.

Two days turned into five before Ari finally felt she could pull herself out of bed and go to the restaurant. She felt almost back to normal after a long warm shower and putting on one of her new maternity tops. As she rubbed her hand across her growing bump she wondered once again, what would be the best choice for her child. After spending the last five days in prayer, Ari felt she knew the decision she had to make. She just didn't want to make it. This decision would be most beneficial to her child, even if it hurt her in the process. From the moment she had seen his face again, she knew that Gage should be a part of this baby's life. Now, she just had to convince herself to pick the phone up and call him.

It didn't take long for her to brush out her blow-dried hair and decide she wasn't up for putting on make-up. She didn't plan on staying at the restaurant more than a couple of hours, just long enough to visit with the lunch crowd and say hi to everyone working in the kitchen. She'd be back at the cottage with take-out dinner in no time. She ran into Sam the minute she set foot in the kitchen. He pulled her into a hug, welcoming her.

"Ari, it's so good to see you out of the house!" His voice boomed throughout the room, causing all the staff to turn in her direction and wave. "We've all been so worried about you."

When he finally let go of her, and she could catch her breath, Ari replied. "I know, Sam. I appreciate the fact that you've all given me the space I needed, and let me think this situation through." She paused and looked around the kitchen, happy to be back in the environment that she loved. "So, I want to get back to work today, and keep it as normal as I can around here. Please, no questions about my choices, okay?"

"I understand, Ari. Just know that if you ever need to talk, I'm here for you...... and so is Beth."

"Sam!" Ari stomped her foot in frustration.

"Sorry Ari, but it's the truth. She loves you like a sister and she's worried sick about you. Won't you please just consider calling her?"

"I'll consider it," Ari paused, taking in a deep breath and exhaling before she finished, "if you promise *not* to bring it up again, and let me handle things my own way! Deal?"

"You are as stubborn as a mule! You know that, right, Ari?" Sam laughed and pulled her into another hug.

"That's just one of the reasons you love me, Sam."

It was just after the lunch crowd had cleared out and Ari was sitting in a back booth, leaning her head back with her eyes closed, feet propped up, when she heard the familiar voice.

"You look more beautiful than I've ever seen you, Ari."

She opened her eyes and quickly sat up straight, pulling her feet to the floor. Gage stood just inches from her. The look in his eyes as he took in the sight of her, caused her heart to flutter.

Why does he still affect me this way? Why can't I just get him out of my system?

The butterflies in her stomach were working overtime. But she wasn't about to admit any of this to Gage. She refused to be a charity case. He hadn't loved her enough to even stay in contact with her. And now? He'd already found another woman to replace her? There was no way Ari would give in and show him just how much he continued to affect her. She squared up her shoulders, ready to take on the battle.

"Gage, what are you doing here? How did you even know I would be here?" Ari scowled, putting up a tough front.

"Did you get the flowers I sent you?"

Oh, I got the flowers alright. But I have to wonder what your new wife would think if she knew about them. Ari bit her tongue and tried to keep her thoughts civilized.

"Gage? I asked what you are doing here." Ari's voice quivered as she spoke, feeling slightly uncomfortable with him in such close in proximity. She had wanted more time to think things through and prepare for their discussion before she met with him face to face.

All of the emotions that she had fought to contain for the past few months were rising to the surface just by being in the same room with him. His blue eyes mesmerized her. Ari combed his body from head to toe, and settled on his thick, muscular biceps. She remembered how good it felt to be in those arms as he'd held her. There were so many good things to remember; and she couldn't deny she still loved him. She would spend the rest of her life loving him. But could she forgive him and move forward as friends? Especially now that he was in love with somebody else?

Suddenly the words of Isaiah 40:29 flashed in her mind. *He gives strength to the weary and increases the power of the weak.*

Okay, Lord, I need your strength more than ever. Please fill me with your peace and help me to let go of my bitterness.

Gage eagerly took a seat across from her, his eyes never breaking contact. "Ari, I just want to talk with you. Please? There's so much we need to discuss." He reached across the table and took her hands in his.

I can't do this, Lord. His touch is too much, I can't.....Lord, give me strength!

This was not how she imagined their talk. She had told herself that she was going to be in control. She would determine how much she allowed Gage in back into her life. But sitting alone in this booth with him, proved to be more difficult than she'd imagined. She couldn't wipe the image from her mind of he and Stephanie that day on the street.

"Gage, I don't think I'm ready for this. *Please*, give me time."

Gage's voiced was steeped in frustration. "Ari, I *can't* wait! You're carrying my child and.......and I want to be a part of my child's life. Of your life, Ari. I want us to be a family."

That was more than she could handle. Every emotion that she'd tried to hold back, spewed from her lips in anger.

"*Family,* Gage? Don't you already have your own *precious* family to think about? Why can't you leave me alone and go on with your life with Stephanie?" Ari pulled herself up out of the booth and stood before him.

"What are you talking about, Ari? You think that me and Stephanie—"

"I don't want to talk about you and Stephanie, okay!" Ari started to walk away but Gage jumped from the booth and caught her by the arm, turning her to face him.

"Ari, it's not what you think. Please, just sit down and talk to me. I love *you*!"

"Gage, I really think you should go now. I know that we need to talk at some point but it's not going to happen today. I'm sorry." Ari pulled out of his grip and walked away, leaving Gage to stand alone.

Gage watched Ari exit the room as quickly as she could. It was obvious she couldn't stand the sight of him. Why else would she be running? He had never imagined her reaction would be so harsh. Filled with uncertainty, Gage sat back down in the booth and lowered his head.

How do I get her to listen to me, God? I just want her to know how sorry I am. Please, if it's your will that we get back together, let her heart be open to my words. Just create an opportunity for me to tell her I'm sorry, where she won't run from me.

Gage knew the truth. He'd taken so much away from Ari, and then walked out on her. He didn't deserve her love. But he begged God for another chance. A chance that he promised not to take advantage of.

Maybe I don't deserve her, Lord. But I have to try, for our child's sake if nothing more.

He had forgiven himself weeks ago, but Ari had no idea of the changes that had taken place in his life. He *had* to get her to sit down, long enough to listen to him. If he couldn't get her to forgive him, things would never be right between them. Baby or no baby!

Sam came busting through the kitchen door, breaking into Gage's thoughts. Spotting him, Sam made his way over to where he sat.

"Now I know why she's crying again! Gage, what did you say to her this time? Have you told her the truth yet?" Sam didn't even try to disguise his frustration.

"She wouldn't give me time, Sam! She thinks I'm in some sort of relationship with Stephanie for crying out loud!"

"Well, what did you expect her to think when she saw the two of you together? Gage, you've got to come clean about what happened in Iowa, and *soon*."

"So, you know everything? Beth told you the rest about what happened?"

"She told me bits and pieces. I suppose that's why you wanted to speak to me on your way through town?"

"Look, Sam, I need your help. I don't know any other way to get her to talk to me." Gage pleaded him.

"Oh, brother." Sam shook his head. "Somehow I knew I would be in the middle of all this before it was over. What's on your mind, boy?"

The slightest of smiles made its way across Gage's face. "Thanks, Sam. Okay, this is how it's going to go down."

Moments later, with everything in place, Gage *knew* Sam was scared that Ari would never speak to him again.

"I can't believe I let you talk me into getting involved in this fiasco." Sam shook his head slowly. "Are you sure this is the only way, Gage? Wouldn't something a little more private, be better?"

"She won't be alone with me, Sam. Now, I've run it through my mind a million times and this is the only way it's going to work. Are you on board?"

Sam looked up to the ceiling as if he was talking to God. "Forgive me, but,—yes. I'm on board."

"Great!" They both stood up and Gage wrapped the bartender in a hug. "I promise you won't regret this, Sam. There's no way she won't agree when she realizes the truth."

"I'm not so sure about that," he raised a worried eye brow in Gage's direction. "This may turn out to be the biggest disaster to *ever* hit Rock Haven!" Sam mumbled as he made his way back to the kitchen.

Ari had just finished taking a long, hot shower, preparing for a relaxing evening of Netflix, when the phone rang.

"Hey, Ari, I'm sorry to bother you."

"Sam? What's wrong?" Ari immediately sat up. Is everything okay?" Sam usually didn't call her at home, after work hours, unless it was urgent. Ari waited for his response, as panic threatened to set in.

"No, everything is *not* fine, unfortunately. I've got a problem down in the lower level and, I hate to ask this of you, but I'm going to need you to come back over."

Ari groaned in response. "Really, Sam? Are you *sure* whatever it is, can't wait until morning? I was just about to put my feet up for the night. It's been a very long day." The thought of having to change out of her comfy sweats and back into regular clothes was just depressing.

Sam paused a long while before he responded. "I wouldn't ask if it wasn't an emergency, Ari. I'm so sorry, but it really can't wait."

"Fine." Ari stood up from her comfy spot on the couch with just a little chip on her shoulder. She'd hoped to remain there for the rest of the evening. "Just give me time to change and I will be there in ten minutes, okay?" Begrudgingly, Ari made her way down to the restaurant to investigate.

Chapter 25

Gage *scrubbed his sweaty palms* down the front of his pants. In ten short minutes, Ari would be standing in front of him, and he had one last shot to plead his case. This was the moment he had been working towards for the past couple of months. The moment that would define his future. His heart beat erratically inside his chest as he thought about her possible reactions to his confession. Would she accept his apology and see how much he'd changed? Would she be willing to give him the second chance that he so desperately wanted? The chance to be a good husband to her, and father to their child? Or, would she tell him it was far too late to win her back. The latter left a sick feeling in the pit of his stomach. He didn't want to be a part-time father. Didn't want to sit on the sidelines watching Ari live her life from a distance. He wanted the whole package. He wanted his family! He silently began to pray as the minutes ticked away.

Please, God. I've waited for this very opportunity for what feels like a life time. Please give me the courage to bare my soul to her and share with her the changes I've gone through. Please let it be enough for her to realize how much I love her and need her. Help her to see we can make it work together, Father.

Pastor Dave had shared many verses with him over the course of their time together in Iowa. But as Gage prayed now, he remembered Isaiah 26: 3-4 clearly. It was one of the verses that had continued to give him the strength to get through each day, while he had been in Iowa working through his past.

"Those of steadfast mind you keep in peace—because they trust in you. Trust in the Lord forever, for in the Lord God you have an everlasting rock."

That's right. Lord, you are my rock and I trust you. I have faith in you, and I believe your words. My roots are planted deep and I will cling to you in time of need. No matter what Ari's reaction, my life is in You, Lord. You are my hope and my stronghold, and I can overcome anything, when I remember my future lies with you.

Gage felt a peace wash over him that only the Lord could provide. He'd made so many mistakes in his past, but he refused to live in fear of them anymore. He was made new in Christ! He would live out the rest of his days glorifying and thanking the Lord for the sacrifice He'd made for him. Gage wasn't sure how God *could* love him, after everything that he'd done. But he believed in the Lord's word, and His word was clear. God had created him, knowing well in advance the mistakes he would make. God gave His life on the cross, because He loved Gage enough to die for him. Horrible sins and all. That overwhelming, powerful truth continued to give Gage chills.

"Are you doing alright over here?" Sam's deep voice cut into Gage's thoughts. Gage turned to hug the man that he'd come to greatly admire.

"Well, I can't lie. I'm more than a little nervous about her reaction, Sam." Not knowing what to do with his shaky hands, Gage stuffed them into his pockets. "I know that God is in control, but I'm still a little weary thinking of her initial reaction. I'm wondering now if I should have planned this out a little better. What if she still walks away from me, even after all of this?" Gage nodded to the decorated room and the guests that occupied it.

"I'd say it's just a little late to be thinking of that now." Sam slapped him on the back, but when he spoke again his voice was much softer, laced with understanding. "Ari's a smart girl, Gage. Just speak the truth to her and let it sink into her heart. It may still take a while before she's ready for what you're asking, though. You have to remember what Ari's been through. She's still hurting, Gage, and she will need time to heal."

"Patience has never been my strong point, Sam." Gage chuckled.

"Well kid, I think it might be time to start practicing then!"

"Guys, I think she's here. Everybody quiet!" Beth called out into the room.

"Heaven help us all," Sam whispered, just loud enough for Gage to hear it. The comment did nothing to help his already frazzled nerves.

It became eerily silent as they waited for the door to open.

Ari fumbled through her purse, searching for the backdoor key to Francesca's. *This is ridiculous!* She thought to herself. *I should've stayed home and had Sam fix whatever's wrong.* After hanging up from her phone call with Sam, Ari had climbed back into her clothes, pulled her hair up into a loose bun, and tossed her dinner on the counter, the entire time grumbling to herself about the inconvenience of owning her own business. She had planned to sit and soak her tired feet tonight and devise an agreement between she and Gage that would allow him to be a part of their child's life without interfering too much with hers. It had been all she could think about for the past five days.

Just envisioning Gage and his new wife, settling down in Rock Haven to raise their child, was enough to make Ari sick to her stomach! Knowing that he and Stephanie would be living in Rock Haven, Ari realized she was going to have to toughen up to endure the oncoming days. There was no doubt that she would come face to face with them again, and she had to accept that they were now a couple.

There were so many questions still to be answered where the baby was concerned. Did she allow Gage to be at the doctor appointments? Would he want to be at the birth? How would they share custody? What role would his new wife play in all of this? The thoughts had consumed her for days but she was determined to strategize and plan, until she was comfortable with a decision and could face the ugly truth. The truth that she and her child's father were never going to be together. Their sins had consequences. And even though she knew God forgave her for her part, they would all suffer for it. Especially their child.

Finally fitting the key in the lock of the lower level entry, Ari slowly turned the knob and pushed the door open to a dark room. "I was sure Sam said the trouble was down here," she spoke out loud to herself. Her fingers fumbled along the wall searching for the light switch. Before she could find it, the room grew bright. Ari realized as she looked up, that the room was filled with dozens of faces she knew, balloons galore, and beautiful birthday decorations.

"SURPRISE!"

Startled, Ari jumped back, her hand upon her chest. "What is going on?"

"Happy Birthday, Arabella," the crowd yelled in unison, as noise makers sounded in the background.

Ari cautiously took two steps inside, a fake smile plastered across her face as she scanned the room in search of Sam. He was in serious trouble!

What Arabella found to be staring back at her, however, wasn't Sam at all. But rather the same blue eyes that had been haunting her dreams for weeks.

"*Gage?*" A bag of mixed emotions enveloped her mind, as she contemplated the distance to her car and how quickly she could get there. Gage walked over and reached a shaky hand out to her.

"Happy birthday, Bella," he smiled weakly. "I wanted to make it special for you. I hope," he looked down momentarily before looking up again, his sincerity evident in the shimmer of his eyes, "I hope you like it."

"Gage, why are you—"

"Arabella, come in and say hi to everyone," Sam interrupted. Gently he wrapped his arm around Ari's waist and guided her towards a cluster of people she knew from church.

Too stunned by everything happening around her, Ari played along for the next twenty minutes or so, greeting and conversing with those there to celebrate with her. As she made her way around the room with Sam, she continued to keep a watchful eye on Gage. What she didn't understand was what he was doing here. If he was in love with, and married to Stephanie, why on earth would he be here celebrating *her* birthday?

Finally, after she was convinced she'd talked with enough guests and noticed that most of them were now filling their plates with appetizers and birthday cake, Ari pulled Sam into a far corner.

"What is going on, Sam?" Ari demanded.

"Ssssshhhh, Arabella," he pressed his finger to her lips, "I know that you are upset, but please, I want you to sit down and talk to Gage. *He* is the one that planned all this for you. He deserves a few minutes of your time, don't you think?"

"Wait, you were in on this *with* him? Ugh," she growled. "Will I be able to trust *anyone, ever* again?"

"Ari, we will work through that later. For now, just sit down and talk to—"

"Sam, this is hardly the place!" Ari argued in an angry whisper.

Sam just smiled at her, speaking through clenched teeth. "You didn't leave us much choice, young lady. Now sit here," he gently nudged her into the closest booth, "and stay put until I get Gage. Understand?"

Ari was too overwhelmed to argue anymore. Surely, her heart couldn't handle any more confrontation or confusion. The only upside she could think of to the situation, was the fact that she might feel more comfortable with a crowd close by. She knew if she faced Gage alone, her emotions would get the best of her.

I can do this. I'm strong enough to face the truth and God will see me through it!

"Fine, Sam! You win. I will talk to him. But I *won't* like it!"

Fear thrust itself upon her the moment she agreed. Knowing her own strength would never get her through the messiness of what was about to take place, Ari reached out to the Lord for strength.

Lord, I'm scared and I don't want to talk to Gage. Please don't leave me. I need you more than ever.

Tranquility washed over Arabella. She reminded herself that God was on her side. She stared out the window, into the dark night, as she patiently waited for Gage.

Surely, we can find a way to have an amicable relationship, can't we?

"Bella?" She turned as he slid into the booth across from her. Ari's breath caught as she gazed at the man sitting just inches away from her. A million times since he'd left Rock Haven, she'd thought about this moment. Never once had it played out like this in her mind. The effect he had on her hadn't lessened while they were apart. No, if anything, she felt a stronger pull towards him as she looked into his eyes, feeling the shiver that raced down her spine. She longed to feel his arms around her again. To share in the joy of having a child together. But, now that he loved someone else, that could never be.

"Gage," Ari tipped her head up slightly, hoping to convey a confidence she didn't have, "I hear you're responsible for this," Ari waved her hand towards the action going on all around them. "What I don't understand, is why?"

"Actually, Bella, I thought of if it, but the one who truly deserves credit for pulling it all together and making it so great is Stephanie. And the reason why—"

"You can't be serious!"

All thoughts of being cordial were gone with just one word. Stephanie. What Ari couldn't understand, the thing that was driving her crazy, was why under all of the anger she was holding on to, was there such a desire for the man that had betrayed her?

Daggers shot from her eyes across the booth at Gage, anger welling up inside her. "Why on earth would you ask *her* to plan a party for *me*?"

"That's what she does for a living, Ari," Gage answered flippantly. "Why on earth wouldn't I ask her?"

Frustrated at how ridiculous the entire situation was, Ari slid to the edge of the booth and prepared to stand.

"You're really something, Gage Russell. I never thought you would stoop low enough to ask your wife to work on your ex-girlfriend's birthday party. That's an all-time low, even for you!"

Ari stood. But before she could take one angry step, Gage jumped up and wrapped his hand around her wrist.

"My *wife*, Ari?" he shook his head. "Stephanie is not my *wife*. She's the event planner I hired to put together this party for you."

"But—," Gage released his grip on her as she stumbled back against the booth, shock distorting her face. "I saw you! You were together.....and she's *pregnant*! I assumed—" Ari continued to shake her head, unable to make sense of the situation.

"Yes, Ari. I am indeed pregnant."

Ari turned to her left, in the direction of that voice she could never forget. There, she saw Stephanie approaching the booth, her arm wrapped around the waist of another dark-haired man.

"And my husband and I are very excited and eager for the arrival of *our* little one." She patted her swollen mid-section.

Ari stood rooted in place, completely dumfounded. Her eyes darted back and forth between Stephanie and the stranger.

"Ari, I would like you to meet my husband, Matthew."

"*Matthew?* But I thought—," Ari looked back at Gage and then to Matthew once more.

Matthew reached out to shake Ari's trembling hand.

"It's nice to finally meet you, Ari. I've heard great things about you from Stephanie. She was so excited when she ran into you at the doctor's office, and that's all she's talked about since. It was really a great coincidence when she found out that you were the one Gage was planning the party for."

Arabella couldn't seem to close her mouth, or make a sound, as she turned to Gage in astonishment, waiting for further details.

"This is what I've been trying to tell you for days, Bella. I came back to town for your birthday and- well," he paused briefly, "and to tell you that I love you."

"You, you love me?" Ari struggled to catch her breath. "Wait a minute." She turned back towards Stephanie and Matthew. "So, when we met in the doctor's office and you talked about your husband, you were talking about *him*?" Ari pointed at Matthew.

Stephanie chuckled. "That's right, Ari. And when you ran into Gage and me downtown, we had just met to go over your party details. That's all. I had only met Gage that day. We had been planning your party by phone for weeks, and Gage was finally able to get to Rock Haven that morning."

"I think I need to sit down." Ari was as pale as a ghost. Reaching behind her with trembling hands, she found her way into the booth and sat down.

"I know this is a lot to take in, and I hate to run, but Matthew and I have plans to go out of town. So, we need to get going. I'm so sorry that we caused you any confusion, Ari. It was never Gage's intention for you to see us together, or for you to come to the conclusions that you did." Stephanie extended her hand. "I am glad we got things cleared up though. I'll give you a call in a week or two and maybe we can get together for coffee?"

"Co.....coffee," still stunned by the news she'd just been given, Ari nodded her head slowly. "Sure, coffee would work." She still had the deer-in-the-headlights look on her face as she agreed, shook Stephanie's hand, and watched her and Matthew leave. Before Ari could even turn back towards him, she heard Gage's voice.

"Bella, I never meant for it to happen like this. You've *got* to believe me! All I wanted was to surprise you for your birthday. And to make amends."

Ari looked up at the man standing before her. "I don't understand, Gage. Why? Why haven't you called? It's been *months*! Every single day I've wondered how you are and what you are doing, and how you could—"

Gage's face hardened. "I guess I could ask you the same questions, Ari. Why? How long have you known that you are carrying my child? And never *once* did you pick up the phone and think to tell me! Didn't you think I had a right to know?"

"Gage, I never intended to keep you from our child, but—"

"But what?" Gage prodded her to continue, a slight edge to his voice.

"I didn't want you to come back just for the baby. If I allowed that, then I would always wonder if you really loved *me*!" Ari looked down at the table and whispered, "I needed to know that I was enough."

Gage reached out, brushing away her tears with his thumb as he cradled her face. "Enough? Arabella, you've always been enough for me. My leaving had nothing to do with you."

"But...."

Gage climbed into the booth across from her, holding his finger to her lips to quiet her. "Bella, now that you know the truth about Stephanie, can we just enjoy the party and have this discussion later? In private? Maybe tomorrow? I really wanted your birthday to be special, and not tainted by this discussion."

Ari nodded slowly, and agreed that it was a lot to take in all at once. "Yes, Gage. A different time and place would be better. I've got a *lot* of thinking to do. And," she confessed, "I am a little hungry."

"Okay, then. How about we get our baby something to eat?" Gage's grin spread across his face, his eyes dancing with joy as he spoke. "Come check out what Stephanie has prepared."

Gage reached towards Ari and helped her from the booth, then moved towards the buffet, still holding her hand. But food was no longer on her mind. Her thoughts were stuck on those two little words he'd just spoken.

"*Our* baby".

That, and the fact that he'd come back to town just for her. Maybe, she wondered, it wasn't too late to find the happiness she'd always dreamed about, after all.

Ari was much more relaxed by the time she'd eaten and talked with Sam and Beth. Apologies seemed to be the only conversations she had anymore. But Ari and Beth worked their way through it, and forgave each other once again. The men had stepped away for minute, leaving the girls alone to talk, as the guests began to dwindle.

"I'm so sorry I couldn't tell you the truth, Ari. Looking back now, I wish I'd handled things differently."

"Beth, I feel horrible for thinking the worst of you. It seems like all I do is ask for your forgiveness these days."

"I know you've been through a lot in the past six months, Ari. But, please remember that I only want what's best for you. I would never intentionally hurt you."

"I do know that, Beth. Again, I'm sorry."

"Okay, enough of that." Beth dismissed the conversation with a flip of her wrist. "Now that you know the truth about Gage and Stephanie, and the whole party thing, have you and Gage talked about *your* future?"

"Our *future*? He planned a birthday party for me Beth, nothing more. He hasn't mentioned a future together. I think that might be a little presumptuous, don't you? I mean, I definitely would be more inclined to hear him out with all that's come to light, but—"

"I see. Apparently, you two haven't talked much then have you? Well, I hope that you'll listen with an open heart when he does share his thoughts, Ari. Gage has changed a lot in the past couple of months."

"I sense you know a lot more than what you're letting on, Beth?"

"Let's just say he had to get through me to get to you, and that involved a lot of truth telling!"

"Oh, Beth. I'm so thankful for our friendship and that you love me enough to look out for me." Ari reached across the table and tried to hug her best friend, but her growing tummy got in the way. Both girls looked down at her baby bump and giggled.

"Maybe just one too many scoops of Butter Pecan at Kilwins?" The girls' laughter grew louder. "Just wait! Your time is coming, Beth!"

"What's all the giggling about over here?" Gage smiled as he approached them.

"Oh, you know, just girl talk," Beth replied. "I'm feeling a little tired so I'm going to say my goodbyes, find my husband, and head home for the night if you don't mind." As Beth found her way out of the booth, Gage pulled her into a hug.

"Thank you, Beth, for everything."

"You're welcome, Gage. Thank you for allowing me to be a part of it. I'm sorry for anything negative that I might have said about you in the past. I shouldn't have judged you. I was wrong for that. I hope we can be good friends."

"I would really like that."

Beth waved goodbye one last time, and made her way through the thinning crowd to find her husband.

"You okay?" Gage noticed the shimmer in Ari's eyes.

"I'm fine, Gage. I just never thought I would witness what I just saw. I guess I'm a little awestruck."

"Beth's a great friend, Ari. She was right to be concerned about the way I was treating you. You're lucky to have her. I know I've got some ground to make up too, but I hope she and Anthony can find it in their hearts to put what's happened in the past."

Ari sat speechless, still dazed by all that had transpired tonight.

"What do you say, Ari? Are you ready to go home and get some rest? I don't want you to overdo it. Stephanie hired a clean-up crew, so we have nothing holding us back."

Home? Ari immediately tensed at the word. Wasn't this what had gotten her into trouble in the first place?

"Gage, maybe we need to clear some things up first."

"Ari, I know what you're thinking, and don't worry. I didn't plan on staying with you tonight, as much as I would love to. I know that we have a lot to work through and it's going to take time. But I want you to know that I love you. I'm not going *anywhere* until we figure this out. Okay?"

"Okay, Gage."

Did he really just say he wanted to stick around and work things out? This has to be a dream.

Ari allowed the hope of a reconciled relationship with Gage sink into her soul.

Gage rested his forehead against hers. "I like the way *this* feels," he said, his eyes moving over Ari's mid-section, as it nearly prevented him from hugging her.

Ari melted into his arms. It had been far too long. But, as hard as it was going to be, she knew she had to take this slow. She refused to let Gage come and go in her life like a yo-yo. He had to be serious about working things out. And he had to be serious about God!

Help me to be strong, Father. I have to do this right if it's going to work between us. And Gage has to commit to that before we go any further.

"How about I drive you home?" Gage offered. "We can worry about getting your car tomorrow."

That sounded like heaven to Ari. After all, letting Gage drive her home wouldn't be that risky, would it? It wasn't like she was agreeing to go back to him. Unfortunately, even *that* sounded good to her right now. She was so confused.

"Ari?"

"Sure, Gage," she looked up at him. "But the first thing we need to do is set some boundaries. Agreed?"

"Whatever you want, Ari. I will do whatever it takes for you to realize how serious I am about being a part of your life. And our child's."

His smile melted her heart. It was going to be a long night.

Chapter 26

Arabella slept like a rock that night. Gage had given her a foot massage and she'd soaked in a long, warm bath. Their time together had been pleasant, void of the pressure to figure out where their future was headed. In fact, they hadn't discussed their past or their future at all. It made Ari happy, if only for one night. She knew there was much to work through, but seeing Gage's face light up when he saw the baby's nursery, how he'd touched her growing tummy and professed his love to their child, well, it was enough for her right then.

Despite all the rest she had last night, Ari felt a little off-kilter today. Gage was coming over for lunch, and they'd promised each other that *today* would be the day they would be completely honest. Today, they would bare their hearts to one another about their relationship.

Gage was prompt and arrived exactly at one. He'd picked up some take out from Nina's and ice cream from Kilwin's on his way, along with a dozen pink roses.

"Gage, you really shouldn't have." Ari took the flowers and placed them on the table with all the others he'd sent that week. "It's beginning to look like a florist shop around here," Ari joked.

Gage held up the box from Nina's for her to see.

"Oh, how did you know? I've been craving that for days." Ari grabbed the box from him and disappeared into the kitchen to get plates and silverware. Gage followed along and placed the ice cream in the freezer for later.

"Thank you, Gage, this was very nice of you."

Gage closed the freezer door and stepped over to the counter where Ari was dishing out Spanish rice and black beans onto their plates. He wrapped his arms around her waist and pressed his lips against the smooth of her neck. "I've missed you so much, Bella. I miss *everything* about us. The way we talk, the way we breathe." He paused momentarily, before slowly continuing. "The way....we touch."

"Gage, we ca—"

"I know, Bella, and I'm trying my hardest to go slow." Gage released his hold on her and stepped back. "You just don't know how much I missed you."

Ari couldn't deny how good it felt to have his arms around her again, but she knew she couldn't give in. They simply couldn't go back to the way things were, no matter how much of a struggle it was.

"I know exactly how you feel, Gage, because I've lived it too. Not a day has gone by that I haven't prayed you would come back to me, especially after finding out about the baby."

"Bella, if you'd only told me, I would have come back."

Sensing the conversation was taking a turn towards the serious side, Ari changed the direction quickly. "Let's eat first, and then we can talk, okay?" Ari pulled away from Gage and carried their plates to the dining room.

They picked up right where they had left off, as if a day hadn't gone by since they were last together. Only now, it was better. This time, Bella *knew* that Gage wanted to be with her and that he wasn't scared about a future as her husband or father to their unborn child. When they were finished eating, Gage began telling her about some of the improvements that he was planning on doing at the farm.

Ari tried to be patient, but his talk of the farm was a bit confusing, as she listened about Max's retirement and the expansions that he intended to make. When she voiced her concern, things started to go south quickly.

"You're keeping the farm? *And* you're expanding it?" Before she gave him a moment to answer, Ari continued. "Gage, I thought you were back in Rock Haven to stay?"

"Bella, before we jump into that subject can you just let me explain what's been going on in my life for the past couple of months?"

"Maybe we should have this talk another day, Gage. I don't think I'm ready for it." Ari stood up from the couch and began to pace the floor, fear filtering into her thoughts once again. Gage was quick to guide her back, wrapping his arms around her and calming her. He gently pressed a kiss to her forehead.

"We've waited long enough. It's going to be okay, Bella. I promise. Come sit down, please."

Arabella nodded and allowed Gage to pull her back to the couch where he sat, facing her.

"Arabella, I love you and I know that I hurt you." Gage ran his thumb along her cheek, brushing a strand of hair. "I was a selfish person when I met you, only seeking what felt good to me or what was beneficial to me. I know that I can never take back our first night together. And you……Bella, will *never* know how sorry I am for that. I had no right to take that away from you."

Ari's face tensed. "Gage, let's not go there again."

"Bella, we *have* to go there. Don't you see? That's where all the trouble started! I've spent the last few months of my life trying to figure out how to forgive myself for that."

She'd been determined not to bring this into their conversation, but suddenly as Bella heard the blame Gage heaped upon himself, something snapped inside her, and she knew she had to make him understand the truth. "You couldn't *take* something that I was so willing to give. Don't you understand that, Gage?"

"No, Bella, you're wrong! I made you give in; I accept full responsibility for my actions."

Bella lifted her hand to his cheek, calming his emotions. "Gage," she leaned in closely, as if doing so would drill her words deeper in to his heart, "no matter what you said or did, in the end it was my decision to be with you. Everyone is held accountable for their own actions. I had to accept that and learn to forgive myself, too."

Gage struggled to understand. "I couldn't come back from Iowa because I could see every day how far you were drifting away from God. And *I*," Gage pointed at his chest, "was the cause of it. I told you I loved you, but I didn't treat you like I loved you."

"But you're here now, right?" Ari asked, full of expectation, and more than happy to close the door on that part of her past.

"Yes, Bella, I'm here. But there's so much more you need to know. After I lost Nonnie, I felt my world spinning out of control, and I didn't know how to stop it. I'd lost or walked away from everything I'd ever loved. But Max was there at the ranch with me, and he talked with me about God, and took me to church with him. He introduced me to the pastor, he showed me Nonnie's bible, and the messages that she left there for me. I knew I had to make a change. That's when all the pieces started to come together."

"You went to *church*, Gage? On your own?"

"Yes, Ari, I went to church. And I'm going to continue to go. I've given my life to the Lord. I'm a changed man now; I don't ever want to go back to who I was before."

There were tears of joy in Ari's eyes as she hugged him. "Gage, you don't know how happy I am to hear this. I've prayed repeatedly for you to find your way to God. And now, I just can't believe it's true. This is the best news you could've given me, Gage!"

"Ari, I've spent weeks with Pastor Dave reading the Bible and growing my relationship with God and I finally found the peace in my life that I was missing. I couldn't be the man you needed before, but I want to be that man now."

Am I really hearing this right? Gage has given his life to you, Lord?

"Bella, every minute that we were apart was torture for me. But I had to put my feelings aside, and do what was right." Gage looked away briefly, appearing to be holding back the emotion that threatened to spill down his face. "Bella, I love you so much that it physically hurts me to think of a future that doesn't include you. I don't even want to think of one more day without you."

Gage pulled back slightly and took Ari's hands in his. "Ari, I know that we have a long way to go, but I will spend the rest of my life if I need to, to get you to trust me and believe in me. I love you, Arabella, and I love our child! Please say you'll let me be a part of our baby's life. And yours."

"Gage, I promise. I will *never* stop you from being a part of our child's life. Ever! I love you, Gage. I want nothing more than for you to be here with us."

When he kissed her, Ari felt every ounce of his commitment clear down to her toes. She relaxed in his embrace, momentarily forgetting everything around them.

It was when he released her, and she was able to catch her breath, that her thoughts found their way back to the fact that he was expanding the farm. She had to know the truth before she got her hopes up.

"Gage?"

"Yes, Ari?"

"Are you staying here in Rock Haven, or are you moving back to Iowa, because I can't—"

"You know, I could never understand how my mother loved the ranch as much as she did, and yet she made her life in New York with my father. Until now. My intention when I first came back to Rock Haven was to take you back to Iowa with me."

"Gage, I—"

"But, Bella," he interrupted, "my love for you is so deep, that wherever you are is where my home will be. *And*, I do love Rock Haven. But—"

Ari's stomach dropped as she interrupted without hesitation. "But….. what……Gage? You know this is my home, and I can't possibly leave. I have a business to run."

"And I have a business to run as well, Bella. There has to be a compromise that we can agree on, because I refuse to let you go. You and our child are my future."

Ari shook her head defiantly and crossed her arms over her chest. "Gage, I won't budge on this. I'm sorry, but I'm staying in Rock Haven. This is where I will raise our baby, and if you want to be a part of my life and our child's, then you will stay here too!"

She expected his disagreement, but what she got instead was his smile. "It doesn't matter, Ari. Whatever your choice is, I will agree to it. I love you that much. But I won't give up the farm. I will just have to commute back and forth and spend some long weekends away. I promise, though, I will make it work."

Her defenses slowly began to dissolve with his promise. "You would do all of that for me?"

"For you and our child, Bella," Gage placed his hand on her growing belly. "I can't imagine my life without either one of you."

"And you'll never *have* to know what that's like, Gage. You will always be a part of our lives. I promise."

"Bella, I don't just want to be a small part of your lives." Gage slowly slid down to the floor. Before Bella even realized what was happening, Gage was on one knee holding open a red velvet box, a sparkling diamond staring back at her.

Ari gasped as Gage took her hand. "Gage, what are you doing?"

Surely Lord, this cannot be what I think it is. As much as I love this man, we simply can't move back into a relationship this fast! Can we?

Bella strained to hear an answer, a prompting, a word of direction from the Lord, but she heard nothing. Doubt and fear began digging and crawling its way through the assurance and love she felt only moments ago.

Gage stared deep into her eyes. "Bella, I know that we'll face trials, and I know being only human that I'm bound to let you down at times. But I can promise you one thing—I will never walk away from you again. If you will have me as your husband, I promise that I will spend the rest of my days, loving you, and doing everything that I can to make you happy."

"Gage, this is so—"

"I know, Bella. It's happening fast. But, we have a child to think about now! Don't we owe this to him or her? What do you say? Will you agree to spend forever with me?"

"Forever, Gage?"

"Oh, Bella, yes! Forever! Eternity will never be long enough, for me to feel like I've had long enough to love you."

Unable to speak around the lump that had formed in her throat, Arabella hung her head and sat motionless.

Gage cocked his head. "Bella, you're scaring me. Say something."

She raised her head until their eyes met, her words as soft as the wind, whispering through the summer grass. "I'm sorry, Gage. I can't marry you."

"Bella...... you can't be serious," Gage pleaded. "You *have* to marry me."

"Gage, I *want* to marry you, I do. You have to know that."

"But?" Gage's voice was edged with fear.

"But, I can't rush into this simply because of the baby. I need to see the changes you've made before I walk down that aisle with you. Then, and only then, will I agree to say, 'I do'."

His next words were rich with excitement. "So, you're not telling me no? You're telling me yes, just not yet? Is that what you're saying, Bella."

Thankful for the sudden adjustment in his attitude, Ari giggled. "Yes, Gage, that's what I'm saying. Just give it a little time, okay?"

Again, Gage pulled her left hand into his. "Then will you agree to wear my ring, Bella, as a token of my promise to you, and the hope of our future together."

"Yes, Gage. Put that ring on my finger!"

Chapter 27

James dropped the letters onto the table once more, and began to open them slowly. One at a time. Just as he'd done countless times since his son's departure. In the past month they had become his most precious possession. His fingers trembled as he pulled out the pages of the first one, and began to read.

Oh Mama, New York is the prettiest place in the world. Well, except for the farm of course. I can't wait for you to visit us here. And James? Well, he is one of the smartest men I've ever known in my life. He's going to open his own business someday very soon.

How are you and daddy? I sure do miss you both a lot. How are things at the farm?

I'm sorry Mama, for leaving like I did. I know that you aren't angry with me, but I also know I hurt your feelings. It's just that I love James so much. I can't imagine my life without him. I know I'm young and you wanted me to wait, but I know there will never be another man that I could love as much as I love James. I pray that you can forgive me, and that you can find a way to love him as much as I do.

A tear dropped onto the envelope as James stuffed the letter back into place. *Why was I so selfish? Why did I make Glory choose between her family and me? She could have loved us both. She did love us both.* His hands continued to tremble as he pulled out the next letter out and continued.

I'm sorry I haven't written in a while, Mama. I love you and miss you so much. I wish you were closer. I miss the way we used to talk. It gets kind of lonely being at home so much while James is at work. I know he has to work hard to get his business going, but I feel so isolated most days.

How is daddy feeling? I'm glad that he has Max there to help him now, since the accident. I'm sorry I couldn't be there to help you through his recovery. James' business requires every extra penny we have right now. Tell him I said to be careful and not over do things. I love you and miss you both. I pray every night that someday soon God and James will see fit for us to be together again, if even just for a visit. All my love, Glory.

By the time James made it to the sixth letter, he was crying openly for the past mistakes he couldn't change.

Mama and Daddy, you wouldn't believe how much your grandchild is moving inside me! I know it must be a boy by the way he kicks about so much. I'm sorry it's been so long since I've written, but I'm very tired these days, and it won't be long now. I know you both want to be here when the baby arrives, but James thinks it would be better for our family if it was just the three of us. Oh, mama, I wish just once you could lay your hand on my growing tummy and feel your grandchild. I know you would love it. I certainly miss all the advice you used to give me. I can't admit this to James, but I'm really scared about the delivery. I wish you were here. Keep praying for us, please? I love you both.

"How could I keep her from her parents? Why," he cried out into the room in anger. "Why was I so selfish?"

Humble yourself before me, and I will lift you up.

There it was again. That soft whisper that James and been hearing day after day, and week after week. Where was this voice coming from?

Let go of your pride and cling to my love, son.

Son? James shook his head and pushed the letters into a pile. This couldn't be. Is this what Gage meant when he talked about the wisdom he'd received from........*God?* All those years Glory had talked about hearing from God, how He whispered into her soul. Is this possibly what *she* was talking about, too? But why? Why now? James wasn't totally sure there even was such a thing as God?

Don't you think it is time to stop running, and come home, child? I love you, and I'm here for you.

"No!" James cried out. "Leave me alone, whoever you are!" He slammed his fist onto the table.

My son, I've loved you since before you were born. And still, I love you now. No matter what you've done.

Sobs shook James' body as he collapsed back in his chair. "Oh, what have I done? If it's true, there really is a God and you love me, *please* help me now."

I'm here for you.

Suddenly James found himself on his knees, his head cradled in his hands as he cried out, "Help me, please, before it's too late. I need you. Show me the way."

Without realizing what he was doing, or where he was going, James reached into the closet and grabbed a jacket, closed the front door behind him, and found himself behind the wheel of his car. He weaved in and out of traffic, not sure where he would end up. Just sensing that he had a need to be somewhere. He finally came to a stop in front of a large structure on 34th Street.

For a few moments all James could do was stare at the building. *What am I doing here? This has to be a mistake. I don't belong here.*

Your search is over, son. *Just walk through the doors. I'm waiting.*

James felt his hand on the door handle, but it wasn't his strength that opened it. The next thing he knew, he was sitting at the altar in the very front of the large church, weeping for all of the years that he'd lost, and the pain he'd caused his beautiful wife and son.

I'm so sorry. I know I've run from you! I've tried to hide and pretend you didn't exist, and I've made a mess of things in the process. Please forgive me.

"Sir, would you like me to pray with you?" James felt a hand on his shoulder and turned. As he looked into the kind eyes of the stranger, James felt a peace wash over him. Slowly, he reached his hands out towards the pastor he didn't know.

"Yes, sir. Please, can you pray with me? I don't know the Lord but.... but I think I would like to."

"*Let me see it one* more time," Beth squealed as she admired the ring on Ari's finger, shining brilliantly before her eyes. It was the second Monday of the month. The girls had just secured a table at Luna's and ordered hot chocolates. "So, have you decided to go ahead and do it then?"

"Not right now, Beth, even though that's what Gage wants to do. He wants to be married before the baby arrives, but I have to make sure this time. I need to see him grow in his relationship with the Lord and I need to know how things are going to be between us with him still running the farm."

"He's keeping the farm?" Beth asked in wonder. "How does he expect to run it from here?" Beth closed her menu as the waitress appeared with their drinks and took their orders. "I'll have a whole wheat bagel, plain cream cheese and a fruit bowl, please."

"That sounds amazing. Make that two, please." Ari smiled at the waitress as she handed both menus to her and watched her disappear into the kitchen. She turned her attention back to Beth.

"I don't know, Beth. He seems to think he can run it fine from here, maybe making a few short trips a month to stay on top of things, but," Ari stopped.

"Uh oh, I sense there's more?"

Ari nodded in agreement.

"Well, this is the perfect time for the two of you to be talking and working through all these decisions," Beth offered.

Ari shifted in her seat and took a sip of her steaming cocoa. "I know he wants to be there on the farm, Beth. He's so happy there, and I *don't* want to be the one to hold him back from happiness. But, I can't walk away from my family's business, either."

Gage and Ari had talked about this non-stop for the past several days. They hadn't spent one day apart since he'd proposed, but every night Gage willingly went back to the loft and kept his promise to Ari. Ari was just having a hard time seeing how this situation with the farm was going to work. She wanted to raise her child in Rock Haven. She couldn't imagine budging on that topic. Yet, it wasn't right for her to ask Gage to give up the place that *he* loved. The place that reminded him so much of his mother and grandmother.

"Gage is happy here with you, Ari. I can see it every time you're together. I've never seen a man dote on a woman like he does with you. And once the baby arrives in a few months," Beth shook her head slightly, "he won't want to be miles away and missing out on everything."

Ari shrugged. "I just wish we could come up with some kind of compromise."

"What if you went to Iowa with him one of these weekends? You know, just to see how it feels once you're there."

Ari took another drink of her cocoa and set it down. "Boy, you're full of good ideas today! Did that little one," she pointed to Beth's enlarged mid-section, "finally let you get a good night's sleep?"

"Not only that, Ari. You and Gage have just really been on my mind. More than usual."

"Hmmm. Any particular reason why," Ari was intrigued.

"That's what I'm trying to figure out! Now, how about you making a trip to Iowa?"

"It might be good idea," she agreed with a lift of her shoulder, "I guess."

Beth sat back in her seat and crossed her arms. "Are you sure that's all that's on your mind, Ari? I feel like there's more to it that you're not saying. And maybe, this is why you've been on my mind so much."

Ari shook her head, her lips curving into a partial smile. "Of course, you would notice. That's why you're my best friend." Ari set her cocoa down. "I probably should have come to you before, since you're the pregnancy expert. But.....it's kind of.....awkward to talk about," her voice grew quieter, "and I don't know if it's just me or the raging hormones."

"Oh, don't even get me started on the hormones this morning, girl! I'm telling you, this one," Beth pointed to her pregnant belly with the most sarcastic look on her face, "has to be a boy as much trouble as I'm having! I sob when the mailman drops of my dailies. What is *that* all about?"

The waitress approached their table carrying a tray of food and delivered their breakfasts, while Ari laughed hysterically at Beth. When the waitress was gone, Ari reached for her best friend's hand and asked her permission to bless their meal.

"Lord, I thank you for the friendship that I share with Beth. I ask your hedge of protection around us and over our unborn children, Father; and I ask that you help Gage and I come to an agreement that is right for both of us. Lastly, Lord, we ask that you bless this food to our bodies. In your name, we pray, Amen."

Beth looked across the table to her best friend. "Thanks, Ari. I really appreciate your prayers and your friendship." She squeezed her best friend's hand.

Ari grinned. "Don't make me cry before breakfast. It's hard enough to get through the day with all these crazy emotions!"

Beth joined her as they laughed about the stage of pregnancy they were both experiencing, before both attacked their breakfast.

Beth stabbed her fork at a piece of watermelon. "So, are you going to tell me, or leave me hanging?"

Ari set her bagel down and slid her chair closer to the table, leaning in as close as she could to Beth. "I'd be embarrassed if I talked to anyone but you about this."

Beth's expression grew serious. "Ari, you know you can trust me."

Ari let out a deep breath. "I know I can, Beth. And that means everything to me." Her nervous hands continued to shake. "So here goes nothing." Ari looked to her left, and then to her right, her facial expression as serious as a someone about to share a life-shattering secret.

Ari leaned in to whisper in her most serious tone, "Gage doesn't find me attractive anymore, Beth."

Hot cocoa spewed from Beth's mouth, shooting across the table and landing on her friend's face before Beth erupted with laughter. "I'm sorry, Ari....um," Beth picked up her napkin, "here," she attempted to wipe Ari's cheek.

"Go ahead and laugh, Beth. But this is serious!"

"Oh, honey," Beth patted Ari's hand, a knowing expression replacing the laughter, "why do you think Gage isn't attracted to you? I see the way he looks at you, there's no denying how he feels."

"I'm as big as a hippo, Beth. Why *would* he find me attractive?"

"I promise you, Ari, that is the crazy hormones talking!" Beth released her hold on Ari's hand and sat back.

"Beth, he doesn't ever, you know, make a pass at me. In fact, I'm the one who's always trying to get him to kiss me. And I have to wonder, if he's only here because of the baby."

"Now wait a minute!" Beth argued defiantly. "Aren't *you* the one that told Gage he had to take it slow?"

"Well, yeah.....I guess," Ari cringed. "But—"

"Oh, no! Beth cried. "If you want my advice, then sit there and listen. Ari, you can't have it both ways. You've been telling Gage since the day he returned, to take it slow. He goes home to his own apartment every night. He spends every waking minute with you that he can. He's being a gentleman and giving you *exactly* what you ask for. How can you find fault in that?" Beth continued without taking a breath. "And as far as you being a hippo? You've got to be kidding me, Ari." Beth slapped her hand down on the table. "You're going to have a baby and you're beautiful. So quit listening to your crazy pregnancy hormones!"

"Hormones?" Ari cringed. "You really think that's all it is?"

"I promise you, Ari. If you told Gage tomorrow that you were ready to walk down the aisle, you would see just how quickly the fireworks would start in your love department."

"Just hormones, huh? How long is this going to last, Beth?" Ari reached for her fork and took a bite of pineapple from her bowl, feeling somewhat relieved that she'd come to Beth with her worries.

"Just being honest, it's going to last until the baby's six months old. At least!"

Ari dropped her fork.

"So then," Beth tapped her fingers on the table with just the hint of a smile, "how long are you going to make him wait for the wedding?"

Ari rested her hands atop her growing bump, mortified at the thought of what her wedding pictures would look like if she got married now. "I don't want to be walking down the aisle looking like this! Can you imagine that?

How would I even find a dress to fit this?" She pointed at the basketball shape under her shirt. "But, I don't know if I can fight with my hormones for that long!" Ari broke out in a small giggle. "And," her expression grew serious again, "I want to make sure he's right with God first."

"I understand your concern, Ari, and I can't believe I'm about to say this, but........" she twisted in her seat uncomfortably, "you are already tied to him forever because of the baby. The marriage is just a formality at this point, don't you think?"

"I guess you're right but, I think just a little more time would be wise."

"Well, okay, that's *your* choice. But that," Beth pointed towards Ari's midsection, "is not getting any smaller before your due date. Just keep that in mind."

"Now," Beth stood up and grabbed the check, "we have got some shopping to do today, so let's head out."

The girls made their way to the cash register and settled up before they walked outside and climbed into Beth's car.

Ari watched their small town slowly drift past the window, her thoughts on a conversation she overheard the night before.

"His father called him last night."

Trying to focus on the road in front of her, Beth could only gasp as she stared out the windshield.

"Wow, I can't believe it." Beth shook her head. "What brought that on?"

Ari turned in her seat to face Beth. "When Gage was in New York last month, he left behind a stack of letters his mom had written to Nonnie back at the farm. I guess his dad finally broke down and read them. And now he wants to come out to Michigan and talk to Gage about it. Believe me, I'm as shocked as you are."

"So, when is he coming?"

Ari thought back to the bits and pieces of the conversation she'd heard from where she'd been sitting on the sofa.

"Dad? Is that you?"

"No, I'm not in Iowa. I'm in Michigan.... with Ari."

"You want to see me? Is there something in particular you wanted to talk about?"

"Oh, I see. Ummm....well sure, that would be fine....I guess. I have room at the loft if you'd like to stay with me."

"Right. Well, just give me a call when you think you're ready to head this way then."

Ari had been resting on the couch next to Gage when the call came in. As Gage hung up the phone, she made eye contact with him.

"That... was... my father."

Ari wasn't sure how to read his vague facial expression. "Are you okay, Gage?"

Gage didn't respond for the longest moment. "Just a little stunned, I guess. It's not in character for my father to call. Let alone tell me he wants to come for a visit."

"He's coming here to Michigan, then? Gage, that's great!" She and Gage had prayed constantly for his relationship with his father. Maybe this was a sign that it was all going to work out. Maybe, just maybe, this was the answer to their prayers.

Ari continued her conversation with Beth. "I don't think Gage has a date, yet. Poor guy has so much going on right now. He's doing all he can to make it up to me for his leaving, and then my crazy hormones have him guessing my mood constantly. Then there's the farm, and his responsibilities for that. Now, he's got his dad wanting to bring up the past. I mean, don't get me wrong, I'm glad his dad wants to talk about it. I just feel bad for Gage right now. That's a lot of emotion to have to be dealing with."

"Yes, it certainly is a lot." Beth agreed. "Maybe we should pray extra hard for Gage right now. And all of the decisions he is facing."

Chapter 28

"Wow! Did you see that?"

Ari nodded at Gage to confirm that she indeed saw the foot, arm, or knee of her child, moving across the inside of her tummy. "Not only that, but I *felt* it!"

Gage moved his hand across Ari's belly, feeling their child continue to move about inside her. Suddenly, he jumped to his feet and pulled Ari up from where she lay on the couch to stand next to him. "I still can't believe I get to feel our baby move!" He hugged her as tight as he could with her protruding belly between them. It was getting harder to do every day.

"Oh, Bella, I can't believe how happy I am." He kissed her on the cheek and then kissed her belly one more time. "This is your daddy, little one. I want you to know how much your mommy and I love you."

Ari smiled and ran her fingers through Gage's hair, as he continued to "chat" with their unborn baby. She loved to hear the interactions between the man she loved, and the child they shared. There wasn't any doubt in Arabella's mind how much Gage loved them both. He made sure each and every day to let her know just how important she and their child were to him. There wasn't an ounce of evidence left of the selfish, self-serving man Gage had once been.

The past three months had flown by. As their child had continued to grow inside her, she and Gage too had become stronger in their relationship. Her due date was now only six weeks away and Ari was becoming nervous about her delivery. Gage had made a commitment to his employees back at the ranch that he would spend at least one weekend a month there, so Ari feared that he'd be gone when the baby arrived.

"I still think we need to pick out a boy's name. Just in case," Gage offered.

"I think we're safe with a girl's name," Ari smiled. She'd had a feeling from the first day she'd learned the news, that the Lord was giving her a girl.

Ari took a seat on the couch, her legs already tired from being on them. "Gage, do you really need to go to the farm this weekend? Can't you just put it off until after she arrives? I'm nervous about you being gone."

"I don't like being away from you either, Bella. But we had an agreement. My employees are expecting me to keep my promise to them. I agreed to make my home in Rock Haven; but I will not give up on my Nonnie's farm. Ever." Gage sat down on the opposite end of the couch and pulled her feet into his lap where he began to massage them. "Why don't you come with me this time, please? You're still far enough away from your due date that it would be safe."

"Gage, I just don't feel up to making the trip."

"Come on, Bella. I wouldn't ask you to put our baby at risk. It's just a car ride. We can stop as many times as you need to for walking or bathroom breaks. I promise."

Ari knew that the timing couldn't be better. She'd finally hired an assistant manager to help out at Francesca's. Now that she was fully trained and doing great, Ari had just decided to cut back her own hours, in preparation for the baby's arrival. Besides, the tourist season was nearing the end, which would mean less business. And, she was really enjoying this stage in her pregnancy. With no morning sickness, she'd been feeling great for weeks now. There was really no excuse for her to not make the trip to Iowa, and it would be nice to see Max again.

"Okay, let's leave in the morning."

"What?" Gage asked with surprise. "Did you just agree to come with me?" Gage slid her legs off his lap and scooted next to her, taking her by the shoulders. "For real, Bella, you're coming with me?"

"Yes, Gage," Bella rolled her eyes dramatically, "I said I would!"

"Oh, Bella, this is going to be great. You have *no idea* how lonely these trips are without you."

"Just one thing, before we leave tomorrow." Ari's tone grew serious.

"Anything, Bella, you name it. Kilwin's ice cream, a new outfit, whatever you want!" Gage jumped up off the couch, ready to pack her bags before she changed her mind.

"Gage, the last time we were at the farm together, you refused to sleep in separate rooms. You have to promise me that you'll stick to our agreement, as it is now, since we aren't married yet. Separate sleeping quarters, okay?"

"Is that all, Bella?" Gage smirked and pulled her face into his hands. "I promised you I would wait until we are married. Besides, I'm not that man anymore. Haven't I proven that these past couple of months?" Gage leaned in and brushed her lips with a gentle kiss. "I love you, Bella, more than anything."

The seven-hour trip turned into nine by the time they made more than a half dozen bathroom and snack breaks. But, even still, Gage and Ari enjoyed the quiet time alone, talking about their future with their little one.

"I wonder if she will have your blue eyes?"

"You mean if *he* will?" Gage chuckled. He was determined that Ari was carrying a son. In fact, Gage was so certain, he had planned to design an entire baseball themed nursery at the loft. He had joked with Ari about her "neutral yellow" nursery at the cottage. "That's way to girly for my son," he'd say. "I guess we'll have no choice but to live in the loft after *he* arrives." Those comments were always met with a playful swat on the arm.

"Well, who knows, maybe he or she will have my green eyes. I know one thing I can be sure of though, is that he or she will have your athletic ability! I can't believe how much this little one moves around and kicks me!"

Gage reached for her hand and wove his fingers through hers. He could do this all day, talking with the woman he loved about their child and their future together. God was certainly amazing. Gage had hoped this would be his good fortune, but after all of the mistakes he'd made, he struggled to imagine it. He could still remember the first time he saw Ari, standing across the room from him at Francesca's. He'd "wanted" her all right. But that desire had led them both down a horrible winding path of sin. He praised God silently once more at the thought about how far they'd come since then, what a different person he'd become since then.

"Have I told you how much I love you lately?" Gage brought her hand to his mouth and kissed it.

"Only four or five times, *this hour*," Ari smiled as she turned to face him. "But I never get tired of hearing it."

"And I never get tired of saying it."

"So, how about Morgan? or maybe Cassidy?" Their differences surrounding the baby's gender made deciding on a name especially difficult.

"How about Mason or Benjamin?" Gage bartered.

"Gage, do you think you'll be disappointed when it turns out to be a girl?"

Gage sucked in a breath, surprised at Ari's words. Trying to keep his focus on the road in front of him, he replied. "Arabella, I am going to love our child no matter what. Boy or girl does not make one difference to me." And then, just because he loved to tease her, he added, "But tell me something, Ari, how are you going to handle having another boy in the house? Because you are having a *son*."

Ari tossed her candy bar wrapper at his head. "You're so sure of it, aren't you?"

Gage took the next left turn. They were only a few minutes away from the farm now.

"I wonder what Max is going to think when he sees me."

"Oh, he'll be surprised. That's for sure." Gage briefly took his eyes off the road and glanced towards her beach ball shape.

As much as Ari was looking forward to seeing Max again, he could tell she was starting to get nervous as they pulled into the driveway. She hadn't been back to the farm since last December, before Nonnie passed away. So much had happened on that trip. Gage was sure she was feeling a little anxiety.

"Ari, it's okay. I know you're nervous about being back here. But, trust me. We will get through it together."

She smiled in response and squeezed his hand gently. "Thank you."

Max rushed out of the house as soon as they pulled into the drive, and went straight to Ari's side of the car to help her out.

"Well, my, my. You certainly have changed a bit since I saw you last, haven't you?" Max's eyes roamed over Ari's mid-section. "You couldn't look any prettier, dear."

Ari blushed and leaned in for a hug. "Thanks Max."

"Don't worry about me back here. I can handle the luggage *all by myself*," Gage jokingly hollered at the two of them, as he pulled the last suitcase from the trunk.

"Wow, Ari! What all did you pack? We're only here for four days!"

Max and Ari looked at each other and laughed before Max dashed over to help Gage with the bags.

"Just the necessities, babe. I promise."

The boys headed towards the back door with Ari following closely behind.

"Well, let's get you both settled in before I head out for the evening."

"Wait." Gage turned. "Max aren't you staying for dinner? I thought we would have a little time to catch up on things tonight."

"Gage, you and I will have plenty of time to talk about farm stuff tomorrow. You and Ari just relax a little tonight after your long trip. Dinner is in the oven."

Ari followed the men into the kitchen, closing the back door behind her. On the small kitchen table, Max had placed two candles, along with an ice-filled bucket of sparkling juice.

"Aww...Max, you didn't have to do all this for us." Ari started to get emotional.

"Whatever you made for dinner smells wonderful, though." Gage turned to shake Max's hand. "Thanks, Max."

Max tipped his hat towards them. "You get some rest now, you hear? And I will be back bright and early in the morning so we can take a ride around the perimeter together, and talk with the employees, okay?"

"I look forward to it."

Ari stepped forward and hugged the old man one more time before he left. As she closed the back door, she turned to Gage. "I can't believe he did all this for us."

"He is such a great man, Ari." Gage peeked out the small kitchen window as Max's truck disappeared down the driveway. "I still can't believe how fortunate I've been to have him in my life. I can't imagine how I would have turned out if he hadn't been there for me when I needed him most."

"I think Nonnie was pretty lucky to have him too," she whispered.

Gage heard the emotion in her voice. He walked up behind her and wrapped his arms around her belly. "It's definitely different here without her, huh?"

"Yeah." She relaxed against his chest. "I guess I wasn't prepared to feel like this. I mean, it's been months since she's been gone. But just being here, remembering the last time we were here together—it's emotional for me, in more ways than one."

Gage tucked a piece of Ari's hair behind her ear and whispered to her. "I'm so sorry, Ari. I didn't think about how hard this would still be for you."

A comfortable silence slipped between them as Gage continued to hold her. "It was Christmas night wasn't it?" His hands moved to rub her tummy, remembering their last night at the farm together.

"I'm sorry, I don't mean to be so emotional, Gage." Ari turned in his arms and gave him the slightest smile. "Why don't you go ahead and take the bags upstairs, and I'll get dinner plated. Okay?"

Gage kissed the tip of her nose before he released her. "Perfect. I'm starving."

"I think that was the best lasagna I've ever eaten!" Ari wiped the corners of her mouth with her napkin and stood up to take her plate to the sink.

Gage couldn't help but snicker, causing her to turn around. "What's so funny?"

"Babe, you say that about everything you eat these days. I'm sorry, it's just so cute."

"Cute?" Ari turned sideways and ran her hands down her enormous belly, exaggerating the size dramatically. "You think *hippo* is cute?"

Gage made his way to join her at the sink. "I think hippo is more than cute." He waggled his eyebrows at her. "I think it's downright gorgeous!"

"Gage!" Ari swatted him with the kitchen towel as he tried to kiss her neck. "Stop that!" she cried through her laughter.

"Oh no, you're the one that started it, Miss 'I look like a hippo!'" Gage continued to nip at her neck and tickle her until she was breathless.

"Okay, really now, Gage," Ari panted. She bent forward, holding her sides. "You're going to send me into labor if you keep that up."

Gage released his hold on her immediately and stepped back.

"Gage? You okay?" Ari reached for his hand. "I was just joking about going into labor, you know."

He took another step back, needing to put some space between them. It wasn't the going into labor that he worried so much about. It was the touch of her skin on his. The way her familiar perfume drove him crazy. This weekend would mark the first time they would sleep under the same roof since he'd moved back to Rock Haven and back into her life. Staying in Rock Haven was easy. He went home to the loft every night without question. But here, without having anywhere to retreat to for the next four days, Gage was feeling a little anxious. Was he man enough to keep his distance and not do something he'd regret? Would he be strong enough to say goodnight and walk away, knowing she was only a few feet away?

Unsure of himself, Gage quickly moved on to another subject. "Honey, how about I throw some wood on the fire and you can go relax on the couch for a bit? How does that sound?"

"Like heaven." Ari waddled to the living room and collapsed on the couch, not even aware of the struggle raging within him. "It's been such a long day."

"Hey, would you rather just go take a hot shower and go to bed early? You really should rest as much as you can, honey." *And the more distance from me, the better,* Gage thought to himself. His doubts were working double time.

Ari sat back up, thrilled with his suggestion. "You know, that doesn't sound half bad." She struggled to get back on her feet. "Which room do you want me to take?"

"You probably better take the one closest to the bathroom." Gage chuckled, "since you'll be the one using it all night."

"Ugh!" Ari huffed in response as she stomped towards the stairway. "If only you knew what my body was going through to give you this baby! Men have it so easy."

"Yes, dear. I know," Gage nodded in agreement. He'd learned quickly to just agree with her on that. "I'll bring your bags up as soon as I grab some more firewood from the porch."

He'd barely made it back inside the house when he heard Bella's scream echo through the house. "GAGE!"

Dropping the wood, and taking the steps two at a time, Gage hurried towards the bathroom. His mind raced with the possibilities of what could be wrong. Had Ari gone into labor? Had the trip been too much for her? Could there be something wrong with the baby? Was she hurt?

She screamed again. "Gage!"

"Bella?" Gage flung the bathroom door open, expecting the worst. All he saw was Ari, standing in the tub, soaking wet and shaking like crazy.

"What's wrong, Bella? Is it the baby? Are *you* hurt?" Fear rang out in his voice as he made his way to her.

"*What?*" Bella's faced scrunched up with confusion. She looked away long enough to grab her towel and attempt to wrap it around her. With her growing figure, the task was slightly daunting. "The hot water turned ice cold! I'm *freezing*! I think you need to check the water heater."

"I thought you were—"

She must have recognized the fear in his eyes. "Oh, Gage, no! I didn't mean to scare you like that." She reached her hand out, and tried to hold back her laughter, pressing her palm to his cheek. "The baby and I are fine, really."

Gage stood frozen in place, the soft touch of her hand on his skin paralyzing him. The realization of their safety slowly sank in. He let out the breath he'd been holding and sagged with relief. It was then, as his eyes traveled the length of her, that Gage noticed just how little the towel was able to cover. He hadn't seen Bella *that* way since he'd walked out of her life all those months ago. Flames of desire quickly spread; his gaze locked on her. Everything around them disappeared; leaving nothing but his heightened passion for her.

"Hellooooo," she waved her hand in his face, "you okay, Gage?"

He hadn't moved a muscle, for fear he wouldn't have the strength to leave the room. He thought seriously about pulling her into his arms, and kissing her the way he'd been wanting to for weeks.

"I really didn't mean to scare you," she muttered effortlessly, obviously unaware of the conflict racing through his mind.

"Bella," he whispered hoarsely taking a step backwards "I need to go. I....I shouldn't be in here with you like this."

"Are you serious? Gage. It's not like you've never *seen* me."

But Gage continued his path backwards, his eyes never once leaving her, until he'd reached the door.

"I need to go, Bella. Please, try to understand," he pleaded. With that, Gage turned and bolted into the hallway as if his life depended on it. Once he was certain she wasn't going to follow him, Gage raced down the stairs, through the living room and into the kitchen, where he finally released the breath he had continued to hold. Bent over, his hands on his knees as he attempted to steady his breathing, Gage realized this was *never* going to work. Why hadn't he thought of this before now? The layer of protection that they counted on every night, when he went home, alone to the loft, was no longer any help. Gage was beside himself with fear. The last thing he wanted to do was jeopardize the relationship that he and Ari had *finally* started to rebuild.

"Think, Gage, think!" He mumbled out loud to himself as he paced the floor, his head hung down in defeat. Realizing he was going to need something to help him release his frustration, and help him to refocus, Gage walked over and lifted his work jacket off the hook, sliding his arms into the sleeves. Stepping outside into the chilly night, his eyes wandered to the large wood pile. He wondered, as he headed towards it, if there would be enough to keep him busy all night. Chopping wood had never held such appeal.

It was past eleven o'clock, and every muscle in his body was screaming in pain, before Gage finally gave up and headed back inside. Covered in sweat and utterly exhausted, he prayed Bella was fast asleep. Sleep for him, however, didn't come easy. Even after a long, hot, shower to relax his aching muscles. Gage tossed and turned throughout the night, thoughts of Bella filling his mind. He didn't know how long he could keep this up. If Bella didn't agree to marry him soon, he would surely go insane.

Thankfully, Max arrived at the crack of dawn, ready to get busy on the list of repairs they planned to tackle that day. After a cup of hot coffee and a couple of donuts that Max had picked up on the drive over, the two of them made their way out to the barn and filled the back end of the gator with tools and fencing. The rest of the crew wouldn't be on site for a least another two hours and Gage was pleased that there would be plenty of work to keep him busy. *Something* had to keep his mind off her. His plan was to stay away from the house until noon, when Max and the others would join him for lunch, preventing him from being alone with Ari again. If he had to look into those beautiful eyes that so easily drew him in, feel her presence so near that his hands ached to touch her, Gage was certain he'd never be able to keep his promise.

Max was unusually quiet as the two of them began to make their way around the perimeter of the property, checking the fence line and the cattle. Gage didn't offer any conversation on his end, thankful that Max was giving him the space he needed. It was well after they had begun their repairs on the second section of fencing before the old man finally spoke up.

"You doing okay?"

"Hmm...what's that?" Gage continued to work, oblivious to the concern Max expressed.

"I *said,* are you okay?"

"Yeah Max, I'm fine." Gage turned towards him with a questioning glance. "Why do you ask?"

"Son, you're a million miles away this morning! Something going on that I can help with?"

"Things are fine, Max. Couldn't be better!"

"Is that right?"

Gage didn't bother to respond.

"Well, okay then. If you change your mind and want to talk, you know where I'm at."

They finished the section they were working on in silence, before picking up and continuing down the fence line. And that's how they continued for the next half hour or so. Until finally, Gage couldn't stand it. He figured Max had stayed quiet out of respect, understanding there was a lot on his mind, but the silence was killing him.

"I can't do this, Max!"

Max spun around just as Gage threw the wire cutters on the ground and stepped away. "Gage, if you didn't want to work on the fence you should have just told me. I can get one of the others to finish it for you."

Gage shook his head and kicked the dirt with his boot. "I'm not talking about the fence, Max. I can't do this with Arabella any longer."

For the first time in his life, Gage saw a side of Max that he never imagined existed. The rancher came towards him, his finger pointed directly as his chest, a fire blazing in his eyes.

"Now you listen here, Gage. That woman and that child of yours are depending on you! You can't just back out of this. You are about to become a father! So, you better get your head on straight. I can't believe you would even *think* about leaving her after everything the poor girl has been through."

"No! That's not what I meant, Max," Gage hurriedly explained. "I love Bella. And I love our child. It's just," he dropped his head toward the ground again, feeling completely defeated, "being here with her, that I *can't* handle."

Max was visibly relieved as he took a step back, his face no longer twisted in anger. "I'm lost, Gage. What is it about being *here* that's so bad?"

"Not being *here*, Max. Being *alone* here." Gage walked over to an old log lying on the ground and took a seat, motioning for the old man to join him. "Back in Rock Haven it's easy. I go home every night and I know that's how it has to be. But here," he motioned to the land all around them, "we are alone in the house and I have no where to go. I want to *be* with her, Max."

Max nodded his head in understanding of what Gage meant. "Gage, you knew walking back into this relationship wasn't going to be easy. And the devil seems to be working overtime on you right now. He wants you to feel defeated. He wants you to believe you're not strong enough. But the truth is, you *are* strong enough, when you let God be your strength."

"But, Max—"

Max held up a hand to stop him. Then the old man bowed his head and began to pray out loud.

Gage lowered his head to his hands and cradled it as he listened to Max petition the Lord on his behalf. He needed the Lord's strength more than ever right now.

The other ranch hands caught up with him and Max not too long after. Between the six of them, they were able to get nearly all of the fence line repaired before they got too hungry for lunch.

"Alright boys, you want to join us back at the house for some food?" Gage pulled off his work gloves and picked up his cooler of water, taking a long drink.

"I left the fixings for some stew with Ari this morning. And there's more than enough for everyone," Max added.

There was a collective nod of heads as they all agreed. After packing up the gator, Gage and Max were followed by the other four on horses as they made their way back to the house.

"Mmm...whatever is in that crockpot smells heavenly!" Mark, one of the ranch hands, closed his eyes, obviously savoring the smell.

"You'll have to excuse him," Josh, another ranch hand, poked Mark in the side jokingly, "his wife isn't much of a cook!" They all had a laugh at Mark's expense, and were still laughing when Ari walked into the room.

Gage kept his distance, but Max immediately went to her side and hugged her before turning back to the others. "Arabella, I don't think you've had a chance to meet the boys before. This here is Mark, Josh, Calvin, and Mitch," he pointed to each one accordingly. "Boys this is Arabella."

Arabella smiled. "It's nice to meet you all."

The four of them all mumbled their greeting to Arabella at the same time, causing her to blush. Gage stepped forward to interrupt the fun.

"That's enough. You boys don't need to be flirting with a pregnant woman. Don't you have better things to do with your time?" Gage tried to maintain a playful gesture, but his underlying intention was received.

"Relax, Gage. No man here would be foolish enough to hit on your old lady!" Calvin piped up.

"She isn't his old lady yet!" Mark was foolish enough to say, and the roar of laughs continued.

"You know what......" Gage got in Mark's face, his hands balled into fists at his side. He had subdued his feelings all morning long, and couldn't take much more. Especially from some loud-mouthed ranch hand who hadn't a clue to the trial he was going through.

Ari gasped at his reaction, then turned quickly and made her way towards the stairway.

"Gage! What in tarnation is wrong with you?" Max grabbed him by his collar and yanked him away from Mark.

"Dude, I was just messing with you!" Mark apologized. Lifting his hands in his defense, he added, "I would *never* hit on your girlfriend, boss!"

"You know what, boys? I think I have a better idea for lunch." Max reached into his wallet and pulled out some cash, handing the money to Josh. "Why don't you head into town and stop by Ms. Anne's. I'm certain her daily special is calling your names. After that, you can take the afternoon off with pay."

"With—"

"Yes, *with* pay!" Max interrupted before Gage could finish his protest. "Let the foreman you hired handle the employees, Gage!"

Gage kicked the leg of the chair and mumbled under his breath, furious that Max had belittled him in front of his employees. After all, wasn't *he* the owner of the ranch?

"I think Gage is going to need something to burn off his energy, so he can finish with the fence. Check back in with me bright and early tomorrow morning."

Gage felt every muscle in his body tense. His heart rate began to increase. He turned away, feeling shamed, as the four boys stalked out the back door. He was so embarrassed. What right did Max have to treat him like a child? After all, Mark had it coming. How *dare* he hit on Ari!

"Gage, what in the world were you just thinking?" Max had seen the boys out and then rounded on him, his jaw clenched in anger.

"I don't know, Max," he argued loudly. "Maybe I just didn't feel right sitting back and watching while Mark made a fool out of me by hitting on Arabella!"

"You have *got* to be kidding me!" Max stammered. Pinching the bridge of his nose, Max took a deep breath in and exhaled before he continued, slightly calmer than a moment ago. "Gage, have you lost your ever-loving mind? Mark wasn't hitting on anyone. Least of all your *very* pregnant girlfriend!"

"She's not *just* my girlfriend, Max! She's going to be my *wife*!"

And that's when it hit him. That's what all of this was about. Ari was still holding back on their marriage, and Gage was beyond frustrated. Not willing to share with Max the revelation he just had, Gage simply stared at the old man, the same fire still burning in his eyes.

Max walked over to the sink and looked out the window above it. "Gage, I think maybe you need some time to cool off and think about what's happened here."

Gage didn't make a move or comment.

"I'll be back tomorrow," Max turned towards him. "If you feel like you can't stand to be here again like you did last night, feel free to finish the fence line." Max walked out the back door and seconds later Gage heard his truck start up and roar down the driveway.

Gage sat down at the table, completely beside himself. How had this morning gone so wrong? Heck, how had the entire trip gone so wrong? And Mark? He hadn't really been flirting with Ari. Gage was just feeling insecure in her love for him, because she still hadn't agreed to walk down the aisle. Not really, anyway. And then there was the whole shower fiasco. One look at Ari, and it felt like every promise he'd made to her and God had flown right out the window. What kind of man has those thoughts about a woman he isn't married to? Not the Christian man that Gage wanted to be. Feeling out of sorts and frustrated with his own behavior, Gage stood up from the table and marched over to the door. It was going to be a long afternoon, and he was hoping by the time he ran out of energy tonight, he'd have worked through all the craziness going on inside his mind.

Arabella was softly crying in the stairway when she heard the backdoor slam shut again. She had overheard everything. Every horrible word. What in the world was going on with Gage? She had never seen or heard him act as he had today. Jealousy was not something he'd ever displayed in all the time she'd known him. And what about last night? Well, that just left Ari flabbergasted. Gage was definitely not acting himself. But she couldn't understand, for the life of her, what was going on in his head.

After waiting a few minutes to make sure Gage wasn't coming back inside, Ari stood up and went down to the kitchen, taking a seat at the table and rewinding the events of last night in her mind. At first, she thought that Gage was just embarrassed about seeing her in the bathroom. But that didn't make sense. Obviously, he had seen her like that before. Then, she had to wonder if maybe he was just disgusted with the way she looked. That was the thought that kept her up most of the night. She had waited and waited for Gage to come back upstairs, but when he didn't, Ari made her way down to the living room and eventually into the kitchen. That's when she saw him out the back window, in the light of the barn, chopping piece after piece of wood. Anger seemed to fill every swing of the axe as he struck each log. Ari finally gave up and went to bed sometime after ten. It had been a long day, more exhausting from emotions than from the drive, and her body ached for sleep.

This morning, she woke with a new hope that Gage would be in a better mood. But when she came downstairs just after seven, she found that he and Max had already gone. She kept busy after breakfast and a shower, first putting the ingredients for stew into the crockpot, then deep-cleaning the house as best she could in her condition. With Nonnie gone, and Max only using the house for meals during the day, a heavy layer of dust existed throughout the home. She'd just put the cleaning supplies away when she heard the backdoor open and the guys walking in for lunch. The next fifteen minutes had turned into a nightmare.

Ari stood and walked over to the cupboards. Pulling down a bowl, she moved to the stove where she ladled up some hot stew and then sat down again. She was silent and motionless, staring into the bowl for a long moment.

"Who am I kidding?" She laid her head on the table as the tears came, overcome by her own negative thoughts, as well as Gage's uncharacteristic behavior. This entire trip had been a mistake. Why had she let Gage talk her into it? And where did they go from here? Apparently, he was no longer talking to her, although she had no idea what she'd done to deserve it. No longer hungry, Ari pushed her chair back and stood up, making her way to the living room. She tossed a small log on the fire before flopping down on the couch and snuggling up with a blanket. She was exhausted again, and she hadn't even done anything! These days it didn't seem to take much to wear her out. It wasn't long before her eye lids grew heavy and she drifted off to sleep.

"*Bella?*" Somewhere in her subconscious she heard the melody of her name.

"Bella?"

"Bella!" Gage shook her gently this time, causing her to stir and eventually sit up. She rubbed her sleepy eyes.

"Gage?" she whispered. "What's wrong?" She straightened and looked around the dark room. "How long have I been asleep? "Why is it so cold in here?" she shivered.

"Bella, its after seven, honey."

"*Seven?*" she asked, looking around the room again as if searching for evidence. "But I just laid down a minute ago."

"The fire was completely out. You must have been asleep for quite a while," Gage smiled and rubbed his hands down her arms to warm her. "I just came in from outdoors and it was cold and dark in here. You scared me."

Slowly, it was coming back to her. The incident at lunch, the crazy behavior last night. Maybe she should just close her eyes and go back to sleep. But Gage *was* talking to her. Touching her even. What happened to his anger?

"Gage, why—"

He pressed his finger to her lips to quiet her.

"Bella, I know I don't deserve your forgiveness. But, please, I'm so sorry for the way I've treated you. Can you ever forgive me?"

Ari slowly nodded her head. "I just don't understand, Gage."

Gage made to move away from her, but Ari reached out to stop him. "Don't go!" she pleaded.

He smiled back at her. "I'm not going anywhere, Bella. Let me throw a couple of logs on these hot embers to get the place warmed back up." When he was finished, he made his way back to her, sitting down beside her. He wrapped his arm around her shoulders, drawing her near to him, and kissed the top of her head.

"I'm sorry for walking away from you last night. It's just—" Gage paused, and Ari instantly was filled with worry. "Do you know how beautiful you are to me?" He reached over, turning her face towards his and she saw the shimmer in his eyes. "Bella, when I saw you standing there, it took every ounce of strength I had to turn away. The desire that I have for you now, is a hundred times stronger than it was before. You're carrying *my* child. And your body has changed because of that. I wasn't prepared for the way it would affect me."

"*You think I'm fat, don't you!*" Ari whimpered as tears threatened to spill from her eyes.

"Don't say that, Ari!" Gage forced her to look at him. "Every single inch of your body is beautiful. And I'm not trying to be disrespectful when I say that. It's not lust I feel for you, like before. I *love* you! And I desperately want to be your husband. When I look at you, and see the way your body has grown and changed because of the child God has given us, it's difficult *not* to desire you. Do you understand what I'm saying?"

She nodded slowly and swallowed the lump of emotion in her throat. "I just thought you didn't want me."

"Bella, I will always want you. Not just physically. I want you as my wife. For the *rest* of my life. I love you so much it hurts. That's why I got so upset with Mark today. I thought he was flirting with you and that pushed me over the top!"

"He wasn't flirting with me, Gage."

"I know." Gage sat back against the couch and sighed. "It took me five hours of working on the fence, alone in my thoughts, before I could come to that conclusion. But I know the truth. It was just my jealousy getting out of control."

"Gage, I've never known you to be jealous. Why now?" Ari prayed that he would continue to talk, to open his heart and share his feelings. They'd broken through a barrier in their relationship, and she knew the more they opened up to each other, the stronger their bond would grow.

"Honestly, Ari?"

"Yes, Gage. I want you to be honest with me. Otherwise, our relationship will suffer. Tell me."

"I get scared."

"Scared?" She asked cluelessly. "Of what? I don't understand."

"Of losing you again. That you don't really want to marry me. That I will never be good enough for you. Should I keep going?"

Ari could feel the desperation in his eyes as he pleaded with her, searching for the answer he needed to hear. Had she made him feel this way? Had she said or done things to make him think she didn't love him?

"Gage," she cupped his cheek in her palm and looked directly into his eyes, "why would you think those things? I love you more than I've ever loved anyone or anything. You are my entire world. How could you think that you weren't good enough for me?"

"Then why haven't we gotten married yet? Are you still afraid my walk with the Lord is not real? After all this time, do you think the changes I've made are not genuine?"

"Oh Gage, is that why you think we haven't gotten married?"

"Well, yeah. I mean, that's what you told me when I first proposed. That you had to see the changes."

"Gage," she chuckled, "I have no doubt that the changes you've made reflect a new man of God. This isn't about you, anymore. Honestly, it's about me walking down the aisle the size of a whale!"

Gage wore the look of confusion this time. "*That's* why you won't marry me?" he cried. "Bella, you are beautiful! Are you kidding me?"

"Yada, yada, yada," she rolled her eyes. "It's so easy for everyone to sit around and say I'm beautiful. But I'm the one that's feeling stretched, and pulled, and far too overweight to be anything but *fat*!" She crossed her arms and pouted. And the snickering started once again.

"What?" she growled at him. "Why are you laughing?"

"I just wish you could see yourself through my eyes, Bella. You really are the most beautiful woman I've ever known. And you get prettier every day. Your face has this glow like I've never seen. Pregnancy looks wonderful on you!"

"You're just saying that so we won't argue anymore. Hmph!"

"Woman, you are driving me mad! Come here!" Gage jumped up from the couch and reached for her hand, gently tugging her up next to him. He began walking towards the stairs.

"Gage, where are we going?" Ari cried, hesitant to continue.

He only pulled harder, not saying another word, and not letting go. They made it all the way up the stairs and into the bathroom where they paused to stand in front of the over-sized mirror.

"Really? You pulled me all the way up here so that I can *see* how fat I have become! Great, thank you." Feeling a little more than awkward for staring at her own reflection, Ari attempted to turn away. Gage didn't let her get away with it. Standing behind her, he wrapped his arms around her mid-section.

"Bella, look at this. God has created this precious little person, growing inside of you. And he's trusting us with his or her care. How could *anything* be more beautiful?"

Ari's shoulders sagged. Her emotions were all over the place. She sure didn't feel as confident as Gage seemed.

"Gage, let's just go back downstairs," she begged.

"No. Not until you look at yourself in the mirror and realize how beautiful you are! How beautiful God created you. Before the pregnancy, during the pregnancy, and after the pregnancy. Beautiful! I will *always* love you and remind you of how beautiful you are." He turned her in his arms and placed a kiss on her forehead. "Say it."

"What?"

"Say you are beautiful."

"Gage, this is silly!" she whined.

"Say it until you believe it."

"Fine," she stomped one foot and exhaled, "I'm beautiful."

"Say it like you mean it!" He turned her back to face the mirror. "Tell yourself that God created you, and that you are *beautiful.* It's the truth Arabella. You are so beautiful. Inside and out."

The smallest smile found its way to her lips. "I'm beautiful." Her smile grew to match Gage's.

"With more enthusiasm."

"I am beautiful!" she cried out and they both broke out in laughter.

"Bella, please don't ever second guess the beauty God created in you. And please, don't *ever, ever* second guess my love for you."

With that, he kissed her soundly on the lips.

"Are we okay, now?" he asked, holding her in his arms.

"We're perfect, Gage. Forever."

"Forever, Bella? So, do you promise that sometime soon, before I'm an old man, and before I go crazy from not being able to hold you like I long to hold you, you will agree to walk down the aisle and say forever to me?"

"I promise, Gage."

Two days later, Ari stood at the open dining room window, watching as Gage loaded his and her luggage into the back of their SUV. She turned at the sound of Max's truck chugging up the driveway, followed by a cloud of dust. Gage met him as he climbed out of the cab of the familiar old blue Ford.

"Looks like you're all set to hit the road." Max smiled and patted Gage on the shoulder.

Ari's heart overflowed with joy. The disagreement between Gage and Max from two days ago was long since dispelled. Gage had apologized the following morning, not only to Max and Mark, but to everyone that had witnessed his poor behavior. The remaining two days on the farm had been wonderful for she and Gage, as Gage learned to let go of the reigns, at her persistence. More and more he let the ranch hands handle the work they normally did without him, allowing him to spend more time basking in the love Ari showered upon him. For the first time in their relationship, they began to pray together in the evenings, learning to let go of the day's stresses, and seeking strength and wisdom as a couple. Ari was so happy with the progress they'd made in their relationship, and she felt closer to Gage than ever before.

"Yep, this is the last of the luggage," Gage slammed the door closed. "Ari's still inside though, if you want to go in and say goodbye. I was going to head out to the barn one last time and check on that new foal."

"Hey, Max!" Ari called from the kitchen doorway where she now stood.

Max smiled at her, then turned back to Gage. "You go right ahead and check on that foal. I've got something to discuss with this beautiful woman of yours."

Gage gave him a smile and winked. "I wouldn't think too fondly of myself if I didn't warn you. She's been on the brink of tears all morning. Poor girl's emotions are really messing with her head. Just remember when you're talking to her, that it's me that has to ride nine long hours in a car with all of that!"

Ari shot Gage a look through the window that she was certain would scare him. "I can hear you, you know."

Gage and Max just chuckled as the old rancher walked through the back door and into the kitchen, calling out to her.

"Ari, I have something for you."

Thirty minutes later, Max had hugged them both goodbye a dozen more times. At last, Ari and Gage piled into their SUV and started their journey back to Rock Haven. Ari's gaze wandered out the window as they pulled out of the driveway. A sadness grew in her heart as they left the farm behind. She continued to think about all that Max had shared with her that morning.

"Are you going to keep it a secret all the way home?"

"Hmmm?" She turned away from the window to look at Gage, her face expressionless.

"The tote." Gage nodded towards her lap. "We've been on the road nearly thirty minutes and you've been oddly quiet. Are you going to tell me what's inside?"

"Oh, its just a little something Nonnie shared with me when we were here over Christmas last year."

"So?"

"So, what?"

"So, are you going to show me what's in the tote, Bella?"

It wasn't just the contents of the tote that had made her break out in tears again this morning. It was the letter that Max had included *with* the tote, that had pushed her emotions to the breaking point. She'd read the letter three times before they ever left the farm, and the words were still burning in her mind.

My dearest Arabella. If Max has given you this tote, instead of me, then I will never have the chance to meet my first great grandchild. I pray that someday you and Gage will have a house, filled with little feet for wearing these. Each one was knitted with love.

I'll never forget our time together on the ranch, Arabella, and what you've come to mean to me. You're special, don't ever stop believing that.

More than anything Ari, I hope you remember your promise to me. Your promise to love Gage and to be patient with him. He loves you more than anything. But sometimes, as you know, men can be stubborn! You do make him happier than I've ever seen him. Please don't ever give up on his love.

The letter was signed in Nonnie's beautiful handwriting. Ari remembered well, the last conversation they'd had, the evening before she and Gage made their journey back to Michigan. It was the last time Ari had seen her alive.

You're right Nonnie. I promised you I would never give up on him. He gave his life to the Lord, he's come back to me, and instead of embracing that and allowing him to be the husband and father he desires to be, I've been worried about me. About how my waist will look in a wedding dress.

Ari hung her head as the tears raced down her cheeks.

"Ari, if you don't want to tell me, it's okay."

Ari turned to face Gage as if she just remembered he was next to her. Even though the tears continued to stream down her face, she smiled through them as she opened the tote. Gingerly, she pulled out a couple of the little pink and blue booties.

Gage's mouth hung open. "I don't understand, Ari. How did Nonnie know?" He turned his eyes back to the road, but there was no mistake in where his thoughts were.

Ari shook her head. "She didn't know about *this* baby, Gage. But she shared with me her dream, that someday, you and I *together,* would have a house filled with babies."

A knowing look came over Gage. "She knew how much I loved you the minute she saw us together. She told me that so many times." Gage smiled this time as he turned quickly to see Ari. "So, are those happy tears, then?" Gage questioned.

"Yes, Gage, they're happy tears." What Ari didn't tell him was that they had only become happy tears once she realized what she needed to do. She couldn't wait; Gage was going to be so surprised. She directed their conversation onto a new topic. "Do you remember we have the ultrasound appointment this Wednesday?" As if the baby knew they were talking about it, Ari felt a sudden jab to her side, causing her to gasp.

"You, okay?"

"Yeah, she's just moving."

"I do remember the appointment. And I couldn't be more excited. I do, however, have to work in the afternoon. I would much rather have lunch in town with you, but I promised Mr. Spencer I'd get this project finished by week's end."

"Gage, you don't have to be at every appointment with me. I understand."

"Honey," Gage reached for her hand, "a team of wild horses couldn't keep me from my baby's ultrasound. I was just hoping to spend the *whole* day with you, and that won't be possible. You know," he brought her hand to his lips and kissed it, "we aren't going to have many more days alone. Just the two of us."

Ari turned in her seat as much as her belly would allow. "Don't take this the wrong way, Gage, but I couldn't be happier that our time alone is running out. I can't wait to meet her!" Ari's smile extended clear to her eyes at the thought of holding their newborn child.

"I can't wait to hold *him* in my arms, Ari."

"*Her*, Gage."

"Mmm hmm. We'll see."

Chapter 29

"*Gage, you have to turn* the air on before I get in! It's a hundred degrees out here!" Ari waddled next to Gage as they crossed the parking lot of the hospital, sweat breaking out across her forehead.

"Give me just a second, babe. I've got it all under control." Gage unlocked the car and reached in to turn the ignition, before walking back over to help Ari into her seat.

"Wasn't he beautiful, Ari."

"Yes, *she* was, Gage." Ari backed into the seat and then swung her legs in front of her, as Gage closed the door.

The ultrasound had been amazing. They were both awestruck by the baby's growth and development, since the last one. The day was getting closer, and Ari could barely contain her excitement at meeting their little one. She opened her purse, and pulled out the strip of photos the doctor had given them, glancing at them once again with admiration.

"I'm so happy she's healthy."

As they pulled out of the parking lot, Gage apologized to her once again. "Ari, I'm sorry we can't spend the rest of today together. I was really looking forward to lunch with you."

Ari waved it off. "Gage, I'm not upset. We both have job commitments. I get it."

"It gets harder each day to be away from you. You know, the closer you get to your due date."

"Awww, you're going to make me cry again, Gage. Haven't we had enough tears today?" Ari chuckled. "Anyway, don't you worry about anything. In fact, I was going to have you drop me by the loft instead of taking me home. I haven't been up there since you finished the nursery, and I wanted to tidy things up a bit."

"Are you trying to say I'm not keeping the place clean?" Gage joked.

"No silly, I just feel like cleaning a bit. I don't know. They say women 'nest' and have bursts of energy before they go into labor. Maybe that's what I'm doing." She shrugged her shoulders to dismiss it. "Whatever it is, I just feel the urge to be at the loft."

"Just be sure you don't overdo it today."

"Don't worry," she patted Gage on the leg. "I'll take it easy. At least the doctor said everything looks great with our baby girl. She already weighs over seven pounds from what the ultrasound says."

"Let's just hope our *boy* decides to stay in there a little bit longer."

"Feeling nervous, daddy?"

"Just a little, dear."

"Gage, you're going to be a wonderful father. I see you with Chloe and how patient you are with her. The way your eyes light up when you're having tea parties, how she loves to sit on your lap as you read stories to her. You've got nothing to be nervous about."

Gage braked for a red light and turned to her. "Aren't you the slightest bit nervous, Bella? I mean Chloe is a toddler, not an infant. I have no practice with a newborn. They're so tiny! What if I drop him or hurt him?"

Ari nodded at him. "I think I'm more nervous about the labor than anything else. I don't want to be one of those crazy women, screaming like I'm possessed when I'm in the middle of labor. And Gage, don't worry about how small she is. The first time you hold your daughter in your arms, all of those fears will disappear."

Gage laughed as the light turned green, pressing his foot on the gas pedal. "I hope you're right."

He dropped Ari off at the back door of Francesca's twenty minutes later. She grabbed a quick lunch, chatted with Sam for a few minutes, and then headed upstairs.

"What are you doing at the loft?" Sam asked.

Ari had already headed for the stairwell, but she turned back long enough to answer him. "Just cleaning up a bit, Sam. I probably won't be up there more than an hour."

"Well, let me know if you need anything. I'll be here all afternoon," Sam replied.

Expecting to see a bachelor pad mess when she opened the door, Ari was pleasantly surprised at how clean the place looked. Gage had always been good at picking up after himself when they'd lived together, but Ari was certain that he would be like any other messy man when a woman wasn't around to gripe at them.

"Hmmm, I'm impressed." Ari made her way from the living room to the kitchen where she spotted a couple of cereal bowls in the sink. Rolling up her sleeves, she ran a bit of soapy dishwater and washed them up. Next, she moved onto the bathroom where she scrubbed the sink and toilet. Finally, she made her way down the hall to the room she'd been waiting all afternoon to see. The nursery.

Gage had done a fantastic job with the baseball mural he'd painted. Ari ran her hands over first base as she thought to herself how funny it was going to be when she delivered a little girl and Gage would have to repaint the entire room pink.

The knock at the front door caught her off guard. Nobody ever came up to the loft. All mail and deliveries were accepted downstairs.

Thinking it must be Gage, who'd probably changed his mind and decided to join her after all, and was just trying surprise her, Ari made her way to the door as quickly as she could.

"Very funny, Gage."

"Excuse me?"

Ari looked up into the eyes of a man she didn't recognize. Startled at first, it took her a moment to catch her breath.

"Sir, I think you must be lost. Deliveries should go to the restaurant." There was something familiar about his face that Ari couldn't quite put her finger on.

"Delivery? No," he smiled, "Sam sent me up."

"Sam?" Ari was confused as she looked past the man into the hallway.

"Aren't you Ari? I mean you look just like the picture Gage showed me."

Ari shook her head, even more confused. "I'm sorry, I—"

"I'm James. Gage's father." He reached out his hand to her.

Ari's felt her jaw drop.

"I'm sorry, if this is a bad time—"

"No," Ari sputtered, realizing how rude she must seem. "Please, come in." She took two steps back, and motioned to him. "Did… Gage… know… you…were coming……..*today?*"

"No, ma'am, I thought I would surprise him." James took in the sight of the room before him. "Wow, this is a nice place you and my boy have."

"Gage designed it." The memory brought a smile of pride to Ari's face. "It was just a cold and empty space before he got ahold of it. He really did a great job, didn't he?" Ari took a few more steps into the living room and offered James a seat on the sofa. "Please, have a seat. You must've had a long trip. Can I get you something to drink? A water?" Before he could answer, Ari walked towards her purse and dug for her phone. "I think I will just call Gage, and let him know you are here."

"Wait, Ari." James stood up and reached his hand out to her. "Would you mind if I talked with *you* for just a bit? Alone?"

"Alone? Um...sure, I guess we can sit down and talk for a bit."

"Great! Could I get that glass of water, by chance?"

Ari was more than happy to excuse herself. Still holding onto her phone as she reached the kitchen, she dialed Gage's number as fast as she could.

One ring. "Please answer, Gage," Ari whispered.

Two rings. "C'mon Gage!" She spoke a little louder.

"Hello?"

"Gage, I need you."

"Bella? What's wrong? Is it the baby?"

"No, it's not the baby!" Ari stuck her head out of the kitchen to see if James was still sitting on the couch. "Your father is here! At the loft!"

"*What?* Ari, are you serious? He's here now? He didn't even call?"

"This is no joke, Gage. He is here *now*!

"I'm sorry, honey. It's going to be a little bit before I can get home."

"He wants to talk to me alone, Gage. I'm nervous. What could he possibly want to talk to *me* about?" Ari peeked out into the living room again.

"Honey, relax!" Gage chuckled. "Just sit down and talk with him. I will finish up here as fast as I can and be over there, okay? He's not going to hurt you, Ari. He's my father."

"I'm not worried that he'll hurt me, Gage, I'm just a little nervous, that's all. He's a complete stranger for crying out loud. And your stories of him haven't been all that great. Just get home as quickly as you can, *please*."

Ari hung up, straightened her shirt, and grabbed a bottle of cold water from the refrigerator. She tried to confidently make her way back to the living room. Acting calm and collected, she handed the water to James and took a seat in the chair, opposite of the couch where he'd chosen to sit.

"So, what made you decide to *surprise* us today?"

James took a long drink from his water and set it on the table in front of him. "I didn't know Gage wouldn't be here, Ari. I hope I haven't upset you by dropping in unannounced. I just thought you and I," his pause was a reflection of his discomfort, "well, I was kind of hoping since Gage isn't here, that you and I could get to know each other a little. I realize this situation is a bit unusual, so, if you would like me to leave, I completely understand."

Recognizing how uncomfortable she'd made James feel, Ari felt a twinge of guilt. Afterall, the man was Gage's father. "That won't be necessary, James. You are more than welcome to stay."

James made small talk at first, inquiring a little about Rock Haven and Francesca's, before he moved on to a more personal topic.

"Looks like you don't have very long to go before that little one arrives, huh?" James smiled as he took in the size of Ari's round shape.

Ari had relaxed a bit by now, happy to be discussing something she was comfortable with. "Just a few more weeks, actually. We just had an ultrasound this morning." Ari was struck by an idea.

"Would you like to see the ultrasound pictures?" She stood up and walked towards her purse.

"Pictures of the baby? *Inside* you?" He paused, seeming a little hesitant, before responding. "Well, sure. I guess I could do that."

Ari pulled the black and white squares from her purse and walked back over to the sofa, taking a seat next to James. The dread she'd felt previously, now vanished.

"This is her head," Ari pointed to the first picture, "and this is her hand. See how she's sucking her thumb?"

"Wow, isn't that something?" James shook his head slowly. "You say she? You know you're having a girl then?"

Ari sat back against the couch, releasing a comfortable chuckle. "I'm certain we're having a girl. But Gage," she paused, "welllll, he's certain it's a boy."

"I see. Well I suppose as long as it's healthy, that's all that matters. Right?"

Ari explained the rest of the pictures, and the two of them carried on a normal conversation over the next hour. Ari was beginning to feel right at home with James. He wasn't anything like what she'd expected from Gage's stories. She did most of the talking, sharing about the restaurant and the pregnancy, and just a little about she and Gage. James didn't say a whole lot, but what he did say was filled with emotion. Ari could tell he was struggling.

Ari placed her hand on his arm as he began to talk about the letters Gage had left him. The letters his wife had written so many years ago.

"It made me see things from a whole different perspective."

"You don't have to share this with me, James," Ari offered.

Just then, the door opened and Gage entered the room. "Dad, what are you doing here?" He crossed the room to stand next to the couch. Ari gave Gage a reassuring look. With a much calmer tone he added, "I mean, why didn't you let me know you were coming?"

"Son!" James stood up and wrapped Gage in a hug. Ari watched Gage's expression from the other end of the couch. She could tell the hug was something new for the two of them.

"Hey," Ari stood up. "I'm going to see if Sam can drive me over to the cottage. Give you boys some time to talk, okay?"

"Don't leave on my account, dear," James was quick to respond. "What I have to say to Gage is not a secret."

"No, no, that's quite alright. You two deserve a little time alone." Ari snagged her purse and nodded toward the door, encouraging Gage to follow her.

"See you in a couple of hours? I'll be anxious to hear everything."

"I'm going to let him crash in the guest room here tonight if that's alright? And I'll be over to the cottage in a bit, okay?" Gage leaned in to kiss her on the cheek. "Thanks for staying with him until I could get here."

Arabella was awakened by the sound of Gage's key turning in the door. She'd already eaten dinner alone, and had taken a long, warm shower before curling up on the couch with a book. Apparently, she was more exhausted than even she realized. With no idea how long she'd been asleep, Ari sat up and stretched. Gage made his way into the living room, dropping his keys on the table, before taking a seat next to her on the couch.

"I'm sorry it's so late, Bella. If you want, I can head back home and let you go to bed."

Ari placed her hand on Gage's arm. "Are you kidding me? I can't wait to hear all about the conversation with your father. Do you want me to warm you up some dinner first, and then we can talk?"

Gage shook his head. "I just made a sandwich at the loft."

"Well, start talking then." Ari turned sideways, leaning back on the arm rest of the sofa, and pulling her feet into Gage's lap. "And massage while you're talking, please."

Gage seemed happy to oblige.

"I don't even know where to start, Bella. My father could never have surprised me more by his words. I guess the letters I left for him were exactly what he needed."

Gage continued to share over the next half hour, as Bella received the best foot massage ever and learned every detail about the transformation in James' life.

"I still can't believe he gave his life to the Lord, Gage. Talk about miracles. You have to be excited about that, huh?"

Gage leaned in to kiss Bella's tummy one more time, looking at her through the top of his eyes as he spoke. "Yeah, and it couldn't have happened at a better time. I want him to be a part of his grandchild's life more than ever. Oh!" Gage sat up quickly. "I forgot to tell you. I've sold the business. An old associate of dad's is buying it. I should have a check in my hand by the end of next week!"

"Gage, that's great news!" Ari beamed.

"One less thing for me to stress over. Now, I can focus all my attention on you and the farm. And with the extra money, I can add that new barn I've been talking to Max about."

The farm. That was a topic she didn't want to get into tonight. Bella shifted, growing uncomfortable once again. "Did your dad say how long he was staying?"

"He doesn't have a return date set as far as I know. You don't have a problem with him staying at the loft with me, do you?"

Bella pulled herself to her feet and turned to face him. "Of course not, Gage. After all, it's your home now."

She didn't miss the way Gage flinched.

"I'd rather call *this* home, Bella." Gage joined her as he stood, reaching out for her shoulder. "You know the baby's going to be here before we know it. I can't imagine having to leave you both at the end of the day. It's hard enough just leaving *you*."

His eagerness to move forward with their wedding wasn't lost on Bella. In fact, that was all she'd been able to think about since reading Nonnie's letter.

Ari made her way to the kitchen without responding to Gage, her mind going a hundred miles an hour with what she was about to share with him.

She started to walk back into the living room but stopped when she saw Gage, his head cradled in his hands, seemingly having a private word with God.

She waited and waited until she couldn't stand it any longer! "Gage, it's time," she yelled.

He jumped up at the sound of her voice and met her half-way, as she strolled back from the kitchen.

"It's *time?* For the baby, Bella? Now? *Right* now?" Panic spilled out with his words.

Ari erupted in laughter at the terror in Gage's voice. She came to him and wrapped her arms around his neck, staring into his terrified eyes. "No, silly. It's time for *us*." When the confusion on his face didn't disappear, she continued her explanation. "I think it's time for us to get married, Gage."

He took a deep breath in and exhaled slowly, before reaching up and touching his palm to Ari's forehead. "Are you feeling okay, babe. You're sure you're not in labor?"

Ari playfully swiped his hand away. "I'm not in labor, Gage." Her smile quickly turned into something more serious. She placed her hand on his cheek and stared all the way into his heart. "But, I am in love with you, and I'm sorry that it's taken me so long to figure out what I wanted. You've went beyond proving your love for me and your commitment to the Lord, and I want to marry you before this baby gets here."

Gage responded, with eyebrows knit together, intensity filling the air around them. "Baby bump and *all*?" he questioned.

She chuckled as she answered. "Baby bump *and all*. I guess we'll have a wonderful wedding story to share with our daughter someday about how the Lord works in people's lives, huh? We're living proof of that."

"You mean our son," Gage slowly swayed back and forth, dancing with Bella in his arms, his eyes never leaving hers.

"We'll see about that."

"So, how soon are you thinking? We have to get a license you know."

Ari stopped dancing. "We'll get the license tomorrow and hopefully Beth can help me find something other than a white bedsheet to cover this," she pointed to her bump. "Let's see if pastor can marry us this Saturday."

"*This Saturday*, Bella?"

She nodded with a smile.

"You have no idea how happy this makes me. Bella, you're more beautiful now than I've ever seen you." Gage leaned in to kiss her on the tip of her nose.

"Beached whales are *not* beautiful!" Ari laughed.

"Stop saying that about yourself, Ari. God has given us the most beautiful gift in the world."

"I know, dear, I'm just joking. I can't wait to meet her."

"*I* can't wait until you're my wife."

The next three days rushed by in a flurry for the two of them. Between getting their marriage license and speaking with the pastor, to planning a simple reception at Francesca's, Ari felt like she had run a marathon. Beth was ecstatic when she called to tell her the news. Ari was very clear that she needed help with finding something to cover her baby bump, and Beth was more than happy to help with said chore. Ari chose a simple, sleeveless, white-silk maternity dress, and opted to be a barefoot bride, as her legs and feet were so swollen that she couldn't find shoes to fit comfortably.

Friday morning, continuing their weekly tradition, Gage, Sam, and Anthony loaded up their fishing gear and drove to the lake with Anthony's boat. This time though, they were joined by James for a couple of hours of male bonding. Gage had been ecstatic about his father's presence. Ari had seen a change in Gage over the past few days; a change that could only be God's doing. His confidence was off the charts, as every day his father showed less interest in leaving Rock Haven. James had said he wanted to stick around and be a bigger part of Gage's life. For that, Ari was thrilled.

Friday night they held a small rehearsal at the church and dinner afterwards at Francesca's. The wedding would be small and intimate, just a few close friends from the congregation, besides the wedding party. Beth had found an adorable peach dress that matched hers for Chloe, so she could walk down the aisle with a basket full of rose petals. And, since they didn't have a ring bearer, they'd tied the rings to the front of Chloe's basket. Her squeal of delight confirmed how excited she was to be a "big girl" for Auntie Ari's big day.

With her belly nearly the size of Ari's, Beth was no help with painting Ari's toe nails Saturday afternoon. In the end, it was Gage that came through for her. Not one bit nervous that he'd jinx his marriage by seeing his bride before the ceremony, the groom marched into the dressing room and promptly sat on the floor with Ari's feet in his lap. When he was finished, her toes wore a beautiful shade of pink.

"Now, *that's* a man in love!" Beth exclaimed as Gage left the room. Turning her attention back to the bride she asked, "Are you nervous, Ari?" The two of them stood, staring into the full-length mirror, Beth's hand on her best friend's shoulder.

"Not to marry Gage," she shook her head. "Nervous about how I look in this dress," she nodded her head and held up her thumb and forefinger, "maybe a little." The space between her fingers grew. "Okay, maybe a lot!"

"Arabella, you're stunning and everyone out there loves you. There's no reason to be nervous."

"I know you're right." Arabella looked down towards her feet, not bothering to hide that something was wrong.

"Want to talk about it?"

Ari looked up and dabbed at her eyes, trying to keep the tears from sliding down her face and ruining her makeup. "Don't take this the wrong way."

Beth rubbed her arm. "Oh, Ari, whatever it is, you can tell me."

"I wish my family were here. I mean, you are like family to me, don't get me wro—"

Beth pulled her into a side hug, interrupting. "Ari, you don't have to explain that. I would give *anything* to have your family here with you today."

A tap on the door interrupted them. Sam stuck his head into the room.

"It's time, girls."

Beth pulled back and looked at Ari. "Are you ready to do this?"

"More than ready," Ari smiled.

Beth picked up both flower bouquets from the table and handed the bridal one to Ari.

"Thanks for everything, Beth." Ari wanted to make sure that Beth knew how important her friendship was to her. "You are the best friend a girl could ever ask for, and I couldn't love you anymore if you had been born my sister."

Before they both broke out in tears, Sam ushered them out the door and down the hall. They made their way to the back of the sanctuary as the music began to play.

As Arabella walked down the aisle on that Saturday afternoon, holding on to Sam's arm, she couldn't have been happier. Gage's eyes shimmered under the light as he watched his beautiful, barefoot, and *very* pregnant bride, making her way down the aisle towards him. Anthony was at his side and his father watched from the first row.

"My beautiful Arabella," Gage held her hands in his, prompted by Pastor Ron at the point in the ceremony where they recited the vows they'd each written.

"Words simply can't express how much you mean to me. From the first moment I saw you across the room at Francesca's, I knew some day you'd be mine. What I didn't know then, was how much the meaning of 'having you' would change. Bella, you shared a world with me that I knew nothing about, and because of your willingness to speak truth to me and to let me go, I've now had the opportunity to not only fall completely in love with *you*, but also with our Lord and Savior. I owe all that I am to you and I promise that I will spend the rest of my life loving you, caring for you, and respecting you, and," Gage's throat grew thick with emotion as his eyes traveled to the roundness of Ari's belly beneath their hands, "I promise to raise our children knowing the love of Christ by being an example to them. Bella, you've made me the happiest man in the world and I can't wait to spend forever with you."

"Forever, Gage?" Bella didn't wait for the pastor's permission to begin and he simply let her continue, stifling a chuckle at her eagerness.

"Yes, Bella. Forever." Gage grinned and nodded in Ari's direction and she responded with a smile of her own. "Forever is as far as I'll go, and I can't wait to share it with you."

Trying to keep her make-up from running, was useless. The man had her undone at forever.

Fumbling through her emotions for the strength to speak, eventually Ari was able to continue. "Gage, you have owned my heart since the first time you kissed me, and you're the only man I'll ever love. I promise to be faithful and true, to support you in times of weakness and to always encourage you to be the best that you can be. I will respect you and raise our children to know and love the Lord. When there's gray in your hair and wrinkles around my eyes, I promise that the love we share will only grow deeper. Nothing can separate us now, Gage, not even death. I thank God every day for bringing you into my life, and allowing me to love the wonderful man that you are. Forever, Gage, is as far as I'll go with you."

Now, it was Gage's turn to cry. And there was no stopping the silent tears that flowed from his eyes.

"Well then," the pastor began, "may I please have the rings?"

Ari looked over her shoulder just in time to see Beth nudge Chloe in their direction. The pastor continued with the symbolization of the wedding rings and how they represented union and commitment for life. "It is a ring of love, and a promise that you make here today. These rings," he held the bands up together, "will never tarnish, symbolizing your love as it is today and will be forever. There is no mistake in the fact that wedding rings are created in a perfect circle, signifying that your love, Arabella and Gage, will remain forever without end. Each and every day over the years, as you look down upon your ring, may it bring you joy, as you reflect on the happiness you share today and let it also be a reminder of your promise to honor and cherish one another."

Gage and Ari recited the words Pastor Ron led with, followed by the placement of the rings on each other's fingers, and finally turning them to face their guests.

"Gage?"

"Yes, sir?" Gage responded quickly, barely able to contain his enthusiasm for the next part of the ceremony.

"You may now kiss your bride!"

Gage didn't move. The guests watched with anticipation in their eyes.

"Pastor?"

A look of uncertainty covered the pastor's face. "Yes, Gage?"

"Could you hurry up and announce her as my wife first? He shrugged. "I've been waiting a long time to hear those words."

Unable to contain himself with this first ever request, the pastor, along with the bride and the wedding guests, broke out in laughter.

"Ok, then. As you wish." Pastor Ron turned the couple towards their guests and stepped to the side.

"Gage and Ari, I know pronounce you man and wife!"

"Thank you, sir!"

Gage stretched across Arabella's mid-section and kissed her gently on her lips as the church came alive with celebratory clapping and cheering. After a few dozen photos, and a whole lot of congratulations, the newlyweds made their way to Francesca's to join their guests for a short reception.

And for the first time since he'd walked out of her life, Arabella allowed Gage to take her home that night and hold her in his arms until the sun came up the following morning. Ari had fallen asleep five minutes after her head hit the pillow, exhausted from the days' events, but it was a moment in time she would never forget.

Chapter 30

When she woke up at 4 a.m., Ari knew that something wasn't right. Her back had ached the entire day before, but she hadn't thought too much of it with the excitement of the wedding and all. Now, the pain had increased greatly, and she was having one contraction on top of the other. She was certain she could no longer consider them Braxton Hicks, by the intensity and frequency. She hadn't wanted to spoil the ceremony yesterday, keeping quiet about them when they first started. This morning, they were growing stronger and lasting longer. Ari was overcome with fear, uncertain that she was prepared for the life-changing event about to happen. Not wanting to wake her very sleepy husband, she tried everything to get her mind off of the pain. The contractions, however, wouldn't stop. They continued to assault her tired and achy body until she couldn't take anymore. It was time.

"Gage honey, I need you to get up." Ari tried to pull free of his embrace, but his grip around her only tightened. With his eyes still closed, he mumbled a response.

"Don't worry, Bella. We got married yesterday, honey. Everything's okay. Just go back to sleep now."

Ari nudged him less gently this time and pulled his arm off of her as she sat up in bed. "No Gage, it's really *time*. Time for the baby!" Another contraction, this time more intense, seized Ari. She cried out in pain.

"Gage!"

In a split-second, Gage jumped from the bed, all his senses on high alert. "Are you sure, Bella?" The fear in Ari's eyes, left little room for doubt.

Gage ran to the closet and grabbed the overnight bag they had prepared in advance. Holding on to her elbow, he attempted to guide Ari towards the front door.

She stopped abruptly, forcing him to halt. "Gage, we can't go in our pajamas!"

Ten minutes, and one very strong contraction later, they were both dressed and ready to race out the door.

"You have to call Beth!" Ari yelled, as she quickly brushed her long hair into a ponytail. "What if we don't make it to the hospital in time?" Gage must have sensed her fear. He pulled her to a stop, and held her face in his hands.

"Ari, look at me. You have to calm down and breathe, honey. It's going to be okay. We are going to meet our baby today."

Somewhat soothed by her husband's words, Ari nodded her head in agreement, and focused on her breathing, as he buckled her into the car and sped towards the hospital.

Once they arrived at the hospital, and the nurses got Ari set up in her room, Gage made all the necessary phone calls. It wasn't long before the small waiting room was filled with anxious friends, and one very nervous, grandpa-to-be.

Watching his new bride struggling with so much pain, was nearly more than Gage could stand. The admiration he held for her was beyond anything he'd ever known. She was amazing. And she was all his. Thinking back over the past twenty-four hours, Gage still couldn't believe how lucky he was. He was a married man. If anyone would have told him two years ago, that he would be married at this time, he surely would have laughed in their face! Sometimes he had to pinch himself, just to know that it was all real. And now, he and Ari were going to be parents! It was a lot to take in. Even though he'd had a few months to prepare for it, Gage felt anything *but* qualified for this next phase of his life. Was he ready to be responsible for another life? Competent enough to do the job right? He couldn't lie about it. He'd been second-guessing his parenting abilities for weeks now. Ari always seemed so confident and sure of herself. Why couldn't *he*? Would the poor relationship he had with his father during his youth, hinder him from being a good parent? Ari's youth, and relationship with her parents, was comparable to a fairy tale. That, Gage knew beyond a doubt, was what allowed her to feel so secure in her new role as a mother. Would he ever be that confident?

Gage leaned back against the coolness of the wall and sighed. He'd stepped out of the room to get a breath of fresh air in between Ari's contractions, but he knew his time was running out. The baby was coming, ready or not. Standing up straight and taking a deep breath, Gage told himself that he was man enough to be what Ari and their child needed. He headed back into the room.

Ari was crying again. The doctor was looking at the baby's monitor, analyzing the heart rate when Gage came to her side. The baby was breech. After six intensive hours of contractions, and hoping the baby would turn, the doctor prepared them to face a cesarean section.

"I think it's time we prep you, Ari. We need to get this little one out."

Gage felt helpless as he watched his unbelievably strong wife, who had barely made a noise all through her labor, crumble.

"I don't want a c-section, please," she begged the doctor.

Gage went to the head of the bed and with two strong hands, pulled Ari's face towards his. "Bella, you need to listen to the doctor. I don't want anything to happen to you or the baby. Please, just agree to the c-section."

"Please... just... ten.... more.... minutes.... doc," Ari's pleading came in between quick gasps as another contraction began to seize her, "and theeeeen," she exhaled and took another breath in, "I will agree to the c-section."

"Ari, I don't think it's going to make a difference, but I will agree to five minutes. After that, if the baby is too stubborn to turn, you're *going* into surgery."

"Gage," she panted, her eyes full of fear, "pray with me please." Ari clung to her husband's arm as he leaned his forehead on hers and prayed for their child.

It was surely the work of God. Four minutes later, just as the doctor had ordered the staff to prep her for surgery, the baby finally gave in and somersaulted into position for delivery. It wasn't long after, that the doctor gave the go ahead.

"Okay, Ari. This is what you've been waiting for." The nurse stood on the opposite side of Gage, coaxing her. "The baby's head is in good position. Now, we need some strong pushes."

Things moved very quickly from that point. Soon, Gage's worries about the delivery turned into excitement, as he saw the baby's head crown.

"Bella, you're *so* close honey! And you're doing such a fantastic job!" Gage tried to encourage her with his words. Her grip on his hand grew tighter.

"One more push, Bella. You've got this." Gage's focus went back and forth between his wife and their newborn about to arrive. The baby's shoulder had just emerged.

"All right, Bella," the nurse encouraged, "one more big push on three. One, two—"

Like Gage, Bella couldn't wait. He watched her bear down with every ounce of strength she had, and push like her life depended on it.

The tears he'd shed at his wedding, were nothing compared to the flood that streamed down Gage's face when he heard his son cry for the first time.

"Bella, it's a boy. We have a son!" He raced back to the head of the bed where Bella collapsed against her pillow, utterly exhausted.

"It's a boy?" she asked with a smile.

"A very health boy," the doctor responded, as the infant's cries rang out through the delivery room. It was the sweetest sound Ari had ever heard.

"You did it, Bella! You are so strong!" Gage kissed her forehead. "I love you so much!"

Nervously, Gage cut the umbilical cord, before the nurse placed their son against his wife's chest. It was the most beautiful thing Gage had ever laid eyes on. All nine-and-a-half pounds of him. He had a head full of jet-black hair and amazing blue eyes.

"He looks just like you, you know." Ari kissed the infants head again. "Are you ready to hold him?"

The fear that he'd felt earlier, vanished the moment he heard his son cry for the first time. Immediately, Gage had felt a calming peace wash over him. He would be the best father he could be. And he was certain that would be enough. He silently prayed his thankfulness to the Lord. The three of them spent the next hour together, bonding. Then Gage went to share the news.

It had been nine long, exhausting hours, when Gage finally bustled through the labor and delivery doors into the waiting room with his arms raised high in the air. The smile on his face so big, it touched his eyes.

"It's a boy!" He announced. "We have a *son*!"

Beth and Anthony were sitting close to Sam and Karen. James was a few chairs away. However, at the announcement, they all jumped up and cheered before making their way to Gage and hugging him in congratulations.

"It's a boy? I have a grandson?" James was the first to speak.

"Yes, Dad. A healthy, nine-and-a-half-pound, baby boy. Would you like to meet him?" Gage was overwhelmed with emotion, as his father wrapped his arms around him in another hug.

"Congratulations, son. And yes," he pulled back and nodded eagerly, "I would love to meet him."

Gage turned towards the others, knowing they were all excited to meet the little guy. "Ari wants you all to know she is doing fine. You'll each have a chance to meet the little one in a few minutes."

He could tell his father was nervous, as they pushed through the double doors and down the hallway lined with newborn baby pictures.

"It's okay, Dad. Remember, this is a time to celebrate!"

"I remember the day you were born, Gage." James stopped just outside of Ari's room and looked up at his son with emotion pooling in his eyes. "It was the happiest day of my life, you know."

"Dad, let the past be the past. I know that you love me. Let's look forward to the future, okay?"

"I just wanted you to know, son."

Gage made his way to Ari's bed side where she placed the swaddled infant in his arms. "Dad, we would like you to meet your grandson and namesake, James Isaac Russell." Gage closed the gap between he and his father, offering him the opportunity to hold the newest member of their family.

A tear slid down James' face as he pulled the baby tight against him, breathing in his new baby scent. "You, you named him…… after *me*?"

James looked down into his grandchild's tiny face, then up to his son and new daughter-in-law.

"Gage," he called out to his son, "your mother would be so proud of you. I only wish she were here to meet her grandson. I'm so sor—"

Gage wrapped his arm around his father's shoulders. "Don't worry, Dad. She's here. All around us. And she will continue to live on through me. One thing I can promise you, is that my children will know all about their grandmother.

James nodded in agreement. The pride he felt for his son, was evident in his smile.

Gage stayed at the hospital that night, never leaving his wife and son's side. He barely gave Ari any time to hold the baby. He was head-over-heels in love with little Jimmie.

"Are you done nursing him yet? My arms are aching to hold him!"

"Gage, sit down and relax while you can. I promise you, within a week you're going to be begging me to take him from you."

Gage shook his head. "Won't happen. I could *never* get tired of this."

When he was done nursing, she tightened up her gown and adjusted little Jimmie's blanket. "Would you like to hold your son now?"

Gage was next to her before she could finish her sentence, his arms held out for the baby.

"I still can't believe you were right. I thought for sure it was going to be a girl."

"Speaking of that," Gage spoke up, "does this mean you are going to re-paint the nursery at the cottage?" He sat down in the recliner next to Ari's bed. "And I won't say I told you so," he grinned.

Ignoring his boasting completely, Ari answered. "Actually, what would you say about us living at the loft again, and giving the cottage to your dad when he visits?"

Gage's face lit up. "Bella, I would love that." Proud of the space he'd transformed into their home, Gage was beyond excited.

"We will still have to re-paint the nursery at the cottage, though. I'm sure your father would prefer not to have a pretty yellow bedroom in his house," Ari chuckled as she lay back against her pillow.

Later that afternoon, while Ari and little Jimmie napped, Gage snuck out to the hallway and made a couple of phone calls.

"Sam, its Gage. I need your help with something."

Sam chuckled. "Ari isn't going to get mad this time, is she?"

"I'm pretty certain this time she's going to love it!"

"Well then, what can I help you with?"

Gage went over all the details with Sam, and asked him to call Beth and Anthony, while he called his father. This was a big project, and they had very little time to get it accomplished.

When Gage and Ari arrived at the loft Tuesday afternoon, it didn't take long for the tears to start flowing. Again.

"Gage, how did you get all of this done?" Ari circled around, taking in the bassinet next to the couch, the baby swing in the corner, and the bouncy seat on the floor.

"I had a little help. But, there's more." He pointed down the hallway towards the nursery. As she moved in that direction, Gage unbuckled baby Jimmie from his car seat and, snuggling him tight in the crook of his arm, followed her down the hall.

"Oh, Gage!" Ari's hand came to her mouth. "You thought of everything." The dresser and changing table had been relocated and re-filled with all of the baby's items, the closet filled with boxes of diapers and wipes. "Even the rocking chair? How on earth did you manage to pull this off in *one* day?" Ari made her way to the rocker and took a seat, reaching her hands out for the baby.

"All the credit goes to my dad, Sam, and Anthony. Everyone wanted it to be perfect for you and Jimmie when you came home."

Home. The word wrapped around her heart, filling her with a comfort she'd never known. Yes, home felt good.

It was then that her attention was drawn to the new mural. It hadn't been here the last time she was in the nursery, just six days ago. She stood and slowly made her way to it, taking in every single inch of his work. It was far more precious than the baseball theme on the opposite wall.

"Gage, this is beautiful." Her hands trembled as they touched the painted man and woman standing side by side, his arm around her waist and the jet-black hair sprouts of a baby peeking out from under its blanket in her arms, watching the sun go down over the water.

Gage moved from the doorway and strode across the room where he leaned his head against hers. The thought that she had come so close to losing everything they now shared, was overwhelming. Caught up in her thoughts of their too recent past, Ari apologized again to Gage, as she'd done so many times in the past few months. "I'm so sorry that I didn't tell you, Gage."

He turned Ari around to face him. "No looking back, Bella. Our past is what brought us here, and we only look ahead from this point." He kissed her lips gently before little Jimmie let out a squeal.

"I think someone's hungry."

Chapter 31

Jimmie was five weeks old when he made his first visit to the ranch. Gage had been refusing to make the trip for weeks, not wanting to leave Ari or his son. When he got the call from Max that the main barn had burned to the ground, he knew he couldn't put the trip off any longer.

Ari had just come home from work at the restaurant, and settled into the dinner that Gage had waiting for her, when he decided to share the news. Jimmie had just been put down, giving the two of them a few quiet moments alone.

"Bella, honey, I need to make a trip to Iowa. Max called today. There's been a fire."

Ari looked up from her plate with wide eyes. "A fire? Is the house gone?"

Gage reached for her hand and held it in his. "It wasn't the house, Bella. The main barn burned to the ground, though. Luckily the horses were all able to get out. But I need to get out there as soon as possible, and deal with the insurance company. I've got to get a new structure in place before the weather turns too cold."

"So, when do we leave?" Ari's quick response caught Gage by surprise.

"We?" He gave Ari a puzzled look. "Meaning, you are willing to pack up little Jimmie and make the trip *with* me?"

Ari shook her head and grinned like it was silly for him to even consider anything else. "Of course. I wouldn't expect you to be away from Jimmie that long."

"Just Jimmie?" Gage ran his fingers across her bangs and down through her long dark tresses. "I thought maybe *you* couldn't stand to be away from *me* that long."

"Well, it sure would be an adjustment without you." Ari looked around the spotless kitchen and living room. "You amaze me, Gage. Between the laundry, dishes, and grocery shopping, to walking the floors with Jimmie when he cries, even changing dirty diapers. You're so good with Jimmie. And to me. You take better care of me than I even deserve." She pointed to her plate of salmon, steamed broccoli and rice. "I never would've expected to go back to work as early as I did, but you've taken care of everything for our family. I don't know any other father or husband that's more devoted than you."

Gage chuckled. "Well, to be honest, I never pictured myself wearing a baby carrier across my chest. But," Gage's eyes grew misty, "I wouldn't have it any other way. I love you and Jimmie so much it hurts, Ari. I can't imagine a day without either of you."

"You're a good dad, Gage. Jimmie's lucky to have you." Ari opened up her napkin and laid it across her lap before looking back up. "And so am I."

"Well, if you're sure you and Jimmie are up for the trip, I would like to leave tomorrow?"

"Tomorrow *is* a little sooner than I expected. But," Ari smiled up at him, "I'm sure we can make it work. This is just one good reason why I now have an assistant manager. Let me just give Tracy a quick call."

"Ari, honey, why don't you eat your dinner before it gets cold? You can call Tracy in a bit."

An hour later, after dinner had been eaten and arrangements made, baby Jimmie began to stir in the nursery.

"I'll get him changed while you get ready to nurse him," Gage was quick to jump up and retrieve the little guy. It had only been two hours since Gage had laid him down, but he missed his son like crazy. He couldn't imagine filling his days with anything other than being a husband and father, or how he'd ever lived without it before. He chuckled as he pictured the expressions on his ranch employees' faces, when he first told them he was going to be a stay-at-home dad. They had been video chatting, shortly after Jimmie's birth, when Gage mentioned he was going to be doing the housekeeping and grocery shopping, along with diaper changes and cooking. He quickly earned the nickname "Mr. Mom." It might not be the normal thing in most people's minds, but it was right for their family.

As he bent over the crib and watched Jimmie stretch his little arms and legs, Gage thought back to how close he'd come to losing both he and Ari.

He prayed a thanksgiving to God, once again, for blessing him with all he had. Then, it was onto Gage's favorite subject.

"I sure can't wait to teach you all about the farm, little one. Some day you will have your very own pony! Your grandma and great-grandma would have loved to have met you, Jimmie." He reached down and picked the baby up just as Ari walked into the room.

"Already talking about ponies, huh?

"Never too young to start! He's going to love the farm as much as I do some day." Gage's smile brightened the entire room.

It was a good thing Gage had insisted on the new SUV they had purchased three weeks ago, because there wasn't an inch to spare, once all of the baby's essentials had been packed. Jimmie handled the long drive well, only fussing to eat once during the entire trip.

After everything had been unpacked, Ari got little Jimmie settled inside the old farmhouse, while Gage went right to work, checking out the fire damage. He had talked non-stop the entire drive, excitedly sharing his designs and dreams for the new structure, and the positive impact it could have on the farm. Ari had to admit, even she was inspired listening to him. And touched. Seeing Gage filled with this much enthusiasm tugged at her heart. He was in the element he loved; that much was obvious. It was like Gage came to life when he was on the farm. A happiness filled him to the core and he radiated joy. Gage's enthusiasm was contagious, and soon Ari began to feel as excited as he did about the new red monstrosity that was to be twice as big as the last barn.

Gage had already been in contact with the insurance company, and had placed an order for the majority of the supplies he would need, not bothering to wait for the claim to be processed. Already there had been mention of purchasing more cattle and horses. Ari was certain that meant Gage would need to hire additional workers and maybe plan to spend more time in Iowa, away from her and Jimmie. That thought continued to bother her as the days sped by.

It was their third day in Iowa, and from the back-porch swing, Ari watched her husband directing the clean- up, organizing the new building crew, and picking up a hammer himself, all while little Jimmie was nestled against his daddy's chest in his carrier. Ari had never seen a more beautiful sight. Gage was an amazing father! Although Jimmie was far too young to understand a word his daddy said, Gage carried on a conversation with him throughout the day, explaining all of his plans and dreams, as if he were old enough to comprehend it all. Ari's admiration grew as she watched their interaction day by day. She couldn't help but wonder, after seeing him like this, if Gage could ever be this happy back in Michigan. Of course, Gage would never admit that to her, and Ari had no doubt that he loved her and Jimmie. But he would do whatever he felt was right to support his family. He always did what he promised her. No matter what the cost.

The days passed by quickly, and before Ari knew it, it was their last day on the farm. They were already packing for the trip back to Rock Haven. The barn had been completed, and the ranch was ready to face the fall and winter seasons that were quickly approaching. Ari had made a commitment early in their stay, to pray for discernment and wisdom, regarding the choice she now faced. With their departure quickly approaching, she felt the time had come to share her thoughts with Gage.

They'd been finished with dinner long enough for Ari to clean up the kitchen, as Gage gave Jimmie a bath and then rocked him to sleep. Now it was just the two of them, relaxing by the warmth of the fire. With her head resting upon his shoulder, Ari reached for Gage's scuffed and scraped hand, evidence of the work he'd done on the farm over the past two weeks. She interlaced her fingers with his.

"You're happy here aren't you, Gage?"

Gage turned to her, one eyebrow raised in question. "Am I happy at the farm? Of course, I'm happy here, Bella. You know that. Why do you ask?"

Ari traced her finger along his chin. "Happier here than in Michigan, huh?"

Gage leaned in to kiss her. "Bella, I'm happy wherever you and my son are. Whether it's Michigan or Iowa, it doesn't matter anymore."

"I think it does, Gage. I've watched you every day for the past two weeks. It's like you come alive when you're here at the farm! You know," she chuckled, "not many dads would be carrying their infant son around while they were trying to focus on work. But Gage, I watch your face light up every time Jimmie's with you, the excitement in your eyes as you share the ranch with him."

Gage reached for Ari's face and cupped her cheek in his hand, his expression growing serious. "Bella, I love Jimmie. I don't want to miss a moment of his life. I refuse to be the dad my father was. But I can do that anywhere, whether it be Rock Haven or Iowa."

"I know, Gage, and that's what I love about you. You are such a great father and—"

"And what, Bella?"

She pulled away, stood up and walked towards the fireplace. "And I don't want to stop you from teaching Jimmie all that you want to teach him. That's why—"

"Bella," Gage stood up and walked towards her, "you don't have to—"

Ari lifted her hand in the air. "No, please let me finish, Gage." Gage stopped, evidently aware of the determination in her voice.

"I've made a decision, and I need you to hear me out." After a moment, Ari's face softened and she closed the distance between them, wrapping her arms around Gage's waist.

"I want to split our time between Michigan and Iowa. I want Jimmie to learn about living on a farm, as much as I want him to enjoy living at the beach, and learning about my family restaurant. I know we can make it work, Gage! It's all I've thought about for the past three days."

When Gage didn't respond with words and Ari instead saw the emotion in his eyes, relief flooded her. Yes, this was the right thing for their family. It might take some adjusting, but she was certain they could make it work.

"Does that mean you agree, Gage?"

Apparently too emotional to speak, Gage pulled her to him and kissed her soundly. With too much excitement in the air, the two of them stayed up until Jimmie woke for his two o'clock feeding, putting together a plan on how to make their new arrangement work. In the end, they decided to split their time equally, and Ari agreed to let her new assistant manager take on more responsibility.

"Six months at our ranch and six months on the beach. Sounds like the perfect compromise."

"Our kids will have the best of both worlds," Ari smiled down on little Jimmie as he nursed. "I can't wait until he's big enough to ride his first pony!"

"Speaking of *kids*," Gage raised his eyebrows in his wife's direction, a teasing grin on his face, "Jimmie really should have a little brother or sister to play with. Don't you agree?"

"Gage!" she whispered loudly. "He's seven weeks old! You can't be serious." Ari tried to contain her laughter so as not to wake the baby in her arms.

"Well, to be fair," Gage made his way to the rocking chair, his eyes full of desire for his wife, "I never got a honeymoon with you, Bella."

"The *one* negative to marrying a girl who's nearly nine- months pregnant," she teased.

Gage reached down and gently picked up his sleeping son from her arms. "I think now that he's got a full belly, he's ready to go back to bed. And," heading towards the stairway, he looked back long enough to make sure Ari couldn't mistake his intention, "so is his daddy."

Back in Michigan, the next four weeks were filled with making new schedules; allowing Ari more freedom, as the assistant manager took on more responsibility. They designed the remodel that would take place at the farmhouse, and worked on figuring out just how they could manage two households. Thank goodness Gage's father had decided to stay in Rock Haven indefinitely, and was occupying the cottage. It was one less thing on her plate to worry about. Ari was beyond exhausted. She was a very busy new mother. It wasn't until Gage asked her over dinner one night, that she'd even considered the possibility of her fatigue to mean something else.

"I think I'm going to turn in early tonight, if you don't mind? I'm having a hard time keeping my eyes open."

"Between being tired and having no appetite," Gage hinted, "I would dare ask my beautiful bride if she's expecting again."

"Pregnant?" Ari quickly dismissed the idea. "I can't be pregnant. I'm still nursing Jimmie."

"Want to bet on it?" Gage's teasing grin had Ari suddenly nervous. "I'll run to the pharmacy if you promise to take the test first thing in the morning. Deal?"

Pregnant? Again? I can't be! How in the world could we ever take care of TWO infants? If Gage is right, that means……oh, my….only eleven months apart? No, he has to be wrong.

"Sure, if you want to run out tonight, that's fine with me. But, don't be disappointed when it comes back negative," Ari smirked, "and I say 'I told you so'." Oh, she hoped that would be the case!

Gage had his keys and wallet in hand, and was out the door almost before the last word left her lips.

Ari made her way down the hall to the nursery, where she stood beside the crib, watching little Jimmie's chest rise and fall with each breath he took. It never ceased to amaze her the amount of love she held in her heart for her child.

Lord, you have blessed me with so much. Thank you for giving me Gage and this healthy, beautiful little boy.

Ari walked over and sat in the rocker, gently gliding back and forth, losing all track of time. She was still there when she heard Gage come through the door, twenty minutes later. She got up and walked to the kitchen for a drink of water before telling Gage goodnight. As she was making her way back down the hall to their room, she tried her hardest not to put too much stock into Gage's enthusiasm. Tomorrow would come soon enough.

Bella tossed and turned for hours, unable to get comfortable or get her mind off of Gage's suggestion. Finally, fed up with not being able to sleep, she climbed over the side of the bed and made her way to the bathroom. The anticipation was nearly as bad as the first time she'd taken a pregnancy test.

Five minutes later, with eyes full of tears, Bella was shaking Gage awake.

"Gage, wake up."

No response.

She shook him harder and raised her voice slightly.

"Gage, wake up! I'm *pregnant*! The test is positive! What are we going to do?" She flopped down on the bed beside him, as he sat up and tried to get his bearings. After she repeated it the *third* time, it seemed to finally hit him.

"*Pregnant*? For real, Bella? This is the best news ever!" He jumped up off the bed, nearly knocking her over in his excitement.

"Best news, Gage? How do you figure? We have a baby that's less than three months old! What will we do with another one?"

Gage took her face in his hands. "Bella, you can't argue with God's plan." Too hyped up, Gage couldn't stand still. "I can't believe it; Jimmie is going to be a big brother!"

Bella sank back onto the bed feeling completely defeated.

An entire hour passed before Gage calmed down enough to talk with her about it.

"Honey, aren't you happy? I thought we planned on having a whole houseful of little ones?" Gage's eyes found Ari's and held them. "Isn't that why Nonnie crocheted all those booties?"

"It's just a little sudden, Gage, that's all. It's not that I'm *not* happy. I'm just...... overwhelmed."

Jimmie's cries sounded from the nursery across the hall. "Speaking of overwhelmed," Ari nodded towards the sound.

"C'mon, Ari," he reached for her hand and pulled her in the direction of the escalating wails, "I'll stay up with you and help keep you awake while you nurse him. We're in this together, you know."

The next morning, Ari sat at the breakfast table, picking at the eggs and toast Gage had fixed her before running to the grocery store. She'd had a meltdown and cried again, as soon as he left, thinking about what having another little one in the house so soon would mean for them. She reached her hand across the table to her phone, but it rang before she could even pick it up. Ari was happy to see Beth's number across her screen.

"You must have known how badly I needed to talk to you. You're not going to believe what I'm about to tell you."

"Ari, I'm in labor!" Beth squealed with excitement.

So much for worrying about her pregnancy. That would have to be put on the back burner for now. Her best friend was having a baby!

"Oh Beth, that's great!" Wait," Ari began to panic, "is Anthony home with you?"

"Yes, but we are about to leave for the hospital," she replied rather calmly. "Contractions are pretty steady at eleven minutes apart."

"And you're as cool as a cucumber," Ari couldn't believe the sure and soothing tone of Beth's voice.

Why couldn't I be half that calm, Lord? I'm a complete basket case over the news of my pregnancy!

"As soon as Gage gets home from the store we will head towards the hospital. Have Anthony call me if anything happens before we get there." Ari paused, ready to hang up, before remembering, "Oh, and good luck, Beth. You're going to do great!"

Beth delivered a healthy baby boy, five short hours later. Gage and Ari stood at the nursery window looking at the little guy, as the nurse gave him his first bath. Gently, she placed a blue cap on his tiny head. It was then, that Ari felt the first little wisp of excitement in her heart over the news she had yet to share with her best friend.

She laid her head on Gage's shoulder as his arm wrapped around her waist. "I'm sorry, Gage. I didn't mean to sound unhappy about being pregnant."

Gage kissed the top of her head. "Isn't this amazing? Just look at little Jacob all swaddled up snuggly." He released his hold on her and turned her to face him. "I know it's sudden, Ari. I just can't help being excited, though. I'm so happy with you and Jimmie and all that the Lord has blessed us with. I love holding him and feeding him and talking to him. I can't wait to teach our kids about the ranch and raising farm animals, to take my boys fishing and hunting, and watch our little girls doing ballet. Life just doesn't get any better than that."

"You really love that old farm, don't you? You must have had the best summers a kid could ever have."

His strong hands came up to gently cradle her face. He pulled her close once again, and stared deeply into her eyes. "You'll see, Ari, when you experience it with our kids. I promise you won't be sorry."

"Well, we have the rest of our lives to enjoy it, Gage. As long as you and I are together, I will be happy."

"Forever, Bella?"

"Forever, Gage."

"Good! Now, let's go hold our godson, and Jimmie's new best friend!"

Epilogue

"Sammie Jo?" Arabella called out again in desperation as she marched through the house, searching for her former bartender's namesake. The three-foot, two-inch ball of energy that dominated their household, was nowhere to be found.

Oh, please, don't be in the mud again! Not before church. They are going to think I never wash this child!

"Sammie, where are you?" Ari cried out, searching every one of the little tyke's normal hiding spots. The hall linen closet. Behind the bathroom door. Even under the kitchen sink.

She was nowhere in sight.

Ari sighed, and for the first time this morning, realized how eerily quiet the house was.

This can't be good. Quiet always means trouble when you have a houseful of kids.

She glanced quickly at the clock hanging on the kitchen wall, noting they had only twenty minutes before they needed to leave for church. Luckily, the baby was still sound asleep in his crib, giving her a quick moment to figure things out. She hadn't gone five feet towards the back door, when it flew open, allowing a cool spring breeze, and one very muddy three-year old, to meander inside.

Ari's eyes widened at the sight.

"Look mama, I got a fwog!" Two tiny, dirt-covered hands reached out to her, holding the biggest frog Ari had ever seen. And with two older boys in the house, three counting Gage, Ari had seen her share of frogs and snakes, spiders and bugs, and anything else they could chase down and catch.

"Jimmie and Max helped me catched him!" Sammie's grin was so big, it consumed her entire dirt-covered face. Her obvious joy made it hard for Ari to get upset.

"Oh Sammie, what am I going to do with you?" Ari's hope of making it to church on time, just once, surely wasn't happening today. She knelt down and found the cleanest spot she could on her precious daughter's tiny face, and kissed her. Then she stood, and turned the tyke around, marching her in the direction of the back porch.

"Let's go see what mess your brothers have gotten into this time."

"And daddy too!" Sammie squealed with pure delight.

Of course. And daddy too.

"Gage, boys," she called out loudly as she stepped outside and into the back yard, "it's time for church. C'mon now let's get—"

From the corner of her eye she detected movement and quickly turned towards the side of the house where she saw not one, not two, but *three,* covered head-to-toe with mud, figures. All of them with their faces turned towards the ground.

It was useless to get upset. She had learned that when Jimmy was still a toddler. Besides, she loved the fact that her husband was so involved in their kids' lives. Even if that meant he acted like a ten-year old most days. He was a great father and his children adored him, especially little Sammie. She had her daddy wrapped so tight around her finger, she could've asked for the world and Gage would've found some way to give it to her.

Ari couldn't hide her grin any longer. With a smile as wide as the ocean, she bent over and scooped up a fistful of mud from the puddle at her feet, and chucked it at Gage, hitting him in the arm.

The thought to run had barely registered in her mind, when she felt Gage's strong arms around her waist, drawing her to the ground, where she was gently tackled by three giggling children and one very large frog.

"Gage Russell," she laughed as he tickled her sides causing her to squirm, "we are going to be late for church! *Again*!"

"Say you're sorry for throwing mud at—"

"We can't be late, Mom!" Max and Jimmie said in unison as they scrambled to their feet, panic seizing their faces as they looked to her.

"We've got to practice our soldier parts for the Easter play and this is our last week," Jimmie grabbed his younger brother by the arm and began to pull him towards the house.

"Yeah, this week we get our weapons!" Max added as he made a sword with his hand and swung it around his head as Jimmy continued to drag him along.

"It's going to be okay, Max. You'll have plenty of time for practice, I promise," Ari encouraged the boys.

"Ok, guys. Play time is over!" Gage pulled himself up from the ground and extended a hand to help Ari as well. "Run upstairs quick and get some clean clothes on."

"And *please*, at least wash your face and hands," Ari begged as she watched them head for the house, knowing from experience there wasn't a chance of them actually getting clean.

"I'm going to be the best Roman soldier ever!" Excitement filled Max's words as the screen door slammed closed behind him.

Gage picked little Sammie up in his arms and headed for the door. "Sorry, honey. I guess we got a little carried away," Gage said as Ari walked beside him. "Again."

Oh, he knows that grin and those mischievous, sparkling eyes are the straight path to my heart.

Ari stopped and cocked her head, narrowing her eyes in his direction. "You can pay me back by getting yourself and Sammie cleaned up, while I change and get Liam ready." She followed him the rest of the way to the house, stepping over two pair of muddy dress shoes and four, once-white socks.

"Better grab an extra bottle for Liam too. I forgot we are having lunch with the Monroe family after church."

Gage nodded in agreement. Standing in the kitchen, he plucked Sammie's dress and tights off of her, and set her in the over-sized farmhouse sink. "Does that mean we are eating at the trough again?"

Ari laughed over her shoulder at her husband's favorite nickname for the all-you-can-eat buffet. "Be nice, Gage." She stopped and turned back towards him. "Remember, they have a lot of little mouths to feed. Eight to be exact! And this way, everyone gets something they like. *You* can even have dessert if you behave during church this morning," she teased. "Now, get cleaning!" When Gage pulled the sprayer from the sink, and turned it on their tot, Ari heard Sammie scream excitedly.

"Spray me, Daddy! Again! Again!"

Sammie's loud giggles followed Ari all the way up the stairway.

Pastor Will Benson, the newest addition to the staff at White Oak Methodist Church, was twenty minutes into the sermon by the time all four kids had been delivered to their individual classrooms. Ari and Gage quietly slipped into the back pew. Pastor Benson had been hired as the new Lead Pastor when Pastor Dave finally retired after thirty years of leading the congregation. If Ari admitted the truth, she had been really nervous about the new pastor before he started. She and Gage had formed a strong bond with Pastor Dave, not only from years of attending weekly service, but from the two years he'd been a personal mentor to them both. His heart, and life, were completely devoted to the Lord and sharing His love with the world. He wouldn't be easily replaced.

But the first sermon Pastor Will preached, had settled all her fears. He was a younger version of Pastor Dave, and he radiated joy and exuberance, standing at the pulpit declaring God's goodness and love for His people.

With her husband's arm draped across her shoulders, and after the crazy, but fun, morning she'd had with Gage and the kids, Ari felt like the luckiest woman in the world. She placed her hand on Gage's leg, and scooted closer to him, as she listened to the second sermon in a series leading up to the Easter holiday.

"Can you just imagine the emotion that must have filled their minds, as they made their way towards the tomb that early morning, preparing to anoint Jesus' body with spices? The cool air of spring surrounding them, the sun slowly creeping over the mountains and the bright morning star, a symbol of hope, could still be seen in the northern sky. But for the small group in route to the tomb of Jesus, hope was surely in short supply.

They were discouraged and saddened, their spirits pierced the same way nails had pierced His hands and feet. But," Pastor Will pointed his finger upward, "I would dare to say their emotions must have gone from one end of the spectrum to the other, when they realized the large stone that covered the entrance of the tomb had been rolled away."

Pastor Will moved from behind the podium, his excitement building as he paced back and forth across the stage.

"And not only had the very large stone been mysteriously rolled away, but it tells us in Matthew 16:5 that as they entered the tomb, a young man dressed in a white robe was seated on the right side.

'Do not be alarmed,' he said to them, for he knew they were expecting to see Jesus' lifeless body. 'You are looking for Jesus, the Nazarene who was crucified. He has now risen'. Then he instructed them to share the good news with Jesus' disciples.

"Church, can you even *fathom* what must have been running through their minds at this time? Depression has given way to fear as they flee from the tomb, and that fear gives way to joy, as Jesus meets them on their way and they fall to His feet in worship."

Pastor Will stopped, and turned towards the congregation, speaking a single word. "Hope." He let that word sink in for a minute before he continued. Now, standing behind the pulpit again, he browsed his notes. "The definition of hope in the Merriam-Webster dictionary is 'to want something to happen or be true; to cherish a desire with anticipation. I suppose they had plenty of hope that day. And church," he stepped from behind the podium, once again, and made his way to the very edge of the stage, his face full of emotion. "As this holiday approaches, and we remember all that has been given and sacrificed on our behalf, share the hope that has turned into faith of a secured eternity! With those that are lost and broken. With those in desperate need of a Savior. Hope," he paused briefly once again, allowing the word to fill the minds of those before him, "hope can make even the darkest hour shine brightly. It can bring peace to those facing trials, and give the destitute a reason to believe."

Pastor Will wrapped up the sermon as the church joined him in worship and the band came back to the stage and performed two songs.

Afterwards, out in the café, Ari had confirmed their lunch plans with Sheryl Monroe, as Gage gathered the kids from their classrooms. Both Max and Jimmie had crafted their cardboard swords during service and were now having a dual in the middle row of their SUV. Poor Liam, safely strapped into his car seat, was stuck right between them as they headed towards the all you-can-eat buffet in town. Ari chided herself for not remembering to put one of the older boys in the very back seat with Sammie Jo.

"Pretty good sermon, huh?" Ari asked Gage over the backseat ruckus.

"It was," Gage nodded. Then looking in the rearview mirror, he talked to the boys. "Remember the swords stay in the car when we get to the restaurant."

Two defeated groans were his feedback. "Awwww, Dad!"

Ari jumped in to support her husband. "Boys, you will have plenty of time to practice this week," she winked at them. "Scouts honor."

Turning back to her husband, she continued. "Hope," she nodded, "I really like the sound of that and what it stands for."

"Well, hope is what got me through my days in Iowa after I'd left you. So, I would have to agree. I like the word. A lot." Gage glanced quickly in her direction and smiled, before turning his attention back to the road.

Lunch went as smooth as it could for the adults, with a total of twelve kids to be looked after; six of them being under the age of four. But they survived with minimal casualties. One toddler ended up with a carrot "spike" in their blonde hair, when two of the older boys had given them an "orange mohawk". Another was left with soaking wet clothes after an entire glass of chocolate milk had been spilled. Apparently, it had gotten in the way of the boys' 'race track.' But with only one casualty drawing blood from an accidental elbow to the nose, they felt like they had conquered the day.

Later that night, long after the kids had been bathed and tucked into bed, Gage caught up with Ari in their room. Intently focused on what she was holding in her hands, and how she planned to break the news to her husband, she didn't realize he was in the room until she felt his arms wrap around her waist. She relaxed in his embrace, enjoying the familiarity and peace it brought her. He leaned in and kissed her on the neck before he noticed what she held in her hands.

"What's that you've g—oh, is that what I think it is?" Gage's interest was quickly piqued when he realized that she held a pair of pink booties in her hand. Another pair from the blue tub that Nonnie had filled, so many years ago.

"Ari? Is there something you want to tell me?"

"I really liked the sermon today." She smiled as she thought about what her husband's reaction was going to be. She already knew he would be crazy excited. The thought of sharing it with him warmed her heart. "In fact, I like the word hope so much, that I was thinking it would make a nice name for our daughter."

Gage turned his wife in his arms, narrowing his eyes on her. "Bella, you're not saying that you're pregnant, are you? I mean, usually I figure it out before you do. And I haven't noticed any mood swings. Or morning sickness."

Ari could sense his excitement beginning to build. Gage had been very vocal with her about his desire to have a large family, but it hadn't taken much to convince her, once she saw what a great father he was.

"Well, if you remember right, when I was carrying Sammie, I didn't have any morning sickness. Must mean this one's another girl."

Gage's grin widened. "You're sure? Have you taken a test?"

"I wanted to wait until Easter to surprise you, but I couldn't stand it any longer. I took the test three weeks ago and if my calculations are right, I'm about seven weeks along." Her grin mimicked Gage's. "We have an appointment next week with Dr. Connors."

"Bella, this is the best news ever!" He picked her up and spun them in a circle before setting her feet back on the ground. Cupping her face in his hands, he placed a gentle kiss on her lips. "God is so good to us. I still can't believe how much He has blessed us!"

And they certainly had been blessed. Their three-hundred-acre farm, where they grew corn and raised a few cows and horses, had more than doubled in size over the past year. Gage had approached Ari, not too long after Sammie's birth with the news that Mr. Bivens, the cattle rancher that had four hundred and fifty acres backed up to Nonnie's place, had decided at seventy-five that he was ready to retire and sell the land. With no children or grandchildren interested in continuing the farm, he'd offered it to Gage, based on the fact that he'd known Gage and Nonnie for so long, and held nothing but respect for them. Gage had always been a helpful hand with problems that would arise on Mr. Biven's farm. They had developed a strong and mutual respect for one another.

Up until that point, Ari and Gage had been dividing their time between Rock Haven and Iowa. But Ari couldn't tell Gage no, even if that meant giving up more time in Rock Haven. So, with the money that they'd put aside after the sale of his business in New York, they were able to put a huge down payment on the land. It was then, that Ari had also decided to sell the restaurant. She had been mulling it over in her mind for several months, tired from the constant travel back and forth with the children, and realizing how happy the kids were on the farm. She'd finally approached Gage with the idea, late one night.

"Gage," Ari climbed into bed next to him where he sat reading yet another book about raising beef cattle, "I think it's time to sell Francesca's."

He couldn't have looked more shocked as he turned to her. "Ari, we can't sell your *family* restaurant. Why would you even suggest that?"

"Gage, our life is *here*. I see how happy you and the kids are on the ranch. That is all the happy I need. Our kids love their animals and all that you teach them about raising them. Max and Jimmie want to do 4H so badly. They love their friends from church and honestly, I'm tired of trying to keep tabs on the restaurant. Not that Beth isn't doing a fine job." When Ari's assistant manager had given her notice eighteen months ago, Beth had stepped in without question. To this day, she ran the place with only occasional help from Anthony.

"But, Bella—"

"I want to offer it to Beth," she interrupted. "And I was thinking we could still keep the cottage instead of renting it all summer. We could add an addition and use it as our vacation house. If you add a second floor with a couple more bedrooms, it could work. That way the kids will still get a small taste of beach life without us having the pressure of business commitments. We will have more time to enjoy the beach."

"Wow, you've really thought this through, haven't you?"

"I had been considering it for a while. When Mr. Bivens offered to sell you his land and cattle, I knew it was the right answer."

They'd agreed that night to take thirty days to think and pray about it, and at the end of that time, they were both in agreement. With no doubt in their minds, they placed the call to Beth. It took less than two months to have everything drawn up and finalized. Ari couldn't have been happier that the restaurant would stay with someone she considered family. Someone that would continue on in their traditions.

With the money from the sale of Francesca's, Gage was able to nearly double the number of their cattle, increase the size of their corn and hay crops, along with the addition of three new barns. After all was said and done, Ari and Gage owned one of the largest cattle ranches in Davis County. Shortly after, the kids had been thrilled to purchase their own chickens, eager to start earning money from the sale of their eggs.

It was a busy place, that farm, and full of more love than Ari or Gage could have ever dreamed possible. It wasn't only cattle and chickens they had, but six horses and fifteen goats, along with three dogs that roamed the property.

"So what you're trying to tell me, is that you would like to name our daughter Hope. Is that right?"

"Do you like it, Gage?"

"Well," he tapped his finger against his chin, "you let me name Jimmie, and the names you picked out for the other three, I love. So, yeah, I think we can agree on Hope. If it's a girl, that is."

"*If* it's a boy, which it won't be," Ari grinned, "then you can pick out the name. Deal?"

"Deal!" Gage agreed. "Now, I think it's time I let my pregnant wife get some rest." He leaned over, placed his book on the nightstand, and turned off the lamp before finding Ari's face in the dark. He leaned in to kiss her. "I love you, Bella."

"Forever, Gage?"

"Yes, Bella. Forever, my love."

About the Author

Brandy Bennett-Baker, a devoted wife and mother, was struggling with empty nest syndrome, when she felt the Lord tugging at her heart, calling her down a path she never dreamed of taking. After much debate, and lots of prayer, she finally gave up the reins and allowed the Lord to lead her down this path that she didn't feel qualified to walk. Putting her faith to paper, she began to write her debut novel, Forever, My Love. Like many of her favorite inspirational novelists, Brandy's greatest hope is that women of all walks of life may come to know God, or deepen their relationship with Him through her writing.

Together she and her husband have five children and five grandchildren. They currently reside in Battle Creek, Michigan and enjoy spending time with their growing family.

CPSIA information can be obtained
at www.ICGtesting.com
Printed in the USA
BVHW030707070319
541952BV00024B/44/P

9 781973 650584